Is This Apocalypse Necessary?

"The characters are convincingly alive, the kind that quickly involve the reader."
—KLIATT on *A Bad Spell in Yurt*

"Those of you who have read *A Bad Spell In Yurt* will need no further notice than that Brittain is at it again … This is a fun, fast-paced entertaining read. And it's meaty enough to keep you turning the pages, humorous enough to keep a smile on your face."
—RANDOM REALITIES on *The Wood Nymph and the Cranky Saint*

"Contains humor, romance, and adventure—something for everyone!"
—KLIATT on *The Wood Nymph and the Cranky Saint*

"… some real chills as the climax approaches."
—DRAGON on *The Wood Nymph and the Cranky Saint*

"… imaginative and entertaining."
—VOYA on *Mage Quest*

"… delightful, with its magic-based modern conveniences and organized wizards in amiable rivalry with the medieval church."
—LOCUS on *A Bad Spell in Yurt*

"… entertaining encounters with monsters, old school chums, gypsies, and an amorous nixie. For balance, there are also some serious subjects under consideration, such as the fundamental conflict of magic and religion."
—LOCUS on *The Witch and the Cathedral*

"A fast moving story that wraps all of its many separate plot threads into one coherent whole."
—SCIENCE FICTION CHRONICLE on *Daughter of Magic*

to learn more about the Yurt books—see www.Daimbert.com

Is This Apocalypse Necessary?

C. Dale Brittain

The Wooster Book Company
Wooster • Ohio
2000

The Wooster Book Company
205 West Liberty Street
Wooster Ohio • 44691
www.woosterbook.com

ISBN: 1-888683-06-6

Cover art: The Issenheim Altar: *The Temptation of Saint Anthony* (detail), Matthias Grünewald
© *Musée d'Unterlinden,* COLMAR, *photo Octave Zimmermann*

Library of Congress Cataloging-in-Publication Data

Brittain, C. Dale
    Is this apocalypse necessary? / C. Dale Brittain.
    p.   cm.
ISBN 1-888683-06-6 (alk. paper)
    1. Wizards—Fiction. I. Title.

PS3552.R49719 I7 2000
813'.54—dc21   00-032054

First Printing: September 2000

Dedication

for David and for Donna, friends of Daimbert

contents

Is This Apocalypse Necessary?

part one ✢ the master

I

THE MIDNIGHT KNOCK came sharp and hard. I had no way of knowing that the knock meant that in two minutes I would be kidnapped and in three weeks dead.

I rolled over, too sleepy to bother with a spell. It had to be someone from here in the castle, so eager for my wizardly wisdom that he couldn't wait until morning. "Mmm?"

The knock came again. "Come in," I mumbled, not recalling for the moment how rarely my wisdom was sought this eagerly. "The door's unlocked."

It slowly creaked open, letting in a cool, damp wind but at first nothing else. It was the darkest hour of the night, the hour when it seems that the sun must this time be gone for good, and the furniture has taken advantage of its absence to metamorphose into something large and predatory. I sat up, abruptly wide awake. Through the doorway stepped a pair of hooded figures, barely visible in the shadows.

Just inside, they paused to light a magic lamp, but their hoods hid their faces from the lamp's glow. The aura of wizardry emanated from them like heat from a stove. Two strange wizards, in a kingdom where I was the only one? My heart slammed against my ribs as I scrambled belatedly for a spell.

"Don't struggle, Daimbert," said one, "and don't make a sound." His was no voice I recognized, though he seemed to know who *I* was. "Is anyone here with you?"

"No!" I said loudly and stretched out a hand, adding the

two quick words that should have knocked them flat. The words had no effect.

Instead a loop of air around my chest suddenly became solid. They were using a binding spell on me.

I struggled to free myself, but with two of them joining their magic together I didn't have a chance. The binding spell held me tighter than any rope and kept my mouth closed, so I could do no more than thrash and make inarticulate grunts as they advanced toward the bed.

"We told you not to struggle, Daimbert," said one reprovingly. "And stop making that sound before we have to paralyze you, too. Good thing we practiced our binding spells before we came!"

So they wanted me alive. I stopped grunting and rolled around so that I could look at them. I could see their faces now but still didn't recognize either one. The first wizard's hair was snowy white above a pink and youthful face that looked as if he usually wore an expression of enthusiastic good-humor, though now he was frowning and shielding his eyes from the glow of the magic lamp. The other had a prominent cleft chin which he carried with pride. It was he who had addressed me. Young wizards, I thought, with the complacency that comes from having carefully-practiced spells work right the first time, but without the experience to know that no wizard's command of magic is ever flawless.

And I had better find the flaw in their magic, and fast.

The one with the chin said the words of the Hidden Language to lift me slowly into the air and move me toward the door. I let him do so, lying still as though in resignation but probing furiously at the binding spell that held me. It was very tidily done, just like in the book—a spell right out of the wizards' school.

A student prank? I wondered as the cold night air hit me. The last time I had been at the wizards' school I seemed to remember spotting a white-haired, pale-skinned young man among the students, but I didn't get to the City very often and had not paid much attention. And I had tended to avoid the school ever since Elerius had joined the faculty.

In my own student days I had carried out a certain number of pranks, and Whitey looked as if he would enjoy a joke at someone else's expense, but it seemed unnecessarily elaborate for them to have flown two hundred miles, from the great City to the tiny kingdom of Yurt, just to play a trick on its Royal Wizard, me.

They extinguished their magic lamp and looked cautiously from side to side, but the castle courtyard was dark and quiet. Everyone must have long been asleep; there was no sound but the whispering of the wind. The only sign of life was a faint glow from the watchman's lantern, near the gate. I considered trying somehow to attract his attention, but he would have had even less luck against these wizards than I was having.

"This way," said Chin quietly. He seemed to be the leader. "Back over the wall." They sailed me up over the castle battlements while I silently cursed myself for not having magical spells in place that would have alerted me to any invader. I had placed such spells at one time, years ago, when Yurt was attacked by unliving warriors made of hair and bone, but the spells had been too hard to keep going during the peaceful years that followed.

Beyond the moat I could make out a squat, winged shape, which in a second I recognized as an air cart. It was the skin of a purple flying beast which, even long after the beast had died, would keep on flying if given magical commands. The school's air cart? I thought in amazement. Could Chin and Whitey have stolen it? Either these two young wizards had gotten themselves involved in a student prank so serious that expulsion from the school would be a pathetically weak punishment, or else others were involved, faculty as well as students.

As they tumbled me into the air cart and Chin gave the command to lift off, I thought I knew, with a cold certainty that chilled me much more than the night wind. Elerius. He had to be behind this. When I looked toward Chin and Whitey, darker silhouettes against the dark sky, I seemed to see not them but an older, black-bearded wizard, contemplating me from under peaked eyebrows with thoughtful, tawny eyes.

And all the time I kept on probing their binding spells, weakening them a tiny bit at a time, first here, then there, so small a change in any one spot that they might never notice that the solid air that held me was gradually diffusing back to its natural state, until—I hoped—it would be too late.

The air cart's wings beat steadily as it carried us away from Yurt and through the night. The rain had ended, but clouds half covered the stars. It was impossible for me, lying at the bottom of the cart, to determine our direction, but my guess was that we were heading toward the coast and the great City. I hoped that by staying perfectly quiet I might lull the two young wizards into an unguarded conversation that would allow me to learn where we were going and why, but they too were silent, except for occasionally giving a low command to correct the cart's course. At one point Whitey seemed about to say something, but Chin shushed him.

The last of the binding spell that held me came apart. But I remained still, eyes shut, breathing very shallowly.

Whitey bent over me and this time did speak. "Did we knock him unconscious?" he asked, sounding worried.

"He's only realized it's no use struggling against superior magic," said Chin, sounding unconcerned. "Isn't that right, Daimbert?" addressing me derisively. "I told you this would work," he continued to Whitey. "I looked up Daimbert's old academic records once, the time I got into the main office at night, and, you know, he nearly flunked out of the school. He never stood a chance against the two of us—in fact, one alone could have done it."

Don't check your binding spell, I thought desperately. Whatever you do, don't check your spell.

He didn't check his spell. *Much* too unconcerned, I thought. If these were Elerius's agents, he should have trained them better. I might indeed have almost flunked out of the wizards' school, but that had been over thirty years ago, and I had picked up one or two magical tricks in the meantime. Chin was going to pay for that remark.

Very slowly, so cautiously that even an experienced wizard might not have noticed, I started putting together a transformations spell. The danger of having one's magic work perfectly, as I had learned from experience over the years but hoped they hadn't, is that it makes one careless: even a spell that comes out just like in the book may not be sufficient. Chin and Whitey, thinking me securely tied up, must have forgotten that I still had a great deal of magic available to me. Being turned into tadpoles would remind them. Once they were safely transmogrified, I would give the air cart my own commands and get back home to Yurt.

But I hesitated with my transformations spell incomplete. It might be better to wait until actually brought before Elerius. I had always known I would have to face him sometime, even though I would have preferred not to do so wearing crumpled yellow pajamas. Much as I would have liked to distance myself by several hundred miles from him and his schemes, I knew that if he wanted me he would keep coming after me. Better to confront him now and learn his plans at once than to go home and wait for his next attack.

Especially if I confronted him carrying his two treacherous agents wiggling in a jar.

Elerius was the best wizard to come out of the school in my generation, or probably any generation since it was founded. He had long played a waiting game, readying himself for the day when he could take over the leadership of organized magic and reshape it to suit his own vision. His ideas and mine on the purposes and goals of institutionalized wizardry differed enough that I doubted he had sent for me to ask my opinions. But he had—rather inexplicably, I always thought—concluded some years ago that I was a better wizard than I actually was (though he had neglected to tell his agents this), and must have decided to silence me before I could disrupt the plans he was even now putting into effect.

But he couldn't be planning to kill me, I tried to reassure the cold fear at the pit of my stomach. Chin and Whitey could have subjected me to much worse had they wanted; clearly I was required intact. Of course, the logical conclusion struck me with depressing force, it was also possible that Elerius wanted to kill me himself to make sure there were no mistakes—and no survivors.

I jerked my mind from the question of my personal safety to the question of what might actually be happening at the wizards' school. All I could conclude was that Elerius had managed to embroil some of the students in his schemes, but that was not nearly enough to go on.

For starters, what *were* his schemes? It was no secret that he intended some day to become the new Master of the school, but so far he had been content to wait. He had always been enormously ambitious, and because he was smarter than anyone else he had quite early decided that whatever he thought best actually was for the best, but so far his self-assurance that he would always work for the benefit of everyone had restricted his ambition. But had he now thrown aside waiting and assassinated the old Master? Was he bringing to the City, one by one, any other wizards he imagined might be rivals and killing them too?

"I don't even know why he's so interested in Daimbert," Chin commented in an irritated tone, startling me out of my train of thought. "You'd expect he'd trust us enough to tell us why he wants him. What's so special about this wizard anyway?"

Oho, jealousy, I thought. I wasn't going to learn Elerius's plans by eavesdropping, but might I be able to play on that sense of aggrieved pride enough to swing these young wizards over to my side?

Of course it would have helped if I could talk. But doing anything beyond grunting would advertise that I was no longer held by a binding spell. And this time Chin might make his threat good and paralyze me, at which point I wouldn't even be able to think.

Time to take action. We had been flying long enough that the eastern sky, behind the air cart, was gradually lightening from black toward gray. The clouds had rolled away, and I could see the stars fading out. The two wizards' faces were just visible as I peered up at them from behind lowered lashes.

"There's the City on the horizon," said Chin quietly, gazing ahead and giving the final magical commands that would guide the air cart to a landing at the school. I waited until they both were looking away, then muttered under my breath the words of the Hidden Language to make me invisible.

In the space of one second my body disappeared, and I was up and over the edge of the air cart and flying along beside it, the wind whipping at my invisible beard. It might be interesting to see how they explained my absence to Elerius.

"He's gone!" gasped Whitey. So they still taught them at the school to recognize the obvious.

Chin sprang forward, feeling around the bottom of the air cart as if thinking I might have just rolled to one side and been hidden by the shadows. Before us in the west the sky was still dark and star-studded, but the yellow lights of the never-sleeping City, ahead of us and a quarter mile below, made an island of brightness at the edge of a dim landscape. Beyond, still black and unfeatured, stretched the sea.

Both young wizards were on their feet now, looking around wildly, with the desperate expression of those who realize they have just made a major mistake and are wondering what they can possibly do to correct it. I recognized that feeling; I had had it often enough myself.

"He can't have gone far," said Chin in sudden resolution. "I should be able to detect somebody working magic. In fact—"

He was just too late. He discovered and was dismantling my invisibility spell as I turned him and Whitey into frogs.

I collapsed back over the edge of the air cart, whose wings kept resolutely flapping, and wiped my forehead with a pajama sleeve. The frogs looked at me with human panic in their amphibian eyes. One of them was mottled green and brown, with an unusually prominent lower jaw for a frog, but the other was the color of chalk. I slowly caught my breath and waited for my heartbeat to return to normal before trying anything else. Flying was hard enough physical and mental work by itself without having to do so while invisible, much less transforming young wizards into frogs at the same time.

At the last moment I had decided against tadpoles. I had no jars of water with me, and if they had dried up and died while transformed they would have been just as dead when turned back into wizards. It seemed a bit excessive to put them to death for kidnapping me.

Besides, they were not my real enemies. Elerius was, and he was waiting just ahead.

II

The air cart began spiraling down, toward the sharp spires of the school on the highest central point in the City. The school was not one building but many, built or added to over the last two centuries and all connected together, glittering both with magic lights and with illusion. Below the spires, below the maze of offices, meeting rooms, lecture halls, and library, were storerooms, the rooms where the teachers had once kept a very small dragon (strictly for instructional purposes), and silent rooms closed with magic locks where, the new students told each other, demons lived, though I had always found that unlikely. I expected the cart to settle, as usual, into the school courtyard, but instead it tucked its wings tidily and dropped like a stone the last thirty feet, to land on a balcony jutting out from one of the towers.

The frogs were catapulted upward by the force of that bone-jarring landing. I grabbed one in each hand and stuffed them into my pajama pockets. Maybe there was an additional magical command one was supposed to give to make the final approach easier, a command I didn't know because I would never have presumed to bring the air cart down here—this was the balcony of the private suite belonging to the Master.

Which meant that Elerius must indeed have already disposed of him. I took a deep breath and climbed out. The frogs were giving their calls, which I had thought frogs gave only to attract mates, but presumably they had no other way to scream in terror—or warning? I paused for a second to cover my pajamas in illusion: a white linen shirt with lace at the cuffs, dark red velvet jacket and trousers, embroidered all over with the moon and stars, a golden pendant around my neck, and a long black cape over all. Then I stepped through the tall open window and inside.

A voice spoke from somewhere ahead. "Did you bring the wizard?"

The corridor before me was dark, but a magic lamp's glow came from an open doorway. In two strides I was at the door. "No thanks to your assistants," I said, "the wizard brought himself."

But something was wrong. That had not been Elerius's voice, and this was not Elerius before me. It was the old

Master of the school, lying in bed propped up with pillows, looking up at me from frost-blue eyes.

I was so flabbergasted I didn't know what to say, and instead gave him the full formal bow, first the dip of the head, then the widespread arms, and finally the drop to both knees. Even if he'd ordered me kidnapped, he was still the head of organized wizardry in the west, and had been for forty years both my superior and the closest thing I had to a father.

"Is that illusion, Daimbert?" he asked. "No offense, but you usually don't dress this ostentatiously. And where are my assistants?"

My finery was already starting to fade. I stood up, snapped my fingers to end the illusion, and drew the frogs out of my pockets. "I decided they'd be safer like this," I said. "Less likely to paralyze me and drop me out of the air cart by mistake while it was flying. Think how upset with them you'd have been."

He looked at them thoughtfully, stroking his snowy beard. Whitey's hair was white because he had been born without pigmentation; mine had turned white overnight due to certain hellish experiences shortly after I graduated from the school; but the Master's was white because he had lived far longer than any wizard ever known: at least four hundred years by most accounts, though some said five hundred or even six.

"I told them to bring you at once and to bring you quietly," he commented. He spoke with his accustomed assurance and authority, but there was a tremorous undertone to his voice I did not recall hearing before. "Perhaps they went beyond their orders. Could you turn them back into themselves?"

A year ago he would have worked the magic himself in a second. I made no remark but set about undoing my spells. If Chin was jealous because the Master considered me special—

certainly more special than he was—but wouldn't tell him why, he might well have chosen to misunderstand his orders.

But why was I, Royal Wizard of one of the smallest of the western kingdoms, suddenly so special?

In a moment I had turned my frogs back into young wizards. They staggered for a moment, then straightened themselves up, heels together. A minute ago I had thought of them as the power-drunk agents of Elerius. But if these were indeed the Master's assistants, I had to change my opinion of them. I saw them now as thoroughly humiliated students a whole lot younger and more inexperienced than I was, even if they might, given a chance, someday turn into better wizards. Though they now were grasping at dignity, they knew perfectly well that they had been showing off their newly-learned spells by trying to bring me here forcibly, and not only had they failed to do so, they would now have the shame of trying to explain why they had thought it such a good idea.

The Master shook his head almost imperceptibly in their direction. "I'll talk to you two later," he said, and they turned around and shot from the room, slamming the door behind them without waiting for further dismissal.

"By the way," I commented, "when you talk to them, ask them about breaking into the office and looking at old academic records."

The Master's eyes twinkled, and for a second I allowed myself to think that he was in bed merely because it was still before dawn, a time when all sensible wizards should be sleeping off last night's dinner and wine. "I expect that in that case they discovered the results of that disastrous transformations practical exam of yours," he said, "where you had all that trouble with the frogs. Perhaps it will be educational for them to realize that wizards can keep on learning even if they're past thirty."

They were never going to let me forget that incident here at the school. I managed a small smile. But I was distracted from humiliating memories by seeing a little pile of silver bells lying on the table. They brought back much happier memories, of learning the spells that would make such bells rise and fall in a constantly-repeating waterfall of soft and musical sound. An elegant touch for a wizard's chambers, but these were dusty and still, as though their spells had not been renewed for a long time.

"But I didn't bring you here in such secrecy, Daimbert," the Master continued, suddenly completely serious, "to joke about frogs."

I hooked a chair closer with a foot and sat down beside him. I was still recovering from the shock of discovering I would not have to face Elerius after all, but now that I thought about it, it seemed very strange that if the Master had something to say to me he had not simply used the magic telephones.

He held my eyes for a moment. "Daimbert, I'm dying."

My immediate reaction was to think that this must be one more prank. The Master couldn't possibly be dying. He had founded the school—it was *his* school. It was neither morally nor physically possible for him not to be here. He must have meant something quite different.

I found myself speaking. "Are the doctors sure?"

Dawn was breaking at last, and the first light came in through an eastern window. He smiled a little, but I could see clearly now the pallor of his cheek. His face had been lined as long as I knew him, but the lines had deepened and multiplied. "It's no use asking the doctors. All they have are the herbs and simple spells we wizards gave them generations ago. *I'm* sure. After all these years, I know this body better than any doctor ever could. Magic can slow aging, as I would have to be the first to affirm, but it has no ultimate power over the cycles of life and death. As long as one lives old body parts keep wearing away, and there are only a certain number of times one can renew the material."

The blow hit at last, the realization that this was not a joke gone wrong, or any kind of joke at all. I put a hand over my eyes; he didn't need to see my sudden tears.

"You are," he said quietly, "the first I've told."

I lifted my head. Again, why me? "I'm terribly sorry, sir."

"You needn't be sorry on my account," he said with something of his old energy. "I've had a much longer and much richer life than any man could possibly expect to deserve, though all those priests with whom you're such good friends will probably tell you I should have spent more time thinking about my soul."

"I am not," I said crisply, "good friends with 'all those priests.' The bishop of Caelrhon is my oldest friend, but that has nothing to do with him being a priest."

Sorrow made me speak more sharply than I intended, but he let it pass. "Well, if he asks you can tell him I'm still not particularly worried about the afterlife. Instead I'm worried about the school."

So was I, though it was still a secondary concern, much less important than the idea that I would never see him again. I nodded and waited for him to continue.

"When I established the school a hundred and fifty years ago," he said slowly, "I did not originally intend to establish an organization and structure that wizardry had never before had. At first my thought was only to regularize the teaching of magic, so that there would no longer be the enormous variety of training and methods that made it so difficult for wizards when we wanted to work together—as when we stopped the Black Wars." He caught my expression and lifted an eyebrow in amusement. "Yes, I know that for you it's something out of ancient history, but I remember the Black Wars."

"But I've never heard you speak of them before," I said eagerly.

"At one time," he answered, looking out the window, "I'd

planned to write my memoirs before I died, and I would have put everything in there. It's too late now, but it really doesn't matter. There are enough written histories of that time already, and enough stories remembered among the wizards, all close enough to accurate that the accounts don't need my own view. I became a teacher rather than a historian. And I've succeeded much better than I ever expected. There are virtually no wizards left in the west trained under the old apprenticeship system, or at least not wizards in important posts. As of last month, I believe that every Royal Wizard in the Western Kingdoms has been trained here, under me."

My predecessor at Yurt had learned his magic as an apprentice over two centuries ago and had trained would-be wizards of his own in his time, but I had never been nor had an apprentice.

"Which means, Daimbert," the Master continued, looking back at me, "that magic now has the kind of centralization that even the Church has never managed. I'm not just the head of the school. I'm the central authority over the way that wizardry is approached, understood, and practiced. Whoever became Master after me will be able to direct how wizardry functions for the next two centuries."

"In that case, sir," I asked tentatively, "why haven't you told Zahlfast you're dying? I mean, he's smart, I'm sure he's realized you're sick, but if he's suddenly going to have all this authority—"

"Who said anything about Zahlfast?"

"But," I said, still tentative, "he's been for years your second in command in almost everything here at the school. I know officially he's only head of the Transformations Faculty, but he's had a hand in all your decisions. So if you're not here—"

"—he'll just take over," the Master finished for me. "At one time I thought so too, Daimbert. I've never asked him what he thought himself."

He paused for a moment, breathing rapidly and shallowly. He was trying his best to treat this as a normal conversation, but I could see that, even aside from the subject matter, he was having trouble talking this much. Doctors might shortly be arriving to see how their patient had passed the night, regardless of his opinion of their abilities. I leaned forward; this could be the last chance I would ever have to speak with him alone.

"But Zahlfast is smart, as you observe," he continued after a moment, lifting a hand from under the covers to wipe a bead of sweat from his forehead. "He will recognize that he is old, not as old as I am but old enough that he will not outlive me by very many decades. What the school needs now is a younger man."

I closed my eyes. He was trying to break it to me that he had designated Elerius to succeed him. He knew that Elerius and I had had our differences in the past, and he was going to reassure me that someone that intelligent and that skilled would do an excellent job of reshaping the school in his own image.

Or—since the Master had apparently not told anyone else that he was dying, did he expect me to carry this glad news to Elerius myself? He could not have chosen a messenger less willing to carry such a message.

"For years," he said slowly, "I acted as though I thought I would live forever. Of course I was sick a few times, and of course I knew that magic can only delay, not deny, the natural rhythms of life and death. But I never arranged for my succession. The faculty has never even discussed what method might be used to find a new Master. Well, if I had been suddenly killed somewhere along the way in the last century or so, which indeed almost happened several times, I presume they would have talked it over, become very irritated with each other, refrained by sheer will from turning each other into caterpillars, and finally settled on the same method the Church uses to elect new bishops: having the men who will be governed by the new Master choose him from among themselves. Probably an admirable method in its own right, but as long as I am here, as long as I know that I'm dying far enough ahead of time that I can do something about it, I consider it far too risky. I want to designate my successor myself."

Here it comes, I thought. Should I smile and make some comment about Elerius's remarkable magical abilities—not that they needed any praise from me? Or should I make a desperate attempt to talk him out of it?

"I think you know what I'm about to say," he said with a faint smile, "though you're doing your best not to show it." I was indeed doing my best not to show how truly worried I was about the future of organized magic. "Daimbert, I want you to succeed me as the new Master of the wizards' school."

III

This was all a dream. That was the only explanation. Yes, that was it. Very soon now I would awaken to a knock at my door, and it would swing open not on mysterious hooded wizards but on a pretty serving maid, who would bring me tea and cinnamon crullers.

I waited expectantly, but no tea and crullers appeared. I toyed with an alternate explanation, that the Master in his illness had mumbled something hysterical that only *sounded* as if he wanted me to succeed him, and in a minute he was going to say something else on another topic altogether. But he was watching me with an intensely pleased smile. Perhaps I should answer.

"This is an even better joke, sir, than having me kidnapped."

He shook his head, still smiling. "No joke, Daimbert. I can see you didn't expect this. And that's exactly why it has to be you. I acquired the kind of power and authority I have here in the West essentially by accident. No one, especially not a wizard with awesome powers, can be trusted to take charge of institutionalized magic if it is his driving goal to do so."

"You mean, you want me as the new Master because I don't have any particularly awesome powers?"

"I want you as the Master because you are the only one who can stop Elerius."

I covered my eyes again. "I'm sorry sir," I mumbled. "I know you're sick and I know you're trying to do what you think is best. But there's no possible way I can keep Elerius from becoming Master." Even as I spoke I was thinking with a kind of amazement, So he knew all along that Elerius couldn't be trusted. He didn't always think, along with everyone else at the school, that Elerius's opinion was as certain as the sunrise to be good.

"You're the only one who has been able to curtail any of his plans in the past, Daimbert," said the Master, still smiling. "I've been watching you since you first climbed up to the school from the warehouse sector of the City to beg me to take you on as a student. Several times I almost despaired of you, but you've got an improvisational flair that makes up for a grasp of academic magic that has sometimes been, shall we say, patchy. Every time you've had to face a challenge, even a challenge that would have daunted many more experienced wizards, you've risen to it. I believe indeed you have abilities of which you are not yet even aware yourself. Part of it may be your capacity to make friends who will be there to aid you when you most need them. And you've got a quality I hardly ever see in a powerful wizard: you're good-hearted toward the weak, not just because you've been sworn to help them, but because you're personally concerned about them."

"And it's that concern," I said at once, "that makes me know I would be your worst possible choice."

"You've also got an unparalleled improvisational flair, and you have never been proud and boastful." He continued to smile, enjoying using what might be his last strength to surprise someone who was not delighted at the surprise but horrified. "You invented the far-seeing attachment for telephones, one of the more useful breakthroughs in technical magic of this generation, but I still hear you modestly insist that you know no technical magic."

"Sir, that was over thirty years ago, and I did it by accident!" I had spent those years quietly proud of my accomplishment, but if I didn't repudiate it fast I would find myself, with no experience whatsoever in organization, trying to supervise a group of wizards who were all much older and better than I was, failing miserably, and seeing Elerius take over after all.

The Master nodded, as though I had just unwittingly proved his point for him. "That's exactly what I mean, Daimbert. And you recognized Elerius for what he is long before the rest of us. Even now most of the faculty would vote for him if there were an election, which is why I have to make certain there will not be one."

I realized slowly what the Master was really saying and went cold inside. Even before his present illness would lead to his death, it had already taken his magic from him, so that he did not trust himself to oppose Elerius directly. But where had he gotten this idea that I somehow could?

"He'd be more than delighted to take over the school," the Master continued, "with his calm belief that he knows better than people do themselves what is best for them, and that if a few rules have to broken along the way it scarcely matters as long as his own self-evidently laudable goals are reached. I've run this school as successfully as I have for as long as I have by realizing that grand organizational plans won't work—the world is too messy and too unpredictable for any wizard to direct it all, even one as good as Elerius."

I closed and opened my eyes as the Master stopped for breath. For twenty years I had distrusted Elerius. The entire time, whenever I didn't doubt my own judgment of him, I had been convinced that no one else would accept the opinion of someone who had graduated from the school only by the skin of his teeth over that of the school's newest and most honored faculty member.

But was the Master himself seeking to establish his own laudable goals through the faulty means of forcing me on an unwilling school? And in the highly unlikely event that I actually became Master, was I then supposed to ram through my own choice of successor, regardless of whether everyone else wanted Elerius and his followers?

No time for theoretical speculation. "I'm very glad, sir, you realize Elerius would be nearly your worst possible successor, but there could still be one thing worse than having him in charge of the school. And that would be having a mildly competent wizard, who had almost flunked out himself thirty years earlier, suddenly elevated from Royal Wizard of a tiny kingdom into a position of power where he hypothetically could, if he wished, make even the mightiest kings obey him."

The Master stopped smiling at last. "You're going to try to refuse the position?"

I had been squeezing the arms of the chair so tightly that my palms were slick. I made myself let go and wiped my hands on my pajamas. "I'm sorry, sir, I appreciate the honor enormously, but I'm afraid you're entirely mistaken in your estimation of me. You tried to put me on the faculty once before, and I told you then to wait fifty years to see if I'd be ready. It hasn't been fifty years—it hasn't even been fifteen."

"Well, I foolishly thought then I might live another fifty years. Neither one of us has the time he thought he might have. The school needs you, Daimbert—the western kingdoms need you."

This was taking on a nightmare quality, and exhaustion didn't help. "How could the school possibly need me?" I burst out. "I know nothing at all about how it's run. I don't have the first idea of its financial arrangements. I don't know what you have down in the cellars. I couldn't name you all the members of the faculty. I'm not even sure what the graduation requirements are—except I *am* fairly sure I never actually met them. There are whole branches of magic where I don't know even the simplest spells. There are—"

He interrupted me, a hand raised. The veins stood out like cords on the hand's back, brown-spotted with age. "That isn't what matters," he said quietly but firmly. "It's all in the files, and anyway Zahlfast can acquaint you with the principal details you'll require. What the school needs in its new Master is not someone who's memorized the library's shelf-list but someone who can set the direction for the next two centuries, both how students are trained and how the practice of magic is coordinated among all the western wizards."

I took two deep breaths, then spoke fast before I could change my mind. I had been keeping this a secret from the school for years, and even here, snatched from my bed for a dawn conversation with a dying man, it was hard to break that silence. Theodora was going to be furious with me for betraying a secret that was hers as much as mine, but I had no choice. "You can't possibly make me Master, sir. You couldn't even put me on the faculty. I've gone against all the traditions of wizardry. I'm married, and I have a daughter."

It was not until I saw how he had to turn his head to look up at me that I realized I had jumped to my feet as I spoke. He did not appear nearly as horrified as I had expected—he didn't even look surprised. After a moment I said, "Perhaps you didn't understand me."

For a second his eyes twinkled again; I noticed they had become bloodshot. "My body's going fast, and my grasp of magic isn't nearly what it used to be, but my mind is still perfectly functional, Daimbert. I've know for some time that you were married."

"To a witch," I said, sitting down faster than I intended.

"To a witch," he repeated.

"Elerius told you?"

He nodded. "I suspect in an attempt to turn me against you. And I have other sources of information as well. But this isn't nearly as startling news as both you and Elerius seem to think it should be. You needn't look so shocked! Wizards really don't marry in the normal course of things, because our first allegiance is to magic itself, but you certainly aren't the first wizard in the West to establish a long-term relationship with a woman, or to father a child." I started to say something, but he was still speaking. "Haven't you, for example, ever wondered about Elerius's own parentage?"

Too stunned to answer for a moment, I turned this over. The Master already knew my deepest secret, and Elerius had a secret that went even deeper. I had several times suspected he had grown up in an aristocratic court, although he never talked about it, and if he had grown up, say, the son of a Royal Wizard somewhere, and if that wizard had already begun teaching him magic when he was a little boy—the way I had begun teaching Antonia—

"Elerius's father was not school-trained," the Master continued, with an almost boyish delight in revealing what someone else had thought hidden. "And Elerius keeps his private life private much better than you do—if anyone else had the same interest as I do in the Royal Wizard of Yurt, they too would have found out all about you and your witch. But the head of a school for wizards has ways of learning things. No, Daimbert, I can appreciate why you're reluctant to take on the responsibilities of leadership so abruptly, and perhaps I should have brought you to the school much sooner. But the fact that you've had a woman back home whom you've thought of as your wife won't stop you from becoming Master here."

The way he phrased it made it clear that for him Theodora and Antonia were no more than a trivial distraction, one I'd be happy to put behind me. One more reason to refuse to become Master. But we were interrupted before I could answer.

A bird called suddenly above my head, causing me to jump. I looked up to see that it was not a real bird but an automaton, silver inset with chips of quartz. It perched on an irregularity on the wall above the door, singing through its metal beak. Its silver was tarnished but the note was almost unbearably sweet.

"An announcement that someone's here," said the Master, enjoying my surprise, "someone to whom I've taught the spells to activate the bird from outside. Melecherius brought it back years ago from the East, where I gather the mages make such automatons. Didn't I give you his book to read once? Come in!" he called.

The door opened and Whitey came in, carrying a tray which he placed on the bed. He stood silently, doing his best to pretend I didn't exist, until the Master nodded dismissal.

"Have some breakfast with me, Daimbert," he said when we were alone again. He pushed himself slowly and carefully to a sitting position and then poured tea. "Were you thinking I was about to expire this morning?" he asked, looking at me sideways in amusement. "You found me lying in bed because that's where all sensible wizards spend the night, not because I'm completely incapacitated. You'll still have several months to get used to your new position."

I shook myself and took the cup he offered. I appreciated his effort to make light of his approaching death, but I didn't believe him. The hot tea did only a little to take the chill from my insides. "By the way," I said, "do you think Elerius can hear us?"

He drank tea thoughtfully for a moment. "I do not believe so. Of course, he could theoretically overhear any conversation in the school if he wanted to, but not even he could be paying attention to what every single person is saying at all times. I brought you here in the dead of night, telling no one beyond my two young assistants, to make sure he would have no reason to pay attention right now."

The Master was eating dry toast with his tea. I forced myself to eat a piece, but it crumbled and seemed almost impossible to swallow. I had been wakened in the middle of the night, kidnapped, brought two hundred miles, and told I was going to have all the administrative responsibilities for western magic as soon as I stopped a wizard who would transform me into a tadpole without a qualm if he thought I stood in his way.

IV

"Are you sure, sir," I ventured slowly, "that it would in fact be truly terrible for the school to have Elerius at its head? After all, he really does always try to act for the best ..." And a few years back, I thought, he had summoned creatures of wild magic to attack the City, as part of one of his schemes. Well, I never had been able to prove that one on him definitively. But there were several other incidents I could think of in which he had sought to gain power, ranging from having a fanged gorgos attack the cathedral of Caelrhon, to working closely with a king who had sold his immortal soul, to digging up a dead body for his experiments ...

"Elerius's rule would be the end of wizardry as you and I know it," the Master said soberly, looking at me from under shaggy eyebrows. "You know the old expression: There are three who rule the world, the wizards, the Church, and the aristocracy. And I suppose one really ought to add a fourth, the mayors and city councils of the commercial centers throughout the Western Kingdoms. Elerius doesn't just want to be the head of the wizards' school. He wants to be the head of everything."

I stared at him a minute without comprehension. "Nobody can be the head of *everything*."

With breakfast inside him, the Master seemed to have revived a little. "You haven't been out of your little kingdom much the last few years," he said, "or you'd know what's been happening. You perhaps heard that the king whom Elerius had long served died last year?"

My immediate reaction was that Elerius must have killed him. But that would be a little too much for someone who prided himself on working for everyone's benefit. "Yes, I knew. My own king traveled to the funeral."

"As did many of the western kings. His was one of the wealthiest and largest kingdoms. Perhaps you didn't know that Elerius had continued as Royal Wizard there even after joining the school faculty?"

When I had earlier been offered—and refused—a position on the faculty, it had been clear that I would have to leave Yurt permanently if I accepted. "But he couldn't do that!"

"Well, he persuaded us that he could. After all, his kingdom is located just south of the City. And then last year, when the king died and the young prince was still too young to inherit, Elerius also became regent."

I had already had too many shocks this morning. "You mean he's acting as king? Of the West's most powerful kingdom? And now you're going to tell me he's planning to become head of the Church as well?"

The Master shook his head, for one moment looking amused again. "I don't think even Elerius would try that—for one thing, the Church doesn't have a single head, any more than there's a single emperor over all the western kingdoms. But he *is* hoping to become mayor of the City."

"I hadn't heard that the old mayor had so conveniently died," I said grimly.

"He hasn't. But his six-year term is almost up, and Elerius has become a candidate, and is actively campaigning against the old mayor's reelection."

My teeth were clenched; I made myself relax in the forlorn hope of coming up with better ideas. "Timing," I said after a minute. "Elerius has always held himself ready, incorporating whatever opportunities arise into his long-range plans. Last year he became a king, this year he'll become mayor of the West's largest city—are you *sure* your illness now isn't due at least in part to him?"

"Quite sure. But he's always known I couldn't live forever—even if I sometimes forgot that myself. And he knew he could prolong his regency and keep on having himself reelected mayor until I did die, at which time his plans would be complete."

"That is," I said, mostly under my breath, "now."

"So you see, Daimbert," said the Master, pushing away the breakfast tray, "I have no choice. I need to name my successor immediately, to ensure it will not be Elerius."

"Then," I said darkly, "he will just spend the time between now and when—when the issue of succession arises—in getting me out of the way: by telling the rest of the faculty, for example, about me and Theodora, or by reminding Zahlfast about the more hilarious aspects of that episode with the frogs, or even by ensuring that I have an unfortunate accident."

The Master had started to lean back against the pillows, but at this he sat up again. I could see the strain on his face, which he was doing his best to keep out of his voice. "Then we will not give him any time to formulate such plans," he said decisively. "Instead of announcing my decision to the rest of the faculty now, as I had intended, I shall give you a letter to show them immediately upon my death." He reached for paper and a quill from the table by the bed and began to write. His handwriting was just a little shaky. "As soon as you hear of my death, come straight to the City with this letter." He finished and held it out for the ink to dry, waving it gently. "You'll be elected at once, and Elerius will be stymied."

I took the paper as he handed it to me but did not look at it. I had almost expected him to write in letters of fire, or to put a spell on the words so that they would be invisible until another spell was spoken over them, but he had worked no magic on it. All he had done was write out what might as well be my own death-sentence.

He fumbled on the table for a book. "I should also give this to you now."

"What is it?" I asked without interest. The book was small but very thick, bound in crumbling leather; the cover looked as if it had once been stamped in gold.

"It belonged to the man who taught me magic—and I'll leave it to you to work out how long ago *that* was. He had it from even further back, from his own master. It's an account of the Dragons' Scepter."

"The Dragons' Scepter," I repeated dully. "I've never heard of it."

"Few people have. But the wizard who taught my own teacher had become a friend of the dragons."

I looked at the floor. A story that old was bound to have been improved greatly over the years. No one became a 'friend' of dragons. Next he was going to tell me that this ancient wizard had taken a thorn out of one's claw.

"This is his own account." I looked up, suddenly intrigued in spite of myself. The book had fallen open to show parchment pages, closely written in faded ink. An old book of tales was one thing—a ledger of spells written down by the man who had once worked them might be something much better. "He became not just the dragons' friend but to some extent their master, developing extremely powerful spells that even they had to obey. But still he, probably the greatest of the wizards of antiquity, found the magic very difficult, so he bound these spells to a special scepter. With it, anyone could force the unchanneled wild magic of the land of dragons into the structures of wizardry."

"And what became of this Scepter?" I asked, highly if unwillingly interested. "Do you think it still exists?"

"I am certain it does, Daimbert, or otherwise I would not be telling you about it. But when he felt his own death coming, he decided it was much too powerful to allow to fall into another wizard's hands."

"He feared someone like Elerius among his own pupils," I suggested. But it wouldn't have to be someone like Elerius. The thought of any wizard with authority over dragons made me all cold inside again.

"So he left it in the land of the dragons, concealed by spells that should elude even the best wizard—unless that wizard had his ledger."

"Then do you have the Scepter here?" I said excitedly. With that kind of power, the Master should be able to dispose of Elerius all by himself, and he certainly wouldn't need me.

He pulled the sheet up to his chin, shaking his head. "The spells, as far as I could puzzle them out, are enormously difficult and enormously dangerous. At first, when I acquired this book as a young man, I thought I would wait until my own mastery of magic had deepened. But with maturity came the realization that I could not trust myself with that much power. I did occasionally toy with the idea of how I could reshape the earth in the image of my own vision if even the dragons obeyed me ... But like my own master I finally set the spells aside, thinking I would reserve finding the Scepter until a desperate time arrived and I had no other choice. Now such a time has arrived, and I find my ability to work magic has weakened too much to try the spells."

Part of the quiet despair I thought I could now hear in his voice was from loss of the powers that had been his for centuries, but part, I thought, was due to him being genuinely afraid of Elerius. That made two of us.

"So you want me to have a dragon eat Elerius, is that it, sir?"

"You always were one for the joke," the Master said, half-closing his eyes and smiling. I had not been joking. "I want you to locate the Scepter before Elerius does and keep it from him."

"So he already knows about it," I said flatly. I might as well jump off the balcony without bothering with a flying spell and make it easy on myself.

"I told him a little about it some years ago," said the Master, his eyes closed and voice low. "At that time— Well, at one point I believed he was the person I would want to find it if anyone did. And I thought it would help that he knew some of the old magic of earth and herbs, as well as the modern scientific spells we develop and teach here at the school— you know some of that old magic too."

Though I had never apprenticed under him, my old retired predecessor as Royal Wizard of Yurt had taught me a lot of his herbal magic, when I first arrived with my brand-new and precarious school spells, and he'd left me his books when he died. Over the years I had also picked up other tidbits of the old magic. "But if Elerius already knows the spells to recover the Scepter ..."

"He doesn't," said the Master, eyes flicking open again. "I never showed him this book I am now giving you."

Unless Elerius had at some point quietly borrowed it.

"When you have the Scepter, Daimbert," the Master continued, "you'll have enough magical power that even Elerius won't dare oppose you. Now that I think about it, perhaps it would be best if you recover it at once, so you'll already have it by the time I die." We were interrupted before he could say more by the silver bird announcing someone. "It seems very early for that doctor Zahlfast insists I see," he grumbled.

I opened the door. This time it was Chin. He too tried to imply that he couldn't possibly have kidnapped me because I didn't even exist. "Excuse me, sir," he said to the Master, staring past me as he would past a piece of furniture, "but would you be able to have a visitor? Elerius wants to see you."

The Master gave an abrupt start, but he managed to say calmly, "Bring him up in about five minutes." As soon as the wizardry student had shut the door behind him he pushed the book toward me. "Go! Go at once! He can't find us together or he'll know. If I don't have a chance to talk to you again, be sure to bring that letter to the school as soon as—well, you know."

I sprang toward the window but stopped myself. "Goodbye, sir. And—" There didn't seem any good way to say it, so I didn't. Instead I said, "Thank you for accepting me into the school all those years ago, and for having faith in me."

And then I was gone, shooting out the window and across the City, a small yellow-clad form that Elerius should not even deign to notice. That is, unless Chin happened to mention that the new piece of furniture in the Master's chambers was also the Royal Wizard of Yurt. I flew eastward, the newly-risen sun in my eyes. It was that and exhaustion, I told myself, that made me start weeping.

The letter designating me as the Master's choice for his successor was folded and stuffed inside the cover of the old ledger book. I had no intention of ever producing that letter. I considered letting it flutter away to oblivion, but sentiment, the knowledge that it was the last thing I would ever have from his hand, stayed me. After all, I thought as I doggedly flew toward Yurt, I had promised the Master nothing. He might assume that when he was gone I would blithely try to use his dead influence and some long-forgotten spells out of the old magic to keep Elerius from heading the school, but I had never said I would do it.

Dear God. I was about to defy the dying wishes of the man who had made me a wizard.

V

It was a long flight back to Yurt, tired as I already was, so it was late afternoon before I came across the last stretch of woods to the castle. It reposed peacefully in the sun, its towers whitewashed, its moat dotted with swans. The royal flag snapping from the highest tower showed that the king was in residence.

I hovered for a moment, looking down. The staff was playing volleyball in the courtyard. Among the players I spotted the chestnut-colored braids of my daughter. I smiled and quietly descended.

Antonia was in most ways the same little girl she had always been, but her legs had become startlingly long in the last year or two, and her shape had begun subtly to change; before too long it would be a woman's, not a girl's. She was flushed and laughing from the game and did not at first notice me.

A player on the other side spiked the ball downward, apparently a sure point, but just before the ball touched the ground it abruptly stopped and reversed itself. Another player on Antonia's side batted it up and toward her. She and the ball rose majestically into the air, waiting until the opposition had jumped and come down again. Then she struck the ball hard and true over the net and slowly descended to the ground while her side cheered.

That was interesting, I thought. She'd used a lifting spell on the ball, but it was not the standard school spell. It looked like something she'd improvised herself.

A stable boy spotted me. "Wizard! Antonia's cheating again! Make her stop!"

She saw me then and ran toward me, pushing loose hairs away from her forehead. "There you are! Did you go somewhere exciting? Why didn't you take me along? And I'm not cheating! I told them I wouldn't work spells any more than once every five minutes, and I didn't."

"I just had to go to the City," I said, taking her comments in order, "and you wouldn't have found it exciting. Antonia, I think they'd really prefer if you played without working any magic at all, so why don't you try it that way for a while?"

"But she can't stop now!" a serving maid called to me. "Your daughter worked lots of spells when she was playing for the other side, so now it's our turn!"

"Make her stop, Wizard!" the stable boy protested again. "Can't you cast a spell that will keep someone from working any magic?"

"Well, yes, but it's a very complicated spell, and I don't want to take risks on its side effects just for a game." This was something I really didn't need to get into. "Besides," I said to Antonia, "you're all hot and sweaty from playing—I'm tired just looking at you! Why don't you take a little rest?"

She gave me a saucy look that could have been her mother's. "And are you *hungry* as well as tired? Shall I have a little snack too?" When I couldn't help laughing—probably undercutting months of conscientious fatherly discipline— she added, "And what are you still doing in your pajamas? Did you wear them to the City? If so I'm glad I wasn't along! It would have been *so* embarrassing."

I and the last shreds of my dignity retreated into my chambers to wash and change. The volleyball game started up again behind me.

Antonia and her mother lived in the city of Caelrhon, but I visited them and Antonia visited me frequently. Theodora still made her living as a seamstress and always insisted that the kingdom of Yurt didn't need a Royal Witch to go with its Royal Wizard, especially not one who would always be expected to sew on other people's buttons for them.

Two days later I took Antonia back home, her visit to Yurt over for this month. She hadn't seemed to notice that I was saddened and sober; now all I had to do was try to keep it from Theodora. She would be very sympathetic to hear that my old teacher was dying, but how was I going to explain that I had been offered the position of Master of the wizards' school and had refused?

I had an air cart of my own, in which we flew under the late summer sun toward the cathedral city of Caelrhon. Antonia's flying abilities might allow her to cheat at volleyball but were not yet up to a forty-mile flight. But she insisted on saying the spells herself to direct the skin of the purple flying beast, as it carried us across woods and ripening fields.

The old ledger with the centuries'-old spells was hidden behind other books at the back of my shelves. I was not even going to look at it, I told myself. I had seen enough books of spells out of the old magic over the years to know that between over-optimism on what a few herbs could do, a tendency not to bother writing down the steps that seemed self-evident to the writer, and badly-faded ink, most of them wouldn't work at all without extensive revision. Even aside from the impossibility of facing Elerius, I had no intention of going into the lair of dragons and using a defective spell in an attempt to reveal a Scepter that would, theoretically, make them treat me as their master rather than swallowing me in one gulp. Being swallowed whole remained by far the most likely outcome. The second most likely outcome was that a dragon would chew me up a little first.

Since this made such good logical sense, why did I feel so miserable?

But in the meantime I should try to enjoy being with Antonia. "Isn't your school starting up again soon?" I asked to make conversation.

She pulled her mouth into an expression of disgust. "I wish I didn't have to go to school in Caelrhon. I already know all the things they want us to learn! And they never teach us anything interesting, like about the land of dragons or secret treasure. I bet I could start at the wizards' school already if you and Mother would let me." I started to say something and changed my mind. "Besides, she says I can't do even the tiniest little spell while I'm at school. She says she doesn't want people to know that we're witches! I told her that I was a wizard instead, but it didn't make any difference."

"Um, well, at least nobody minds if you work spells in Yurt," I said. I wasn't going to get into the volleyball issue again.

"I know," she said thoughtfully, "but Mother still told me not to turn anybody there into a frog, not even for practice. But there's this bully at school," she added with new enthusiasm, "and I bet *lots* of people would be happy if I turned him into something. Do you think I could transform him into someone who wasn't a bully? Do you think I could do it in a way that no one would know it was me?"

"Spells can be traced," I said quickly and evasively, "and a transformations spell won't change someone's character. Besides, I think your mother would figure it out pretty quickly even if no one else did." How, I wondered, had a daughter of mine gotten so good so young on transformations spells? She would never have had trouble at Zahlfast's practical exam. But then I remembered. Elerius had taught her.

Theodora was sitting by the open casement window, sewing, when I brought the air cart down into the quiet cobbled street where she lived. Timbered house-fronts leaned over the street, but a ray of sunlight shone on the sea-green silk she was embroidering.

"Is that a skirt?" asked Antonia, kissing her mother. "Who is it for?"

"One of the mayor's daughters," Theodora answered. Then, when Antonia took her little bag off to her room, she added to me with a smile, "It is in fact not a skirt but, if you'll believe it, a dress. It's the latest style for young women at fashionable late-night dances. This skirt-part sits on her hips and keeps her legs decently covered, though the slit on the left side is designed to make sure that no one speculates in an untoward and uninformed way that those legs might be unattractive! And then this rather filmy part I'm embroidering now makes a tactical advance northward from the waistband, just about keeping her decent, as long as she doesn't dance too hard and disarrange the straps. And lest you fear that too much bare skin might be exposed, you'll be pleased to hear that she'll wear it with green ribbons wrapped around her left leg and both arms."

"Wow!" I exclaimed. "Is she coming by soon for a fitting? Do you need a helper?"

Theodora laughed, gave me a push, then relented and kissed me. So far, I thought, I was doing a good job of suggesting nothing was wrong.

"How about this black crepe?" I asked, noticing a pile of scraps on the table. "Are fashionable young ladies of the merchant class now wearing black for dances?"

"No, that was for a funeral just two days ago," Theodora said more soberly. "One of the masters of the dock-workers' guild was killed when a whole pile of crates fell on him. Apparently he lived just long enough for his wife to get down to the docks, and he told her, there in front of everybody, about this illegitimate son he'd had years ago! It turned out the lad knew perfectly well whose son he was, but they'd always kept it from the wife. But she was very gracious about it, even invited the son to the funeral."

"Would you invite *my* illegitimate son to my funeral?" I asked teasingly.

Theodora gave me a quick look from amethyst eyes. "If I learned you'd had a child I hadn't known about, of course I'd invite him or her to your funeral: a funeral which would happen *very soon*!"

We both laughed, and I was kissing Theodora properly when Antonia came back. "When I get married," she pronounced, "you aren't going to catch *me* doing that mushy stuff all the time."

After Antonia had gone to bed that evening, Theodora and I sat a little while by the dying fire, me on the couch and she on the hearth-rug, her head leaning against my knee. I worked my fingers through her curly hair to find and trace the edge of her ear, staring the while into the red and orange coals before us.

"At least Antonia isn't interested in boys yet," she commented. "A good thing, too. Even if she's just been away for a few days she always surprises me when she comes back by how grown-up she looks. She's going to be a lovely young woman."

"A young woman who's going to be locked up for ten years from the time she first looks at a man with interest," I said firmly.

Theodora laughed and squeezed my leg, although I had been at least partially serious. "Have you spoken recently to the bishop?" she asked.

"Joachim? No. Is there something I can do for him?"

Theodora embroidered altar cloths and sewed vestments for the cathedral, and it sometimes seemed these days that she saw my old friend the bishop of Caelrhon more than I did. "Apparently he's worried about something to do with the

bishop of the great City," she said. "I was just wondering if
you'd heard about it, since the wizards' school is also in the
City. I told him you were coming today, and he left a note for
you."

Affairs of the Church held no interest for me. "The
Master of the school is dying," I said suddenly.

Theodora turned then to look up at me. "I'm very sorry.
Is that what's been bothering you?" When I cocked my head
at her she added, "You should know me better than that,
Daimbert! Did you expect your light-hearted joking this
afternoon would make me think everything was fine?"

I touseled her hair. "Well, everything in Yurt is fine. And
the Master is very old—we all knew he couldn't live forever."
I was thinking, if I had agreed to pursue the Master's idiotic
dying scheme, I would be here telling Theodora good-bye
forever.

"So will they just elect a new head from among the faculty?" Theodora asked thoughtfully. She shook her head and
squeezed my hand. "I'm sorry, I know in some ways the old
Master was like a father to you, but I'm afraid I'm thinking
not about him so much as how the school might change. You
know you've said several times that some members of the faculty seem open to the idea of starting to accept women as students as well as men."

"Well, by the time Antonia would be ready to go to the
school," I said noncommittally, "there may well have been
some changes." Elerius might once have taught my daughter
some magic, I thought, but I was absolutely determined that
he would not have a chance to get his hands on her again.
Theodora and I would train her ourselves.

"I visited the Master the other day," I continued slowly,
"probably the last time I'll ever see him. And I—I told him I
was married to you. We've always kept this from the school,
and I'm sorry I didn't ask you about it first, but I thought for
various reasons that I should tell him now."

Theodora rested her chin on my knee, her amethyst eyes dark in the shadows. "But you don't sound as though the school is planning to cast you out of institutionalized wizardry."

I shook my head. "No, no," I said, not meeting her eyes. "In fact, just the opposite! I think," I added in a rush, "that the Master considers this a temporary situation, and that I'll tire of you sooner or later. He is, of course, completely wrong."

Theodora smiled and rose to her feet. "Time for bed," she said, taking my hand and pulling me up with a tug. "You can show me just how tired you are or aren't of me!" I slipped an arm around her waist, but she paused by her cloth scraps. "Here," she said, digging among them. "I should give this to you before I completely lose track of it."

It was the note from Joachim. I stuffed it into my pocket and nuzzled Theodora's hair, wanting distraction from thoughts of the school.

But she stepped away. "I won't think you're tired of me if you want to read your letter first. After all, it's from the bishop!"

I pulled her toward me again but obediently broke the seal on the letter with the thumb of my free hand. "Didn't anybody ever tell you," I asked with a chuckle, "that witches aren't supposed to have any respect for the Church? It can't be anything very important or he would have telephoned."

Joachim's note was short—he had never had any use for chit-chat. But it turned out to be very important after all.

"There is a problem with the election of the new bishop of the City," it read, "and the cathedral there has asked other western bishops for assistance. Normally I would never bother you with this, but there seems to be a difficulty with the wizards' school trying inappropriately to influence the election. I need your advice on the wizard Elerius."

part two ✢ naurag

I

So now that he's effectively a king, is about to become the leader of the wizards' school, and also mayor of the City, it sounds as if he also intends to dominate the Church."

I sat in Joachim's office at the cathedral, the morning sun shining on the polished woodwork as if nothing was wrong. Faint in the distance were the rumble of winches and workmen's shouts from the ongoing construction of the new church. I had just been filling the bishop in on the approaching death of the Master and on Elerius's intention to work it into his schemes. All I omitted was the Master's desire to make me his successor, which, because I was not going to do it, was irrelevant.

"This is even more serious than I had thought," Joachim commented gravely.

"So is Elerius trying to get himself elected as bishop of the great City?" I asked, feeling both furious and helpless.

"It's not quite that simple, Daimbert." Joachim drummed his fingers on his desk, something I had never before seen him do. He must be wondering if it was appropriate for a church leader to be asking the advice of a wizard. Not that I had any good advice to give him. "Normally the cathedral priests of each diocese elect new bishops on their own," he continued, "with little if any advice from outside. And when the old bishop of the City died two years ago, that is just what they did. They had a dispute within the cathedral chapter for a while, with two if not three contenders as I understand it.

Eventually they compromised, taking a path many cathedral chapters have taken before them. They elected none of the various candidates, but instead a holy hermit from up in the hills, one whom some people were already calling a saint."

"Don't tell me," I said bitterly. "The holy hermit has decided that being the head of the most important diocese in the West is much too active a life for somebody who wanted to devote himself to solitary prayer. *Especially* since an angel has been showing up, telling him it's fine to step down: an angel with a black beard and illusory wings."

The sun was a glint in Joachim's dark eyes. "I do not believe Elerius has been quite that blatant. But when the hermit indeed did, as might have been expected, return to his hermitage a few months ago, the cathedral chapter was faced with resolving the same internal split they had been unable to resolve two years ago. And Elerius, expressing what he says is a deep yearning for the wizards' school and the Church to work together for the betterment of humanity, has thrown his support behind one of the candidates."

"Where is he *getting* these ideas?" I demanded.

For a moment Joachim looked amused. He could find amusement in the strangest places. "He may have gotten this idea from you and me."

If Elerius intended to turn even my friendship with Joachim into part of his schemes, there was nothing he would not do. "So is it too late?" I asked quietly.

The bishop stopped smiling. "His candidate has not yet prevailed. Too many of the cathedral priests are uncomfortable either with the man himself or with his backing from the wizards' school. As much as I myself believe that some of my colleagues are too quick to dismiss the idea that any good can be found in a wizard, in this case their caution is salutary."

I didn't answer. For all I knew he was being amused again. He turned his enormous black eyes on me. Even after all these years, I still sometimes found Joachim's gaze disconcerting. "So, Daimbert, what are you planning to do to stop him?"

First the Master, now the bishop. What had I ever done to make the two men I respected most think I might somehow be able to stop the best wizard ever to come out of the school? "I'm not going to do *anything*," I snapped. "You priests can try to find a way to keep his influence out of the Church, but there's nothing I can do to keep him out of the direction of the wizards' school. I guess there's still a chance that the citizens of the City will have too much sense to elect him mayor, and maybe King Paul and some of the other western kings can prevail upon his royal family to have someone else act as regent there, but all the faculty at the school will be delighted to have him as their new Master."

"I can see this will be very delicate," said Joachim thoughtfully. "I am sure you wizards don't think of God as speaking through the electors, as cathedral priests do when they elect a new bishop, but it may still be difficult, at least at first, to persuade others to join you in opposing a man whom they have just chosen to head organized wizardry."

"Didn't you hear me?" I burst out. "I just said I *wasn't* going to oppose him. Even if I didn't know perfectly well that any magic I tried against him would blow up in my face, at least I'd recognize the horrible danger—to Theodora and to Antonia, and for that matter to everyone in Yurt, as well as to me. I'm going to stay quietly at home and hope he doesn't think about me at all."

"Yes," said Joachim as though I had made a different comment altogether. "I understand that you might not want to trust even me with your plans, at least at this early stage. Secrecy may be vital, though I rather doubt Elerius has spies here in the cathedral. But I do want you to know that I shall always pray for you and will help you in any other way that I can. All you need do is ask."

It was a good thing, I thought as I flew home to Yurt, that I hadn't told Theodora all of Elerius's plans. Normally I hated to keep things from her, but this was different. She— and for that matter Antonia—would probably have offered their help too in what could only be a suicidal effort. The thought of Antonia trying to oppose Elerius, armed only with a few transformations spells he had taught her himself, made my blood run cold.

But it wouldn't hurt, I thought grumpily as the air cart banked over the castle, to take a look at the ancient wizard's spells. Then, once it was conclusive that what the Master seemed to think was my only hope was instead completely impossible, the issue would stop nagging at me.

King Paul met me in the castle courtyard as I carefully set my air cart down outside my chamber doors. "How is your wife?" he asked with what seemed unusual enthusiasm. "It must be delightful to be married—being with the one you love best, acknowledging your love to all."

"Theodora is fine, thank you," I said, wondering what could have caused this sudden interest. He had been a witness, standing next to me at a side altar in the cathedral when Joachim married Theodora and me, but he had never before burst into paeans in praise of matrimony.

"You wizards probably don't know what it is to be afraid," he added in an apparently abrupt change of topic.

"Actually I have an excellent idea," I said testily, but he gave no sign that he'd even heard.

"I'm going to do it, Wizard," he continued with a rather forced grin. "But I may want you there in case I start to get cold feet."

I didn't have the slightest idea what he was talking about

and told him so, just barely keeping full-blown irritation out of my voice. He still didn't seem to notice.

"It's wondering what Mother is going to say about my choice that's the worst," he said. It slowly dawned on me through my own concerns that my liege lord was extremely nervous about something.

And the most likely explanation was that he had finally decided to get married. Ever since Paul had become king of Yurt, over ten years ago, there had been a steady parade of princesses and well-born ladies who just happened to be traveling through our part of the Western Kingdoms and stopped to visit the royal family. The existence of a handsome young king with emerald eyes and an excellent temper was bound to attract attention. Some of the young ladies had stayed a few days, some a few weeks. Paul was friendly to all of them, gave balls in their honor, and waved cheerfully from the battlements as they rode away at last. His mother was equally friendly to all, but her own candidate for new queen of Yurt remained Princess Margareta of Caelrhon. Margareta had been selected as queen of choice when she was not much older than Antonia, and while waiting for Paul to make up his mind she had grown into an elegant and languorous young woman.

"It's silly to be this nervous," said Paul, wiping his hands on his trouser legs.

I didn't want to worry about my king's romantic life on top of everything else, but I reminded myself firmly that it was of primary importance to everybody else in Yurt. And since wizards, even incapable wizards like me, lived longer than anyone else, if I was going to stay holed up here forever it should also be important to me who would give birth to the king I would serve after Paul. "Your mother must have figured out by now that you're not interested in the Princess Margareta."

"It's not that," he said, stepping back and forth from one foot to the other. I saw him realize what he was doing and make himself stop. He clenched his fists and looked full at me for the first time. "Wizard, I'm going to marry Gwennie."

"Well, I guess that's wonderful, sire," I muttered, since some answer seemed called for. Inwardly I was much more stunned than I dared show. It was one thing to think in the abstract about two young people who suited each other very well, another to imagine what the kings of the surrounding kingdoms—and for that matter the masters of the wizards' school—would say if Gwennie actually became queen of Yurt. "I hope you'll be very happy together."

"She said she'd meet me here," he said, glancing from side to side. This time of the day my end of the courtyard was generally deserted. "So I'm going to ask her now."

"Then I'll just step into my chambers and—"

But he caught my arm. "Keep your window open. I'd really feel better if I knew you were right there."

I obediently tied the air cart to a ring outside my door and went inside, where I could look out and watch Paul fidget. Even with the window open I was fairly well screened by climbing roses. I had previously thought myself that he ought to marry Gwennie, but now that it came down to it all the reasons why it would be an incredible social gaffe rushed to my attention. And I could certainly appreciate why he was nervous about telling his mother.

There was a rapid click of heels, and Gwennie came around the corner. Blonde like the king and exactly the same age, his childhood friend, his trusted assistant in everything to do with the functioning of the castle, Gwennie was the daughter of the castle cook and was castle constable in her own right. "Sorry I'm late, Paul, uh, sire," she said with a smile, pinning back stray tendrils of hair. "That messenger from Caelrhon brought a whole pile of tradesmen's bills this morning, and I'm sure some of them can't be right. For example, you didn't have a jeweler set a diamond into a ring last week, did you?"

"Um, well, actually, Gwennie, I did." There was a brief pause. "Gwendolyn."

"You did?" She sounded surprised. "In that case, I won't send the jeweler the rather sharp message I've just been composing. But I wish you'd told me."

Paul seemed momentarily unable to continue. In many ways he was still the same good-hearted, reckless, perennially cheerful young man he had been when he assumed the throne, so easy-going that it sometimes seemed that the only thing to stir his passion was his stud stables. His mother focused on the need for a royal heir to the kingdom; I kept thinking instead that he ought to become more sober and regal—more like his father, except that his father had already been very old when I knew him. A nagging voice in the back of my mind liked to point out that I hadn't been any more mature when I was Paul's age, but I had an answer to that one: I'd been a brand-new graduate from the wizards' school, whereas Paul was a king.

"The ring was supposed to be a secret," he brought out. "A splendid secret."

Through my curtain of roses I could see Gwennie stiffen. "Shall I be the first, sire," she said in a formal and artificial voice, "to wish you and the Princess Margareta joy?"

"No, no, no," said Paul quickly. "I'm sorry, Gwennie. I'm going at this altogether wrong." He took her arm and dropped it again. "But you don't need to worry about Margareta."

She raised one eyebrow quizzically. "Then what *do* I need to worry about?"

Paul floundered for a second, then threw himself resolutely onto his knees at her feet. "Gwendolyn," he said in a high voice that didn't sound anything like him, "Gwennie, dearest, I want to ask you to be my queen. The ring, this ring," fumbling it out of his pocket, "is a symbol of the love and harmony we shall share together." After a moment he

added, as if reciting a lesson, "A diamond, the hardest of all
the minerals, stands for the permanence of our bond."

Gwennie seemed unable to speak. Paul rose to his feet and
dusted off his knees. "Here, go on, put it on your finger," he
said in his normal voice. Gwennie's hand closed around the
ring but she did not put it on. "Glad that's over!" he continued conversationally. "I'm sure you're surprised. After all,
you've doubtless loved me for years, but you believed I
thought of you as just the castle constable and my oldest
chum."

Gwennie started to say something but Paul was still speaking, and she drew back a step without interrupting. Her lips
narrowed into a straight line I would have found ominous,
but the king wasn't paying attention.

"Didn't you ever wonder why I never married any of the
young women who've been thrown at me?" He sounded
cheerful now, confident of the answer she had not yet given.
"I realized a long time ago that none of them could ever be
the same comfortable companion you've always been. And
yet it was obvious I couldn't very well marry my own cook's
daughter! And I didn't want to insult you by asking you to be
my mistress. So I thought I might be like Father, who didn't
marry anybody until he was so old he should have been a
grandfather! In the meantime you and I could still be friends,
and by the time we were old maybe no one would care anymore if we did get married."

From my window I could see a furious red working its way
up Gwennie's cheeks. Paul didn't notice, and I had a feeling
that my suddenly shouting out to him that he was doing this
entirely wrong, and had to stop before he made it even worse,
wouldn't help the situation anyway.

"So you're probably wondering why I'm asking you now.
Too surprised to say anything?" he added, as though realizing
for the first time that she was standing stiff and silent. "Well,
I've decided that Mother has a point, I really do need an heir,

and besides I've always liked kids myself. So I concluded it probably wasn't a good idea to wait too long if I was going to marry you eventually anyway. Then I had an idea: I can ennoble you! The royal chancellor over in Caelrhon just retired after serving two kings for years and years, and King Lucas gave him a patent of nobility as a reward for his faithful service. So I decided if I did the same for you, then nobody could throw your parentage up at us. Would you rather be a countess or a duchess—before, of course, becoming queen?"

II

Gwennie took a deep breath and found her voice at last. "Let me thank you," she said in a low tone, "thank you warmly for the honor you have done me. I'm sure it required considerable ingenuity to find a way that we might be married without your totally embarrassing yourself. But it will, I am certain, still be a considerable relief to you when I refuse."

Paul had been listening, his head tilted to one side, a smile on his lips. When she paused, it took several seconds for the smile to dissolve. "What do you mean, refuse?" he demanded then.

Gwennie took his hand, pressed the ring into it, and stepped away. "I mean I will not marry you," she said. Her voice trembled for a second, but she steadied it. "And therefore you need not worry about making me a countess or a duchess or anything else. But I shall always be grateful for the thought."

"Gwennie, I— I'm flabbergasted! It never occurred to me you wouldn't want to marry me!"

"It can occur to you now," she said briskly and turned on her heel. "Now, if you will excuse me, sire, I need to return to my duties."

Paul jumped to block her path. "Gwennie, wait! You can't just leave me like this!"

"You've had your answer," she said, not meeting his eyes. "What more do you need?"

"A reason! I thought you loved me."

She kept her gaze resolutely fixed somewhere beyond his left ear. "My feelings do not come into this. As castle constable, I am sworn to uphold the best interests of Yurt, which precludes allowing its king to become a laughing-stock through such a misalliance."

"Laughing-stock! Gwennie, you can't be serious. It's— I see it now! You love somebody else! You don't want to marry above your station because you'd feel uncomfortable being a queen. It's that stable man, isn't it!"

For a second Gwennie looked as though she might laugh but changed her mind. "Do not make yourself jealous, sire, over any stable man. But you are quite correct." Her voice had turned to ice. "I have no interest in marrying someone who thinks I am aspiring 'above my station.'"

"No, Gwennie, that didn't come out right." He took her arm, and she, looking imperious, stood stiffly while waiting for him to release it. "I mean, don't all young girls dream of growing up to be queen?"

"I dreamed of becoming castle constable," she replied without any expression.

At this Paul burst out, "Damnation, Gwennie, I love you!"

"It would have helped," she said through frozen lips, "if you had mentioned that before, and not in that tone of voice."

This was becoming almost too painful to observe. I retreated back into my chambers, but I could still hear their voices clearly through the open casement, and after a few seconds I silently stepped back to where I could see them again.

"Of course I love you," Paul said defensively. He had

released her arm but still blocked her path, and she made no attempt to get by. "I said so! I said the ring stood for the 'love and harmony we would share together.' I know I said that."

"Then let me remind you of what *else* you said," she answered, able to restrain her fury no longer. "I would have had to refuse you no matter how you proposed, but you've made it remarkably easy for me, sire! You told me you couldn't possibly marry your own cook's daughter. You told me the only reason you decided to marry now was because you liked children. You told me you'd always been sure that I loved you, and that all girls want to grow up to be queen. What am I *supposed* to make of this, sire?"

"Can't you even call me Paul like you usually do?" he broke in plaintively.

"I'll tell you, *sire*, what I make of this." She faced him squarely, fists on her hips, eyes flashing—both beautiful and terrifying. Paul's own features seemed to turn to stone as she spoke.

"You're comfortable as king of Yurt, so you didn't want to complicate your life with anyone new. What better way, you thought, to resolve the problem of the inheritance than to make your oldest chum serve as a brood mare as well? After all, you decided, thinking of the years I've faithfully served you and sure that I must love you—without ever asking if I did!—I would serve you in this too. An entirely reasonable fear of social stigma held you back for a while, until this 'patent of nobility' notion came to your attention. The last inconvenience out of the way for a convenient and comfortable marriage. Well, let me tell you something, sire. You say you didn't want to insult me by asking me to be your mistress. I would almost rather that you had. In that case, you might have least have felt compelled to say from the outset that you loved me!"

Her voice broke with the final words. She spun past him, and this time he made no attempt to stop her. The tears were already running down her cheeks as she fled away across the courtyard.

Paul hesitated until she was almost out of sight, then shouted, "Gwennie! Wait!" and started after her. I could hear a door slam over on the staff's side of the castle long before he had a chance to catch up.

Several minutes later there were rapid hoof beats on the stones of the courtyard, and Paul's red roan stallion shot out of the stables, the king leaning low over his neck. For a second the hooves sounded hollow on the drawbridge, then they were gone.

I slowly shook my head. Paul would not be back until dark, if then. My own personal life had had a few disasters along the way, but the king seemed at the moment far ahead of me.

"And if the chief authority of a kingdom can't even make a cook's daughter do what he wants," I said to no one in particular, "then it's completely hopeless for wizards to try to control all of humanity."

Something caught my eye, sparkling in the sunlight out in the courtyard. I went out to take my air cart around to the stables, now that things were quiet again, and stooped to pick it up. It was the diamond ring.

Neither Paul nor Gwennie was at dinner that evening. No one said anything about overhearing them, or about seeing the king belatedly chase a weeping Gwennie toward her chambers, and there weren't even any whispers. But there was a distinct undercurrent of *knowing*. Conversation was stilted, and topics that might generally come up—such as marriage and children, jewelry, even Paul's and Gwennie's names—were not even mentioned.

"I believe," commented the queen mother as we ate, "it must be at least a month since the Princess Margareta has visited Yurt. The poor girl will think we're neglecting her. I'll call the royal court of Caelrhon this evening and invite her."

After dinner I determinedly took out the old wizard's ledger and pulled close a magic lamp. It couldn't hurt, I told myself again, to have a look at the old spells of the wizard who had taught the wizard who had trained the Master and founder of the school. The thought occurred to me as I reluctantly sat down at my desk that my time this evening would be much better spent out looking for Paul, who was still not home, but I told myself firmly that the king could take care of himself.

I started conscientiously at the beginning of the book. Dust from the crumbling cover made me sneeze as I opened it. The first page said, in letters that still twinkled like stars in spite of the passage of centuries, "I, Naurag, most wise of all wizards, record herein my experiences and my spells. Let only the stalwart of heart and most learned of mind peruse them." The handwriting was careful and clear—to me it looked like a very young man's.

The volume started off with a few weather spells, that appeared remarkably like what we still used at harvest-time, then turned to what seemed a highly improper spell, which would allow one to see inside another's clothes—if, I supposed, one still had doubts about the shape of the mayor's daughter. "This most cunning and mischievous spell have I devised myself," the long-dead wizard Naurag had written proudly at the end of it. But I should not let myself be distracted. The spell for the Dragons' Scepter should be in here somewhere.

The next several pages were blank, to be followed not by new spells but by a sort of memoir, written in a more rushed hand. "Having been most grievously maltreated, I shall bid adieu to the confines of this kingdom and cast my fate and that of my purple companion to the eddies of the air."

Purple companion? I bent closer, growing more interested in spite of myself. This purple companion, it appeared as
I continued to read, was winged, and the wizard rode upon it.
Naurag seemed to have had some sort of quarrel with his
king, although I couldn't determine over what—all that he
told me was how his enemies had conspired against him,
"casting truth from them as one would a spent gourd."
Gourd? I read on.

"For belike 'tis the jealousy of that magic-caster whom I
drove hence which now poisons the thoughts and actions of
the man I believed ere now to be my faithful lord. That one's
aim is e'er bent on securing my purple companion to himself."

I knew that back in the days before the wizards' school was
founded, western wizards quarreled with each other constantly, and in this case it looked as though a disagreement
with another wizard had escalated until Naurag, whose
ledger I now held, had been forced to flee his own kingdom.
And what was this 'purple companion'?

The creature seemed as devoted to Naurag as a large dog,
readily obeying the wizard's magical commands even while
he was still working out the exact words to use for them,
sleeping with its wings spread over him at night as they fled
across the Western Kingdoms, expecting in return only a
steady diet of melons and gourds.

Suddenly I realized what it must be. An air cart. Not the
dead skin but the living purple flying beast from which it had
originally been made. I knew that such beasts lived up in the
northern land of wild magic, but I had never seen a live one.
Too bad—this one sounded rather likeable.

I wondered somewhat guiltily how the two flying beasts
whose skins now served as the school's air cart and mine had
happened to die. I rather hoped they had lived long and
happy lives, watching little flying beasts grow up around
them, until, rich with experience, they had expired naturally,

happy in the knowledge that even when they were gone their skins would keep on serving the men who had been their friends.

Out in the courtyard I heard the sound of hooves, then voices—King Paul, home again at last. He always took off for a miles' long run on his stallion whenever he had something to think over. In this case, I thought, turning a parchment page, his thinking was unlikely to have resulted in any satisfactory conclusions.

This part of the memoir was rather disjointed, having apparently been written at odd moments as the wizard and the flying beast fled from their enemies. The kingdoms still had the same names, and it was disconcerting to see places I knew mentioned here as being ruled by cruel kings with savage and volcanic tempers, unlike the rather peaceable lot into which we wizards had, ever since the Black Wars, shaped the lords we served.

"Having perfected the commands which my purple companion is most wont to obey, I hereby record them for the benefit of the next wizard who may essay to tame one of these creatures." The spells, written down carefully in the Hidden Language, were exactly what we still used to direct the air cart—the spells I had recently been teaching Antonia.

I sat back, chewing thoughtfully on a pencil. The castle had grown quiet around me. Was this perhaps not a real memoir at all, but something the Master had created just for me? Were references to what the kings of men could do to each other without organized wizardry to oppose them supposed to make me realize how necessary it was for someone responsible to take over the school's direction?

But I shook my head. The Master was dying, without nearly the energy to have forged an elaborate document that looked so convincingly like something eight hundred years old. Besides, he would have seen no need for such a ruse to work on my conscience—he thought I had already agreed to succeed him.

And if the spells looked familiar, I thought as I pulled the volume toward me again, it was because school spells had not been created in a vacuum. Many were in origin the spells the Master taught to the wizardry students because he himself had learned them as an apprentice, from a wizard who had in turn studied with Naurag.

But in here were spells that had never been taught, spells that were supposed to bind dragons. I found my place and kept on reading. These spells, if anyone was ever to use them again, were to be learned by me directly from Naurag.

III

I kept on reading long into the night, falling into bed only when my eyes began watering so badly I could no longer focus. A knock woke me what seemed only minutes later: not mysterious wizards this time, but my breakfast. "Leave it on the table," I mumbled, rolled away from the light, and went back to sleep.

When I woke several hours later, it was again to the sound of a knock. I pushed the hair out of my eyes, pulled on my dressing gown, and opened the door.

This time it was Gwennie. "I have come for your breakfast tray," she said stonily, not meeting my eyes.

"Um, I haven't quite finished yet," I said, retreating. I took a quick swallow of cold tea and bit into a regrettably stale cinnamon cruller. "Maybe if you came back in a few minutes—"

She followed me inside. Now that I thought about it, it was curious that Gwennie should be running kitchen errands. Ever since she had become castle constable in her own right, her mother the cook had given up her plans to make Gwennie her own successor.

She slammed my door shut and showed no further interest in the tray. "Were you listening yesterday?" she asked, low and intense.

It was clearly no use pretending ignorance. Her eyes were unnaturally bright, her fists clenched at her sides. "I'm sorry, Gwendolyn, I'm afraid I couldn't help it," I said from behind the inadequate shield of a teacup. "My windows were open, and you and King Paul were right outside when—"

"Then let me explain something," she said in a voice of ice. "You in fact heard nothing at all. He did not speak. I did not answer. Is that clear?"

"Very much so," I said quickly, stopping myself just in time from adding, "My lady." At this point she would have considered it the gravest possible insult. "By the way," I ventured to add, "is the king around this morning? I had something I needed to ask him—on quite a different topic," I continued hastily, "than the topic which, of course, never came up in the first place."

"I understand he is still lying lazily in bed this morning," she responded loftily, already moving back toward my door. "Some plaintiffs have come to receive his judgment, and I have been forced to make them wait." And she was gone, without taking my tray.

I dipped the cruller into the rest of the tea and considered what I had learned last night. Paul had doubtless spent fruitless hours lying awake, alternately cursing Gwennie and himself, but I had actually discovered something. Spells to master dragons really might exist after all, and it was possible I could work them.

So far this was just an intellectual exercise, I told myself while washing and dressing. Even if I did somehow manage to master some rather small dragon, this didn't mean I was going to head the school. Such a piece of antiquarian knowledge certainly wouldn't give me the wisdom and authority the new Master would need, much less make me capable of stopping Elerius if all the other faculty wanted him—though I still rather liked my idea of having a dragon eat him.

Naurag and his 'purple companion' had eventually fled entirely from the Western Kingdoms, pursued by enemies about whom he made highly disparaging comments without ever saying explicitly why they were his enemies. They had traveled thousands of miles north, beyond the high frost mountains, to the realm of dragons and wild magic.

I had once reached the borders of this land, and that had been plenty wild enough for me, but Naurag had traveled further and further north. Reading between the lines of his account, I saw a growing intoxication with the power and ease of his magic. Spells worked far better in the land of dragons than in the lands of men, as they had taught us at school; some of the best students (never of course including me) had even been taken on field trips to experience it themselves. Naurag had discovered that everything he wanted to do came easier and easier the further he traveled—until he had arrived one day in a valley full of dragons.

I crossed the castle courtyard to the great hall. As always in the summer, the tall doors stood open to the air. Inside King Paul sat on his throne, scowling, listening to two men who each claimed the other had cheated him disgracefully in a business transaction. I went to stand beside my king.

Back in the days of Paul's father, I had spent many days standing stiff and majestic beside the royal throne, lending I hoped an air of mysterious awe, while Joachim, who in those days before he became bishop was still royal chaplain of Yurt, had stood on the other side, lending a quite real air of spiritual authority. But Paul's law-giving tended to be more informal. In this case, he looked as if he didn't understand what either man was talking about and could use all the help he could get.

I didn't have to stand long. Paul suddenly slapped his knee with one hand. "That's enough!" he roared.

The two plaintiffs stopped short. "Excuse me, sire—" one started to say.

"You're *both* in the wrong! Both of you cheated the other. I don't want to hear another word of your whining! Instead you're each going to pay the royal treasury one hundred silver pennies as a penalty for wasting our time like this. Pay it to the constable on the way out—yes, that's right, the same young woman who showed you in. You're going to have to settle for yourselves whatever sordid quarrel brought you here. Well, what are you waiting for? Is it going to take the edge of the sword to teach you to listen to your king?"

King Paul was not wearing a sword, but the two plaintiffs did not wait to see if he would summon a knight to back up his threat. They fled out the tall doors, while I wondered if back before the Black Wars scenes like this had been more common, except that then the kings and their knights would have followed through with immediate action against those who displeased them.

Paul whirled on me. "What do *you* want, Wizard?"

At least he didn't bother telling me that I had never overheard a conversation he had invited me to overhear. "Um, excuse me, sire, I had a question about my position here."

This wasn't exactly the best time to raise this, but I had begun worrying during the night that Elerius might try to get me out of Yurt. Finding a way to persuade Paul to fire me as Royal Wizard might, he would think, make me more likely to listen to his blandishments.

"I hope you're not about to tell me," the king growled, "that I've been shamelessly cheating a wizard of your caliber by not paying you enough."

So did Paul expect me to ask for a bribe in return for silence on his romantic affairs? "Oh no, sire," I said hastily. "Rather—" It was going to be hard to put this delicately. "If something happened, if you heard, for example, something about me from the wizards' school, would you be in a hurry to hire a new wizard?"

The king was surprised enough to stop frowning. "Are you in trouble, Wizard? Is your school trying to drive you out of Yurt? It isn't that— They aren't going to hold it against you after all this time that you have a wife?"

He winced a little on the last word but kept his concern for me, not himself. "No, well, I might indeed be in some sort of difficulty," I said vaguely. "Nothing serious yet, but it's hard to tell. And I was just hoping, sire— That is, I was hoping that whatever you heard, you wouldn't be too quick to replace me. And by the way," I added in a rush, holding out the diamond ring, "I think you dropped this."

Paul pushed it roughly into his pocket. Then he took a breath, stood up, and slapped me on the shoulder. "I can tell, Wizard, that this is more serious than you like to admit. But don't add to your worries by wondering about your position. You'll always be my Royal Wizard. After all, didn't I award you the Golden Yurt? And in the meantime," his voice dropping, "if you need any help, do not hesitate to ask. Especially," he hesitated, then hurried on, "especially if there's some way to help you that will get me out of this castle."

"I'll let you know!" I promised quickly and mendaciously, then returned to my chambers and Naurag's book. I was certainly not going to take the king along on a doomed attempt to stop Elerius just because he wanted to avoid the embarrassment of daily encounters with Gwennie.

Even in Naurag's rather laconic style, his encounters with dragons sounded terrifying. Only two things saved his life: the rapid flying speed of his 'purple companion,' and the fact that the spells he used to communicate with it had certain affinities to spells that would get the attention even of dragons.

Late last night I had reached a much more powerful spell than anything I had seen so far in the book, page after page written small, a spell in the Hidden Language that would, Naurag claimed, force a dragon to obey. "I compose these words," he interjected at one point, "at the borders of the magical realm, in a homey setting I would ne'er have expected to discover so far from man's accustomed habitations. The people here are wont to climb very high, building their very dwellings in the faces of cliffs. Their toes and fingers are most marvelously long, and their children seem quite taken with my purple companion." I had fallen asleep without seeing the end of the spell.

I looked at it again in daylight to see if it might still appear as feasible as it had last night: if, starting with an air cart spell, one could ultimately gain the mastery of ferocious creatures of wild magic. The letter the old Master had given me, choosing me as his successor, was still tucked into the volume—I had been using it as a bookmark. Not wanting to chance one of the maids coming across it, I stuffed it into the back of a drawer and pondered Naurag's magic.

I recognized what he was doing, beginning with a known spell, making some improvisational leaps based on a sound understanding of basic spell structure, adding other steps that came to him out of sheer desperation, and when even that was not enough, working in entirely different spells that would move one along quite unexpected paths within magic's four dimensions, in the brazen hope that one would eventually arrive somewhere recognizable. I had invented the farseeing attachment for magic telephones much the same way.

At least he didn't leave to the imagination any steps of what he had finally worked out. He broke in again, just as I was trying to decide if the unknown herb he found so necessary for the steps on the fourteenth page was something I might in fact know under a different name, or something for which I could substitute. When I turned the page, looking ahead to see what effect this herb was supposed to produce, instead I found the comment, "But alas! This spell which served me so faithfully in the dragons' valley, when my peril was greatest, turns to ashes here in the mountains' foothills, so that my certainty fades also."

I paused, noticing that my pencil was now chewed almost to splinters. It looked as if one needed not only an extremely powerful spell, but also to be fully into the land of wild magic itself. There was no way this spell could be tested; it would only work if one's magic had already been improved by traveling north until one stood virtually at the door of a dragon's lair.

No longer reading the spell closely, I started leafing ahead. Naurag might have gotten a spell he created on the spot to work for him when several large dragons poked their fire-breathing snouts from their caves to see what strange creature had invaded their valley. But no two wizards' magic ever works exactly the same, unless one has memorized all the steps of the other's spells, and I didn't see much point in asking the dragons to wait while I carefully recited Naurag's spell, pausing occasionally to check the book and make sure I had each word right.

The handwriting here was sloppy. I sympathized with Naurag's despair—I felt it too. He was pushing ahead with writing down the spell, but in knowing it wouldn't work where he was, in the borderlands, he must have started doubting whether he even remembered everything he had done correctly, and whether it would ever again work at all.

Suddenly I stopped reading to stare blankly out the window. I thought I understood at last why the Master had decided I would be a good person to succeed him, and why he had given me this book. At first I was amused, then, the more I thought about it, appalled.

The Master, in reading this account written by the teacher of the man who had taught him his own magic, must have decided that Naurag reminded him of me.

IV

At last I reached the place in Naurag's account that mentioned the Dragons' Scepter, the part for which the Master had given the book to me in the first place. Two wizards stood between me and Naurag: the Master and the man who had trained him. But as I read on it increasingly felt that I personally knew this man whose flesh had for centuries been dust, so that all that was left of him was a tattered ledger—and his spells.

"In day's light," he wrote with new enthusiasm, "I ween that I may be able to improvise a solution to this difficulty which troubles me so sore." His improvisation, as he went on to discuss, centered on a wizard's staff he had brought with him to the land of wild magic. Apparently he had stolen it from some other wizard during his flight from those he considered his enemies. "The power already latent in this staff," he wrote, "shall make it amenable as a matrix for my spells."

I had never stolen anything from another wizard, I thought indignantly. If the Master of the school was likening me to Naurag, I hoped he kept that in mind.

Greatly daring, Naurag, still with his 'purple companion,' had ventured out from the borderlands, north nearly to the central valley where the largest dragons lived, and there worked his spell again, attaching it as he went to the staff. "I baptize this staff the Dragons' Scepter," he wrote proudly, describing it all after the fact as though it had been a much simpler process than I suspected it really was, "baptized not in religion but in spells of my own devising, and with this instrument I can make the fiercest serpent bow its scaly neck to me."

I glanced across the room to where an old wizard's staff leaned in the corner. It had once belonged to my predecessor here in Yurt. I didn't think it had any particular powers latent within it, but it crossed my mind to wonder if I might be able to attach Naurag's spell to it myself, up in the land of dragons, even if I couldn't find the original Scepter. The nagging voice pointed out that this was sounding more and more as though I planned a trip north soon.

This was still an intellectual exercise, I reminded myself. Just because his spell had worked for him didn't mean it would work for me. Not even the Master himself had attempted to reproduce the spells that had created the Dragons' Scepter. Naurag was a better wizard than I could ever be if I lived far long than the Master.

The next few pages of the ledger were sheer boasting. If I could believe him, once Naurag had perfected his Scepter he spent several weeks commanding the dragons, lining them up like soldiers, forcing them to perform exhausting feats of precision flying, leading them, astride his purple companion, on flights to the icecaps of the ultimate north: breaking their will to resist, until when he finally decided to become more lenient they had laid their scaly snouts at his feet in sheer gratitude for his mercy.

The Princess Margareta arrived from the neighboring kingdom late in the afternoon. I was out in the courtyard, getting some fresh air and trying to catch my breath mentally, when I heard the note of a trumpet and spotted a group of riders emerging from the woods below the castle.

As the riders kicked their horses for the final ascent, the bells on their bridles all pealing, the queen hurried out to meet them. King Paul was with her, formally dressed in blue and white velvet and looking uncharacteristically sober.

Princess Margareta drew her white mare to a halt. The knights and ladies with her laughed and called greetings to their friends in the castle of Yurt, but the princess looked around her coolly. Was it a proprietary look she gave the castle's white-washed towers? Or was it a look of ennui at being summoned here once again with no more indication, than there had been on any of her preceding dozens of visits, of progress toward becoming queen?

But this time Paul, who usually treated her like a slightly annoying little sister, took her stirrup and helped her dismount. "Welcome to Yurt, my lady," he said gravely. Maybe he regretted his outburst this morning, I thought, and was trying to make up for it now by being especially polite and sober.

Margareta smiled suddenly and took the king's arm. "I am glad for this invitation, Paul," she said, as if it had been he who called her rather than the queen mother. I also noted that she used his name very familiarly. He escorted her toward the best guest chambers while the stable boys led the horses away. She had grown tall and willowy, and as the queen looked after them I thought at least I could see her point: they would if nothing else be a handsome couple.

"The summer has been infinitely boring," I overheard her continue. She had managed to lose the squeaky voice she had had when younger. "Father had promised as recently as Christmas to take us to Xantium this year, but by springtime he was saying it would be too hot in the summer, and now I fear he will shortly be saying that the autumn winds are too rough on the Central Sea."

"I've never been to Xantium either," said Paul encouragingly, "although my own father went years ago. I hear the journey is long and dangerous, which may be why King Lucas doesn't really want to undertake it. Maybe you and I could go on our own instead."

Margareta stopped in her slow stroll across the courtyard to gaze at him with new interest. I stared myself. I had been on the trip to Xantium with old King Haimeric of Yurt, and

I would not have recommended it to an elegant princess.

"There perhaps I could buy some really unusual and love-ly silk dresses," Margareta said dreamily.

"Then maybe I could have a real adventure and use the skills in which I've been training all my life," suggested Paul.

The princess's own serving maid, along with the maid from here in Yurt who always assisted her on her visits, ush-ered Margareta into the guest chambers, and the king wan-dered back across the courtyard toward the great hall. I glanced quickly around, relieved that I did not see Gwennie anywhere—and wondering if the maid would drop any inter-esting hints about recent developments in Paul's personal life. In a closed community like this, one might as well forget about keeping anything secret, and the staff generally knew the details even better than the principals.

But concentration on Naurag's account made me forget, at least for the next two hours, about Paul and the princess. This section was written in gleeful anticipation. "Those that did most scorn me shall I strike most mightily with the force I now command," he said. Not content with precision drilling in the land of magic, he had decided to take his drag-ons south. Skipping through what struck me as a rather blood-thirsty desire for vengeance, I searched for an indica-tion that the Scepter had continued to work for him even when out of the land of magic.

And it had. But it took me several minutes to realize quite how well it had worked. There were a number of blank pages, with nothing beyond a few odd words jotted on them, then the memoir resumed again. Both the handwriting and the ink had altered; the blank pages, I concluded, must have separat-ed accounts written years apart, even decades.

"Belike even a wizard grows old," his new account began, and I had to modify my conclusions: at least a century must have passed. "My apprentices commence now to take to them-selves apprentices of their own." Maybe even two centuries.

"When I look about me, I see a City at peace, the City where once emperors strutted, now under the benign control of wizardry. The bloody misadventures of my youth could have been those of another man. E'en my purple companion is long gone, though his skin serves me still. But the Dragons' Scepter stays ever at my hand."

He had ruled the City, then, as Elerius hoped to rule it now. He spoke of peace but this, I calculated, must all still be before the Black Wars. Imposing peace on others was not enough without some sort of organization to ensure that wizards themselves were not drawn into deadly quarrels.

His account continued, filling in a few details from the years he had not chronicled as they happened: years in which he used his authority over the dragons to annihilate any who opposed him. Drawn inexorably from their northern lairs, the dragons had been forced to come at his command and bring destruction to Naurag's enemies. The spells attached to the Scepter served him extremely well. His tone here was sober, even regretful, though regret constantly had to fight with pride of accomplishment. Once again I became indignant at the thought that the Master might compare me to Naurag; I had never annihilated anyone in my life.

But then, as he faced his own death, he had also faced the decision of how to dispose of his magical authority over the dragons. A final time he went north, not to summon dragon forces again but only to drill them in formation one last time. "My once-ferocious friends begged me," he continued, remarkably airily, "to leave the Scepter behind when I finally determined to return unto the lands of men. They wished no other hand to wield it as I had." I could see their point.

At dinner King Paul and Princess Margareta were still talking about Xantium. I was the only person now in Yurt ever to have been there, but they didn't ask my opinion.

"All the luxury goods of the East, I understand, are to be found in Xantium," said Margareta. "Not just the silks and spices, but exquisite jewels, costly perfumes, the most delicately crafted gold and silver, ointments that will keep a woman's skin as pure and smooth as a baby's."

"My father's party had to fight off several groups of bandits on his way east, and they almost got caught between two warring armies," Paul said cheerfully, without seeming to hear anything she said.

"I hear the governor's palace in Xantium puts even the greatest castles of the Western Kingdoms to shame in its elegance and beauty," said Margareta.

"Then they were all captured by an Ifrit," added Paul.

When one of the knights asked what an Ifrit was, I was forced to rouse myself. Just as well; thinking about Naurag, I had been staring at my plate and scarcely tasting the food. But I now explained that an Ifrit is an enormous though vaguely man-like creature, imbued with great magical power: some said that the Ifriti had been created first of all creatures when the world was made, to help with digging rivers and pushing up the mountains. They were never seen in the West, but I knew from experience that at least one still lived in the deserts far beyond Xantium.

Ifriti gave Margareta pause, although the king was apparently absorbed in plans of how he could defeat one in battle—plans, I could have told him, that were all quite useless. But I gave their conversation little more attention, wondering instead if I should try some of Naurag's simpler spells on the air cart. If they worked here, at least there might be some hope they would work on a dragon.

"You haven't been here since the two most recent foals were born," Paul said to the princess when it finally occurred to him that she was not captivated by his imagined future battles.

She had been sitting silently for the last ten minutes, but at this she inclined her head gracefully and smiled at him.

"Are they red roans, like your Bonfire?" she asked. Even a princess whose own interests went little further than fine silks and marble palaces must know that the best way to Paul's heart was through his horses. "I understand that the steeds of Yurt are becoming renowned throughout this part of the Western Kingdoms."

"I'll take you to see them a little later," he said, promising a great treat. Dessert had come by this point, and I took a few quick bites of mine before leaving to go try my spells.

The stables were quiet and dim, lit by a single magic lamp—far safer than a lantern with all this hay to burn. My air cart was in a stall by itself at the far end. The horses here had become used to it over the years. Princess Margareta's mare flared her nostrils at me, but as I passed between rows of stalls there was little activity beyond the munching of oats.

Inside the stall with the air cart, I said a few magical words to lift it from the ground, then tried one of the spells that, according to Naurag, had allowed him to assemble the dragons into formation. My cart had no other carts with which to muster, but it obediently canted sideways, lifting one wing high in salute.

Encouraged, I tried a command that should lead to great speed—one of the shortcomings of the air carts had always been their slow though steady pace. The air cart shot away, over the heads of startled horses, and rammed itself against the stable doors, its wings beating madly. Hooves slammed against the stalls, and Paul's stallion trumpeted a challenge.

"I should have tried this outside," I thought, saying the quick spell to stop the cart and bring it back. But there seemed little doubt that Naurag knew what he was talking about.

Though intrigued by this progress, for several minutes I tried nothing more, waiting for the horses to calm down again. Just as I was about to take the air cart out into the courtyard, the stable doors opened, and I heard voices. "The foals are right in here," said Paul.

I ducked down, not wanting to surprise the king and the princess with my presence. I would wait to try further experiments until they were gone.

Princess Margareta squealed at how adorable the foals were. "Look at their legs—how long!" she exclaimed. "And their tiny little noses! Could I feed them a carrot?"

"They're still just drinking mares' milk," said Paul apologetically.

"Have you named them yet?" she asked. "Can I name them? This one is so red she reminds me of a rose—I'll name her Rosie."

"That's actually a little colt," said Paul awkwardly. "He'll grow into a stallion," he added, as the princess seemed uncomprehending.

"Then I'll name the other one Rosie," she said cheerfully. "And call this one Thorn. Won't those be good names?"

Sitting on the floor I couldn't see the king's expression, but he only hesitated a moment before saying smoothly, "Usually I wait until they're a little older to name them, to make sure the names suit their temperament."

"Feel how soft Baby Thorn's fur is," replied the princess. "And the tiny little mane on Rosie stands straight up!"

I could hear Paul take and let out a deep breath. "Princess Margareta. Please turn around for a moment and look at me. I have something to tell you."

Either she didn't catch the quiet intensity in the king's voice or else she chose to ignore it. "And Thorn's little lips are so soft—oh! He's trying to chew a hole in my sleeve!"

"He's just trying to nurse," said Paul, sounding amused for a second. But then he was again all seriousness. "I want to ask you something."

No, I thought. He can't do this! Not at least until I figure out the Dragons' Scepter.

But if I was still thinking about it, the nagging voice at the back of my mind told me, I must really be planning to use it against Elerius, which meant that it should scarcely matter to me whom Paul married, because I would not be alive to see it.

"So is Bonfire their sire?" asked Margareta, just a little too loudly. "He must be, from their coats! Didn't you tell me once that he came from up near the land of magic? Maybe that would be an even more exciting place to visit than Xantium."

There was no question now that she was putting him off. "Well, I was there once, but—" Paul started to say, then realized it too. I would have given up the effort, but my king was nothing if not persistent.

"Princess, please listen to me."

"Didn't you have some yearlings?" she asked desperately, but this time he would not be distracted.

"Margareta, dearest princess, I have come to a momentous decision. I need a wife beside me in Yurt, a woman to be my queen. You must know that I have always loved you beyond all other women, that my heart has been entirely at your command ever since you were the tiniest girl." At least this time he had the words right, but I could have told him the tone, low and flat, was entirely wrong. "I hereby offer you this diamond ring, as an eternal and unchanging symbol of the love between us."

There was a long silence. This seemed all the king had to say, and Margareta for the moment appeared incapable of answering. At last she said, in nearly as flat a voice as his, "Just like that. We're standing here in the stable and you ask me to be Queen of Yurt."

"Because I love you," said Paul, determined to get that detail clear this time. "I couldn't wait any longer. I had to ask you as soon as we were alone."

Margareta made a little snorting noise. "You're acting like

some stable man," she started to say, then checked herself. Paul made a sound that could have been a moan or a cough but did not interrupt. "As a princess," she continued icily, "I had always expected that the man of royal blood who would win my hand and heart would ask for them in the most romantic way possible, not just blurt it out while we were standing up to our ankles in straw!"

"Um, I think my mother's planning a ball while you're here," Paul ventured. "If you like, we can forget about this for now and I'll ask you then. That should be romantic," he added lamely. "I could ask you to marry me in front of the whole court, Gwennie, and then—"

He stopped as abruptly as if his tongue had turned to stone in his mouth. He probably wished it had—only about two seconds earlier.

The princess's breath hissed between her teeth. "Then it's true," she said, so fiercely that if I were Paul I would have backed rapidly toward the exit. "I have heard the rumors before, and heard new rumors when I arrived today. But I have always dismissed them. King Paul, I told myself, has been destined for me since I was a little girl. I might worry about his heart being won by another lady of high lineage, but never, I persuaded myself, *never* would he lower himself so far as to fall in love with his own cook's daughter!"

"Well, no, Margareta, you don't have to worry about that anymore," he said wildly. "You see, just yesterday—"

He stopped short with the realization that he could make this far worse than it already was. But it was too late.

"That's all you think of me?" she cried. "Second best to your own castle constable?" At least Paul seemed to have broken through the princess's accustomed languor. "She turns you down, and so the very next day, to assuage your wounded dignity, you stammer out some completely insincere proposal to *me*?" She gave a sudden little scream. "And your horrible colt has eaten a hole in my dress!"

She turned and ran then, sobbing, toward the courtyard, with more energy than any of us had ever seen in her before. The horses and I put our noses over the edges of the stalls to watch her go. Just before leaving she cast something from her hand. Paul waited much too long before calling out, "Margareta! Wait!" and running after her.

This time it took me several minutes to find the diamond ring, half-buried in the straw. I put a tracing spell on it before dropping it into my pocket, in case this kept on happening.

V

I slipped out of the stables a quarter hour later, deciding to postpone further experiments with the air cart—for one thing, it was getting dark. From the direction of the kitchen I could hear the clattering of washing up and an occasional voice, raised in question or laughter, but the rest of the castle was silent.

Back in my chambers I returned to the battered magical book and found my place, where the long-dead wizard discussed the hiding of the Dragons' Scepter he had created. He seemed to be caught between believing no other wizard would be nearly wise or clever enough to wield it as he had, and wanting future generations to be able to marvel, awe-struck, at his powers if they actually witnessed the Scepter in action. The latter form of pride finally triumphed—even if he doubted anyone else would ever be as skilled as he was, he wanted to be very sure that posterity believed him.

Naurag thus overcame what I read as deep reluctance and described the place where he had hidden the Scepter, including an explicit description of the magic that should help one find its location, even centuries later, and of the spells that would be needed to counteract the spells of concealment he had laid upon it. I paused, chose a new pencil on which to chew, and wondered if it could possibly be as easy as he here suggested.

Armed with a fairly simple set of spells, only a few of which even required exotic herbs, a wizard should be able to discover Naurag's Scepter, activate its power, and command the dragons as he had once done. Once the Scepter was in one's hand, one wouldn't even need to be a wizard to access its powers. But if this was all that was required, why had the Master himself never gone to retrieve it?

Suddenly I understood. I looked again at Naurag's description of the Scepter's hiding place, but it was as I feared. Even though a wizard should, theoretically, be able to make the largest dragons obey him once he held it, the hard part would be holding it in the first place. For Naurag had concealed it in the floor of the mightiest dragons' lair.

That was it, then. I couldn't duplicate the spells Naurag had originally created to tame the dragons, because I would have to be standing in the dragons' valley to do so, rattling off page after page of phrases in the Hidden Language and waving around a handful of herbs I probably wouldn't recognize even if I did find them. I couldn't locate the Scepter to which Naurag had attached the spells, because one would in essence already have had to use those spells to get past the dragon who guarded it. The Master's hope that I could somehow use this centuries'-old magic to oppose Elerius was therefore nothing but a futile dream.

This was all a great relief, I told myself the next morning, standing in my dressing gown eating cinnamon crullers and looking out toward the courtyard, through the climbing roses. A spider had died down in the corner of one of my window panes; her legs were sprawled out and body bleached white by the sun.

It was much better this way, I said to myself again. I wondered absently why the crullers seemed to have no flavor this morning; maybe a new girl was making them. Perhaps I should get dressed, I thought, except that the inferior crullers seemed to have sapped my initiative.

I opened the old ledger again half-heartedly, but saw nothing I had not seen last night. There was the spell for finding the Dragons' Scepter in the floor of a dragon's cave, a blank page, the word "Afterword" written in a shaky hand, and then nothing more.

Voices came from the courtyard and the sound of hooves. Princess Margareta, elegant and slim in her riding habit, led her mare toward the mounting block.

"But you have only just arrived, Margareta!" the queen mother cried, hurrying up to her. "Did you and the king perhaps have some sort of quarrel last night?" she added hesitantly. "Because if you did—"

"No, no, my lady," Margareta answered coolly. Refusing Paul seemed to have given her a resolution she had never had before; she could now refuse anybody. "Nothing like that at all. I had always intended to spend but a single night in Yurt. My parents will want me home again today. I am sorry if you did not understand or if the brevity of my visit has caused you and the staff any discomfort."

The knights from Caelrhon who had accompanied the princess here were hurrying to bring out their own steeds. "We are always glad to have you, Margareta," the queen said, worried but not wanting to give offense. "I'm sure Paul will be disappointed not to have been here to say good-bye, but he seems to have ridden out very early this morning. Do you know yet when you might be free to visit us again? Because you do know that—"

"I will doubtless be very busy at home for some months to come," said Margareta, settling herself into the saddle. "Thank you again for your hospitality. Oh, you might telephone my father's court, just to leave a message with his constable as to what time I left here. They always like to know when to expect me."

"Of course," the queen started to answer, but Margareta had kicked her mare and was off across the drawbridge, the knights hustling to catch up.

The queen looked after her, shaking her head, then started in the direction of the room where we kept the telephone. I sipped the last of my tea, wondering what I should do with myself all day. The hours seemed to stretch before me endless and empty. Perhaps I should leave too, since everyone else seemed to be doing so, and go visit Theodora.

Quick footsteps echoed in the courtyard, and I looked up, surprised to see the queen back from telephoning so quickly. She rapped briskly on my own chamber door and called, "Wizard!" I pulled my dressing gown closer around me and opened the door. "You have a telephone call."

"I must apologize for having you run my errands, my lady!" I said, trying to cover my embarrassment with dignity, then bowed and swept out past her. Who could be calling me? But by the time I reached the telephone room I was smiling. It had to be Theodora, asking if I could come visit her and Antonia for a week. A week with her and away from Yurt right now would be highly welcome.

But the face illuminated in the base of the glass telephone was not Theodora's. It was a black-bearded wizard: Elerius.

I could tell that he had spotted me in his own instrument even before I picked up the receiver—no time to try to disguise my pajamas with illusion or to recreate the frilled white shirt and the cape which had failed to impress the Master. "It must be nice, Daimbert," Elerius commented, "to be the Royal Wizard of such a backwater little kingdom. No responsibilities, nothing to do but sleep 'til noon."

The Master must still be alive, I told the hard pounding of my heart, or Elerius wouldn't be starting our conversation with a joke at my expense. "In the evenings when you City wizards are all down in the restaurants and taverns," I replied haughtily, "I improve my time with the close study of long-forgotten spells." Now I just had to hope he didn't know I had Naurag's book.

Tawny eyes considered me thoughtfully. "Perhaps you would like to try the City restaurants again yourself. I know from experience that the kings of Yurt have always kept good cooks, but I expect it's been months since you've had any fresh seafood. How about coming down to the wizards' school for a visit—say, this afternoon?"

"Why this sudden eagerness to improve my culinary variety?" I asked warily.

"I think it would be a good chance for the two of us to talk about Antonia and her education."

"Antonia!" My heart, which had almost resumed its normal rhythm again, gave a great lurch.

"Certainly. Isn't it almost time for pupils to be returning to their classes for the autumn? I'm sure those teachers in Caelrhon have long since taught her everything they have to teach. But I'm her friend—almost an honorary uncle, one might say." Did he linger a little too much over the word uncle? "I'm very interested in discussing with you what would be best for her and her future."

"Of course," I gasped. "What a good idea. I'm so glad you brought this up, Elerius. I'll be there in a few hours." He continued to watch me, to see if I recognized the threat implicit behind his words.

Oh, yes. I recognized it just fine.

part three ✣ elerius

I

Os I GUIDED THE AIR CART from the stables, projecting so much fury and despair that the stable boys stayed well out of my way, it crossed my mind that I needed to let my king know I was gone. With no intention of letting him invite himself along, I scribbled him a quick note and pushed it into the reluctant hand of a stable boy. "Unexpected business has come up related to the wizards' school," I wrote. "I expect to be in the City for at least a few days but should be back soon." This last was a lie. I didn't know if I would ever be home again.

I had decided to take the air cart to the City even though flying myself would have been faster. This, I explained firmly to the nagging voice at the back of my mind, was not due to any reluctance to face Elerius. After all, I had barely taken time to pack, only tossing some clean socks and my old wizard's staff into the cart. Rather I was taking advantage of a chance to test more of Naurag's spells on the cart. His ledger was the only book out of all my library of magic that I took with me to confront the best wizard of this age.

The spires of the royal castle of Yurt disappeared rapidly behind me. No time to say good-bye, even in my mind, to the kingdom I had served for thirty years. And if I thought too much about the fact that I might never see the castle again, I would not leave at all. As the air cart, zipping along at greater speed than usual due to Naurag's spells, next flew over the cathedral city of Caelrhon, I realized that there was also no time to say good-bye to Theodora and Antonia. I wasn't sure what I was planning to do, even whether I would defy Elerius or seek to persuade him that I was a harmless incompetent who could safely be ignored. My mind kept asserting, obstinantly and without good evidence, that I would think of something, but whatever it was my family would be safer if they knew nothing of it.

The towers of the City rose before me long before I felt mentally prepared. With a history that went back over two thousand years and a modern bustle that came from being the most important commercial center of the West, the City was a spectacular sight. Once I had lived here, one more young man among thousands, but Yurt had for many years been my real home. The school on the peak of the City's highest hill—where, I now realized, Naurag had established himself as ruler centuries earlier—seemed to shimmer with magic: the official spells that protected the school itself, but also the overflow of hundreds of unofficial spells, being worked by serious faculty and by students both studious and carefree. As I directed the air cart down, a flock of insubstantial and rather misshapen bluebirds flew up toward me. One of the classes must be working on illusions.

As a visiting graduate of the school who had once even taught a series of lectures here, I was able to get a narrow room at the top of a tower. It was reached by a twisting staircase with broken stone steps—but then the school assumed that anyone who stayed here would prefer to fly up rather than climb. I realized as I closed the door behind me that the simplicity of living arrangements at the school, which had seemed perfectly normal when I was a student here, must have been the result of a deliberate decision by the Master. The organized wizardry he had established was not an organization of either luxury or display.

My outstretched arms could easily reach across the room from one wall to the window on the opposite side, but the ceiling, shadowy and hung with cobwebs, was at least twenty feet over my head. The window looked out into reaches of air, and by craning my neck I could see the great harbor a dizzying distance below. But I didn't take time to admire the view. I tucked Naurag's ledger behind a few dog-eared books of modern spells which lay forgotten on a shelf, slapped magic locks on both door and window, and went in search of Elerius.

I didn't have to look long.

As I hurried out of the residential part of the school toward the classrooms and the library, wondering distractedly if it might be possible to establish some sort of secret base in the maze of tunnels and rooms down below the school, he came around a corner so fast that he almost ran into me.

"Daimbert! How good to see you so soon!" His lips smiled but not his eyes. He must have had his agents watching for my arrival. "I knew you would be eager to come to the City once I mentioned that we could plan Antonia's future together."

When I had thought that the Master's student assistants were Elerius's henchmen, come to kill me, I had found a way to overcome them, I reminded myself. So why this paralyzing lack of good ideas when facing Elerius himself?

"Let's go down to the harbor and find a restaurant where we can have an early dinner," he said as though he were just making light conversation, not threatening my daughter's safety if by any chance I did not cooperate with him. "I'm so busy with the complicated affairs of the school that I'd like a break, and it's too easy to be distracted if one stays here, with wizards and students always running in and out of the office with questions and ideas."

He did an unconvincing job of suggesting that the responsibilities of supervising so many other wizards was a task he would just as soon give up. I followed him down the corridor and out one of the many doors that gave on open air—much faster to descend to the waterfront by flying than on foot. Roofs, narrow streets, and hidden courtyards showing an unexpected green, all flashed beneath us, all of them sheltering citizens who must know that they were always under the eyes of the wizards, but who had much too much else to do to worry about us.

As we descended I glanced back toward the tower in the school where I had been given my room. As long as I was with Elerius I knew he himself couldn't be trying to circumvent my magic locks, but there must be people here who would be only too eager to perform little chores for him. My only hope was that he wouldn't know to look for Naurag's book because he didn't know I had it—sitting hidden on a shelf with other books of spells, it would do nothing to draw even a wizard's attention to itself.

"You're awfully quiet, Daimbert," Elerius commented as we descended, the cool sea air fluttering our clothing and giving me a shiver. "Don't tell me that after all these years and all that we've done together you're still suspicious of me."

You got that one right, I thought, but I still didn't speak. Even a wizard shouldn't be able to hear another's thoughts unless that other person was trying to communicate mind-to-mind, but just in case I tried to stop thinking too. It didn't work—my brain kept churning.

"By the way," he added as though casually, "I heard that you visited the Master last week. And you didn't even stop by my office to visit! At this rate I'll start thinking you really don't like my company."

If he had hoped to surprise me by mentioning my dawn visit to the Master, I was ready for him. Either Whitey or Chin, angry at me for how I treated them, were likely to have mentioned something—if not to Elerius himself, then to someone else who then told him.

"The Master wanted to tell me himself that he thinks he's finally dying," I replied soberly. A partially true answer would be more convincing than a completely false one. "I expect that in the next few weeks he'll be summoning many more of his former pupils to let them know."

"So he told you that directly?" Elerius shot back, more sharply than I expected. "Curious, Daimbert, because those of us who work most closely with him have of course recognized that his current illness will surely be his last, but I do not believe that he has yet said as much to any other wizard."

Jealousy, I thought, almost smugly. The Master loved me more than he loved Elerius, and Elerius knew it. I imagined for a second how even more jealous he would become if he knew the Master wanted me to succeed him, but it was hard to be smug for more than a few seconds about events so sad—and so terrifying.

The waterfront approached rapidly beneath our feet, and the increase in noise, of shouts, the creaking of pulleys and rigging, the clatter of cargo shifting, and music from the taverns, gave me an excuse not to answer. We reached a street of restaurants a short distance uphill from the harbor, where it was a little quieter. A few people glanced up, startled, as we came down from above to land near them, but then shrugged and continued about their business—flying wizards were after all a common sight here in the City.

"I've heard fine things about this restaurant," said Elerius, opening a door for me, his good cheer back in place. "It's not cheap—but don't worry, I'll pay. I know a little kingdom like Yurt can't afford very much for its Royal Wizard!"

I allowed him to act patronizing; I had to save my attention for something much worse. We ate lobster, sitting in an alcove under a low wooden ceiling that appeared to be made from the hull of a dismantled ship, looking out through the front windows toward the sea. Late afternoon sunlight flashed golden on the water and put a halo around the many

islands that made the approach to the City docks so dangerous to those who didn't know it.

Afternoon moved into early evening as we finished lob-
sters, steamed clams, salad, and apple tart. The harbor itself,
inside the breakwater, was calm, with only a few ships now
moving: merchant ships rowing in at the slack of the tide, a
pilot with a lantern standing at the prow, or small fishing
boats preparing to go out for the night catch. Beyond the
breakwater, however, white waves splashed high, and for a
moment I saw the dolphins riding the swell. It was a curious-
ly reassuring sight. No matter what Elerius did as Master of
the school, seeking to bend all of organized wizardry, and
eventually the kings, the cities, and even the churches of the
Western Kingdoms to his bidding, he was unlikely to have
much success against the ocean and the dolphins.

Elerius didn't mention Antonia once during dinner.
Instead he regaled me with a complicated story of a young
wizard who had run into all sorts of problems—even a
demon—when he took up his first post after graduation, a
story which was probably supposed to be funny. That young
wizard was fortunate, I thought. No one was ever likely to
expect *him* to become Master of the school and thwart
Elerius.

"Let's go for a walk," Elerius said, wiping his lips. "That
was an excellent dinner, but I could use the exercise." The
waiter smiled as he accepted payment and didn't detain us
while having someone try to make sure our money stayed
money even in the next room. But then, though that was the
kind of trick student wizards liked to pull, the masters of the
school had always been scrupulously honest. And after all, I
thought loftily, nodding to the waiter, I had an august white
beard even if Elerius didn't.

We strolled past the chandlers and outfitters, past the co-
ops where the fishermen brought their catch, past noisy inns
and disreputable boarding houses that catered to the sailors,

past the moorings of cargo ships, fishing skiffs, and pleasure barges. The smells especially, the mixture of fish and salt, were vivid with memories of my childhood. I had known the harbor area well years ago, when my family wholesaled wool imported from the Far Islands, but it had been a very long time. The boy who had run through these streets, always more interested in peering up at distant magical lights, burning in the windows of the school, than in the shipping schedules that controlled when great loads of wool might arrive, had looked no further than becoming a wizardry student.

I thrust my hands into my pockets while we walked and found something hard, which startled me until I realized I was still carrying Paul's diamond ring. I glanced over at Elerius, but he seemed content to stroll in silence: apparently I was worth a lot if someone who considered himself so busy with the complicated affairs of the school had this much time to devote to me.

Sunsets were coming earlier these days, and the low sun sat surrounded by plumes of red and orange. But still we walked, away from the harbor now, and along the strands where the shipbreakers worked. The partially dismantled bodies of ships lay beached like dead whales, their sound timbers and hardware being salvaged, but at this time of day the workshops were quiet. It occurred to me that just as most wizardry functioned the same whoever might head the school, most of the activities of the City continued unaffected by whoever might be elected mayor.

I had almost persuaded myself that therefore it would not ultimately matter if Elerius took over, when at last he began to speak of Antonia.

"The school has never admitted women as wizardry students," he said suddenly, looking out toward the sunset. "But I see no reason why that tradition should be continued, and I think your daughter will be an excellent candidate for our first female pupil. When do you think she'll be ready to start her formal studies, Daimbert? Do you want to wait for a few years, or is she ready to begin now?"

He had caught me unprepared; I had expected open threats. "Why do you think the school's policy is suddenly going to change?" I inquired warily.

He turned then to look at me, eyebrows peaked over thoughtful hazel eyes. "Come now, Daimbert. You don't feign ignorance very well. As soon as the old Master dies—and you yourself just told me he finally realizes himself that he is dying—the wizards here at the school will need to elect a new head, and it will scarcely be a surprise to you that many have already told me that I will be their choice. The older wizards know that it is time to turn the reins of authority over to a new generation, and it is not boasting for me to say that I am generally regarded as the best of our generation. Welcoming women into the school—starting with Antonia—will be one of my first official acts."

The last place I wanted my daughter was under Elerius's control. "She's much too young," I said hurriedly, not meeting his gaze. "She's only twelve. I was past twenty when I started my own magical studies."

Every time I looked back toward him it was to see his eyes fixed on me. Maybe I should be flattered that he found me so fascinating. "Perhaps one of the mistakes of school training has lain in waiting so long to begin," he said slowly. "After all, if one is to study a foreign language one learns it most readily as a child. Should the Hidden Language of magic be any different? Even aside from Antonia—who learned spells more easily when she was five than do most second-year wizardry students—I could point to the days before the school, when would-be wizards often started their apprenticeships as boys."

"The last place for a twelve-year-old girl is all by herself in the middle of a group of unruly young men," I said firmly.

This wasn't what I had planned to argue with Elerius about, but it would do for now. And it was a point from which, I thought, nothing was going to sway me.

"Not by herself," he said, nodding slowly. The last burning rim of the sun lingered on the horizon, but very soon it would be dark, and the air was rapidly growing cold. "I propose giving her a study companion, another twelve-year-old who has also demonstrated an early flair for magic, who is far too serious-minded to be easily distracted from study, and whose abilities deserve to be trained and developed by the world's greatest teachers of wizardry."

"And where are you going to find another girl like this?" I asked suspiciously.

"Not a girl. A twelve-year-old boy. My son."

II

This was why he had brought me here, I told myself, thinking furiously. This was why we had strolled for miles along the shore away from the school, to where we couldn't possibly be overheard, even with magic. Elerius stood with the sea air stirring his beard, waiting for my reaction to a secret that even the Master, who thought he knew about all of us, had never uncovered.

And I thought I understood why he had told me that secret. The gesture would, he believed, guarantee to me that he would not spread the story of Antonia's parentage if she did come to the school, as well as tying the two of us together in a bond of fatherhood.

I had no intention of being tied to him by any bond. "What's the boy's name?" I asked as if casually.

"Prince Walther."

It took me a second. But then I spun around to stare at him through the dusk. "*Prince* Walther? Prince of what? Where did you find a princess?"

"Prince of my kingdom, of course," he said, not at all embarrassed, "and heir to the throne. He will be a king as well as a very good wizard—the first kingly wizard, I believe, the West has ever had. And I didn't 'find a princess,' as you rather coarsely put it. His mother is the queen."

For one second I felt a surge of jealousy; the queen of Yurt had never been the slightest bit interested in *me*. Yet Elerius had somehow lured the queen he served out of the royal bedchamber and into his, even while his king was still alive. No wonder his queen had been happy to have him acting as regent while their son was still a boy! Elerius and young Walther would rule the City and the wealthiest of the Western Kingdoms as father and son, and neither wizards or nobles would stand in their way.

Out of several things I might have said I chose, "Does the boy know you're his father?"

For second there was a crack in his confidence. "Well, no, not yet. We could not tell him when he was very young, of course, for no child could be trusted with a secret like that. And now— Well, he's at a delicate stage, at the threshhold of manhood, having lost the king he'd always thought of as his father not long ago— The queen and I shall find a suitable time to tell him in a few years. But in the meantime I am teaching him a little magic; he has quite a flair for it!"

"So you're waiting until he's eighteen," I said, mostly to myself, "until he's been crowned king, so that neither he nor anyone else can raise embarrassing questions about his hereditary right to succeed until it's too late."

Elerius didn't answer, although I couldn't tell if this was because he felt uneasy about misleading his own son about something this important or because he didn't deign to share any more of his plans for the young prince with me.

"Why did you risk telling me this?" I burst out. "Aren't you afraid that even if I don't tell the nobility of your kingdom I'll tell all the wizards at the school? They are shortly supposed to be electing you Master, yet you've broken the oldest traditions of institutionalized magic by a liaison with a woman!"

"I'm telling you this because I trust you, Daimbert, and I know no surer way to show it. I keep no secrets from you because I trust that you will keep none from me, once we are established as co-rulers of the Western Kingdoms."

This whole evening had taken on a nightmare tone. Maybe the seafood had been tainted and I was hallucinating. It sounded as though Elerius had just said that, rather than ruling jointly with his son, he wanted to rule jointly with me. The sky above us was still pale, but the broken shapes of hulls and spars had dissolved into formless shadow.

"Me," I said slowly at last. "You want me as your co-ruler." First the Master had thought I was capable of leading organized magic, and now Elerius. I wondered wildly if they had somehow confused me with some other wizard, much more skillful, also named Daimbert. "You're twice as good as I could ever be, and yet you want to share your authority with me?"

"You've spent the last twenty years thinking you had to oppose me," said Elerius, a smile in his voice. "And somehow, I've never known how, you've always been successful. Won't it be a relief to give up the struggle? Instead you can work beside me, making sure that I always keep wizardry's moral principles in mind if that is your concern, rather than having to fight me in secret. You notice that I am not just offering you a position of some authority under me, but rather suggesting that we ask the school's wizards to make the position of Master a joint one. You and I will train our children to be even better wizards than we are, and when they grow a little older and marry each other—"

"Marry!"

He chuckled at my shock. "Don't you think by that time someone besides you will have been able to overcome the old notion that wizards are married only to magic? And I know you still think of Antonia as a little girl, but she's going to be a lovely young woman, and it's not too early to start planning. She'd be a charming queen. You don't think I'm going to be fussy just because she lacks royal blood!"

"I'm not arranging Antonia's marriage to anybody," I muttered. Irrelevantly I wondered if young Prince Walther would be interested in marrying Gwennie.

"And I do need your help, Daimbert," Elerius continued, not feeling that the marriage he planned between Prince Walther and my daughter needed any further discussion. "You've probably heard that I'm a candidate for mayor here in the City, and between running the school, ruling my kingdom as regent for at least a few more years, and supervising the city council, I'll have more than enough responsibilities for one wizard to handle."

"And I hear you're trying to influence the election of the new bishop as well," I said in a flat voice.

"That's *especially* where I'd like your help, Daimbert. You've always gotten along well with that bishop in Caelrhon."

"Joachim," I said coldly. Nobody was going to call him "that bishop."

He didn't respond to my coldness but continued as though we were just having a friendly chat. "My candidate for bishop here is someone who also seems willing to accommodate himself to wizardry, but you're much more experienced at influencing priests than I am, so I'll leave him to you."

Joachim had never 'accommodated' himself to wizardry, and to the best of my knowledge I had never influenced him in anything, but it hardly seemed worth bringing up.

"I realize you've spent very little time at the school since you graduated, but I don't want you to hesitate because you feel unsure about taking up supervisory tasks," Elerius continued, in apparently full confidence of my agreement—and also apparently not caring if he sounded patronizing again. "Let me give you an example of how you could help me right away. The Master once told me about a Dragons' Scepter, hidden up in the land of wild magic. Retrieving it, so that we could use its powers for the good of the school, is exactly the sort of task for which your improvisational brand of magic should be well suited."

I made the slightest affirmatory noise, trying to cover my surprise with nonchalance. Did he then know all about my last conversation with the Master?

"So, what do you think, Daimbert?" I could no longer see his features, but as he turned a gleam from the lantern on a fishing boat far out to sea seemed to flash in his eye. "This is finally the opportunity for wizardry to do what it has always had the potential to do: mold mankind in the direction it ought to have taken all along. You and I are at precisely the right point to do it, both at an age where we've acquired experience and wisdom, an age where many men start to find their strength waning but which we as wizards find to be but an extension of vigorous youth. Even now, school wizards have been able to end most warfare in the Western Kingdoms, but you and I together can also bring peace to the Eastern Kingdoms. We'll end corruption and petty bickering in city governments and ensure that their economies are well managed. By working with the bishop of the City, we'll quickly be able to end the foolish superstitions that distract people from practical considerations. And though we rule absolutely, with an authority that will make our names legendary for millennia after our deaths, we shall always know that we are improving the lot of humanity through our rule. Don't you find this a tempting offer?"

At one time it might have been tempting. But if I had learned one thing as a wizard, it was that it is impossible for someone, beneficent as he might imagine himself, always to know exactly what another needs, much less arrange for that to appear. Naurag, brash as he might have been, had recognized this well before he died; in fact, I thought, this might have been what he intended to spell out in the "Afterword" to his ledger which he never wrote.

Ending warfare was fine, but not if we replaced the tyranny of kings with tyranny of our own. Trying to regulate the economy, however, beyond assuring access to opportunities, was outright impossible. Elerius and I would never know what was better for hundreds of thousands of people than they did themselves. Ending 'foolish superstition' was not just impossible but highly dangerous. If we decided to tell people what they could and couldn't believe we might as well declare ourselves gods and make the people worship as well as fear us. "I'm sorry," I said, very quietly. "I won't be your co-ruler."

I couldn't see his face, but his breath came short and sharp. I had surprised him then. He had thought the combination of bribe and veiled threat would be more than enough to bring me to his way of thinking—especially since he himself was genuinely convinced he was right. "Are you going to fight me, then, Daimbert?" he asked after a moment. "Is your plan to wrest control of the school for yourself?"

It might have been the Master's plan, but it most certainly was not mine. "I have no interest in control over anything," I said as clearly as I could. I was defying the Master's dying wishes, but there was no way I could either join in absolute authority over the West, or try with my limited resources to oppose the man who would wield that authority.

"This is, of course, exactly what you would say if you did plan to oppose me," Elerius commented after a moment.

"That may be. But it's nonetheless true. Do whatever you like as head of the school and head of whatever other institution will have you. I'm going to stay quietly in Yurt."

The Master wouldn't be alive to know about it, and Theodora wouldn't be surprised to hear that Elerius had been elected. But how, I asked myself in dismay, could I possibly tell Joachim?

After a moment Elerius said in a tone of forced cheerfulness, "If you really mean that, I'll be very sorry not to have your assistance. It would have been good to have your ideas and your magic working beside me. This won't, of course, change anything in my plans to bring women into the school. Antonia can begin her wizardry studies this winter, or even earlier."

A hostage for my good behavior. But how could I keep her away from the school without making Elerius think I was plotting against him?

"Well," he added, "there was something I had planned to show you after you agreed to work with me. I might as well show it to you anyway. It should help reassure you that my motives are only for the best."

I'd never had any doubt about his motivation. The fact that he was convinced he was acting for the best only made it worse.

He rose, flying, over the shore and headed out to sea. I followed him, wondering if he really did have something to show me or was leading me into a trap.

But this didn't seem to be a trap. He flew out about a mile to a low, rocky island, circled by phosphorescent breaking waves. A half moon hung in the sky, casting just enough light that I could see that the island's surface was pitted and without vegetation. And coming out of the pits—

"No," I said, and my heart went tight and cold. "No. You can't have done this, Elerius. Not if you claim you're acting for good."

I could see now what crept around the island: creatures manlike yet not human, creatures made of hair and dead bone but given the simulacrum of life by spells out of the old magic of earth and blood. They turned their misshapen heads up toward us, and their eyes glowed in the darkness. The eyes were the only features in those heads.

"So you recognize them, Daimbert," said Elerius, pleased. I could see his face now, without color or expression in the pale light. "As you'll recall, I first encountered creatures like this in your kingdom."

"I recognize them all right," I growled. They had come very close to killing all the inhabitants of the royal castle, including me. "You must have made them yourself, but I can't have forgotten where you found the model. You're planning to attack Yurt if you think I'm opposing you, is that it?"

He laughed in what sounded like genuine amusement. "You have the strangest sense of humor sometimes, Daimbert. Of course I'm not planning to attack anyone's kingdom." He seemed easily capable of simultaneously chatting and maintaining his position high in the air over the island; I on the other hand was fighting to maintain mine. "And you misjudge me badly if you think I would threaten you in any way."

Not threaten me, just threaten Antonia?

"Although the creatures like this that you and I initially encountered," he continued, "were indeed made for war, I have shaped mine quite differently. For one thing, I have no dragons' teeth, which all the old books agree work best for such creatures. They're modeled on the same spells, of course, but mine are made for peaceful purposes. My intention is to teach them agriculture."

"Agriculture!" Maybe Elerius had lost his mind—but he sounded entirely rational.

"Of course, it's possible that I'll have to use them as soldiers a few times while establishing peace throughout the West—or even try them out in the Eastern Kingdoms. But wizardry has less messy ways of stopping armies than creating other armies: that's why I have additional plans for my creatures. The farmers in all the kingdoms always have to work so hard during harvest time. Once I've perfected the spells on these I can use them as additional field hands during busy periods. They'll work without pay, of course, and even without food and rest. Think what a boon to the farmer this will be!"

The metaphysics of making undead creatures from old bones, then turning them into slaves, was much too complex for me, but I had a pretty good guess what Joachim's reaction would be. "I— I see," I said slowly.

"Maybe if you don't want to help me with the Dragons' Scepter," Elerius suggested, turning to fly back to land, "you could at least give me a hand with my creatures. I know you studied the old magic yourself at one point, so you're just the person to assist me. So far they've been a bit harder to govern than I had hoped, even violent, which is why I've had to keep them isolated on this island until I'm quite sure they're safe."

Undead soldier-slaves who were in revolt even as they were created. The metaphysics didn't seem complicated after all.

"So you see I'm being perfectly open with you," Elerius said as we landed back on the docks below the school. The harbor had become quiet now, other than distant notes of sailors' songs. I leaned against a bollard to catch my breath. Sick horror had drained the strength from me. Useless to oppose him if I couldn't even stand upright trying. "No secrets, merely an invitation that still stands. Perhaps you just need more time to think it over. After all, we don't know how long—"

He was interrupted by the sound of a bell ringing, a steady dark note tolling again and again. One of the City's churches? But that didn't sound like any church bell I knew.

Then Elerius and I whirled to stare at each other in the faint light, both recognizing it at the same time. That was the bell that hung on top of the school, the bell that was rung only, and then for just three notes, when a group of wizards was graduating. The steady ringing could mean only one thing: the Master had died.

And as we both jumped upward to fly back to the school I realized something else. I wasn't going to defy his dying wishes after all.

III

The school gave the Master a Christian burial. There was no precedent for the funeral because he was the only Master the school had ever had. It was Elerius's idea: part of his effort, I thought, to persuade the cathedral chapter that the wizards were a respectful and tractable group whose opinion ought to be consulted before they elected their new bishop.

We laid him to rest not with the great dignitaries of the City, in the cathedral yard, but rather in a little patch of earth behind a church that stood in the shadow of the school. Elerius made me do the negotiations with the church's priest over what kind of pious gift would be suitable in the circumstances. The priest pronounced the liturgy over the Master's body, and the sexton planted white wooden crosses at his head and feet. I had no idea what the Master's own wishes would have been; as a matter of professional pride, he and the other senior teachers at the school had always avoided any speculation on the afterlife or anything else that might imply that the Church's authority was greater than theirs. But I thought that Joachim would have concurred.

It was a horrible week. The students, most of whom had never had a chance to develop much feeling for the Master beyond fear and awe, milled around uncertainly, unsure what to do with the sudden freedom granted by cancelled classes. I came across Whitey and Chin, however, sitting in the library surrounded by piles of books that were probably for a project he had assigned them, weeping unrestrained.

Many of the teachers too seemed overcome, disappearing into their studies for days at a time, emerging hollow-cheeked to find something to eat and then disappearing again. Once I came upon Zahlfast, who as second in command at the school should have been ensuring that some modicum of organization was maintained, standing leaning against the courtyard wall, staring at nothing with red-rimmed eyes. I did not think he even noticed me.

Elerius alone remained calm and in control. He moved into Zahlfast's office, from which he contacted the rest of the wizards around the Western Kingdoms to tell them the sad news, dealt with the tradesmen who supplied the school, and reassured students that classes would be starting again very soon.

And I realized that I too would have to die. As long as I was alive Elerius would keep after me and, even worse, keep after my family, trying to ensure that I would help him or at least not work against him. If I merely disappeared he would search me out and for all I knew threaten to do horrible things to Antonia until I agreed to reemerge. If I didn't actively want to assist him in running the world I had to thwart him. The only way I could possibly work against him would be to have him think I was dead.

Staging my own death convincingly was going to be difficult. Elerius himself had once helped another wizard disappear by pretending to blow himself up, so he would be alert to the slightest hint that this might be a trick. I couldn't let even Theodora know that I was still alive, much less King Paul, because the burden of having to keep a secret from Elerius, intent on worming it out of them, would be too great.

But my heart contracted at the thought of having to put Theodora through the sorrow that all of us at the school were now feeling at the Master's death.

There was no time to hesitate. The teachers would shortly rally to start teaching their wizardry classes again and realize they needed to choose a new Master; the cathedral priests
were already well behind schedule in electing their new bishop; and I thought the mayoral election was coming up shortly. Elerius was already regent—for the son no one but I knew
was his—in the largest of the Western Kingdoms. The longer
he held the other offices as well the harder it would be to
overcome him. Now I just wished I had the faintest idea how
to do so.

"I've decided to try to find the Dragons' Scepter," I told
Elerius. A partial truth is more believable than an outright
lie, I reminded myself again.

He had moved back into his own office from Zahlfast's—
he had been careful not to appear overeager by taking the
Master's study immediately. He looked up at me with calculating tawny eyes from the book he had been reading. "Is this
to assist me, Daimbert, or to begin an assault against me?"

"Oh, to assist you, of course," I said, passing smoothly
from partial truth to total falsehood. "That's why I'm volunteering to go find it—to show you my good faith. I'm still not
at all sure I'd be any good at running the school, but I've been
doing a lot of thinking the last few days, and here I think
you're right. If wizardry is going to expand its authority, we
need all the magic we can get. And I understand that the man
who made this Scepter taught the wizard with whom our
Master originally apprenticed."

He nodded slowly but did not seem as convinced as I
would have liked. "I understand the Master used to have
some sort of ledger or book about the Scepter," he commented.

"Really? Have you seen it? Is it in the library?"

It sounded forced in my own ears, but he seemed unsus-
picious. "I've never seen it myself," he said, shaking his head.

"It's not in the Master's study now, but you might ask the librarian for assistance—if he's coherent again."

There was the slightest touch of irritation in his voice; Elerius had planned for a period of grief, but in his view that period should be over now. I also noted the admission that, even though he had not presumed to move in, he had taken the opportunity to see what the Master's study might provide.

It wasn't clear to me whether he believed my sudden profession of support for him, or whether he was letting me go as some sort of test. But it didn't matter. Once I was dead he could have no power over me.

I took my air cart north, flying with the augmented speed I had taught it with Naurag's spells. With few supplies beyond his book, I followed the coastline toward the land of dragons.

Summer was nearly over, and low clouds and fog hung over the coastal hills. And autumn with its cold and its dank rain came to meet me as I moved north. I was kept busy as the days passed trying to keep the cart in clear air, but we repeatedly ran into clouds where it was almost impossible to see, and where beads of cold water formed on my hair and beard, making the whole cart clammy. Much of the trip I sat shivering, trying to stay out of the wind.

And all the time I was flying I kept thinking of excellent reasons why I should delay my trip into the lairs and open jaws of the dragons. While the mangled remains of my body would certainly provide convincing proof of my death, there would be the distinct difficulty that I wouldn't be alive to take advantage of the opportunity.

The last coastal towns had long disappeared behind me, and even the last fishing villages, when I reached the range of mountains that separated the land of wild magic from the lands of men. To the east, the mountains rose as much as three miles up to jagged, ice-covered peaks. Up there the school maintained a watch station, to monitor magic creatures trying to head south into human realms—and presumably wizards heading north. But here the mountains sloped down into the water, before continuing out into the western sea as a series of empty, wave-drenched islands.

The air made me feel cold down to my bones, but it carried with it an exhilarating sense of power, of magical ability that gave me the courage to keep trying—and even the belief that I might still succeed. Elerius couldn't possibly have tracked me this far unless he was flying invisible behind me, which I doubted—it would severely restrict his activities back at the school. It was time to appear to die.

First I landed and found a sharp stone to hack at the side of the air cart, making plausible-looking teeth marks, such as a dragon might leave. Thinking about Naurag and his purple companion, much less about the Master, who had given this cart to me, started to make me sad and sentimental, but I gritted my teeth and hacked on ruthlessly. When the air cart was looking fairly tattered it was time to think about blood stains.

On the way north I had considered and rejected a dozen ways to imitate the look of real blood. None of them were likely to fool Elerius. Reluctantly I took my knife and forced the point against a finger tip. A single drop of blood appeared. I smeared it carefully on the inner side of the cart, but it didn't even show.

Several times during the trip, gathering wood for a fire or slicing up the dried meat I had brought along, I had scraped a hand or an arm, but the scrapes appeared all to have healed, not even leaving a scab I might pick. I could kill an animal and spread its blood around, I thought, but this region seemed devoid of animal life—even the plant life was limited to something with large, dusty-green leaves growing close to the ground. Besides, I didn't trust Elerius not to be able to distinguish human from animal blood.

After considering various parts of my body and trying to decide which one I might be able to spare, I finally worked up the nerve to make a cut through the skin of the back of the left arm. It took fifteen minutes and a lot of squeezing, but I managed to extract enough blood to spread thinly but fairly artistically over the air cart, creating a suggestion of someone struggling unsuccessfully against a dragon. A bloody hand print added a nice touch of verisimilitude.

I gave the cart the magical commands to return it to Yurt and watched it flap away, feeling both sorrow and triumph. They would be grief-stricken at home when they thought me dead—or at least I liked to think they would be—but I was underway at last. Before Elerius became master of the world he would have to deal with me.

Then I turned, set my jaw in determination, and started northward. Flying, I thought, would warm me. Before me, though still hundreds of miles away, lay the great valley of the dragons and, if Naurag's spells had continued to work for all these centuries, the Scepter that would control the dragons. I had no idea how I would worm it out from under the dragons' noses without being eaten first, but I was going to try.

And as I flew, into the heart of great, unfocused magical forces, I began to imagine it might not be so difficult after all. I had Naurag's spells—what more did I need? And if for some reason I couldn't get hold of the Scepter, I told myself, then I always had a fall-back position from which to oppose Elerius. I was fairly sure I could find an Ifrit in the East again, and, half-drunk on the magic through which I flew, I decided that I could surely persuade him that he owed me three wishes.

I had flown for about an hour and was starting to feel like trying some spells to practice the greater and greater abilities I could feel coursing through me, when I abruptly paused and rubbed my eyes. Something bright purple flapped toward me, rapidly coming closer. Either I was hallucinating from loss of blood or else my air cart was approaching from before me, from the north.

Had it somehow looped around by mistake and gotten ahead of me? I hovered in the air, trying a far-seeing spell— which worked far more easily than it ever did at home. I thought I had given the commands to the cart quite clearly: did this mean, I thought with an abrupt loss of the confidence I had felt seconds earlier, that Elerius had seen through me and was already blocking my plans before they started?

But this wasn't my air cart. It was not tattered, and over-all it just didn't look right—especially its head. The head had been left attached to the skin of the dead flying beast back when it was made into a cart, but the eyes had been sewn shut and the jaws wired together. Yet this head seemed alert and watchful, looking from side to side as it came. It jerked up sharply as it spotted me, and for a moment its wing-beats held the creature steady in one place, then it approached, slowly but as though very interested.

This wasn't my air cart, but something I had never seen before. It was a living purple flying beast.

IV

The flying beast made an interrogatory noise, apparently as surprised to see me as I was to see it. I dropped to the ground so as not to appear threatening. It circled me slowly in the air, its long neck craned for a better look. These crea-tures were born flying, I had been told, and from below I could see that its feet were extremely rudimentary; no won-der the wizards had had to attach wheels to them in making them into air carts.

This creature had long fangs hanging from the corners of his jaw, which looked as if they could do serious damage if he wanted to bite me, but so far all he seemed to want was to look at me—and at the patch of vegetation in which I stood. I glanced downward and suddenly realized what these low-growing plants were over which I had been flying. They bore wild gourds, newly ripe.

I reached down, plucked an especially large one, and tossed it upwards. The creature shot forward with one stroke of his wings and snapped it out of the air. Two quick crunch-es and he swallowed, then licked his lips with a long purple tongue and looked toward me expectantly. Apparently for a flying beast these gourds were fang-smacking good.

Picking another, I rose into the air and cautiously approached. The flying beast opened his mouth wide, beating his wings hard in eager anticipation. I tossed the gourd from a distance of only a few yards, and again it disappeared into his maw.

"What's the problem?" I asked, keeping my voice low and friendly—the way I had often heard King Paul talk to his horses. "You love these gourds, and you've come here now that they're ripe, but with your tiny feet do you find it hard to stand on the ground to eat them? Would you like me to pick you some more?"

He grunted at me and licked his lips again. I doubted he could comprehend human speech, but so far we understood each other just fine. I picked two more gourds, tossed him the first one, then slowly approached. He backed up a little, but after I tossed him the second and he had swallowed it down, he came slightly toward me. Again I picked a gourd and again I approached, wary in case he charged if feeling threatened, until I could reach out with one hand and touch his scaly pur-ple neck. He gave a quiver but neither retreated nor attacked. I made friendly murmuring sounds, gave his neck a pat, and with the other hand put the gourd directly into his mouth. He backed away with great startled wing-beats that almost knocked me out of the air, but he swallowed all the same.

It took the rest of the afternoon before I felt I had fully tamed the flying beast—or maybe he figured out that as long as he continued to play coy I would continue to pick and give him gourds. Antonia, I thought, would love him—I just hoped we all lived long enough so I could introduce my daughter to the purple beast. At last, when his belly was as round as a gourd itself, he gave me what I could have sworn was a friendly wink from one yellow eye, settled himself into a slow flying pattern a few feet above the ground, and went to sleep.

I sat among stripped gourd vines, contemplating my "purple companion." Naurag's had flown even faster than dragons—at least until the larger and less maneuverable dragons had gotten up to speed. So far I hadn't tried on this beast any of the commands in the Hidden Language which the long-dead wizard had detailed for me—and which we still used for the air carts. But I couldn't help looking ahead, imagining myself zipping under dragon noses—even between dragon teeth as their jaws closed fractionally too late—shouting in triumph and waving the long-hidden Scepter. And then I would return to the City wielding it, a battalion of dragons at my back, and then I would explain to Elerius in words of one syllable that he was going to retire from active life instantly, and then—

In the meantime, it was growing cold. I shivered, wrapping my arms around myself. This plan wouldn't work very well if I froze to death before getting properly under way. There was nothing here with which to make a decent fire; green gourd vines wouldn't cast much heat. I tucked my hands into my arm pits, stood up, and began to pace, thinking I might have to do so all night.

And then I almost jumped out of my skin as something hard and damp touched me in the small of the back, giving a snort that shot hot air up inside my shirt. I whirled around, seizing wildly at spells. It was, of course, the flying beast.

He had descended and was looking at me somewhat quizzically through the dimness. I realized that in his concern for me he had actually set his feet, or at any rate his broad belly, on the ground. In spite of his scaly skin, he radiated heat. I took a step closer and put one cold hand on his warm flank. He gave a sharp wing-beat that knocked me over, and I tried to make apologetic noises as I struggled back to my feet. But then I realized. He hadn't been trying to drive me away. He was trying to pull me closer.

The wing beat again, and this time I let it drag me to him. The skin under the wing was rough, and the odor would not have been my first choice, but it was certainly warm. Tucked up against the flying beast, I relaxed and closed my eyes. As long as he was with me, I might be eaten but I would not freeze in the land of dragons.

When I awoke in the morning it took me a moment to realize where I was. I was stiff and constrained, my arms pinned to my sides, and everything in front of my eyes was indistinct and purple. Besides, it was starting to feel as though I was tipping—

The flying beast, doubtless feeling me wiggling around, graciously lifted his wing to let me out. It was only as I rolled out into the air that I realized that during the night he had used his other wing and his intrinsic flying abilities to rise into the air again.

I caught myself inches above the ground. "Good morning," I told the beast from amidst the remains of the gourd patch. He looked around to make sure we had gotten them all yesterday. "I'm going to name you for a very great wizard who had a friend just like you. I'm going to name you Naurag."

Eager as I was to start hunting for the Scepter, I ended up delaying a few days, practicing riding on Naurag's back, trying out the various spells in the old ledger, and scouring the whole region for gourds. Not much else grew around here. The borderlands of the land of wild magic were barren and bleak, as I remembered from my one earlier trip this far north. Several times we saw other purple flying beasts in the distance, but my own trumpeted loudly in their direction, doubtless telling them that this helpful gourd-picker was his personal property, so they should not expect him to share with them.

Normally the Hidden Language allowed one to alter the shape of reality, by entering into magic's four dimensions and speaking with the voice of the same forces that had created the earth in the first place. But I had the impression in giving commands to Naurag that I was actually *talking* to him, that he was not being forced to obey me so much as listening to what I had to say and happily going along with it. Without human vocal apparatus he couldn't speak the Language himself, but he seemed quite capable of letting me know his thoughts and feelings through look and gesture.

"Ready to face dragons tomorrow, Naurag?" I asked him, leaning against his side while I toasted over a small fire the last of the cheese I had brought with me, preparatory to spreading it on the last of the stale bread. For conversational purposes I preferred the language of men; the Hidden Language was really not designed for general discussions. Besides, I hoped that Naurag would pick up human words the way an intelligent dog might; he already seemed to know his name.

He gave a friendly grunt, and I realized somewhat guiltily that he had no idea what I meant when I said "dragons." A sensible flying beast would stay as far from them as possible. But I was certainly not going to survive an encounter without him.

I had spent the last few days memorizing the spell for finding the Scepter as best I could; the first part, the part with the densest phrases in the Hidden Language, I had already attached to my old wizard's staff. It wouldn't have a tenth of the powers of the Scepter itself, but until I found the Scepter it had to do. Although I had to assume rather optimistically that the herbs also necessary for the old spells would occur to me between here and the dragons' valley, I was starting to believe that I might be able to work them—but only if I had rapid escape transportation.

We started north the first thing in the morning, and within a few hours the landscape began to change. We flew over a row of low hills, brown and desolate as was almost everything here in the borderlands of the realm of wild magic, but beyond lay a small lake the same color as the sky, rimmed with plants of emerald green. I directed Naurag to fly lower for a closer look; warm air, completely out of season, wafted up to us, along with a scent of—melons?

He looked back over his shoulder at me; he had smelled them as well. I banked and swung lower still. Melon vines indeed grew along the edge of the sky-blue lake, along with bushes covered densely with white flowers. No sign of dragons or other danger. "How about if we stop for a snack?" I suggested.

Naurag thought this was a swell idea. In a moment I was seated on soft grass, plucking the sweet, pink-fleshed melons that grew in profusion on either hand, cracking and eating some myself but tossing the rest to my companion, who floated beside me a foot off the ground.

Among the flowering bushes that surrounded us, I now saw brilliantly-colored butterflies, drinking delicately from the blossoms. Though the blooms themselves were white, their pollen was golden, and all the red and yellow butterflies flashed gold from their abdomens as they flew. A splash from the lake next drew my attention, and I saw fish, the same sky-blue as the waters themselves, leaping upward and dropping again, eyeing me with what I could have sworn was interest.

When I leaned back I could see, thrusting skyward, the shimmering white peaks that separated human lands from those of wild magic. A band of mist swirled around the highest points for a moment, then dissipated, letting me look from the comfort of this magical valley up to the bitter snows and glaciers of mountains where man had never walked since the Ifriti first helped push them up from the earth's mud and stone.

It looked a little like a picture of heaven I dimly remembered seeing in a Sunday School book as a child, a flowering and fruitful land beside a lake at the foot of the mountains. Could this in fact be heaven? But if I were really dead I thought I would have noticed. Still, being dead from everybody else's point of view might turn out to be extremely liberating, I thought, and picked and cracked open another melon. There was no reason to do anything at all, except enjoy the pleasures of the land of magic.

With a snap of my fingers I created an enormous illusory beetle, metallic green, who swooped over the lake's surface. Some of the fish dove down in dismay, but others leaped at it with gusto, then fell back in disappointment when their mouths closed around nothing more substantial than air. Another snap of my fingers, and the beetle was gone, but both Naurag and I were invisible, only our shadows marking our continued presence. I had never before been able to make anything invisible beyond myself, and even that was always difficult. The next moment, we were again visible to the startled fish, but now the branches of the bushes started swaying and shaping themselves, to form letters spelling out DAIMBERT.

"I'd better stop," I said to Naurag with a laugh. "Spells are suddenly so easy that in a minute I'll persuade myself that I

can face dragons with my bare hands. We should get underway again. But let's remember this place—when the snow is
blowing in Yurt, it might be nice to have a lake of perpetual
summer to which we could come."

We flew onward for a few miles, rose over another row of
dry hills to the next valley, and almost collided with a giant.

He stood up, stretching with arms over his head, just as we
flew past. Brown, placid eyes stared at us with the same mild
alarm that might be shown by a cow seeing something small
rustling in her pasture. Naurag avoided him with a few quick
wing-beats, seeming unconcerned. The giant grinned at us as
we darted by, showing teeth as big as my head. I nodded back
in salute.

"Did you see that?" I asked Naurag excitedly. "He must
have been the size of a house! And I'm glad you were able to
avoid him—I bet he doesn't perform snappy maneuvers any
easier than a house would. I've heard about giants all my life,
but I never thought I'd see one."

But this giant was only the first of many we saw in the next
hour. They had enormous, bulging muscles, which I thought
they must need to move themselves around even here in the
land of magic, but their strength seemed turned entirely to
domestic purposes. I soon realized that the rather misshapen
heaps of stone that dotted the landscape here were giants'
huts, with tidy garden patches and normal-sized sheep out in
back. The giants all seemed friendly enough, slow-moving,
only slightly curious about us but delighted when I returned
their waves.

"I wonder why I ever imagined the land of wild magic
would be a dangerous place," I said to my purple companion.
Talking to him, I had managed to reassure myself in the last
few days, was entirely different from talking to myself. "I'm
certain the dragons will be a challenge when we reach them,
but everything else here is delightful."

It was at that point that I spotted the fanged gorgos.

At first I had thought the rough pile of stones was just another giant's hut. But rather than having a garden and sheep around it, it had bare, muddy earth and half-gnawed bones. "Is this some sort of outlaw giant?" I was just starting to ask, when a horrendous stench wafted toward me. My head jerked up to see, rising from behind the rocks, a creature five times the size of a man but with the wings of a bat. Its fanged jaws were enormous, even for its enormous head, and its eyes glowed like living coals.

It shot toward us, giving a horrible, slathering sound. I could recognize all too well what that sound meant—it meant hunger.

Without waiting for commands from me, Naurag sped northward, his wings beating faster than I had ever seen them move. The giants quickly disappeared behind us as we raced away across wooded hills and narrow green valleys. I had had no idea Naurag could go this fast—we must be covering many miles in not much more than a minute. Clinging desperately to his neck as I was almost thrown free, I glanced back to see that it wouldn't do any good. The gorgos, its enormous leather wings beating almost lazily and its mouth wide open, was rapidly drawing closer.

V

There was a way to stop a gorgos, a spell I had used on one a dozen years ago, if I could just remember through my terror what it was—

And suddenly the slathering sound and the fetid breath at the back of my neck were gone. Naurag, sensing the change too, jerked his head around. A trick? The gorgos had stopped dead, its winged shoulders hunched. A tiny piping noise in the distance resolved itself into someone's voice, shouting upward from the ground.

The gorgos turned abruptly and started south, back in the direction from which we had just come. It looked as though someone with much more powerful magic than anything of mine had just ordered it to leave, and it had obeyed.

I waited to let my heart slow down and then tried to act nonchalant. No use letting whoever it was see how terrified I had been of something that obeyed him readily. "A wizard from the school, do you think, stationed up here, or some other kind of magical creature?" I asked Naurag. "Do you think whoever it is might be friendly to flying beasts?"

Naurag seemed to think so. He flew quickly toward whoever had shouted at the gorgos, his head up and all his purple scales sparkling in the sun. As we drew closer, I could see it was a person, and for a second I was not sure if it was a man or a woman: someone tall, wearing flowing white robes, crowned with silver hair that rippled loose in the wind.

A face turned up toward me, and I could see now that it was a man, indeed the most handsome man I had ever seen: youthful in spite of the silver hair, with sharply-chiseled features, including a cleft chin that the old Master's pet student back at the school would have envied. "Greetings!" he called up to me, as unconcerned to see a wizard riding a purple flying beast as he had apparently been a moment before at the sight of a fanged gorgos.

"Um, good day!" I called back. "Thanks for stopping the gorgos before it ate us."

He lifted one hand as though to shrug away this minor service, but it appeared to me as if he held something in his other hand, concealed in the folds of his robes. "Come down," he called, his voice deep and melodious. "We see so few humans here it would be a pleasure to meet you."

Then he's not human himself, said a sharp voice in the back of my mind. But, I answered myself, that needn't mean he intended me and my companion any harm. He had, after all, just saved our lives. And if a gorgos would listen to him, I rather doubted I could get safely away if he was so interested in my company.

"The pleasure will be all mine," I called down cheerfully. I pressed Naurag's sides with my knees, and he sailed down to hover next to this man, this being, this—

Elf, said the voice at the back of my mind. When I was a boy listening to my grandmother's stories, the stories that had doubtless led to my decision to become a wizard, I had imagined the northern land of wild magic as a place of elves and fairies. But somehow when I was eight years old I had not thought of elves as gloriously handsome and seven feet tall.

"My name is Daimbert," I said politely, "and my purple companion is named Naurag."

The man's chin lifted in surprise. "Naurag? I once knew someone— But that was many years ago. It is of no matter. You may call me Gir. Come. The others will be interested in seeing a human. And after your fright I am sure you would like to eat and drink."

I considered several ways to suggest that I had not been frightened of the gorgos at all and gave them all up as useless. Gir strode briskly downhill, and as we followed him it crossed my mind to wonder if he could possibly mean the original Naurag, the old wizard who had created the Dragons' Scepter. But I shook my head at such a fancy. This man was younger than I was.

As we went I looked around, seeing that the landscape here was one of steep, wooded hills, a brilliant green as of early summer, and that the air was as warm and soft as at the first little lake we had reached. I saw no sign of human—or elven—habitation other than the neat brick path that Gir was following. But, looking ahead, I thought that the grove of great trees that topped the next hill looked somehow strange—

He strode effortlessly up the steep incline before us, Naurag following with gentle strokes of his wings, and now I could see why the trees seemed so odd. Their trunks bulged outwards halfway up to the crown, and set in those trunks were windows. Gir's people lived literally in the trees.

Several came out to meet us, both men and women tall and silver-haired, beautiful in features and grave in manner. But something about the gathering nagged at me as not quite right.

My flying beast seemed quite comfortable with them, letting them stroke him on the neck and looking around for melons. I told them when they asked that I was a wizard, that I came from hundreds of miles south of here, and that I was more than willing to visit their humble chambers. As they led me up a winding stair inside the trunk of the largest tree— Naurag flew up outside—I realized what was bothering me. This whole group seemed composed of men and women no older than King Paul, without anyone older, and without any children.

A recent settlement, then, of elves who had left the main group to establish a new colony? But the dazzling porphyry columns that circled what they referred to as their "humble" chambers certainly did not suggest a frontier colony.

"This is beautiful!" I said in awe, looking around at stone in shades of ivory, pink, and mauve, all brightly polished and set off by baskets of flowers and ivy. The elves seemed pleased; one made an allusion to how hard it had been finding the right stones, gathered from all over this land. Outside the windows we could see the leaves of other trees, as well as Naurag looking in.

They fed me spring water and fruit, melons like those I had eaten earlier, apples, strawberries, raspberries, and lemons, apparently all in season at the same time here in the land of magic. It was the best fruit I had ever had in my life, perfectly ripe, juicy, sweet, its aroma alone a sensuous pleasure. Gir had the young woman in charge of the gardens come forward rather shyly to describe to me her many years' project to bring the fruit to such a pinnacle. She must, I decided, have been gardening since she was old enough to walk.

Even if I never saw this place again, I thought, it was good to know that it was here: an enchanted spot thousands of miles from home, but to which, in the darkest winters and the harshest times, one might imagine coming.

"And may we ask," Gir asked when I had sampled some of everything and tossed Naurag a melon, "why a wizard has come to the land of dragons?"

I wiped my mouth on a delicate napkin, shining white like all their robes. "Actually, I need to get into a dragon's lair. I realize this may seem foolish to you, and I'm afraid I really can't explain why, but I wonder if you could tell me if it is very far from here."

The others looked at each other, and Gir shrugged. "It is not far at all. A five-minute flight on the beast you name Naurag will take you there."

"Maybe I'd better get started," I said reluctantly, "though first I do want to thank you for this wonderful food—"

But they urged me to stay for the rest of the day and the night: not, I thought, as though wanting to give me a mournful farewell dinner, but rather as though visiting the dragons would be mildly fatiguing event, which it was best to approach fresh.

After my escape from the gorgos, I was delighted to put off dragons and their fangs until tomorrow. "Isn't it dangerous," I asked, "having dragons virtually on your doorstep?"

"It could be, of course," Gir said gravely. "One must never underestimate either their ferocity or their cunning. But long ago we found a way to deal with them, and after all we endured before we came here, we do not find them so bad a watch-dog on our porch. Although our life here requires vigilance, I would not call it dangerous."

Perhaps, I tried to reassure myself, dragons' ferocity had been grossly overrated. But the voice at the back of my mind, which refused to look on the bright side, reminded me that I had met a dragon once, and although it was several decades ago now, time had not obliterated the memory of coming extremely close to being messily devoured.

Gir and his people wanted to entertain me. First the food and then this, I thought, toying with the idea of living here for the rest of my life while Elerius did whatever he wanted. They seated me in the middle of the grove of trees, brought out stringed instruments, and began to play. From the first notes, their melodies entered straight into my bloodstream, drawing me deep into the melody. One of the silver-haired women began to sing, words I could not understand, set in a minor key. Somehow, although I had no idea what she was singing about, her song brought me images: a brave band of explorers lost in a foreign land, their valiant efforts to survive, their sorrow and despair as their numbers began to dwindle, the unexpected discovery that gave them hope—

Something heavy and hot hit me on the leg. Startled, I looked down to see that Naurag was hovering next to me and had put his head across my knee. I put a hand on his head and scratched it as though he were a cat, which he enjoyed tremendously, then went back to listening to the music. But the spell was gone, and the words to this song were no more to me than beautiful sounds in a foreign tongue.

The next song, however, I could understand, for it was sung in the language of men—for my benefit? Three of the women sang together, their voices light and clear, singing of the joys of their grove, their pride in their homes and in their fruit trees, the deep companionship among their group, their love for their neighbors the giants and even, if I understood them correctly, the dragons. I could appreciate why they danced with pure pleasure, robes whirling around them, as they sang this song.

Stories followed, stories of a small group of people living in what I gathered was one of the more northern parts of the

Western Kingdoms, treated with growing suspicion as new neighbors migrated up from the south and settled near them. The story was set long ago, in the days of the distant Empire, but it was very poignant nonetheless. The people were first regarded with amazement and awe, but then increasing jealousy as their new neighbors could not grow food or build with beautiful stone as they did, especially when the neighbors died and they did not. Finally open resentment boiled up when the people did not have the wizardly skills their new neighbors seemed to expect. Attempts to migrate themselves were almost disastrous when they settled first near the lair of a gorgos—a danger with which I could certainly identify. I was pleased when, after a series of even more hair-raising adventures, the story finished with the people finally finding a place of peace.

When the stories ended, my hosts brought out supper, fruit again but also sheep's milk cheese. "We barter for it with the giants," Gir told me, seeing me look around in a surprised search for sheep. He did not tell me what they traded.

"I understand that as a wizard far from home, you may be uneasy about revealing too much of your abilities—at least at first," one of the women said when I had eaten. "But tell me—was that idea of Naurag's of creating a wizards' school ever put into practice?"

They were all politely waiting for my answer, but I, having just worked something out, took a moment to reply. "You knew Naurag, then," I said slowly. "The original one. The wizard eight hundred years ago."

"Of course," said Gir, delighted. "I told you we had. And you knew him too? Your creature is named for him?"

They weren't King Paul's age after all. They were the people of the songs and the stories and had probably been right here since before the kingdom of Yurt even existed. "No, I never knew him," I said cautiously, "but I've read about him." I felt hesitant to tell them specifically about the old wizard's ledger—especially since he had showed a remarkable carelessness in not mentioning that elves lived boldly on the dragons' doorstep. "He had a purple companion just like mine. He did not start a school himself, but one of his apprentices' own apprentices did so, where I received my own wizardry training."

And which I might be expected to head if I could locate the Dragons' Scepter. Well, if I found it I could defeat Elerius, and if I couldn't I wouldn't have to become Master, being dead, so it was a victory either way.

"I guess you could say," I said, stretching, "that interest in dragons continues among wizards even after all these centuries. I'll head into their valley first thing in the morning."

part four ✛ the funeral

I

ORAGONS AREN'T COLD-BLOODED like lizards. The fires that burn in their bellies keep their blood hot enough, or so they had told us in wizards' school, that dragons actually prefer the cooler climate of the northern land of magic. Therefore there was no reason to expect them to be sluggish at dawn. But I started before dawn anyway, slipping out of the gorgeous guest room inside the elves' tree without bothering them with my departure. The more I thought about it, the less I liked old Naurag's failure to mention the elves, and it seemed safest to answer the fewest questions possible about my mission.

My purple flying beast was floating outside the window as I came through it. But he lifted his head from under his wing at once, spotting the melon I had brought for him. I tossed it to him, swung a leg over his back, gave a quick, quiet command in the Hidden Language, and we were off on the final leg of our trip to find the Dragons' Scepter.

The sun was not yet up, and I shivered as the wind hit me. It felt as if it had come straight from the glaciers that lie, unmelting, further north of the land of wild magic. I decided I would skip a visit there this trip. The eastern sky was a thick layer of clouds, tinted orange.

But I forgot the cold the next moment, for the purple beast's steady wing beats brought us over a high knife-edge of rock, thrust up from the boulder-strewn plain, and I saw before me the valley of the dragons.

Warm-blooded or not, the dragons were still sleeping this early in the morning. I pulled up Naurag for a moment merely to gape.

It was a stunning sight. And one seen, I told myself triumphantly, by very few wizards, or at least by very few who were still alive five minutes later. Fifty feet long or more, covered with glittering scales in red or green or blue, long fangs protruding around its jaws, each dragon lay in front of its lair, burning eyes closed in sleep, great leather wings folded, smoke rising from the nostrils. The valley, not surprisingly, was devoid of any other form of life. Any one of the dragons, even the smallest, could have snapped me up as easily as Naurag ate a melon.

My purple companion had thought of this too. He turned his long neck to look at me accusingly. But this was no time to hold back. With or without the final touches the old wizard had put on his finding spell, I would have to use it before the dragons awoke.

I put my heels to Naurag's sides, and to his credit he responded at once, shooting toward the largest one of all. As we flew forward I had to revise my impressions once again: these dragons were even larger than they had appeared from the valley rim.

The biggest lay half in and half out of its lair, its snout resting on its front feet—each armed with talons that looked about the size of wizard's staff I clutched determinedly. This one's scales were not bright as were the other dragons', but a dirty yellow, as though age had stripped them of color. The scales were scarred and cracked at the edges, and the enormous wings folded down the creature's back were tattered, as if from many deadly fights over the centuries. I wondered briefly, as my flying beast zipped past, if this dragon was one of the very ones whom the old wizard Naurag had bent to the Scepter's will.

An eye opened. We had been spotted.

Our only advantage was the very small size—relatively speaking—that would also have made it so easy for the dragons to devour us. By the time the dragon had turned its head we were well out of striking range, flying back along its side and into the lair itself, where the long barbed tail lay coiled. That tail was twitching as I leaped from Naurag's back and started on spells.

This would never have worked anywhere except in the land of wild magic. In two seconds I had released the spells stored in the silver-topped staff and roared through most of the rest of the finding spell the old wizard had recorded for uncovering the Dragon's Scepter. With improvisational abilities I didn't know I had, I created bridges in the spell where herbs were supposed to go, and stepped back, triumphant, by the time the great pale dragon had pulled his tail out of his lair and started shifting around to put his head in instead.

And nothing happened. I smacked the butt of the staff on the floor in wild frustration at the same time as the first tendrils of smoke from the dragon's nostrils curled around me. I *knew* I had the spells right! I had spent days memorizing the words in the old ledger, and with my own abilities enhanced by the powers of this land I could feel my spell taking its correct shape. Right about now the enormously powerful spell that the wizard Naurag had created to keep his Scepter hidden ought to be breaking up, revealing the Scepter just in time for me to snatch it up and keep the dragon at bay.

Talons scratched on the stony floor of the dragon's lair. Smoke was filling the room, and I could hear the dragon's belly rumbling, loud as an earthquake. The flying beast sensibly shot up to the top of the chamber, out of the way.

And then I realized what was wrong. The spell of concealment was not breaking up because it was not there. At some point in the last eight hundred years somebody else had taken the Scepter.

It would have vastly improved my chances of survival, the nagging voice in my head pointed out, if I had known this before rather than after I entered the dragon's lair. Flames licked toward me, and the great yellow eyes had fastened on me.

No time for heroics—just for desperate flight. And sometimes the simplest ways are best. I made myself invisible.

The dragon's teeth snapped shut, but I was no longer there. Invisible, I flew straight up to where my purple companion was doing his best to fly through the ceiling.

He jerked as an unseen hand touched him. "It's me," I told him, low, under the disappointed roar of the great dragon. "Let's get out of here," and tried to wrap him in invisibility as well.

Even here in the land of magic, hard spells worked at impossible speeds did not always function perfectly. Bits of his purple nose and tail protruded from my spell, but I hoped the dragon would not resolve these in the shadows into something edible. The flying beast took us winging toward the entrance to the lair—an entrance nearly blocked by the dragon—while I struggled wildly to hold on.

Right past the dragon's jaws and neck he shot, along the flank and then down under the reeking belly, as its movement threatened to crush us between flank and wall. The tail, outside now, was lashing madly, but Naurag dodged and dodged again, then abruptly was out, free, and whizzing over the heads of the other dragons, while I gave a shout of defiance and tried desperately to cling to his neck with sweaty palms.

The sun broke through the cloud bank on the eastern horizon, and, invisible or not, we cast shadows. Dozens of yellow eyes were open now. With snorts and jerks of leathery wings, the dragons heaved themselves to their feet, swiveling their massive heads to pick us up. One drove its talons straight through our shadows, but another had spotted disembodied bits of purple and launched itself toward us.

Razor sharp fangs glittered in the dawn light, only a few feet away. And Naurag dove. Down to within inches of the massive skull of another dragon that was slower getting started, then upward again at a sharp angle. Just as the first dragon, mouth still wide open, struck its companion with the force of an avalanche.

A horrible roaring rose behind us. Naurag turned south, propelling us onward far faster than I could possibly have flown myself. The purple neck to which I clung, the purple wings beating on either side, were becoming visible again, even to eyes streaming from the force of the wind. My staff was long gone. I glanced back over my shoulder. Two of the dragons were fighting, tearing into each other with fang and talon, their bellows ringing out across the rocky landscape and black blood spurting.

But at least one other still had us in view, as the tattered remnants of my invisibility spell fell from about us. The dragon—this one a brilliant crimson—gave an almost lazy stroke of its wings and covered a third of the distance that separated us.

Illusion, I thought, panic making the words of the Hidden Language that I had known for forty years suddenly seem strange and incomprehensible. Illusion is a lot easier spell than invisibility. And I made us into a cloud, a dark, fast-moving cloud, certainly not a human clinging to the back of a purple flying beast.

The crimson dragon behind us paused as if puzzled. But past its shoulder I saw other dragons coming to join the pursuit. At least one of them must have enough brains in its bony skull to associate this suddenly-appearing cloud with the suddenly-disappearing tasty morsel they had been pursuing.

And I realized we were leading the dragons straight toward the elves' grove.

"No!" I screamed at Naurag. "Not this way!" But neither tugging nor commands in the Hidden Language could alter his direction. He was flying back in the direction of the melon-fields where I had originally found him as fast as his wings would carry him. And the way there led straight over the silver-haired community.

The knife-edge ridge that marked the border of the dragons' valley was a blur below us. I darted a quick look back again, hoping against hope that the dragons would stop at that boundary. No such luck. Dragons of all colors, scales glittering in the early morning light, flames snorting in all directions, raced after us. They might not be able to recognize a wizard and a purple flying beast in an illusory rain cloud, but they saw something moving fast and were as eager to catch it as a bunch of cats. And the distance between us was rapidly vanishing.

I said a quick prayer in case any saints paid attention to those in the land of wild magic. With luck, we would be past the elves' grove before the dragons caught up to us, and they would have so much fun playing with and eating us that they wouldn't bother the people who, after all, had for many years lived almost on their doorstep.

But *why* had they never bothered them? the voice in the back of my mind asked, still curious even when only moments from death. And then through bleared eyes I saw a tiny, white-robed figue on the ground before us, and heard a voice, tiny and piping at this distance. It was Gir.

And this time, even at a distance, I could tell he held something high in his hand. My flying beast altered course to fly toward him like a frightened child toward his mother.

The dragons behind us were so close I could feel the heat of their breath on my back. But they stopped abruptly at whatever command Gir shouted to them, jostling together in the air, great wings smacking against each other.

As Naurag slowed, panting hard, and drifted down toward the groves, the dragons turned, greatly reluctant but turning all the same, taking a few frustrated snaps at each other's wings as they headed back toward their valley.

II

I fell more than dismounted from the flying beast's back, my arms and legs feeling as if they had no strength at all. "I wish you had allowed me to accompany you," said Gir gravely. One hand was concealed in the folds of his robe, as it had been after he stopped the gorgos. "When you spoke so determinedly of going to the dragons' valley, I had assumed that you, like old Naurag, had wizardly ways to bend them to your will."

"I thought I did," I said, sitting on the ground with my head between my knees. Several things had become clear to me, about one day too late. "But it turns out that you have what I was looking for."

Gir sat next to me, his chiseled features concerned. For a second he bit his lip, as though trying to reach a decision, then he tossed back his silver hair and spoke briskly. "We prefer not to discuss Naurag's Scepter with outsiders, but yes, of course we have it. We have had it for centuries. Otherwise we would never be able to maintain life in our peaceful and beautiful grove. But did you not know? When Naurag gave it to us, he said he would describe the final disposition of the Scepter in the same ledger in which he had, years earlier, recorded the spells by which he created it. We could not, of course, have duplicated his spells, but we had always assumed that some of the apprentice wizards he trained might do so."

I sighed, not looking at him. "No one else ever duplicated his spells," I said, more to myself than to Gir. "They're too hard to work anywhere but right here—and, I believe, too hard for even the best wizards of our age." Could Elerius create a Scepter of his own, given a chance? I wasn't going to give him that chance. "All I could do was work the finding spell that was supposed to reveal the Scepter hidden in the greatest dragon's lair. Old Naurag set out to write an Afterword to his ledger, but I think he died before he could."

Gir contemplated this. "Then you wizards have assumed all these years the Scepter was still there? And the others sent you to find it?" I nodded; he was close enough, and it would be too complicated to explain properly. "But what," he added, "did they intend to do with it?"

I let his question hang unanswered. Something he had said caught my exhausted attention. Elves could not work spells.

A wary sideways glance showed him sitting relaxed, one arm across his knees, frowning as he looked north toward the dragons' valley. With a far-seeing spell I could make out the sun flashing on their scales as they circled, preparing to land again. All my spells worked easily here. In less than a second, far before Gir realized what I was doing, I could have him wrapped in a quick binding spell and the Scepter out of his hand and into mine.

I thought this over while my rapid breathing slowed. The other elves weren't here—presumably still back in their chambers in the great trees of the grove, this early in the morning. But sooner or later they would realize that Gir was gone and come find him, about the time that my binding spell would be disintegrating. By then, of course, I would be far away, already having raced back to the dragons' valley to round them up, to command them to return with me to the City. There I could quickly force Elerius to capitulate, before going on with my terrible winged forces to overcome the evil princes of the kingdoms beyond the mountains, to free the slaves in the East, to annihilate every fanged gorgos in the land of magic…

And suppose the dragons didn't all go with me? the nagging voice at the back of my mind wanted to know. Several, or even one, could easily stay behind, then fly over the ridge and devour elves at its leisure, now that they were no longer protected by the Scepter. Well, I thought uneasily, I would just have to be very sure that every single dragon followed me.

So did that mean I was going to have to spend the rest of my life surrounded by dragons, making sure that not even one ever returned? Brief and completely implausible images floated through my mind, the castle of Yurt surrounded by a great circle of quiescent dragons; a fleet of dragons hovering in the air, wings flapping slowly, high over Theodora's house while I visited her; or dozens of dragons, collared and obedient, sitting like colorful statues on the turrets of the wizards' school.

I shook my head at the thought, which got me a questioning glance from Gir. No, I told myself, it was sad but inevitable that some elves would have to die. They had already had very long lives, and even though Gir had now saved my life a second time, it would be justifiable to sacrifice a few of his people. It was merely sentimental to think otherwise, I tried to persuade myself. After all, my principal goal was to protect the world as a whole from Elerius.

Elerius also believed that the end justified the means, that if a few people died in the pursuit of his own obviously worthwhile goals, then their involuntary sacrifice was well worth it.

Gir spoke suddenly, breaking a long silence. "If you cannot tell me your need, I must respect your reticence. But if your wizards' school needs the Scepter, of course—" His melodious voice began strong but suddenly threatened to break. I sat up straighter and looked at him fully. "Although I wield it, I am not the leader," he continued in a low tone. "We have had no leader since we came here. But I can speak with the others. It might require a certain amount of time to make our preparations, but perhaps we could leave our grove, find some other place where—"

I spoke before I had a chance to consider further, but it was the only answer I could have given. "I came to find the Scepter if no one were using it. Since it was Naurag's and he gave it to you, we of the wizards' school cannot decide eight hundred years later that his gift was wrong."

If I took the Scepter, either by force or else—after a wait that allowed Elerius to consolidate his position—by persuasion, then I would be responsible for at least some of these elves' deaths. I might be able to overcome Elerius by attacking him with dragons, but all I would have overcome was the man, a man that at times I had rather liked. Elerius's plans for world dominance, on the other hand, the self-assurance that his way was the best possible way, those would be alive and well. They would live on in me.

As I rose slowly to my feet all sorts of other reasons why it would never have worked anyway occurred to me. Arriving in the City with a horde of dragons at my back would have been much more likely to begin a devastating battle between the wizards of the school and the dragons—and me—than to make Elerius abruptly reconsider his agenda. Especially since there was an excellent chance that Elerius, with his much better abilities, would snatch the Scepter from my hand as easily as I had snatched it from Gir.

And might the dragons, no longer intimidated by the Scepter, start erupting into the land of men after I brought them back here, even if I succeeded? The wizards' school has always had the announced mission, dating back, I realized, to programs of Naurag's, of keeping dragons well up in the north; and yet keeping them there had never been a particularly onerous task. Gir and his people—and the Scepter—I now suspected, had for centuries been unacknowledged allies in the wizards' efforts to keep humans safe from wild magic. There might be an excellent reason that there were a lot more dragons in the old stories than were ever now seen in the Western Kingdoms.

"No need to worry about moving, Gir," I said with a rather unconvincing effort at nonchalance. "The Scepter would be dangerous for us to use anyway." An understatement. "It was just an idea one of the old wizards at the school had had, but I realize now it would be impractical. There's somebody who's got a plan to take over the world. His name is Elerius. But I realize now that bludgeoning him into submission by trying to wield a Scepter I don't even know how to use just wouldn't work. Keep it here, and keep the dragons—and the other creatures of wild magic—in control."

Gir sprang up with as much youthful vigor as Paul. Looking at the relief and gratitude all over his face, I realized that he had just been having as big a moral struggle as I had. I was relieved that I would not be responsible for his death after all.

"If you have completed your visit to the dragons' valley, then," he said cheerfully, "we should have breakfast. I do not believe you had any blackberries yesterday."

I stayed two more days with the elves. That evening, rather than entertaining me with their music, they had me tell them stories, how old Naurag's original dream of a wizards' school had finally been put into effect centuries later, once the devastations of the Black Wars had made the wizards, fractious and touchy as they were, realize they had to start working together for the good of all humanity. My own grasp of the history of wizardry was always a bit shaky; I hoped the parts I had to make up weren't too far from accurate.

During the day I flew on my purple flying beast over the giants' farms and, carefully avoiding the lair of the fanged gorgos, on to explore other areas of this wild northern land. It might, I thought, be my only chance to see the creatures that I had assumed ever since I grew up were just imaginary: and to find out they all existed here. Some were beautiful, many strange, many dangerous. I thought rationally that I should be bitterly disappointed to have made this trip for nothing, but in fact I knew it was not for nothing. And it was hard to be downcast when the magic flowing through me felt so glorious.

But if there was nothing for me here, then I needed to return to the City. I had to find out how Elerius was doing in his plans to take over all of western society. "Or how would you like to visit the East?" I asked my flying beast. "I'm sure you've never been there, and they do have good melons, though not as good as the elves'." The power of an Ifrit, if I could find and master one in the wild eastern deserts, would certainly be enough to outmatch even Elerius.

Naurag flew south reluctantly on the third day, making sure that I noticed him casting lingering glances toward the elves' gardens and orchards. I hoped he realized I was planning to take him much farther from those orchards than the borders of the land of magic where I had found him. It would, I tried to explain to him, be an exciting new experience for him to see humans.

The trip south, back toward the City, took much less time than the trip north, with Naurag's rapid wing beats carrying us across woods and hills. Finding enough gourds and melons for him occupied much of my attention—attention which I knew I should instead be turning to the question of what to do about Elerius now that it turned out I didn't have the Scepter. But the feeling of loss to be leaving behind all that magic drained me of any initiative. After three days of following the coast line, we started approaching lands I knew.

And I realized that I had headed us toward Caelrhon. It was inland from the City, out of my way though not very far. I had started humming during the afternoon, no longer as depressed as I had been to be leaving the land where my spells worked so well. The vague image floating through my thoughts resolved itself into setting the flying beast down in the cobbled street by Theodora's house, while the evening darkened and the lamplighters came up the street. She would be delighted to recognize my step, and she would draw me in, toss the cloth scraps off the couch—

But Theodora thought I was dead. No visits with his wife for a man who still seemed to imagine that he could force the best wizard since the original Naurag to give up his plans for world domination.

We flew high over Caelrhon's royal castle as evening came on. A large number of tents were set up outside the moat, and I could make out men in armor around them. Perhaps the king had decided to summon all his knights for exercises. The spires of the city of Caelrhon rose before us in the last light of day; my flying beast seemed to be responding to commands I wished I could give. I made both him and me invisible and flew low over the rooftops, just trying a delicate probing spell to reassure myself that Theodora was there and well.

Neither Theodora nor Antonia was there. Not quite allowing myself to worry, I set the flying beast down in the meadow a mile outside the city walls, where the Romneys sometimes camped.

I hadn't picked up Joachim's mind either, but that was less surprising. At prayer in the cathedral, his mind would enter the realm of the supernatural and be inaccessible to my magic. But as I lit a small fire and, visible once again, started preparing supper, I wondered uneasily what had been happening while I was gone. Might Elerius, now elected new Master of the school, have invited Antonia to start her studies in the City at once, and urged Theodora to come along to act as chaperone for my daughter and Prince Walther?

I had bought an earthenware pot of stew from a friendly woman on a farm the day before. She had given me far too much to finish in one day, so I had managed to keep the rest inside the pot today with a careful binding spell. It smelled rich and savory as it began to heat. I sat with my back against Naurag's flank and my face toward the fire.

It cast very little heat or light against the darkness. The evening was chill, and the last of the summer insects called raucously to each other. But suddenly their calls went still. Someone was moving stealthily through the meadow toward my fire.

III

A quick spell lit up the darkness. I did not know what to expect, thief or another batch of student wizards coming to kidnap me, but the light in its brief flare showed instead what appeared to be a boy crouching, startled, a few yards away.

"Come closer so I can see you better," I called as my spell faded. "I won't hurt you, but I don't want to have to use magic to capture you if you try to run off."

The boy hesitated while I waited. The smell of the stew, I thought, had brought him. If this boy was a runaway, he must be hungry. Hunger was stronger than caution, for in a moment he rose to his feet and moved slowly closer, still tensed for flight at any moment.

"If you'd like to share my supper, I have plenty," I said. In spite of my friendly invitation, I kept a shadow over my face until I was sure this was no one I knew. He took one cautious step forward, into the flickering light of my fire, and now I saw that it wasn't a boy after all. It was a young woman dressed as a boy, her hair all cut off under her cap.

"You're a wizard," she said accusingly, dragging her voice down a few octaves. "I don't trust wizards."

I laughed and let the shadow slide from my face. My identity should be safe with her; I couldn't remember ever seeing her before in my life. "You don't need to pretend to be a boy with me. I'm not about to assault you. And you might as well trust me, because if I'd meant you harm I could already have turned you into a frog—but I don't. What's your name?"

For a second I thought she would flee, but then she peered toward me, shrugged, and came a step closer. "I'm Hadwidis," she said, no longer trying to pitch her voice lower. She said her name firmly, as though there might have been some doubt in my mind about it. I knew no one named Hadwidis. "Can I really have some of that, Wizard? I saw your fire and was going to avoid you, but it smelled so good!"

The stew was hot by now. We shared the spoon, and I let her have the larger portion. From close up she appeared even younger than I had originally thought, maybe only five or six years older than Antonia. Her caution all seemed forgotten in her hunger. She couldn't have been running for long, I thought, and wherever she had left, it had been someplace she trusted the people around her. From the way she gobbled the stew down, I doubted she had had anything to eat since leaving that place.

When Hadwidis finally sat back from the well-scraped pot, she took a deep breath and said, "Well! Thank you. I should have thought to bring some food along."

"That's a common oversight with people running away," I said in a tone meant to encourage confidences, but she didn't hear me.

She had finally realized that the large shape at my back was not a boulder. "What's *that*?"

"A flying beast. He's purple, though you can't tell in the darkness. He's very friendly. His name is Naurag."

She peered at him cautiously, and Naurag snaked his long neck around my shoulder to peer back. "He looks like a dragon, only smaller," Hadwidis said at last. "But I thought dragons weren't real."

"They're real enough," I said, more gruffly than I intended. "But he isn't a dragon; he's just a flying beast. Pat him on the neck, he likes that."

She patted him carefully, exclaimed at how warm he felt, then rubbed his scales more enthusiastically. I was watching her in the meantime, wondering where she had run from and where she thought she was going. I had enough to worry about already.

"You know, Wizard," she said unexpectedly, "I don't think you owned a flying beast the last time I saw you."

"Do I know you?" I asked, appalled. Here I had carefully staged my death and avoided telling this young woman my name, and she was about to turn out to be a cousin or something of one of the servants in the castle of Yurt, who would shortly be announcing to everyone that I was still very much alive.

"You probably don't remember me, but do you recall coming to the Nunnery of Yurt once, six or eight years ago? You were spiritual sponsor for a woman who then decided she didn't want to be a nun after all."

I nodded; I remembered that fiasco extremely well. It was the first and only time I had been inside the nunnery. "You were there too? I'm afraid I still don't recognize you."

"I was just a girl then, one of the novices. We probably all looked alike to you in our white robes. But I remember you. After all, that was the most exciting series of events at the nunnery in years! But I'd have remembered you anyway. We'd hardly see a man from one year to the next except for some really old priests, and you looked very interesting. At first we all thought you were old too, because of the white beard, but your face didn't look old. We had quite a few discussions in the novices' dormitory afterwards about whether you were a wizard or not. I said you were, and it turns out I was right! But," more soberly, "I guess now I'll never be able to tell the other girls."

If she had been a novice nun for years, I thought, isolated from the world inside the cloister, she would have no idea that the Royal Wizard of Yurt was supposed to be dead—and in fact, she might not even know I came from Yurt. "So you've decided not to make your final profession as a nun?" I asked.

She hesitated a moment, staring into the fire. Naurag nuzzled her shoulder encouragingly, which knocked off her cap, showing a shaved scalp. But then she hooked an arm around the flying beast's neck, as if for comfort, and slowly shook her naked head. "I did make my profession," she said in a low voice, "two years ago when I turned sixteen. But I've changed my mind. I just don't have the vocation to be a nun."

"So you ran away," I said flatly. For a nun to leave the cloister, I was sure, must be to commit a horrible sin. But I didn't worry about that now. Suppose, I thought instead, Antonia decided to run away from the wizards' school? She would be even worse at planning ahead than this girl.

Now that she'd admitted it Hadwidis was more than willing to fill me in on the details of her flight from the cloister. "You know, Wizard, it's quite a relief to have somebody to talk to about this! I thought it was all going to be easy. Three days ago the plan appeared in my mind, fully formed. The nunnery's having all the windows redone—a chance to see a real man within the walls! The glazier and his son are staying at the guest house. They'd washed out their clothes and hung them up to dry, so I just stole a shirt and cap and a pair of trousers that looked like they'd fit me. Then two nights ago I waited until everyone else was asleep, put on the clothes, unlocked the gates—I know where they keep the key—and slipped out."

This then explained the shaved head. Three days ago it would have been covered by a nun's wimple.

"It turned out to be a lot harder than I thought, running away. For one thing, I realized I couldn't go anywhere in daylight, or everybody would realize that I must have left the nunnery and probably send me back. And I *won't* go back. Also I hadn't remembered that I'd need money outside the nunnery. We nuns don't have money of course—we have nothing of our own. At night I may be able to pass as a boy, but I'll have to find something to eat —and somewhere to stay—until my hair grows out. After that I'm planning to go into the city of Caelrhon and work as a waitress at one of the taverns. What do you think, Wizard?"

"Well, Hadwidis," I said slowly. From nun to tavern wench! She certainly had decided to leave the cloiser thoroughly behind her.

She interrupted before I had a chance to come up with some well-meaning and fatuous advice about not restricting her choices. "My name, for example! That's part of the reason I had to leave. I'm Hadwidis and always will be, but when I made my profession I had to take a saint's name. Well, if you can imagine it, they had run out of women saints! All the women's names the abbess thought suitable for us had already been taken by the older nuns. So my group all ended up with men's names. I tried telling the abbess that I was sure there had been just as many holy women as holy men over the years, if not more—after all, women can become nuns and men don't do anything of the kind!—but that as long as only men decided who was really a saint, women's holiness wouldn't be recognized. Do you remember the abbess, Wizard? She wasn't impressed with my argument."

I remembered the abbess vividly. I wouldn't have tried to argue with her about anything. "So what name did you end up with?"

"Sister Eusebius!" she said as though spitting out the words. "Can you imagine? They call Eusebius the Cranky Saint. It turns out there's always a nun with his name at the house because he's the patron saint of Yurt. They've got his Holy Toe in a reliquary somewhere in the kingdom."

"Umm," I said in vague affirmation, remembering just in time that I didn't want to advertise how well I knew Yurt. I had had only one direct contact with the saint myself, years ago in the narrow valley that housed the hermitage of the Holy Toe, but it had certainly not faded from memory. A saint who responded to a lovely woman's prayer, to cure her of her vanity, by giving her a giant nose-wart certainly deserved the appellation of Cranky. All saints were holy, Joachim had once told me, but that didn't mean they were nice.

"And not only did I not want his name, it turns out the saint didn't want me to have it either!" Hadwidis was excited now, gesturing as she spoke. "I had to make my profession on his holy day, of course, and no sooner had they given me the ring that marked me as a bride of Christ and called me Sister Eusebius for the first time, when all the candles went out by themselves."

"Well, ah, there could be a perfectly normal explanation—"

But she was not listening. "And the candles wouldn't relight! At first the abbess said it was the wind, except the air was perfectly still. It smelled of roses, too—which I thought pretty suspicious, because it was the wrong season for roses. Then the abbess said those candles must be defective, so she sent for some more, and they burned perfectly well until they got within ten feet of me, when they all went out. So I knew that the Cranky Saint was angry, and I think the abbess was starting to realize it too."

"Had you done anything to make him angry?" I asked, fascinated.

"Well," she said, partly embarrassed and partly proud, "I did play him at the Feast of Fools. Did you have the Feast of Fools when you were little? It's the day that everything is turned upside down. It was a lot of fun when I still lived at home, and my little brother would play Father, and I'd be Mother, and all the servants had to do whatever we said. It certainly made things different to have a three-year-old boy sitting on the throne! But I think they only have the Feast at the nunnery because it's such an old tradition. The girl who's chosen to be Abbess for the day always has to be better than good. Anyway, I'd decided to liven things up and play Saint Eusebius. I even made up a song for him to sing: 'Oh, no, I lost my toe, I'm filled with woe, here in the snow, my tears do flow—' But you get the idea."

That would certainly have gotten a cranky saint's attention. "Were there any other signs of his displeasure besides the candles?"

"None that anybody else saw, so the abbess started thinking I was making things up. And I was really trying to be a good nun! Or at least I started trying harder after that. But sometimes during the night services I'd get so sleepy that I'd just sit down on a bench, or sometimes when we were fasting I'd get so hungry I'd just take an apple or something from the kitchen, or sometimes when we were supposed to be reading I'd start making up a funny song in my head and get to giggling, and you know what? Every time, I'd feel a pinch on my arm, or there would be a sudden cold breeze right down my back, or a tap like somebody tapping his foot right behind me. Let me tell you, it was creepy!"

Something she had just said was nagging at me, but I was too interested in her relationship with the Cranky Saint to wonder about it now. "So how did Saint Eusebius react to you running away?"

Hadwidis grew abruptly less animated, and her shoulders slumped. "I think he was pleased," she said in a quiet voice, no longer meeting my eyes. "I tried to be a good nun, but he wasn't happy with me whatever I did. Now, the last couple of nights, whenever I try to get a little sleep lying under a bush, I've had the strangest dreams. They aren't like any dream I've ever had. I think—" and I had to strain to hear her "—I think they're visions."

"Visions!" This sounded far worse to me than unexplained breezes or strange tappings. I put out a hand to feel Naurag's solid, reassuring flank. The night seemed suddenly very dark, and the faint glow of the city of Caelrhon, behind its walls a mile away, looked unreachably distant.

"It was terrible, Wizard," she continued, almost in a mumble, "yet it's also the most intensely spiritual experience I've ever had. I know I shouldn't be telling you this—they taught us in the nunnery that wizards have no use for religion, and I certainly know enough to distrust *one* wizard. But it's been going on for two days now, and I don't know if the saint will appear to me again if I try to get some sleep, and I've got to talk to *somebody*."

I made an encouraging sound, suddenly realizing what it was she had said that might be important. But I forgot it again the next moment.

"He seems friendly enough now that I'm no longer Sister Eusebius—maybe he even appreciates it that I have some gumption. But he's given me a mission. He's told me to look for someone named Daimbert."

"Daimbert!" To the best of my knowledge, there was no one else in the kingdom of Yurt with that name but me. The advantage of belonging to an institution that had no use for organized religion was that normally saints didn't pay any attention to us either, but it looked like all that had just changed. "Did he tell you why?" My voice came out thin and squeaky.

Hadwidis didn't seem to notice. "He said that I could help this person," she mumbled. "But I don't know how. This is awful, Wizard. It's not like worrying if the abbess is going to catch me yawning in the middle of a psalm or something. The saint has looked right into my heart and believed I could do something important, and yet I've already sinned by breaking my sacred vows, and now I'm afraid I'm going to disappoint him terribly."

"You're supposed to help this person named Daimbert," I repeated slowly. I didn't have the slightest idea what she could do for me either. Maybe the Cranky Saint had decided my situation was so hopeless that even a spiritually-confused runaway nun was better off than I was.

"Saint Eusebius may have put the idea to run away in my mind originally," she said in despair, "just so I could find this Daimbert. I think—though I can't be sure—that I know someone or something that would assist him. But how am I supposed to look for someone I don't even know? I haven't even met any men in years, much less ones named Daimbert. I've been praying for guidance, but— I just don't know what to do, Wizard!"

I made a rapid decision. If the saint wanted this girl to find me, I'd better not do anything to thwart him. "Saint Eusebius is helping you even more than you realize, Hadwidis," I said gently. "I'm Daimbert."

Her initial reaction was not relief but shock. She scuttled around to the far side of the fire, looking at me with wide eyes. "Somehow," she said in a small voice, "having my prayers answered this abruptly is almost as terrifying as having a vision."

An irreverent voice in the back of my mind counseled me to be properly appreciative of this first, and doubtless last, instance of being the answer to a maiden's prayer, but I ignored it. "Well, my prayers have been answered as well, if you know something that would help me."

"But what?" she said in confusion. "I can't imagine that the saint wants me to teach you the liturgy, or how to sew a habit, or which months of the year the novices are allowed an extra blanket on their beds. You wizards probably have important magical problems to solve, but all I've known for years is the nunnery!"

I didn't have any better ideas. "Well," I said encouragingly, "if the saint meant for me to find you, so you'd have something to eat, and for you to find me, to tell me something as soon as you remember what it is, then he should be happy now. Maybe you'll think of it in the morning." Whenever Antonia had been frightened or worried, I'd always tried to project calm reassurance.

We soon settled down on opposite sides of Naurag, his warm wings over us, as there seemed to be little we could do tonight. Hadwidis, concerned about visions or not, went to sleep immediately, to judge from her steady breathing. But I lay awake a long time, wondering where Theodora was and what had been happening in Yurt while I was gone, such that Saint Eusebius could possibly imagine a young woman would help me.

IV

First thing in the morning I sent Hadwidis into Caelrhon with some of my money to buy food. I didn't want to risk recognition by going myself. "If they realize you're a girl and not a boy," I told her, "it shouldn't be a problem. But don't sign up to work at the tavern just yet. Oh, and also don't tell anybody you're with a wizard named Daimbert." Then I spent the whole time she was gone worrying that I should be taking her back to the nunnery, though it was clearly the last place either she or the Cranky Saint wanted her to be, and wondering how I was supposed to thwart Elerius if I was carting a runaway nun around everywhere with me.

She came back whistling, carrying a bag with cheese, bread, meat pies, a dozen melons, and my change. "That was fun," she said. "I haven't been in a town in years, and even then the servants usually bought everything for me. Nobody seemed to realize I was a nun, but as I was coming back I started thinking. Suppose the abbess organizes a search party to find me? After all, she's not going to want to tell my mother I've disappeared."

"Or your father," I said absently, wondering if there was some way I could get her to Theodora. Theodora would take care of her—but Theodora didn't seem to be in town.

Hadwidis gave a little sigh. "No, my father's dead. He died last year. And, do you know, Wizard," glaring in my direction, "the abbess wouldn't even let me go to his funeral! She said I had 'left mother and father' in becoming a bride of Christ. Though maybe it's just as well, because if I'd been there—"

I patted her arm in sympathy. "Would you excuse me for a few hours?" I said carefully. "I have to go somewhere. You can eat both meat pies if you're hungry while I'm gone."

Her reaction surprised me. Tears started into her eyes— not as blue as Antonia's eyes, but blue nonetheless. "Wizard, you aren't— You aren't just going to leave me, are you?"

"No, no," I said hastily, resisting the impulse to give her a reassuring hug. She was too big for that—especially as I'd known her only half a day. "I have no intention of leaving you. If I'd wanted to, I could have slipped off while you were in town, but I don't want to. In fact, I hope you will stay here with Naurag. I've never left him alone since I tamed him, and I don't want him following me—or even starting back toward the land of magic on his own."

She wrapped her arms around Naurag's neck, while he looked inquiringly toward the bag of melons. "Promise me," she said, her voice unsteady. "Promise you'll be back. After meeting you I couldn't stand to be left alone again. Swear you won't try to leave me!"

There was nothing for it. "I promise I'll be back," I said solemnly. "I swear on magic itself that I'm not abandoning you here." But how many more promises was she going to extract from me, I wondered, and how was I supposed to stop Elerius while taking care of her? I didn't want to take her into danger any more than I would have wanted to take Antonia.

But she immediately became cheerful again. I shifted her and Naurag into a densely-thicketed grove of trees, so that the purple flying beast would not attract attention. She had already started eating a meat pie by the time I left, and called good-bye through a mouthful.

I flew the forty miles to the royal castle of Yurt wondering about the military exercises that King Lucas of Caelrhon seemed to have begun. He and King Paul had never been intimate friends, but they had gotten along perfectly well for years, so I assumed he couldn't be planning to invade Yurt. But who would he invade—or whose invasion did he want to oppose? Since the end of the Black Wars we wizards had been fairly effective in keeping our kings from going to war with each other.

One more thing to try to sort out. But I forgot about Caelrhon as I approached the castle that I had thought I might never see again. Before reaching it I paused in the air to wrap myself in invisibility. At least for now, the castle must not see me.

Usually blue and white pennants snapped from the towers. But today all the towers were flying black. The royal flag was the only spot of color among them. And while I did not see any tents of bivouacked soldiers by the castle, a large throng milled around in the courtyard—many more people, I thought, than usually lived there. Could Paul be marrying the princess after all, and have invited all the neighboring dignitaries to the wedding?

Not with black pennants. Somebody had died.

Still invisible, I dropped quickly into a shadowed corner of the courtyard. My body, even if invisible, would still block the sun's light, and I didn't dare let anyone discover me. But who could have died? My heart constricted as I tried to scan the courtyard, ascertaining who was still alive.

King Paul for one, dressed formally in black and talking quietly to someone I couldn't quite make out through the crowd. The queen mother and her consort. The queen's aunt, the elderly but lively Lady Maria. Gwennie, apparently answering questions from some priests I did not recognize. A great many knights and ladies, most but not all from the castle. The kingdom's two counts and its duchess, the latter with her husband and twin daughters. But I spotted no one from the royal court of Caelrhon, not King Lucas, not Princess Margareta.

The slightest hint of magic warned me, and I had all my mental defenses up as I turned to see—Elerius.

Elerius? What was *he* doing in Yurt? He stood twenty yards away, not looking in my direction. Another wizard was with him, someone in a tall red hat to whom he seemed to be listening intently. The latter shifted, and I recognized Zahlfast.

My brain churned wildly, trying unsuccessfully to come up with an explanation for why all these different people should be here. Was Elerius going to make an announcement, about his new position as absolute ruler of the world, from the kingdom of Yurt as some kind of final insult to the wizard he thought dead?

And abruptly I realized. This was my funeral.

Immediately I felt much better. Once or twice, while listening to our chaplain drone on about the merits of someone no longer with us, I had thought that the person who would have appreciated the praise the most was the person least able to hear it: the deceased himself. But now I was going to be able to hear for myself all the words of approval and gratitude usually reserved until someone was dead; I wouldn't even care if they weren't all sincere.

Gwennie made an announcement, and those in the court-yard started moving toward the stairs leading to the chapel. I shifted to avoid some priests who were talking about the election of a new bishop in the City at long last—it sounded as though Elerius's candidate had been chosen. But I didn't have time to worry about the Church's affairs. As the crowd shifted I could see at last to whom Paul had been speaking. It was Theodora, standing with Antonia's hand in hers.

I took a breath of profound relief. No wonder I hadn't been able to find them in Caelrhon last night; they had been here, preparing for my funeral. Theodora too, I thought, would appreciate all the nice things said about me, though I wished someone other than the portly and rather self-righteous royal chaplain would be saying them.

But as I looked at her face, pale but composed, I had to fight the impulse to burst back into visibility and take her in my arms. I knew her well enough to realize that she was trying to control enormous sorrow. Could saving the world from Elerius possibly be worth causing this kind of suffering to the woman I loved?

Then I noticed Elerius again, his hazel eyes fixed thoughtfully on Antonia, and grimly stayed invisible.

My daughter was fidgeting, unhappy but more stubborn than grieving. She seemed to be turning something over in her pocket with the hand that her mother was not holding. "I still don't think he's dead," she said to King Paul, before Theodora gave her a sharp tug to lead her up to the chapel.

Denial was not the best way to deal with loss, but in this case she was right, I thought with an inward smile.

I let all the others go up the stairs first, then slipped up silently behind them. Everyone squeezed together on the pews, including the two wizards. Between the old Master's funeral and mine, this made two visits to a church in a month for men who probably hadn't been inside one for years.

Standing at the altar was not our portly chaplain but the bishop himself, formal in the scarlet robes Theodora had embroidered for him. Better and better, I thought, but was surprised to see how much grief was in Joachim's face as well. Candles were ranked on the altar, but none burned, and the chapel was dim in spite of its high stained-glass windows.

I wondered briefly if I ought to reappear now just to save everyone all the embarrassment of going through this unnecessarily, but I stayed invisible, leaning against the door jamb. Very soon I was going to have to take off for the East, or in whichever direction my so-far stubborn brain eventually came up with, and unless I was very lucky this funeral would indeed be necessary—just premature.

"We are gathered here," Joachim said when the general rustling had died down, "to remember the life and commemorate the death of Daimbert, Yurt's Royal Wizard. But he was much more than the wizard here, though he filled that function well for over thirty years. He was a teacher, a husband, a father, and a friend."

I looked quickly toward Zahlfast, who sat looking sober and unsurprised. Elerius must have filled him in on my family situation when they were invited to my funeral. Any disapproval Zahlfast might have felt had been erased by my supposed death.

"It is with heavy hearts," Joachim continued, "that we commend Daimbert's soul to God. His strength and his abilities were always great, but he also gave them a moral dimension that meant he never sought power for its own sake. And his abilities were heightened by his friendship—his reaching out to others. He made friends, real friends, more easily than most, and those friends were as great a source of strength to him as his spells. Wizards, he often told me, live much longer than ordinary people. So I never expected that I should one day be here, officiating at the memorial service of the man I loved most in all this world."

The bishop stopped as though not trusting his voice to continue. There was a faint sniffling from several spots on the benches, but otherwise the room was silent. I felt both guilty to be putting them all through this and enormously gratified.

"When an old man dies," Joachim continued after a minute, "we grieve for ourselves, because of how much we miss him. When a man dies in his prime, we grieve also for all he might have done on this earth, which must now remain forever undone. But none of us can predict the day of death—ours or another's. Nor can we speak with assurance of the status of anyone's soul, for that is known only to God. But in this case we can have little doubt that Daimbert, approved by mortals and by saints alike, has gone to a better place. He has left us behind in the world of flesh, where power such as that he wielded so gracefully can too easily lead to greed and ambition, to sin and false desires."

Actually I hadn't gone anywhere, but I was interested to notice Elerius and Zahlfast shifting uneasily. From them my eyes slid to the gilded statue of Saint Eusebius, Yurt's patron saint, beside the altar. He was depicted here as in the days before a marauding dragon ate every part of him but his toe: dressed as a hermit and leaning on his staff. I still didn't like it that the saint had sent Hadwidis looking for me, especially as I wasn't totally convinced that that meant he approved of me, as the bishop seemed to think all saints must.

Joachim opened the Bible and read, his voice low and somber. "Man is born to trouble as the sparks to fly upwards... As for man, his days are as grass. As a flower of the field, so he flourisheth. For the wind passeth over it, and it is gone; and the place thereof shall know it no more... He cometh forth like a flower, and is cut down; he fleeth also as a shadow, and continueth not." He lowered the book and looked out across the congregation—directly at me, but his eyes were unseeing. "So the Prophet, in his despair, spoke of humanity unredeemed."

The sniffling on the benches had grown louder. It was not from Theodora, sitting in the front next to the king, for her pale cheeks were dry. Nor was it Antonia, her chin wrinkled in what looked more like anger than grief. My principal mourner appeared to be the Lady Maria.

Joachim flipped forward in his Bible. "But that was before the coming of Christ," he said, and he read again, his voice stronger now. "I am the resurrection and the life: he that believeth in me, though he were dead, yet shall he live... O death, where is thy sting? O grave, where is thy victory? ... I create new heavens and a new earth: and the former shall not be remembered... For now we see through a glass, darkly; but then face to face... And God shall wipe away all tears from their eyes; and there shall be no more death."

He turned slowly then and lit the candles on the altar. Their light flickered and glinted on the crucifix and the gilded statue of the Cranky Saint.

But when he turned around again, Joachim looked old, his hair more streaked with gray than I remembered and his cheeks lined. Only his eyes, enormous and deep-set, burned with the same fire that had always been in them. "Christ came to redeem us from sin and death," he said slowly, "to tell us that the grave is not the end, that we may all yet meet again. We can only pray to believe this."

V

When the bishop fell silent and looked unlikely to speak again, King Paul rose from his place. "I think it would be good," he said, his voice rough, "if those of us who knew Daimbert best were to say a few words in his memory, so that the good he did may not be forgotten. I shall always revere him as the man who saved the castle of Yurt from black magic more than once over the years. I rewarded him with the Golden Yurt, slight recompense for the mortal danger he put himself into for all our sakes. And all the men who receive that reward in future generations will know that they have a difficult model to emulate."

Paul turned toward the wizards then. "It is because of my respect for wizardry that I have invited these two old friends of his from the City to be here." He spoke firmly, as though refuting some argument against their presence—had either the bishop or Theodora tried to exclude them? "In Daimbert's honor, I have rejected any insinuation that wizards should not be governors of men. Nor shall I participate in any force joined to oppose wizardry. But it is not for Daimbert's use of magic that I shall principally remember him. I shall remember him as a counselor, a companion, and a friend."

Something was going on here that I had clearly missed—was he referring to Elerius's role as regent of his kingdom?

Gwennie rose then when the king stopped speaking. "Daimbert was my friend as well," she said, a quiver in her voice. "Man or woman, great lord or servant—it made no difference to him." She took a deep breath as though intending to say more, but instead put her handkerchief over her eyes and sat down quickly.

Paul turned to look at Theodora, as though inviting her too to say a few words. She shook her head, almost imperceptibly, and the king murmured something low and put a sympathetic arm around her shoulders.

The duchess rose then. "I've worked with at least four different wizards over the years, both royal and ducal, and Daimbert was by far the best. I'm horribly sorry he's gone now. If it hadn't been for him I might never have married," with a tender look for her husband, "so I have a personal reason to thank him, but there was always more. Daimbert had spunk."

But I was distracted from listening by watching Theodora and the king. I wasn't at all sure I liked him sitting with his arm around her in such a proprietary way. Gwennie, looking toward them with narrowed eyes, her handkerchief forgotten, had noticed too.

It meant nothing, I told myself sternly, being only an expression of Paul's affectionate nature. But the nagging voice pointed out that Theodora was now, as far as she knew, a widow, while Paul was the same man who had already proposed marriage to two different women essentially back-to-back. Maybe he thought the third time would be the charm.

Well, I thought with a small smile, he'd have to ennoble her first, and I guessed that Theodora's reaction to that would be the same as Gwennie's.

A number of people looked toward the two wizards when the duchess had finished, clearly expecting to hear from them next. They glanced at each other uncertainly, hesitating, but instead the Lady Maria bounced to her feet.

"I knew the wizard Daimbert before a lot of you were even born," she announced, "back when I was just a slip of a thing myself." She had actually been a mature woman at the time I first arrived in Yurt, but I was certainly not going to correct her. "When he came I was at a difficult stage, but he acted as my knight, polite and gentle, guiding me both in the ways of judgment and the ways of the heart." I remembered this somewhat differently. "And everybody's been talking about their sorrow and the hope for a better place, but I want to say that it's just *terrible* that he's dead! And I want to find out *why*, how he let his guard down, what kind of dragon ate him, and if somebody sent him up there on purpose to get eaten!" It sounded as though my ruse with the air cart had worked perfectly, though I wasn't sure I liked the direction her ideas were taking.

Lady Maria suddenly gave a little scream, cutting off the flow of her words and making everyone jump. "Look! Look there!" she cried. "Saint Eusebius is telling us the real culprit!" And to my amazement I saw that the statue of the

Cranky Saint had taken one gilded hand off his staff and was pointing. "It's *that wizard* who killed our Daimbert!" Maria shrieked. And indeed the saint was pointing straight at Elerius.

The chapel was filled with startled exclamations as everyone started to push forward for a better look, then stopped, overcome with awe. I myself was so surprised that for a moment I almost lost track of my invisibility spell. The air was suddenly heavy with the odor of roses—months out of season.

Elerius was so taken aback that open shock showed on his face, though I didn't think anyone but me noticed. He would have had little contact over the years with the supernatural, only with natural magic: he had dealt with a demon once, but never with saints, who might interfere less than did the dark forces in human affairs, but whose power, when they used it, was such to make all the might of wizardry laughable.

The bishop alone approached the statue, cautiously and reverently. "The saint, the patron of this kingdom, has indeed sought to tell us something important," he said at last. "Perhaps he is merely admonishing the wizard Elerius always to remember the self-sacrifice and the rejection of absolute power which Daimbert demonstrated in his life. We must pray to understand the saint's true meaning."

"I just *told* you his true meaning!" snapped the Lady Maria, completely uncowed. "*That wizard* told us himself he sent our Daimbert up north to the land of dragons, on some 'secret' mission. Why else would he have done it if not to make sure the dragons would eat him?" She whirled toward King Paul. "I'll never understand why, sire, you thought it appropriate to invite the obvious murderer to our Daimbert's funeral!"

But before either Paul or Joachim, must less Elerius, could answer her, a high voice piped up, quavering with shyness and emotion, yet absolutely determined. "Maybe the saint is just telling us to ask Elerius where my father has gone," my daughter exclaimed. "Because I *know* he's not dead."

Elerius, his composure fairly well recovered, spoke then for the first time. "I most certainly did not kill your father, Antonia," he said smoothly, "as I had hoped he would help in the difficult task of making the transition from the old Master's governance of the wizards' school to whatever new order we decide upon. As acting Master, I require all the assistance possible." Still only acting Master, I noticed; maybe the other wizards wouldn't be as pliable as he hoped. "But I am interested to know why you think he is still alive." There was more in his words than an adult's kindness to a bereaved child. Could he somehow have detected my presence?

"Because I'm a witch," Antonia answered, between pride and mortification. "Witches can tell what's happened to people they love—though I must say my mother has given up awfully easily!"

"Antonia, dearest, we *saw* the blood and the toothmarks—" But Theodora did not have a chance to finish.

King Paul sprang to his feet. "You have deceived me, Wizard!" he almost shouted at Elerius. "I did not want to believe it, for I knew that Daimbert had always thought well of his friends at the wizards' school. And I did not credit King Lucas of Caelrhon and his stories about how all the wizards are now planning to eliminate all the kings, or how we have to fight them—Lucas came up with some story like that a dozen years ago, and it was all nonsense then. But this time he may be right!"

Is that what I had seen in Caelrhon? Troops massing to march against Elerius's kingdom—or even against the wizards' school itself?

"For Daimbert warned me," Paul continued darkly. "He made a veiled suggestion that 'something' might happen at the wizards' school, something that would require me to hire a new wizard. At the time I paid little attention. But I see now that he knew he was going into mortal danger when he returned there."

Zahlfast answered for Elerius, who seemed more surprised than angered at this accusation. "But wizards do not kill each other," he told the king. "Not since the Black Wars has there been a single instance of one wizard murdering another, as much as we might sometimes quarrel. What possible motive could Elerius have for wanting to murder his friend?"

Paul, deflated, did not answer, but Theodora spoke for him. "There was in fact a very good motive. I have told no one of this before."

"Except me," put in Antonia. "And in fact I was the one who found it!"

They had the full attention of everyone in the room—including me. Theodora reached into her pocket. "Here I have a letter from the late Master of the school, naming Daimbert as his successor. He was too modest to tell any of us—the letter was hidden in the back of a drawer, where Antonia and I found it as we were going through his effects. But Elerius must have known—and killed him because of it."

"Except that he's not dead," put in Antonia, but no one was listening.

For the first time that I could remember, Elerius was genuinely dumbstruck. This revelation that he had not been the Master's favorite, coming so close after the pointing statue, hit him unprepared. Zahlfast snatched the letter from Theodora, and several other people craned over his shoulder to read the Master's shaky hand.

That's done it, I thought. I had faked my own death knowing that Elerius would want to manipulate me in life. But with this letter he now had a genuine motive to find and kill me.

The bishop spoke into the silence. "The statue of Saint Eusebius is no longer pointing," he said. "He seems satisfied that we have received his message."

Everyone had shifted away from Elerius, even Zahlfast, leaving a wide empty space around him. "The statue means nothing," he said harshly. "Maybe the lady just imagined she saw it move. Or maybe somebody moved it by magic," with a scowl for Theodora.

But then he took a breath, straightened his shoulders, and I could see him becoming calm and reasonable again through sheer will. "And this letter is not the startling document you all seem to think it is. I'm sure the Master was only here confirming something I had already determined for myself: that Daimbert and I should jointly head the wizards' school. I know that my own abilities are such that no other candidate will presume to present himself to oppose me, but I also wanted Daimbert, with his flair for improvisation, to assist in my tasks. Doubtless the Master worried that the other wizards might feel uncomfortable with having someone as their co-head who had as weak an academic background as Daimbert did, and that is why he thought this letter was necessary. Didn't Daimbert tell you he had agreed to rule jointly with me?"

"No," said Theodora and Joachim together, clearly not believing a word of it—though I could have told them that parts were true.

But Zahlfast's reaction was the most pronounced. "You cannot decide for yourself, Elerius, that you are going to head the wizards' school, with or without a co-ruler! We have yet to elect the man to replace the Master, and you cannot simply assume it will be you!"

Elerius's peaked eyebrows gave a sharp twitch; he had miscalculated, something he rarely did, and he knew it.

"I have been second in command at the school for years," Zahlfast continued, almost in a growl, his face close to the other's. "Yet you do not see *me* making any such presumption!" With an open quarrel between powerful wizards, this was going to be the liveliest funeral Yurt had ever seen. "I would have thought your position as regent for your kingdom would have disqualified you for the permanent leadership of the school—especially since you have been widening your activities lately with your campaign for City mayor. I cannot speak for the other wizards, Elerius, as you seem to think you can, in believing that they will all choose you: but I can certainly speak for them in saying that you are presuming far too much!"

Antonia, watching them, was again playing with something in her pocket. She took it out, and it glinted a moment in the candlelight. My attention was momentarily jerked away from the two wizards, for I recognized it. Antonia was holding her mother's old ring of invisibility.

And then she slipped it on. Normally one invisible person cannot see another—in a room full of wizards practicing their invisibility spells one would see nothing but shadows. But I could still see my daughter, seeming to shimmer slightly around the edges as she tossed back her braids.

Everyone else was staring at the two wizards. Antonia looked straight at me and slowly started to smile.

I raised a finger to my lips. Theodora's ring not only made the wearer invisible but, because it had a spell to reveal that which is hidden carved into the gold, it allowed the wearer to see through others' spells of invisibility. Antonia smiled wider and nodded, a finger to her own lips.

Then she slipped back into visibility, just as her mother took her sharply by the arm, muttering, "Give me that ring, now! I told you not to play with it."

While I had been distracted, Elerius and Zahlfast had clearly exchanged further remarks, because both were now flushed. "Why fight me, old man?" Elerius was saying, almost in a shout. "Why fight the new ways, in which wizardry will rule the earth? If you don't want to be part of it, retire, as you should have years ago. We wizards have served society for centuries with our magic—now we'll dominate society for its own good!"

The older wizard did not like this at all, but he did not answer. Instead I realized with dismay that he was trying to turn Elerius into a frog.

He was not going to be successful by himself. Even as I recognized that, even as I tried to shape a spell to assist him that would still leave me invisible, Elerius broke free of the other's magic.

And the statue of the saint raised both hands in horror, dropping his staff, as a great wall of fire rose in the middle of the chapel. Elerius rose with it, laughing defiantly, then both he and the fire disappeared with a shower of golden sparks— and I felt him rush past me, not seeing me any more than I could see him, as he flew from the room and from the castle.

part five ✣ xantium

I

tHIS WAS NO LONGER ME against Elerius. This was a split within institutionalized wizardry.

As I flew rapidly back toward Caelrhon, where I had left Hadwidis and the purple flying beast, I tried to imagine what Zahlfast was telling the rest of the wizards back in the City. I didn't dare get close enough to the telephone room to catch more than an occasional word, but he had shot straight there as soon as Elerius disappeared, missing Joachim's only partially successful efforts to restore the dignity of my funeral long enough for a somber hymn. Zahlfast was talking loudly into the telephone and waving his arms wildly when I left.

Elerius should most definitely not, I thought, have tried to defy him. The older wizard had never been flashy, but he had not become second in command at the school without an enormous amount of magical ability. And he also had the respect of the schools' teachers —of whom Elerius had been by far the youngest. And now Elerius was suddenly no longer the Master's apparent heir and no longer had the school's resources to draw on, but would have to operate from in hiding.

Shadows were long as I dropped from the sky into the grove where Naurag and Hadwidis were hidden. First thing tomorrow, I thought with renewed spirits, it was off to the East. If I could escape dragons, I should be able to master an Ifrit, and with the latter's power I would easily discover

Elerius's hiding place and bring him bound in magic fetters to the school.

Where by now everyone knew that the old Master had wanted me to succeed him. I pushed this thought aside as Hadwidis sprang up to meet me.

It was a little embarrassing to realize how delighted she was to see me, considering I had not thought of her even once all day. There was, I thought, a tinge of relief in her happy smile, but she spoke as though she had never doubted I would return.

"Naurag ate all the melons while you were gone," she told me cheerfully, "and I ate almost everything else, so I hope you had something for lunch wherever you went!" I hadn't but let it pass. The purple flying beast pushed his snout into my chest in a welcoming way, and I rubbed his head above the bony eye ridges. "Did you know, Wizard, they hardly ever let us eat meat at the nunnery? Only when we were sick—though I must say, some of the older sisters seemed to get 'sick' pretty often!"

"I'm going to have to take you someplace safe," I told her, "someplace where you'll have plenty to eat and a warm place to spend the nights until your hair grows out. You know you can't keep on sleeping under bushes—the next person you meet might not wish you well as much as I do."

"That's no problem," she answered, handing me the remains of the bread and cheese. There was what appeared to be a fang mark on the cheese, as though she had tried feeding it to the flying beast but he hadn't liked it. "I'll just stay with you."

I knew she'd say that. I broke off the corner of the cheese where Naurag had nibbled and ate the rest. "I'm afraid I'm going someplace too dangerous for you. But I've thought of a wonderful spot for you to stay. The royal castle of Yurt isn't far from here, and the people there are very friendly—or so I've heard," I added quickly.

Gwennie, I thought, would take care of her. Now I just had to make sure that Hadwidis didn't drop any clues that would allow Gwennie to deduce she had been with the recently deceased wizard of Yurt—without telling Hadwidis that that was who I was.

Her face fell, and she put both arms around Naurag's neck, suggesting that if I left her behind I wouldn't be taking my purple companion either. "But you *can't* leave me, Wizard," she said stubbornly, eyes downcast. "Saint Eusebius wanted me to find you, and there's no telling how cranky he'll be if you take off without hearing the information I'm supposed to give you."

"And have you remembered it?" I asked hopefully.

She gave me a quick, coy look from under her eyebrows—as if, I thought, she had been spending the day practicing to be a tavern wench. "I *might* remember if you took me along."

It was going to be dark soon, and I didn't have time for this. I gathered some fallen wood without saying anything, stacked it to burn against the cold and the night, and used a quick spell to light it. Only then did I remark, "So I gather you remembered during the day the information the saint wants me to have?"

She wanted to say that she had, she wanted to tease me some more, but she had been an absolutely honest nun far too long. "No," she mumbled, head down. "But I might if you took me along!" she repeated defiantly.

"How about if you tell me everything you *do* know," I suggested, "relevant or not, and maybe it will be in there somewhere."

Somehow I had imagined there wasn't a lot to be known about a nunnery and the women who lived there. It turned out I was mistaken. Hadwidis was more than eager to tell me all sorts of things that I would doubtless have found fascinating if I had been planning to take the veil myself. One thing she never said explicitly but I could figure out easily enough:

nuns weren't supposed to talk most of the time, remaining silent to be able to concentrate on their prayers. For a lively young woman coming out of years of enforced silence, being invited to speak at length was as refreshing as being given water would be to a thirsty man.

I learned the history of the nunnery of Yurt, which went back to the days of the long-dead Empire, centuries before the Black Wars, long before the Western Kingdoms even existed as independent entities. I learned the names—both the original names and the names they took as brides of Christ—of all the other nuns in the house. I learned which ones had come there as widows, which as young girls offered by their parents, and which ones, like Hadwidis, had decided for themselves in girlhood that they wanted to avoid the world—the decision she had since regretted. She told me which psalms they sang at which hours of the day on the different days of the week and offered to sing me all of them; I declined, saying I could look them up in the Bible if they turned out to be relevant.

Hadwidis had started off sitting across the fire from me, but after a short time, shivering, she came around and sat close beside me, both our backs against Naurag's warm flank and our shoulders together. As she detailed the differences between fast days on which one was allowed lentils and fish broth and the ones where one was allowed only bread and water, my mind started wandering. The principal conclusion I had reached so far was that the life of a nun disciplined the body and the mind so that a woman would not be distracted from God by the affairs of this sinful world, but that I personally thought a young woman ought to be given a little more scope for action. It was impossible to imagine Antonia in the situation Hadwidis described.

It was also impossible to imagine sending Hadwidis to stay with Theodora and Antonia while her hair grew out and she decided how to break the news, both to the abbess and to her family, that she wasn't going back. So far I hadn't heard anything about her family during her monologue, but I felt sure that would be coming soon. Antonia knew I was still alive, and if the two girls got together it wouldn't be long before Antonia extracted enough information from Hadwidis to realize that she knew me too—and to tell her that the wizard with whom she had spent a couple of evenings was Antonia's missing father. At that point, everyone would know.

I glanced up at the stars, wheeling slowly overhead. "It's getting toward midnight," I said, breaking into an account of how to measure a nun for a new habit. "I'm afraid this isn't going to work after all. We need to get some sleep."

Hadwidis stopped in the middle of a sentence, then pressed herself closer against me. "It's cold," she whispered. "I don't want to sleep on Naurag's other side from you."

"He's a lot warmer than I am," I started to say, then stopped dead. Hadwidis had taken one of my hands in both of hers and started to kiss it passionately.

Gratitude? Loneliness, or a fear of being left alone? I desperately attempted to come up with innocuous explanations, all the time trying to ease my hand out of her hers.

It didn't work. She had me in a grip like iron and had climbed halfway into my lap. Her cap had fallen off again, and her bare scalp brushed my cheek. "Hadwidis, don't be silly," I said, much too loudly. "It's been lovely getting to know you the last day or two, but—"

"Don't, Wizard," she murmured, halfway between sensuousness and tears. "Don't push me away from you. Don't treat me like a child."

"You're young enough to be my daughter!" Pretty weak, but it was all I could think of. A quick jerk, and my hand was free.

So instead she threw both arms around me. "Lie with me," she whispered into my beard, and I realized that she had been planning this ever since I left that morning. Apparently

I wasn't responding the way I was supposed to in her plan. "Lie with me and show me what it's like to be a woman—and make sure I never have to go back to the nunnery."

Joachim was right. Man *was* born to trouble as the sparks to fly upward.

I managed to get a grip on her shoulders and pushed her back so I could see her face in the flickering light. "Hadwidis, this is a tremendously flattering offer you're making. But you're being far too hasty." She shook her head hard and tugged at me again.

It is hard to turn down somebody's heartfelt plea, especially somebody looking up with eyes glittering with tears. In retrospect, I admired both Gwennie's and Margareta's ability to stay steadfast against Paul's proposals.

I took a deep breath and attempted to sound calm and rational, talking to Hadwidis as though she were an adult—and most indubitably trying to talk her out of it. "You scarcely know me—if you want to give yourself to a man, Hadwidis, wait until you find the one you'll love for all your life. I'm not going to force you back to the nunnery, no matter what, but if you fall into sin there are some people who will say that that is an especial reason for you to return, so you can do penance there. And besides—" when none of my arguments seemed to be reaching her at all "—you should know that we wizards don't form liaisons with every girl we meet."

"You're lying," she said, angry now, her eyes flashing in the firelight. "*Lots* of wizards take lovers. I've seen them do it!" Naurag, highly interested, curved his neck around so he could watch.

"As a matter of fact," I said brightly, "I do have a lover—but she's also my wife! So I'm afraid I'm really not available." I knew as I spoke that it would have been better to bring Theodora up immediately. To mention her now sounded like a pathetically false excuse.

"You *can't* be married," she answered stubbornly. "Wizards are supposed to be wedded to magic itself. Even in the nunnery we knew that. If nuns are brides of Christ, wizards are bridegrooms of magic! You just think I'm not attractive because I don't have any hair," she continued bitterly, her voice breaking. When I tried to deny this, she snapped, "Then prove it! Lie with me to *prove* you think of me as a woman! Or else you're going to be sorry in another year, when you come into Caelrhon and find a beautiful tavern waitress with luxurious hair who won't even give you the time of day!"

"Hadwidis, listen," I said, still trying to be reasonable though she was now sobbing. "I'm not one of those wizards who goes around seducing women—" And then I froze, the rest of the sentence unspoken, though I doubted she had heard me anyway.

I had just realized what the Cranky Saint wanted me to know.

II

"Hadwidis," I tried again, more gently. "You mentioned yesterday that you had a little brother. What is his name?"

She was startled enough at this sudden change of topic that she sat up, rubbing her eyes with her knuckles. "Walther. Prince Walther. He's the heir to our kingdom." She glared at me from under her brows. "He's not going to come after you for seducing his sister, if that's what's worrying you."

It wasn't. "He's not really your father's son, is he," I said quietly.

Hadwidis gaped at me. "But how did you know?"

"And that's what made you decide to become a nun in the first place—seeing the Royal Wizard of your own kingdom with your mother, back when you were still a girl. You decided you didn't want to live in a world that had that kind of deceit in it. And when you left the nunnery again it was your most vivid image of worldliness, the one you unfortunately set out to repeat: a woman in love with a wizard."

"I'm not a thing like my mother!" she snapped, but she said it sitting a few inches back from me, her arms resolutely folded across her chest.

"You see," I said, still quietly, "I know your Royal Wizard. His name is Elerius. You may not have heard this, tucked away in the nunnery, but he's acting as regent of the kingdom until your brother grows up. At that point he intends to tell the boy who he really is, so they can govern institutionalized wizardry and the Western Kingdoms together, as father and son."

"Walther doesn't know he's only my half-brother," she said slowly. "I don't think my father ever even guessed—or anyway I hope not."

"So how did *you* guess?" I asked, delighted to have distracted her from her designs on me.

"It should have been obvious to anyone who looked," she answered darkly, but her anger now was turned against Elerius instead of me. "I'm blonde—or would be if I had any hair—as were both my parents when they were younger. I think their parents were blonde too—though one of my grandmothers may have been a red-head. But Walther's got night-black hair—just like our wizard!"

"Well, hair coloring's not an absolute marker of family ties," I interrupted. "Dark-haired people have blonde children all the time. I hope you haven't based everything on your brother being darker than you are."

"Of course not," she retorted, scornful of my limited understanding. "And I used to tease little Walther about his hair, without thinking anything of it. But the time that my father was out of the kingdom, and I woke up with a bad dream in the middle of the night, and slipped into my mother's room the way I had when I was much younger—"

She paused, lips tight together, but I could imagine the rest. Finding her father's supposedly loyal Royal Wizard in her mother's bed would have been a shock to any well-brought-up young princess. Naurag nuzzled her shoulder sympathetically.

"Did your mother say anything to explain herself?" I asked after a moment.

"Well, she sent me back to bed so fast she probably hoped I hadn't seen anything," Hadwidis said reluctantly. "And in the morning, first she denied everything, then she tried to say that he was there to cast some sort of spell to keep out malignant forces, and finally she told me that this was something for adults, that I was too young but would understand better when I grew up, and that I shouldn't say anything to Father—maybe she thought he was too *old* to understand!"

"Does your abbess know?" I asked, wondering how far this might have spread.

Hadwidis turned her face away, but I heard her say, "No," very quietly. "I told her all my sins, but this wasn't about me. This was about somebody else."

I touched her arm and could feel her shaking. I put my cloak over her shoulders. "I'm afraid it's not just about your mother anymore," I said gently. "It's about your whole kingdom. Without a legitimate brother, you're first in line for the throne."

Hadwidis gave a strangled sob. "Did you think I didn't know that?" she demanded.

"In the nunnery, of course," I continued thoughtfully, "you couldn't possibly become queen. You could concentrate on your prayers, without worrying about women who deceived their husbands, and also without worrying about how and when you should tell your brother he had no real claim to be king. If you were out of the way among the nuns, and your mother falsely swore at your brother's coronation that he was your father's true son, then you couldn't possibly do anything about it."

"But Saint Eusebius drove me out," she retorted, sobbing in earnest again.

There didn't seem to be any doubt about it. The Cranky Saint wanted her to become queen.

I shivered involuntarily. Elerius would have thought he had nothing to fear from Hadwidis as long as she was isolated and silent in the cloister, but I didn't like to think what he might feel was necessary if he learned she was out. I put a comforting arm around her without thinking, but it would have been too obvious to take it away again immediately, and she didn't seem inclined at the moment for more romantic overtures.

After a moment she caught her breath and lifted a tear-stained face toward me. "So you see, Wizard, that's why I have to become a tavern wench. I can't very well show up at court, making my mother think I'm about to expose her—and maybe really doing so, and taking away the throne from my little brother, when I'm sure he wants it so much. If I can't stay in the nunnery, I have to go someplace where they'll never, ever think to look for me. Who would think to look for the heiress to one of the largest of the Western Kingdoms working in a tavern in Caelrhon?"

Elerius might. He certainly knew where Hadwidis had gone when she announced her intention of becoming a nun, and he could even now be checking to be sure she was still safely there. When he found out she was gone—especially if he got any hint from the abbess that the Cranky Saint might have his own plans for this girl—she would be in as much danger as I was.

"Well, Hadwidis," I said reluctantly, "you may need to postpone your career in the tavern. Because I'm going to take you with me."

Her head came up so fast that she bumped Naurag on the nose. "Really, Wizard? You mean it?" she cried in delight, though the firelight still reflected on rivulets of tears running down her cheeks.

"I mean it," I said, even more reluctantly. "But you're coming as my daughter, not my lover. In fact, it might be good if we had a chaperone." I could feel her tensing angrily under my arm, so I hurried on. "You need to think this through, Hadwidis. Whether you end up as queen or as a nun again, you'd be better off as a pure maiden. For that matter," with a very forced effort at a chuckle, "don't you think the taverns in Caelrhon would be more interested in hiring on a fresh young girl than someone a wizard had discarded?"

She was starting to make angry muttering sounds, so I pulled myself away from her and leaned my head against Naurag's warm flank. "Try to get some sleep. We'll be starting before dawn, and we have one important stop to make before we leave this region."

I could hear her settling down behind me. Just as I was starting to doze she suddenly said, "By the way, where are we going?"

"To the East," I murmured sleepily. "To find an Ifrit."

"This will be great," said Hadwidis definitively.

Dawn was just washing out the eastern stars when Naurag swept up the hill toward the royal castle of Yurt. I left him and Hadwidis in the old king's rose garden outside the walls—the late roses were all past, even the famous blue rose, but it was still too dark to have seen the colors anyway.

Invisible, I flew over the battlements and down the courtyard, to where a few stone steps led up to Gwennie's chambers. I paused outside her door, listening, but everything was silent. Cautiously I tried the handle. Gwennie had slid the bolt across inside, but a small spell quickly slid it back. Slowly I opened the door, almost silent on well-oiled hinges. Letting my invisibility spell dissolve, I snapped my fingers and said the two words to light the candle on her bureau.

She stirred at the sudden light on her eyelids. "Gwennie," I whispered. "Wake up."

She was awake in an instant, as any good castle constable should be, ready to face whatever emergencies arise. "What is it?" she said, blinking and sitting up.

Then she recognized me. I saw the scream coming and stopped it just in time, with a tiny paralysis spell to her vocal chords. I didn't dare use too much magic, for fear of alerting Elerius if he were still around, but I also didn't want a dozen knights crashing in on us.

"I'm not a ghost," I said quickly. "I'm not even dead." I let her have her voice back. "But I need your help."

Her breath came fast, but she managed to answer fairly steadily. "Then if you aren't dead, why did your air cart come back all covered with blood and dragon bites?"

"It's a long story," I said, listening again to hear if anyone else was stirring. "If you come with me I'll tell you the whole thing. In fact, that's why I'm here. To ask you to come with me."

"Come where?" she asked suspiciously. I knew what she was thinking, only half a minute awake and facing a man whose funeral she had just attended. I had heard the same stories when I was a child, of the spirits who return in the darkest part of the night, just before dawn, to draw the living away with them—

"Take my hand," I said, offering it. "Feel how solid I am. It was all a mistake."

And then she leaped up, smiling radiantly, and not only took my hand but hugged me hard, a startling experience since she had nothing on but a thin nightgown. "Theodora's right here in Yurt! You'll want to see her at once, though maybe you should try to surprise her less than you did me. And the bishop too! He'll be so pleased—"

I was starting to feel a desperate need of haste. Even after as exciting a day as yesterday, not everyone in the castle would linger long in bed, and I wanted to be out of here before anyone else arose. But Gwennie had pulled on a dressing gown and was dragging me out the door, toward the guest chambers where my wife and daughter would be staying.

I managed to stop her. "Please, Gwennie, I don't have time to explain, but I can't tell Theodora I'm alive. It would put her in horrible danger. I need you to come with me."

"Why?" she demanded, starting to be suspicious again.

"There's a princess who needs someone to supervise her— and not the Princess Margareta!" I added hastily, seeing Gwennie's face begin to go hard. There was no good way to explain it. "Please," I said desperately. "Get some clothes on and come with me. I'm going to the East to find an Ifrit," hoping this would be as appealing to her as it was to Hadwidis.

"And we'd be gone a long time?" she said slowly.

"It might be a very long time," I agreed dully, wondering how long it would take to find Elerius again even if I did somehow manage to make an Ifrit obey me. All the stars were gone now, and from the kitchen, at the opposite end of the courtyard, I could hear the first faint clanking of pans.

Gwennie gave a sudden wicked grin. "Then His Most Royal Majesty King Paul will just have to deal with life without a castle constable for a while. Give me five minutes."

She closed her door behind her, leaving me standing on the steps. Far across the courtyard I could see a small figure advancing rapidly toward me.

I donned my invisibility spell again at once, but a voice spoke inside my head. "It's no use trying to hide. I'll just spot you again with Mother's magic ring." It was my daughter.

She raced across the courtyard and sprang into my arms as soon as I was visible again. For a moment I just rocked back and forth, oblivious to everything else in the pleasure of holding her again when I had thought I never might. But then I pulled my face away from her soft hair to look at her. "Antonia," I whispered, "how did you know I was here?"

She smiled quickly but proudly as she whispered back, "I figured out how to set up a spell to detect someone entering the castle, and then I calibrated it specifically for Elerius and for you." She must have felt my start of surprise, because she added as I released her, "He's not here, if that's what you're worried about."

"But how did you do that?" I asked, low and urgent. "Detection spells can't be calibrated for people."

She shrugged and gave me a saucy look. "Just shows that your school doesn't know everything there is to know about magic. I'll tell you sometime how I worked it out. And I was so glad yesterday to find out I was right about you! But did you really see a dragon, even if it didn't eat you? Are you going to stay in Yurt now? Is it still a secret? And why are you here, outside of Gwennie's chambers?"

"I need her to come with me," I said lamely, not wanting even to begin explaining about Hadwidis. "Nobody else can know yet that I'm alive. I'm trying to find and stop Elerius."

"Then I'll come too," said Antonia promptly.

I put my hands on her shoulders, disconcerted to realize how tall she had become. "I'm afraid I can't do that," I said quietly. "Your mother would never forgive me."

"Then take her too." Even in the faint dawn light my daughter's eyes were bright. "We can both help you find Elerius. We'll do a much better job than Gwennie could."

I shook my head. What was supposed to be an extremely brief stop at the castle seemed to be dragging out forever. Any minute now Hadwidis on Naurag would come flying over the wall to see what was keeping me. "If both of you suddenly disappeared, Elerius would guess immediately that you must be with me. He'd know then I'm still alive, so I'd lose any element of surprise."

"So that's why you let us think you were dead," said Antonia approvingly. "Good idea. But," suddenly troubled, "I hope I didn't give you away, by saying in front of everybody that I was sure you were still alive."

"Elerius may have some suspicion, but as long as your mother appears convinced I'm gone, he won't know for sure. That's why we have to keep this secret from her—as well as everybody else. Would you want your friends here in the castle to be subjected to torture if Elerius discovered you'd gone, and thought the rest of them must know where we were?"

But Antonia wasn't worried about the rest of the castle. "Mother's sad," she said accusingly.

"Then you'll have to try to comfort her—" I started to say, when I heard the click of Gwennie's latch.

Just as the door opened Antonia thrust her hand into her pocket and disappeared. Gwennie came out, dressed for travel, and thumbtacked a note to her door. "There. I've said I've decided to spend some time with an old friend. It's even true!" She took my arm with a smile. Smells of cooking were wandering down the courtyard now, and the sun would be up any minute.

"Good-bye," said my daughter's voice inside my head. "Don't go anywhere interesting without me."

Neither Antonia nor Paul would forgive me if they found out I had gone to look for an Ifrit and not taken them along. But then my chances of coming back successfully seemed so small that I was willing to risk their wrath. "Good-bye," I said silently to Antonia. "Let's go," I said aloud to Gwennie. I took her firmly by the arm and rose into the air, over the battlements and back to my flying beast.

Time to go seek help in the ancient magical lore of the East, accompanied by the suitably-chaperoned princess whom the Cranky Saint somehow thought could replace Elerius's son.

III

The last time I had journeyed from Yurt to the East had been on horseback. The trip had taken months, through the Western Kingdoms, across the high mountains, through the constant wars and dark treachery of the Eastern Kingdoms, by ship to Xantium, overland again to the Holy Land, and finally beyond to the vast, uninhabited deserts where Ifriti still lived, almost as old as the earth.

This trip was far shorter, even though Naurag could not fly nearly as fast with three on his back as he had flown coming south from the Land of Wild Magic. We followed the major rivers at first, paralleling the great pilgrimage and trade routes, south through the Western Kingdoms to the Central Sea, and then along its northern shore, east toward Xantium. From the air one could see hundreds of square miles at a glance, and without the waterways to follow we would have been lost at once. Autumn had been advancing rapidly in Yurt and Caelrhon, but as we went south we caught up with the summer, and found again, to Naurag's delight, melons that were ripe.

Gwennie accepted Hadwidis's presence with only mild surprise. I introduced her as a princess who had once been a nun and now had no home, without going into detail about how Saint Eusebius had driven her from the nunnery in order to help me. Hadwidis now knew that I was Yurt's royal wizard, but since Elerius couldn't—I hoped—get to her while she was with me, her knowing my identity scarcely mattered. With another woman present—and several times Gwennie mentioned that I had a family as if this were perfectly normal and well-known—Hadwidis made no more impassioned attempts upon my virtue, which would have been a relief if the voice in the back of my mind hadn't complained that her giving up so easily might have been a comment on my desirability. Gwennie, for her part, seemed to find it entirely natural that I should journey to the storied East with a runaway nun, which told me more about her attitude toward Yurt's Royal Wizard than I felt I really needed to know.

The two young women quickly became friends, but both maintained a certain reserve. It occurred to me that it was ironic that, although neither told the other this, both were running from the possibility of becoming queens: Hadwidis the queen of her father's kingdom, by exposing her brother's parentage, and Gwennie the queen of Yurt by marrying Paul.

The thought crossed my mind as we followed the curving coast of the Central Sea that perhaps the Cranky Saint wanted King Paul to marry Hadwidis. She was, after all, a suitably high-born princess, with a much more exalted ancestry in fact than Paul's own, and her time in and out of the nunnery could, with luck, all be excused as a girlish escapade.

Then I glanced at Gwennie's face, where the enjoyment of the adventure could not entirely conceal a constant low level of indignation and sorrow, and decided not to bring this up.

We came at last to Xantium harbor, an expanse of water as big as the biggest lakes of the West, almost completely cut off from the Central Sea by high rocky cliffs. On the ends of the twin promontories guarding the narrow passage into the harbor stood high towers, watching with both human eyes and magic. The harbor teemed with ships, commercial vessels, pleasure barges, and fishing skiffs, most with their sails rigged differently than those in the great City back home. Mixed with the salt in the air came the scent of oranges, halfway between tangy freshness and rot.

"The Princess Margareta said she wanted to visit Xantium for the silk dresses and ointments," said Gwennie, clinging to my belt and leaning past me for a good look. "Should we maybe bring her home a present?" I couldn't tell if she were being sarcastic.

Naurag's steady wing beats took us across the harbor to the city itself, which sprawled for miles behind its walls. Faint wailing reached us from the minarets below; it must be the hour at which those who followed the Prophet were called to prayer. I looked down at the tangle of streets, plazas, and alleys, the tall white spires and huts built virtually on top of each other, the palaces, inns, lawcourts, churches, and tenements, and decided it would be hopeless trying to find Kaz-alrhun's house after twenty years.

"Kaz-alrhun is—or used to be—the greatest of Xantium's mages," I told Hadwidis and Gwennie. "Oddly enough, he's always been well-disposed toward those from Yurt. He used to operate out of the Thieves' Market; I'm going to see if I can find him there."

The Thieves' Market I could locate even if I couldn't find Kaz-alrhun's house. Over the hill from the harbor, toward the back walls of the city, was a wide open area, packed thick with booths. We hovered high over it, looking down at a web of striped awnings stretched over booths where it seemed everything possible was for sale, from food to jewelry to weapons to clothing to peacock feathers to brightly-colored birds in cages.

I wrapped all of us in an invisibility spell as we descended, not wanting to cause a panic. Voices speaking in a dozen different accents rose to meet us, accusing, cajoling, reasoning, and shouting. A swirl of magic rose too from the booths, spells to improve the appearance of the merchandise and counter-spells to detect hidden flaws, all of it with the wild strangeness that eastern magic has to anyone trained in the West. Hadwidis had been silent since we first reached the harbor, but now she said, "I've changed my mind, Wizard. I'm not going to work in a tavern in Caelrhon after all. I'm going to be a thief in Xantium."

I set Naurag down in a somewhat open spot in a corner of the market. Heat radiated up from the paving stones. "It

would be best for you two to stay here," I said a little uneasily, with visions of slave-traders trying to snatch two attractive
young women. "I think I can make the invisibility spell last a
while—"

But they were having none of it. "We didn't come to
Xantium to cower in a corner," said Gwennie firmly. Though
I couldn't see her, I could imagine her frowning with fists on
her hips. "We'll take Naurag with us—nobody will bother
two women who have what looks like a small purple dragon
flying right over their heads! And besides, didn't you tell us
that the Thieves' Market is one of the few places in Xantium
properly patrolled against pickpockets? I don't know about
you, but I'm not leaving Xantium without doing some shopping!"

Reluctantly I let my spell dissolve. There were startled
shouts around us as the purple flying beast abruptly became
visible, and a number of people left their booths to rush
toward us—then, when Naurag yawned, showing his fangs,
to press back. "What marvel is this?" "Where did it come
from?" "Is it real or illusion?" "No illusion, but is it an
automaton?"

We stayed close together, next to Naurag. I was ready
with the words of the Hidden Language to get us out of here
in case the crowd proved threatening. In a moment, however, our novelty wore off. The boys who had been at the front
of the crowd, staring, were the first to leave, playfully throwing pebbles at each other.

"It's just one of those western mages," someone pronounced. I realized he meant one of the wizards from what
we called the Eastern Kingdoms, though they were still west
from here. "He's probably trying to sell it. They all have
shoddy merchandise." It took a lot, I thought, to impress the
thieves through whose market funneled much of the treasures from around the Central Sea.

After a few more minutes I let Gwennie and Hadwidis go, pushing their way through the crowds, exclaiming over the merchandise in the booths they passed and ignoring the looks they received. Naurag floated lazily ten feet above them. I meanwhile set off to find a booth that sold automatons.

Xantium's greatest mage had always specialized in self-propelled magical creatures, some so realistic it was hard to tell them from creatures of flesh and blood, except that Kaz-alrhun's tended to be larger and more brightly colored than life. Others, however, were little more than simple self-propelled tools. If he was here, the appearance of a strange flying beast had not been enough to rouse him from his booth. When I heard the nightingale's song rising melodiously over the midday babble of the market place, and saw the bird perched on a silver-plated bough, eyeing passers-by with a jeweled eye, I knew I had found the right spot.

The striped awning was drawn across against the sun, with only a slit that showed shadows within, but on the counter in front of the booth several jeweled birds hopped about, and to one side stood a chessboard with ivory and ebony pieces, set up for a complicated puzzle.

I lifted the edge of the awning cautiously. "Kaz-alrhun?" There was a stirring inside and a flash of eyes, and a man emerged.

But not the one I expected. Xantium's greatest mage was enormously fat, almost as dark as his ebony chess pieces, and virtually bristling with the aura of magic. This man was far younger and slimmer, and though there could be no doubt from the instant I saw him that he too was a mage, there was none of the sense of an overflow of spells that seemed constantly to accompany Kaz-alrhun.

The young mage looked at me with inquiring black eyes from under a heavy shock of hair. Abruptly his face lit up, and before I knew what he was doing he had put an enormous pink and purple illusory spot on my chest: school magic.

"Daimbert!" he cried with a flash of white teeth. "In the name of the most merciful God! You should have warned us you were coming! And we received no word from the harbor-master that you had arrived."

And then I recognized him. "Maffi?" The last time I had seen Maffi he had been a boy, just starting an apprenticeship in magic with Kaz-alrhun. He had traveled with us for part of the trip into the distant East, and during the trip I had taught him the rudiments of illusion. I was trying to work out how he had possibly managed to grow up since I last saw him when I recalled that he was the same age as King Paul, who too had been a boy when we left him behind in Yurt to travel east. That is the problem with revisiting a place that one has not seen in years. It rarely has the common courtesy to stay unchanged just because it has not altered in one's memories.

"Well, it was a spur of the moment decision to come," I said as Maffi hustled me back into the shade of his awning. I noted that Kaz-alrhun apparently still maintained his network of contacts that told him when anyone interesting arrived in Xantium. "Since you don't have telephones here, there was no way I could have sent a message that would have arrived before I did. And since we didn't arrive by ship, we didn't sign in with the harbor-master."

I looked around the dim interior of the booth and saw other automatons, piled together, inactive, but no one else was there. "Are you still working with Kaz-alrhun?" I asked as if casually. If Maffi could have grown up, I didn't trust Kaz-alrhun, already very old, not to have died on me. And I wasn't at all sure I had confidence in young Maffi's abilities to help me find and master an Ifrit.

"He does not leave his house often these days," said Maffi. "But he will of a certainty be delighted to see you! There is little business here this day—I shall take you to him at once." He whistled in the automatons from the front counter, put a quick binding spell on the awning that would prevent anyone else from entering, and took my arm to lead me away through the market. Magic came easily to him now; he must have finished his apprenticeship years ago.

"Just a moment," I said. "I need to get my companions."

Naurag was easy to spot, hovering nearby. Maffi and I worked our way through the crowd to find Gwennie and Hadwidis, already carrying several parcels, haggling over the price of a cobalt-blue silk shawl.

Maffi's eyebrows lifted appreciatively when he realized my "companions" were both young women, and he shouldered his way up next to them. "It is not worth nearly the amount this greedy caterpillar demands," he told Gwennie, giving her a smile and an exaggerated bow. Gwennie looked startled but smiled back; Hadwidis, who had had limited experience with handsome young men in recent years, barely avoided gaping at him.

"You should have a garment that brings out the color in your eyes," Maffi continued, "not something as muddy as this shawl truly is. He has improved the appearance with illusion." A few quick words, and the shawl was revealed to be not the brilliant blue that had caught her attention but instead a rather depressing gray. "Try the merchandise in this next booth. His prices are higher, but his colors will stay true when you carry them home."

The merchant frowned heavily at Maffi, who paid him no more attention but instead turned to helping Gwennie bargain at the adjacent booth. "Give no heed to his talk of 'final price,'" he told her confidently. "If that were indeed his final price he would never sell a single item." In a few minutes Gwennie had a silk shawl that was exactly the color she wanted, and for less than she had been prepared to spend.

"Thank you," she told Maffi somewhat breathlessly. "My name is Gwendolyn, constable of Yurt. Are you the mage of which our wizard has been telling us?"

"I hope so, of a certainty," with a grin for me. "But come, and we can make our acquaintance in greater comfort at the house of my master in magic, Kaz-alrhun."

He guided us out of the market place and through the narrow streets, where we of the west with our fair skin received the occasional odd look, but most of the stares were reserved for the purple flying beast, winging his way above us. Even tall, turbaned men with curved swords hanging from their belts stepped aside with marked politeness when they saw a mage and a flying beast coming toward them.

Automatons were cleaning the fountains in Kaz-alrhun's courtyard, self-propelled creatures with half a dozen legs, each leg equipped for scrubbing. They finished and scuttled away as we crossed the flagstones, and the water, quiet during the cleaning, began again to shoot high. Maffi reached up and touched one finger to a bell, which began to swing mightily back and forth, pealing the sweetest note I had ever heard from a bell. "Visitors!" he called cheerfully. "And unexpected ones!"

A door opened at the far end of the courtyard, and I saw Kaz-alrhun at last: older and slower than I remembered, but still accompanied so closely by magic it seemed his spells must burst into visibility. The courtyard abruptly seemed much smaller with him in it. His enormous body was covered with odd bits of colored silk, and his black eyes, which seemed to have no whites at all, stared in amazement.

At first I thought he was staring at Naurag, who had come over the wall, but it was not the flying beast who had surprised him. It was me. Two jeweled birds, which had just begun singing in the branches above us, stopped short, teetered for a second, then crashed to the pavement. "Daimbert," said Kaz-alrhun slowly. "I had heard that you were dead."

IV

When Kaz-alrhun at first seemed to have nothing more to say—either overcome with joy to see me alive after all or, more likely, shocked at the inefficiency of his information network which had given him such faulty information, Gwennie and Hadwidis gave each other quick glances. A princess and a castle constable always have resources, even in awkward social situations. After only the briefest hesitation they stepped forward to give formal curtseys. I realized that everyone who knew I was alive was here in this courtyard— that is, everyone except my daughter. "Greetings, Mage," said Gwennie politely. "I know it's a shock that our wizard won't stay dead," she added confidentially. "He startled me too, appearing like an apparition at dawn last week."

Kaz-alrhun shook himself and slowly started to smile then, showing a gold tooth. "Daimbert plays a subtle game," he said with what I trusted was approval. "If even his friends believe him dead, then his enemies must be quite baffled."

"I certainly hope so," I said, remembering his love for intrigue. The mage smiled again and sent his automatons whizzing off in search of refreshments. Soon we were all seated around a shaded table, eating iced lemon sherbert and candied almonds. Naurag happily settled in a corner with a pile of melons. The air was heavy with the scent of the flowering vines over our heads, and the tinkling fountains made a steady, gentle background of sound that distanced us from the noises of the street. Maffi maneuvered himself into the seat between Gwennie and Hadwidis; the latter turned away shyly and carefully adjusted the scarf over her stubbly head.

It struck me as impolite to start immediately asking questions about an Ifrit, so I asked instead after the Lady Justinia, the governor's granddaughter here in Xantium, who had spent some time in Yurt half a dozen years earlier.

"Did you not observe the turmoil here in the city?" inquired Kaz-alrhun. "Half of Xantium is busy preparing for her upcoming wedding." The city hadn't seemed any more tumultuous to me than usual as we flew in, but then I didn't know it very well.

"Who is she marrying?" asked Gwennie brightly. When in Yurt Justinia had caught King Paul's eye—though I personally had always doubted whether he had caught hers.

"The heir to one of the largest merchant families," Maffi answered her. "The fair Lady Justinia will need all her new husband's wealth and influence in years to come, for she may soon become the governor of Xantium in her own right."

"That is, if the other great families and the bishop will accept a woman as governor," commented Kaz-alrhun.

I had enough intrigues of my own to worry about without getting involved in Xantium's. "Then if she's so busy I'm afraid she won't have time to visit with old friends from Yurt," said Gwennie in ill-disguised relief.

"But you, Daimbert," said Kaz-alrhun suddenly, leaning his elbows on the table until it creaked in protest, "have not come to my house to inquire after the governor's granddaughter. It has been twenty years and more since you were here. And you would not have put out such a plausible rumor of your own death if your mission here now were one you wished to share with the world. Will you yet share it with me?"

With Kaz-alrhun I always had the feeling that he was maneuvering me, using my own activities to further some long-range goals of his own. My instinctive reaction therefore was to say nothing. But if I said nothing then he would not be able to help me. I shook my head mentally and gave him a straight answer. "I'm looking for an Ifrit." Kaz-alrhun's eyebrows went up sharply. "It's the only thing I can think of that will give me the power to overcome the West's best wizard."

"You have decided at last, then, to pit your resources against those of the wizard Elerius," said the mage, leaning forward with interest, so that the table creaked even more alarmingly, and Gwennie had to rescue a sliding bowl of almonds. He was nothing, I thought, if not well-informed about my friends and my enemies.

But he had not heard of the death of the old Master of the school. I filled him in quickly on how Elerius had made himself regent of the West's wealthiest kingdom, put himself first in line to head the school, and had when last seen been running for mayor of the West's largest city, after having just influenced the election of its new bishop. "All went well," I concluded, "until one tiny miscalculation. He tried to tell Zahlfast, the man who has for years been second in command at the school, that he would soon be Master himself, and instead he ended up in an open breach with Zahlfast—and, I presume, the other faculty members at the school. This had just happened as I started east."

Gwennie and Hadwidis followed my account with great interest, because I had so far given them very few details. Hadwidis took in a sharp breath when I first mentioned her kingdom as being run by Elerius but made no comment. Kaz-alrhun, however, seemed to notice her reaction and be adding it to his store of interesting tidbits. I left young Prince Walther completely out of my account as irrelevant; the Cranky Saint might have decided to make queen the unsatisfactory nun who had been given his name, but first I had to deal with Elerius.

Gwennie, however, picked up on a different aspect. "You seem strangely well-informed about what happened at your funeral," she told me, eyes narrow. "I know I told you a little about it, but you speak as though you *saw* it. Don't tell me you let us all sit there being sad and saying nice things about you, watching and chuckling at us the whole time!"

"Well, not chuckling—" I mumbled lamely.

"You let your wife be devastated. You let the bishop speak sorrowfully of all your admirable qualities. And you just stood there invisible, reveling in it all!"

"No, I didn't revel in it, you need to understand—"

Gwennie snorted and turned away with a sharp scrape of her chair, to present me an indignant back. "If you die again," she said without turning around, "I'm not going to any funeral unless I see the body—and drive a pin into it too!"

Kaz-alrhun, however, was impressed. "Perhaps I should let a rumor of my own death spread through Xantium. Then were a service held for me, I might discover the true nature of others' feelings."

Maffi had been trying to distract Gwennie with illusory golden eggs, which hatched forth extremely tiny purple dragons, though Naurag seemed more interested in them than she was. Now Maffi leaned past her shoulder to comment to the older mage, "If you would discover others' true feelings for you, sir, I can start by obliging you with mine any time you like!"

Kaz-alrhun laughed and waved him away with an enormous hand. "But why do you seek an Ifrit, Daimbert? You will need no assistance against Elerius but your own magic. What you term a tiny miscalculation on his part suggests rather that his plans had not yet matured when he suddenly needed to put them into effect. If your school has turned against Elerius, than the city merchants and the priests will not listen to him either, and I expect the kingdom he rules will shortly cast him out as well."

"They won't cast him out," said Hadwidis gloomily but with certainty, speaking for the first time in a while. She blushed and went silent when we all looked at her.

"She's right," I said hastily, to distract the others from her confusion. "The rest of the school faculty may take a second look at Elerius—though I fear many will still support him—but that doesn't mean he will have no resources. And even worse, I'm afraid war is brewing in the west. Some of the kings are already deciding to attack the wizards, and they won't make distinctions between those wizards who do and don't support Elerius."

"Then perhaps you do need an Ifrit after all," said Kaz-alrhun thoughtfully. "Your western armies would be no trouble for one. And I presume, Daimbert, that you have come to Xantium in the expectation that I would help you master one?"

The tone of his voice gave me sudden hope. "Could you? Do you know where one is? I remember you managed to paralyze one once, so I thought—"

He chuckled, which set his mighty belly quivering. "Not one of my most successful spells, as it proved—poor taste to remind your host of that event, Daimbert!" He was right; the Ifrit had soon cast off the spell, taken away the mage's magical abilities for a period, and come close to killing him. I looked at Kaz-alrhun imploringly—hadn't he figured out in the last twenty years where his spell had gone wrong?

"But I may be able to assist you in some modest way," he continued, giving a small smile. Which meant that he was going to expect something in return from me. "Indeed, there are rumors among all the mages of Xantium that it may soon be possible to capture an Ifrit as we never have before … But enough of this. Tomorrow shall be time to discuss these matters. For the rest of today, accept the hospitality of my house and take refreshment from your journey."

I didn't dare push him for immediate details though I was wild with curiosity, for he spoke with a note of complacency. Instead I stood beside Naurag, stroking his neck reassuringly, while Kaz-alrhun and Maffi examined him, both with their eyes and with their spells. "I have often heard of these flying beasts," said Maffi, who I recalled would never admit not having heard of something. "But never have I seen one before." I wondered with a cold touch at the back of my neck if the mage would want to keep Naurag in return for his help. Presumably the Ifrit—if we mastered one—would take us wherever we wanted to go, but how could I leave the flying beast behind?

Kaz-alrhun, however, seemed less interested in acquiring Naurag for himself than in learning how I had tamed him. "Melons," I said. "I fed him melons all one afternoon, and he became my friend."

"And said spells, I might assume?" the mage inquired. "For no wild creature, much less a wild creature from the land of magic, will tame with a few melons."

I rubbed the bony ridge over Naurag's eyes. He was awfully tame now that I thought about it, especially for a creature that looked like a small dragon. But I didn't see how a few air cart spells could have had anything to do with it.

Late in the afternoon, after we had all taken turns in the hot, lemon-scented bath where automatons scrubbed our backs, and as the smell of roasting lamb was just beginning to emerge from Kaz-alrhun's kitchens, I took Hadwidis and Gwennie out again. We walked to the huge church dedicated to the Holy Wisdom of Solomon, to give thanks to God for our safe arrival in Xantium. Joachim would have wanted us to go.

Maffi led the way, through a maze of twisting streets where I quickly lost track of all direction. The day was still hot. Stone walls edged the streets, pierced by doorways opening onto flowering courtyards.

Hadwidis looked around eagerly, at the heavily-veiled women surrounded by body guards as big as Kaz-alrhun but a lot more muscular; at the shadowed shops from which voices emerged, promising love-potions; at the black-robed clerks arguing intently with each other as they walked; at the dark-eyed children playing half-naked in the gutters. I wondered uneasily if she was still planning to become a thief here and was seeing all this as her future habitat. I didn't want to have to explain to the Cranky Saint, if I ever made it back to Yurt, that I'd left her in Xantium.

But she became subdued once we reached the church. Golden candelabra gleamed throughout, sending light flashing across the enormous mosaic depiction of the Last Judgment. We made our way across an onyx floor that was shot with gold, between porphyry columns, to the main altar. A group of pilgrims and purple-robed priests were already there; we knelt briefly in prayer at the edge of their group.

As we rose and stepped quietly back, Hadwidis asked in a whisper, "Do they have nuns here in Xantium?"

"Well, I'm sure they do," I said in surprise. Maffi and Gwennie were walking slowly around the circumference of the church, looking at the mosaics. "But if they're like the nuns in Yurt, I never would have seen them because they'd never come out of the nunnery."

"Just wondering," she said, not looking at me. "In case I got tired after a while of being a thief and a tavern wench here."

I didn't answer but reached up to readjust her head scarf, which had slid down over one ear. She was, I reminded myself, not much older than Antonia. She had never been very successful as a nun, and she was frightened of being forced into being a queen, but her reckless decision to find instead something else wild and irresponsible to do kept worrying her enough that she wanted an escape route.

I wouldn't have minded an escape route myself, but I didn't think I was going to find one.

V

It was still dark when the door to my room creaked open. "Come, Daimbert," came Kaz-alrhun's voice, cheerful with a note I had learned to distrust. "If you would meet with an Ifrit, it were best to do it before dawn."

I rolled out of bed, grabbing my clothes. There had been too many pre-dawn risings lately to suit my taste. "So the Ifrit is near here?"

"Very near, yet very far," he said with a chuckle. "Going may be for you and me the work of ten minutes, yet you may find that days pass in the journey."

The mage set a lamp on the table, which cast just enough light that I could see my buttons, though leaving his face in shadow. "How about my companions?" I demanded in the middle of tying my shoes. "I can't leave two young women alone here."

"Maffi need not accompany us. He will guard them and keep them from boredom."

That was what I was afraid of. "No. I brought them along because I want to keep them safely under my eye. They'll have to come with us."

"Is one perhaps your daughter?" asked Kaz-alrhun in interest. "If so, you should have introduced her as such. I observed you closely, and I would say most definitely that neither is your lover."

"Almost my daughter," I said vaguely. "I'll get them."

"There is one difficulty, Daimbert," said the mage with another chuckle. "The Ifrit's wife has recently left him, having tired of a wild life in the desert and desiring to live her mature years among humans again. I understand that he is searching for a new woman to make his wife …"

Well, he certainly wasn't going to make either Gwennie or Hadwidis his wife, if I had anything to say about it. "Maybe I could turn them invisible—" I suggested uncertainly.

"I have a better plan, Daimbert," Kaz-alrhun announced. "Leave this to me. Rouse them now, but make haste."

In a few minutes, still rubbing the grit from my eyes, I followed Kaz-alrhun out through the heavy doors of his house. Gwennie and Hadwidis walked close on either side. There was no sign of Maffi. "King Paul has been talking for ages about coming to Xantium," Gwennie said in my ear. "He's going to be madly jealous when I tell him all my adventures." She didn't sound sympathetic at all.

The mage carried a torch that flared and hissed as he walked, which he did with remarkable speed for one so old and so heavy. A massive hammer swung from his other hand. I hoped he would say more about the new methods for capturing an Ifrit at which he had hinted the day before, but he did not speak. The streets that had been jammed with humanity yesterday were nearly empty now, and most of the other people we spotted faded away down alleyways as we approached.

But the first morning clatterings emerged from shuttered windows as we reached the city walls, and yellow streaked the eastern sky. The back gates of Xantium's massive walls were locked and barred, but at a few quick words from the mage the bars lifted, and with a loud click the locks came open. The hinges creaked as the gate slowly swung ajar.

We slipped through, then I stopped in sudden doubt. We had emerged into a broad field dotted with low structures. In the dim dawn light I recognized them as domed sepulchres.

But Kaz-alrhun motioned us to hurry after him. "You must be below ground before the sun clears the horizon, Daimbert," he said, leading the way in and out between the low white domes. All had gaping doorways, leading into empty, paved rooms. Gwennie was frowning next to me; she may have been reconsidering how jealous this adventure was going to make Paul.

The mage stopped at one tomb that looked the same to me as all the rest but which clearly was significant to him. He handed me the torch, said a few words under his breath, and swung the hammer against the paving under the dome. On the first stroke it bounded back, but on the second stroke the stones splintered. We jumped to avoid the shards, then, at a sign from Kaz-alrhun, stepped forward cautiously.

Under the paving was not the coffin I expected but rather a flat stone with an enormous iron ring set into it. "Pull up the trapdoor, Daimbert," Kaz-alrhun ordered, his face inscrutable. Half the sun's disk had risen over the horizon, making the torch's light pale.

I checked with a quick spell. There was enough wild eastern magic here to confuse a dozen school-trained wizards, but I was fairly sure no Ifrit lurked immediately under the stone. Slowly I pulled it back, adding a lifting spell to my arm's strength when the stone proved even heavier than I had expected. Below was a dark staircase, smelling of damp earth and disappearing down.

"You will need the torch, Daimbert," said Kaz-alrhun, his gold tooth flashing. "When you reach the bottom, you shall see a black cat with a white tip to its tail. Burn three of those white hairs, and then you shall see a great marvel. Proceed now down these stairs, and your 'daughters' may follow you, but in a form that will make them safe."

"And you?"

"It may be minutes, and it may be days, but when you return I shall be intrigued to hear of your encounter with the Ifrit."

"Wait a minute," I said harshly. "You said you were coming with me."

"And I have. But I come no further."

"What am I supposed to do with an Ifrit? *You're* the eastern mage. You're the one who's supposed to know how to master Ifriti."

"Your spells will serve you well," said Kaz-alrhan, with much more confidence than I felt. "Hurry, for if the sun should rise any higher before you descend, this gate will be closed to you until tomorrow."

Gwennie took a deep breath, then spoke in the voice of Yurt's castle constable. "I may enjoy an adventure, Wizard, but Hadwidis is just a young girl. I cannot agree to sending her down there."

Hadwidis started to protest, entirely unconvincingly, that she thought descending into a black hole under a tomb would be exciting, but she didn't have a chance to finish.

Kaz-alrhun's hands darted out, and he seized Hadwidis and Gwennie by the arms. "I do not intend to risk angering the Ifrit for nothing. If you will not lead the way down, Daimbert, then you shall follow." Before I could react, the two young women disappeared before my horrified eyes, and the mage was instead gripping two black dogs by their collars. With a quick motion, he tossed them down the staircase, where they disappeared with loud yelps.

The last edge of the sun still lingered below the horizon. The mage hadn't left me much choice. I snatched up the torch and leaped after the dogs. The trapdoor slammed shut above me.

I flew downward, holding the flaring torch over my head, with a sick feeling that in a moment I would see the black dogs stretched out awkwardly across the steps, their backs broken. If they were killed as dogs, there was no way my magic could bring them back to life as women. But I descended the entire staircase without seeing them. Near the bottom, a soft light began glowing around me, apparently from the walls themselves. The stairs ended in an empty marble hall, set about with columns of jasper.

I looked around wildly, then jumped as a wet muzzle came up behind me and licked my hand.

Both the dogs were there, looking at me with frightened human eyes. Both had smooth black fur and alert ears. On one the fur on top of the skull had been cut very short.

I dropped the torch and wrapped an arm around each of their necks. "It's just a transformation spell," I said, trying to be reassuring. "I have no idea why the mage wanted to turn you into dogs, but I can get you turned back in just a minute. I've known how to work these spells since I graduated from wizards' school."

Or at least since not much later than that. But before I could start picking apart Kaz-alrhun's spell, different from anything ever taught to western wizardry students, the dogs put their heads up, and one gave a short bark. A large black cat came strolling, white-tipped tail in the air, across the empty hall toward us.

The two dogs wiggled in interest, collars clinking. I kept a tight hold on them and made calming sounds, halfway between what I would have said to them in their own forms and what I would have said to real dogs. The cat froze, all the hair on her back going straight up.

If I was going to have to use magic that involved this cat, she had better not scoot away, or we could spend the rest of eternity beneath Xantium's cemetery. With a last firm word to the dogs—I resisted telling them Stay!—I moved cautiously toward the cat. "Come on, puss puss puss. Don't be frightened." This had better not turn out to be some enchanted princess whom I had just mortally insulted.

But the cat relaxed after a moment, and my ensorcelled companions stayed at the bottom of the stairs, where they both kept wagging their tails. I held out my hand for the cat to sniff, then she allowed me to pick her up, still making soothing sounds. "There's a good puss, don't dig your claws into my arm, that's right, just relax while I stroke you, while I run my hand down your tail, while I pluck out three hairs—"

At that she did dig her claws into my arm and shot away, but I had the white hairs. I returned in triumph to the guttering torch. "Stay back," I told Hadwidis and Gwennie. "Kaz-alrhun said that if I burned these hairs I'd see some marvel, and if it's an Ifrit you'll want to be out of the way." And not in human form, I added to myself. I had once known a woman an Ifrit had considered his wife; she in fact had enjoyed living with him, but it had still been clear that it wouldn't have made any difference if she hadn't.

I dropped the hairs into the flame and waited. They burned with a cat-like hiss, twisting and shriveling for a second before disintegrating. And then, somewhere in the distance, a low note began sounding, like an enormous organ playing at the bottom of its range.

At the same time, tendrils of smoke began wafting out from between the jasper pillars. As I watched, heart pounding, trying desperately to remember what little eastern magic I had once known—all the spells I had been going to review this morning before Kaz-alrhan and I together went in search of an Ifrit—the smoke began to coalesce.

The eyes were the first to take solid shape, blood-shot eyes the size of my head. The black dogs behind me whimpered once. The smoke continued to thicken and take shape, now in a man-like form, but a man bigger, far bigger, than any human ever seen: a man with dark green skin, pointed ears, and clawed hands, whose enormous form nearly filled the marble hall. This is what I had come to the east to find, I told myself, backing until the first step of the staircase caught me in the leg. This was an Ifrit.

"You have broken our pact, Kaz-alrhun!" he roared with a voice that shook the jasper columns. "By what death shall I slay you? We agreed that if I would not disturb you if you would not disturb me. But you have summoned me from my sleep at the hour when dreams are sweetest!"

He snatched me up in one clawed hand, bringing me up to eye level to stare better. "But I'm not Kaz-alrhun," I said as clearly and politely as I could through my panic. No use even trying a spell against a creature whose magic was so powerful that mine might not even have existed. All I had were my wits. "I have made no pact with you."

This technicality did not immediately register with the Ifrit. The fingers slowly started to close around me. I caught a look of horror from the black dogs, pressed under the stairs together. It appeared as if Gwennie wouldn't find it necessary after all to push a pin into my body to make sure I was really dead.

But the Ifrit didn't kill me at once. Instead he loosened his fingers again to turn me this way and that, peering at me as though I were some intriguing insect, and he was hoping I wouldn't sting him before he decided to go ahead and crush me. I smelled his sour breath and looked at the huge pores in the green cheek next to me. There was a very distinctive green mole on the side of his green nose. Just as I feared. It had been over twenty years, but it wasn't the sort of thing one was likely to forget. This was the same Ifrit I had met before.

"You're a mage," he said accusingly. "How am I supposed to keep track of all you little mages? Especially when you anger me?" with a snap of teeth the size of boulders.

"I am not a mage, but a western wizard," I managed to croak out fairly firmly. "And you can't hurt me. I'm from Yurt."

It had worked before. I held my breath, waiting to see if it would work again, and imagining what I would do to Kaz-alrhun if I got out of here alive—preferably something much worse than the Ifrit might do to me.

The Ifrit seemed to be thinking this over for a moment. Ifriti live an extremely long time, and I didn't know if that meant that an event of twenty years ago would seem as fresh as yesterday to him, or whether millennia of memories would keep any one particular incident from staying with him.

But the enormous hand still did not close around me. "Why did you think I wasn't supposed to hurt people from Yurt?" the Ifrit grumbled, as though my words had struck a chord and his slow, dangerous brain was genuinely trying to remember.

"Another one of us little mages," I said as confidently as I could. "He freed you from a bottle, where you had been imprisoned under the dread seal of Solomon, son of David."

"You aren't Solomon, honored be his name," the Ifrit interrupted angrily. "And neither was that other mage."

"But Solomon bound you, remember," I said, knowing I had to spell it out for him. "The mage I mean is the one who freed you. And in return you gave him two wishes. The first wish was that you would keep safe everyone from Yurt."

It was deeply ironic that the "mage" who had, over twenty years ago, found the bottle with the Ifrit in it, and dared to loosen the lead seal, was Elerius.

He had been trying to lure us into the eastern deserts for reasons of his own. As part of his plans, he had ordered the Ifrit he freed to take us captive but not to hurt us. Since he had, as usual, convinced himself that he was acting for the best, he wouldn't wish to actually damage us before he got what he wanted from us.

As it turned out, he'd never gotten what he wanted, which was part of the reason he now seemed convinced that I was a potentially dangerous opponent. But he had most indubitably ordered this Ifrit not to harm anyone from Yurt, and I wasn't going to dwell on the detail that Elerius had expected the Ifrit to keep us safe by keeping us captive. Instead I hoped that, if my luck just held longer than the five minutes it had lasted so far, I would be able to use Elerius's own wish against him.

"But that was before," the Ifrit objected. "That mage couldn't have meant I was supposed to keep people from Yurt safe forever."

"Quite true," I said, extemporizing wildly. "But you granted him two wishes, and until he asks for the second you have to continue to honor his first one."

"Are you *sure* Kaz-alrhun didn't tell you to wake me up this early?" the Ifrit growled, frowning again.

"Quite sure," I said, which was in fact true. "I had no idea even that you had made a pact with him, and I certainly didn't know I would meet you here in this hall."

"I do not like Kaz-alrhun," the Ifrit commented darkly. "And I do not like that other little mage, either. There's a good reason why I never granted him his second wish." His voice trailed off, as though he were trying to remember.

I remembered perfectly, though I wasn't about to remind him. "But until you do, his first wish is still in effect," I said brightly, hoping to change the subject while I was still ahead. "And now—"

"You talk too much, little mage," said the Ifrit, with a scowl that dug a crease in his forehead like an eroded ditch. "And your talk is not amusing. As long as I'm supposed to keep you safe, you're going to grant *me* wishes."

Wishes? How was I supposed to grant wishes to an Ifrit? Slowly the outer parts of his body started going all misty again, though the head and the hand that held me stayed disconcertingly solid.

"Wherever we're going," I said desperately, "I need to take my dogs along!"

The Ifrit saw the two black dogs then, and his expression softened. They did not however seem reassured and cowered under his gaze. "Dogs don't demand wishes," he said agreeably and snatched them both up in his other hand, ignoring their startled yelps. Then he turned and shot through the jasper columns, which dissolved around us. Air like a hurricane rushed past, and it was impossible to see. The world went black and seemed for a second to turn upside down, then slowly stabilized and grew quieter again. I tried not to retch and clung desperately to the Ifrit's thumb.

When up and down had reasserted themselves, I opened my eyes gingerly. It was light again, and we were no longer in the strange, empty hall beneath Xantium's cemetery.

Instead we were on a sunny hillside, amid the tumbled ruins of what might once have been a temple. A few statues still stood upright—next to us a carved creature with the body of a woman but the head of a dog. A hundred yards away, sheep grazed on sparse grass. A sharp peak a few miles distant thrust into the sky. The Ifrit set us down, relatively carefully. He looked even bigger here, out in the open, than he had in the hall to which I had inadvertently summoned him. My legs collapsed under me, and the two black dogs rushed to press themselves against me.

"Time to start amusing me," said the Ifrit. "I think I shall have you work magic. You mages always claim to know so much magic, though I have never been particularly impressed by anyone since Solomon. Go ahead. Make this hillside dissolve into the sea."

part six ✤ the ifrit

I

THIS WAS ALL KAZ-ALRHUN'S FAULT. At some point in the last twenty years he had tried to master the Ifrit and had reached a standoff: both respected the other, and neither would bother the other, even though the mage still had a means to summon the Ifrit if he wished. So he had decided to let me try western magic, with the thought that if I succeeded, then he would have an authority over an Ifrit no other eastern mage had ever had, and if I failed, then at least he wasn't the one who ended up dead. And to think that I had told Hadwidis and Gwennie that Kaz-alrhun was "well-disposed" toward those from Yurt!

"Um, why exactly do you want this hillside to dissolve into the sea?" I asked, when the Ifrit seemed to be waiting expectantly. What he had just suggested was far beyond my powers, probably beyond the powers of all the wizards at the school working together. If I sold my soul, the supernatural forces of darkness could doubtless dissolve an entire mountain if they felt like it, but I doubted my soul would bring that much on the market these days. "How about if I do some tricks for you instead?"

"What do you mean, *tricks*? I do not appreciate being tricked by you little mages."

I rejected the idea of tricking the Ifrit by transmogrifying him into a frog. It probably wouldn't work any better than it would with a dragon. "I mean I'll create exciting things for you to look at," I babbled. "See, I can make this dragon—" I was working fast, and my illusory purple dragon looked a lot more like Naurag than a real dragon.

I didn't get a chance to finish it anyway. The Ifrit stamped an enormous green foot onto my illusion. "You aren't listening, little mage. I do not want to see dragons! I want to get rid of this hillside and all its sheep."

"Just tell me why," I said, stalling, "to be sure that I get rid of it in the way you wish." The hillside, dotted with stones and sheep, seemed perfectly innocuous in the morning sun.

The Ifrit picked me up between thumb and forefinger and dangled me in front of his face, where I had an excellent view of his great yellow teeth. "You talk a lot for something so little. I want to drive the roc away, of course."

"The roc? What's that?" If something would just make sense for a moment, I might be able to think of what to try next.

"You're awfully stupid for a mage," the Ifrit commented. "The roc is a very big bird, of course. He makes his nest on top of that peak. These are the sheep on which he feeds." He pointed, in case I had as little idea what a sheep was as what a roc was. "If his sheep were gone he'd have to go elsewhere, and I could find out what he's gathered in his nest. Rocs like to collect things, and I expect some of what he has belongs to me."

How could an Ifrit be intimidated by a big bird? But then I spotted motion off toward the peak and stared. I should have realized that if an Ifrit called something "very big," it would have to be truly gigantic.

The bird soaring toward us must have had a wing-span of fifty yards. It flew with startling speed—faster than even the greatest dragon. The wind from its wing-beats, reeking with carrion, blew even the Ifrit's greasy hair around. Still held in the Ifrit's grip, I looked up at it in horror. It was a dull black except for its naked head, colored bright orange. It screeched at the Ifrit, then dove and hooked one of the sheep in a single talon. The rest of the flock scattered in panic from under the enormous shadow.

Then it was gone, flying back toward its nest. I realized I had been holding my breath and slowly let it out again. If anything could successfully tangle with an Ifrit, I thought, this creature could. Kaz-alrhun might have had more success recruiting its assistance than he was likely to have with mine.

"Well?" the Ifrit demanded. "Are you going to do it? Are you going to stop asking foolish questions and dissolve this hill into the sea?"

"I have a better idea," I said brightly. "Better" was probably an overstatement, but at least it was an idea. "Rather than driving the roc away by destroying its sheep, I'll slip up in secret to its nest. That way I can find anything of yours it may have taken."

The Ifrit gave me a sour look. "I know your plan. You tricky mages are all alike. You're intending to keep everything the roc has for yourself." For such a stupid creature, he had surprisingly good insights sometimes.

He thought for a moment, absently-mindedly squeezing me tighter, then slowly started to smile. "But if you go up there, and a nasty place a roc's nest is, too, then I won't have to! Well, little mage, I'll let you go, but I'm keeping your dogs until you come back. That way I'll be sure there's no trickery!" He bent over to set me down and stroked the heads of the terrified dogs with one finger. "My wife used to like dogs," he added, almost sentimentally.

I looked again toward the peak and saw the roc starting this way again, clearly visible even at the distance of several miles. It must have young birds in its nest, with gigantic appetites it had to satisfy. With a sinking feeling I wondered if it also had a mate someplace near, perhaps one even bigger.

"Gwennie! Hadwidis!" I called, trying to make it sound as though I were addressing hounds, so the Ifrit wouldn't suspect. "Round up those sheep and get them out of the way!"

Gwennie and Hadwidis, delighted to have an excuse, fled from the Ifrit. Barking wildly and racing back and forth, inefficiently for sheepdogs though not doing badly for young women, they managed to stampede the sheep, which had just started grazing again. They all disappeared over the hill together while I wrapped myself in a spell of illusion.

"This is fairly amusing," the Ifrit admitted, admiring the effect. "I didn't know you little mages could look like sheep."

Covered with illusory wool, I flew toward the center of the hillside, below the ruined temple, where the sheep had been a moment before. The roc screeched again at the Ifrit as it stooped toward where its sheep should be. I was the only one there. It decided to take me.

I managed to time my jump so that the talon, thick as a spear, passed under me rather than through me. Hanging on desperately, I was swept up into the air with a few great wingbeats, as the roc headed back toward its peak. If such unnatural creatures as rocs and Ifriti, I thought, would just stay in the magical lands of the north rather than cluttering up civilized lands and making trouble for well-meaning wizards, life would be substantially easier.

I smelled the nest before I saw it. A reek compounded of carrion and bird-lime wafted toward me. The roc sailed over some towering cedars, no more than small bushes to it, and then, wide wings fluttering, settled toward its nest. It was a tangle of huge logs, some with the leaves still on, stained yellow and white and draped with the remains of sheep, goats, and other animals I didn't care to identify. Stones and metal objects glittered from the interstices, but I had no time for close examination. Amid the bones and branches were three baby rocs.

Nestling birds, all eyes and beaks and disordered pinfeathers, are always ugly. Newly-hatched rocs proved to be as much uglier than standard as their parents are bigger than standard. Squawking fiercely, they jostled each other and opened their beaks for a bite of sheep.

I turned myself invisible just in time. The parent roc opened its talons and dropped me toward those open mouths. With a quick spell, I kept myself from falling and darted over to the edge of the nest.

The baby birds screamed in frustration when the "sheep" vanished from in front of their beaks. The adult roc settled itself, sending the whole nest creaking and swaying, and looked around in surprise. Then it started examining its nest, a log at a time, turning over the branches and slicing at them with its great hooked beak. It appeared as if it were hunting me by feel and by smell.

In which case, invisibility wouldn't work for long. I waited until the roc's head was turned the other way and dropped my invisibility spell for a new illusory appearance. When the roc turned toward me again, there were not three but four baby rocs in its nest.

It was not the most realistic illusion I had ever done, but it was the best I could manage on a few seconds' notice. Someone had once told me birds can't count, and I prayed it was true. The roc's enormous yellow eye fixed me, and I tried waggling my immature wings to give an air of verisimilitude.

The monstrous orange head bent down, and for a horrified second, as the great hooked beak came closer, I thought my illusion hadn't worked at all. But the roc instead seemed to feel parental concern for me. I had been perched on the very edge of the nest, and it now used the side of its beak to jostle me back toward the center, where I would be safe from falling. Concentrating on keeping my illusion going, I let myself be jostled. As half-decayed—or possibly regurgitated?—meat smeared against me, I thought that at least I must now smell like everything else in the nest.

Since there seemed to be no sheep here and the three genuine baby birds were still protesting, the parent roc rose again. The backwash from its wings pressed all of us down. As it soared away, I scrambled through the tangle of branches in search of what I had seen glittering there. I had a few minutes to find whatever the Ifrit wanted before the roc came back.

It looked as though it had, like a magpie, picked up anything shiny that caught its eye. I ignored the swords and bits of armor that were scattered throughout the nest but filled my pockets with shiny rocks—hard to tell, crusted with birdlime as they were, if they were precious stones or just flecked with mica. I tossed scraps of colored cloth aside, rejected a collection of bronze amphoras, and then saw something that winked like gold.

It was under a heavy log. Letting my illusory nestling appearance dissolve from off my back, I applied a lifting spell to the log, just enough to use magic to snatch the object up.

There was a squawk directly behind me. I whirled around to see the three young rocs glaring at me suspiciously. Each of them was appreciably bigger than I was. They might be too young to fly, but those beaks were *sharp*. Madly I tried to reassemble my disintegrating appearance of a newly-hatched bird. They did not seem impressed. The one in the lead lifted a foot where the baby talons were already sharp and pushed.

I lifted into the air just too late to keep my leg from being wrenched between branches of the nest. I gave a completely un-roc-like cry of pain, finding it impossible to keep my illusion going as I jerked the leg free and moved rapidly backwards. I was still trying with magic to hang onto whatever object I had just picked up, plus the theoretically valuable stones now starting to work their way out of my pockets.

The nestlings advanced again. Human or baby roc, they didn't want me in their nest.

My rather limited knowledge of the natural history of birds flashed through my mind. I had the vague memory that in many species the nestlings would drive from the nest any of their number that seemed small or weak. As a baby bird I must seem remarkably defective. All three aimed their beaks at me.

I sprang back again, just in time. "That's fine," I told them from a safe distance. "If you don't want me in your nest, I don't want to be here either." I took a quick glance over my shoulder and saw, off in the distance but quickly coming closer, the roc returning. It must have found one of its scattered sheep—and I fervently hoped not one of the black dogs.

The Ifrit was just going to have to be satisfied with what I'd already collected. I shot away from the nest and hid among the cedar trees until the roc's great shadow had passed overhead. I tried moving my leg experimentally to find out if it was broken or just strained, but it hurt too much to tell. Then, the squawks of the now-satisfied baby rocs ringing in my ears, I flew as fast as I could back toward the ruined temple where I had left the Ifrit.

But what was this I was holding? I looked down as I flew at the golden object, the last thing I had picked out of the nest. Alone of everything I had grabbed, it was clean of filth. It seemed to be a circular plate, about six inches across, carved with symbols I didn't recognize, and attached at the back to a sturdy handle. It looked like nothing so much as an oversize signet, for impressing a seal in wax.

The Ifrit was seated cross-legged on the grass when I returned, seemingly absorbed in two tiny creatures. As I landed on my good leg a short distance away I realized they only appeared tiny in contrast to his size. It was the black dogs.

"Now roll over," the Ifrit was saying. "Sit up! And beg! Good girl. Speak! Roll over again." Gwennie and Hadwidis were rolling and sitting for their lives.

I shuffled the contents of my pockets quickly and flew forward. "I brought back everything of yours from the roc's nest," I said loudly and confidently. I sat down in front of him as casually as I could, not about to let him see I was injured. "You may want to clean these up a little, but here they are." I spread the stones I had gathered out on the grass by the Ifrit's foot, retaining only the gold signet.

He turned toward me, irritated. "These dogs are much more amusing than you are, little mage," he said accusingly. "They're very smart and understand everything I say."

They were also going to kill me for leaving them as dogs for so long, even though I had a very good reason. They flopped down, panting, in the shadow of the Ifrit's knee.

"You are also filthy," added the Ifrit. But he bent, interested, over the stones and stirred them with a stick. After a minute he gave a disgusted snort. "Diamonds and rubies and emeralds. Is this all you could find?"

"The roc had some brightly-colored cloth," I offered. "And there were weapons and armor, some of it pretty rusty."

"Nothing of mine," said the Ifrit dismissively. "Are you *sure* I have to keep you safe? I told you to work the simplest magic, and you wouldn't, and now you have tried to keep me from getting back my rightful property from the roc. I ought to just crush you, Yurt or no Yurt."

II

The sound of barking interrupted us before I could find out whether the Ifrit was just threatening or was deadly serious. Real sheepdogs tore up the hill toward us, furious. I was just thinking that if they were supposed to be guarding the sheep they had been doing a remarkably poor job, when they launched themselves at Gwennie and Hadwidis.

Hadwidis, the dog with the nearly bare scalp, was totally unprepared. The sheepdogs' rush knocked her from her feet, and one sprang for her throat. But Gwennie recognized the danger and reacted at once. With a great growl she leaped in front of Hadwidis, barking defiance. For one moment, surprised by her fierceness, the sheepdogs fell back, then they growled and went for her.

It was impossible to sort out the snarling tangle of fur and fangs. The only way to stop the fighting was to stop them all. In a second I had paralyzed all the dogs. The Ifrit cocked his head, as though deciding that this might prove amusing after all.

Madly I started disentangling their inert forms. Paralyzed, they could move no muscles other than to breathe. There were six sheepdogs to my two; Gwennie's brave defense couldn't have held up more than a few seconds longer. She and Hadwidis both had cuts, but hers looked more serious.

I freed the two of them from the paralysis spells and turned back to the real sheepdogs. But before I could decide what to do, or even begin to guess why they had attacked us, I heard voices, and three men, carrying shepherds' crooks, came over the hill.

They stopped dead on seeing the Ifrit—as well they might. Their swarthy faces became paler, and they staggered as though their legs would scarcely support them. But the Ifrit ignored them. He instead picked up the two black dogs in his hand and held them close to his face, making soothing sounds. If he thought he was making the dogs feel less distressed, I could have told him it wouldn't help.

But with them out of the way I could safely free the sheepdogs from my spell. In a moment they bounded up, looked around for the missing enemy, and seemed to focus on the Ifrit for the first time. They gave startled yelps then, and, spotting the men, raced to them, barking frantically. One dog was limping where Gwennie had gotten his foot between her jaws.

I flew to meet the shepherds and tried to land casually on both feet, though it required magic to keep me vertical. Compared to seeing the Ifrit, meeting a wizard didn't seem to bother these men at all. "You'd better get out of here," I said quietly, looking back over my shoulder. "The Ifrit's totally unpredictable. And there's a roc that comes to this hill to take sheep. No telling when it will be here again."

One of the men recovered from his shock enough to frown at me—or maybe at my filthy clothes. "Of course. It is our roc."

"Your roc?" I felt hopelessly inadequate. These men were not magic-workers, yet they could speak proprietarily of a bird the size of a whale. I noticed that, for shepherds, they wore very expensive clothing—far nicer than mine had been even before I was dragged through the roc's nest.

"Well," said another shepherd, keeping a wary eye on the Ifrit, "not ours the way these dogs are ours." That was a relief to hear. "But we make sure there are always sheep on this hillside—we bring out the dogs periodically to keep the sheep from straying, and to keep anyone else from pasturing their flocks here. That way we can be sure that the roc does not site its nest anywhere else. And that means that in the winter, when the roc abandons its nest for warmer climates, we can freely climb up its peak and search it for treasure."

"The Ifrit brought me and my dogs here," I said apologetically. "I had no intention of interfering with your flocks. I'm afraid that when your dogs attacked mine, mine fought back."

"Flea-bitten old thing," said the first man dismissively, aiming a kick. He was, I thought, so thoroughly frightened of the Ifrit that he was taking out his fear on his wounded dog.

The small pile of precious stones by the Ifrit's foot might, in these men's eyes, belong to them. "I got carried up to the roc's nest," I continued, still apologetic. "That's what I took, those stones over there. I thought they might mollify the Ifrit but they didn't. Do you want them?"

But fear of approaching the Ifrit was far stronger than any greed. "No, no, anything you gathered, you can keep. We'll be back some other day." And, whistling the dogs to them, the men hastened away back over the hill.

I should have asked them if we were anywhere near Xantium, I realized. All the landmarks were unfamiliar—no telling how far the Ifrit had brought us. Somehow I was going to have to either evade the Ifrit and get back to Xantium, or else persuade him that keeping people from Yurt safe meant following me back to the West to oppose Elerius.

In the meantime, what did I have in my pocket? Down at the bottom I still had the diamond ring Paul had tried to offer both Gwennie and the Princess Margareta, but on top of it was the strange oversized signet I had found in the roc's nest. Heartlessly I turned my back on the Ifrit and the dogs, whom he was still stroking with a massive fingertip, to give the thing a better look.

It was a signet all right, carved with letters and symbols that I could not read. But something about it teased at my memory. I was sure I had seen a bottle somewhere, sealed in lead, with this exact imprint in it. It had been—

It was a bottle in which this Ifrit was once imprisoned. I was holding the dread seal of Solomon, son of David.

"I'll threaten the Ifrit with this, and he'll *have* to obey me," was my first triumphant thought. I might not have been able to get the Dragons' Sceptre, but if I could command the Ifrit with this the effect would be the same. The certainty that this seal was exactly what the Ifrit was hoping to find in the roc's nest made my triumph all the sweeter.

But in the next minute I began to have doubts that it could be this easy. If the seal of Solomon itself conferred authority over Ifriti, then the royal Sons of David wouldn't have had nearly as many problems, what with the Great Captivity, the Empire, and the followers of the Prophet, over the last few millennia. It might well have been stolen from them at some point and been wandering around the East ever since, but if anybody had been able to use it to command Ifriti, I should have heard about it.

King Solomon had, it was true, imbued his Black Pearl with some of his greatest powers many, many centuries ago, but the Pearl was now lost beyond recovery in the Outer Sea. Solomon was unlikely to have imbued two different artifacts with his magic. The seal might have the power to keep an Ifrit closed up in a bottle, but to get the effect one would have to capture an Ifrit and imprison it in the first place.

"I think I'll keep these dogs," announced the Ifrit in his rumbling voice. "They remind me of my wife. The only problem with dogs," he added thoughtfully, "is that they die as easily and senselessly as you humans. I've seen it."

"They're really my dogs," I objected, stuffing the signet back in my pocket. "They would miss me if they stayed with you." I didn't know how much longer I could keep this up, distracting the Ifrit from killing me or demanding impossible things, while trying to keep an eye on him so he didn't accidentally crush the dogs he claimed to like so much. My leg was hurting worse than ever. And there was no telling when the baby rocs would become hungry again.

"You could stay here too," conceded the Ifrit, "though if you don't stop wiggling out of everything I ask I shall cease finding you amusing."

"I've heard," I said cunningly, "that you were once imprisoned in a bottle. Can this be true? Can a creature as large as you have ever fit in a bottle? I can't believe it. You'll have to show me."

"Nice try, little mage," growled the Ifrit. "That's one of the oldest tricks there is."

Something was flying toward us. The roc again? But this didn't look big enough to be the roc. And it was purple.

A trumpeting call reached me. I sprang up with delight, which brought a stab of pain to my leg. It was Naurag.

But something was chasing him, something that resolved

itself as it came closer into a flying carpet: dark red and carrying two people. Kaz-alrhun had decided to join us after all.

I threw my arms around Naurag's neck as he landed, and the two black dogs, escaping the Ifrit while his attention was diverted, jumped around him, barking in welcome. Naurag didn't know what to make of the dogs.

No telling whether Naurag and the mage had come together or whether the flying beast had escaped from Kaz-alrhun's house and sought us out while hotly pursued. The flying carpet landed a short distance away, and Maffi and Kaz-alrhun stepped off, the first almost lazily, the second with a bounce.

The older mage was carrying a bottle: a bronze bottle shaped like a cucumber.

Unsealed, I saw. And I certainly didn't have any lead to heat to try to make an impression of the signet. I would have to improvise.

Kaz-alrhun and the Ifrit eyed each other, both giving massive frowns. "I kept our agreement and did not summon you," said the mage firmly, as fury seemed to be building in the Ifrit's green face.

"You humans always like to wiggle out of things," said the Ifrit darkly. "You sent this other mage instead."

Now was my chance, while neither one was paying attention to me. I snatched the bottle from Kaz-alrhun's hand before he could protest. Into it I tossed a pebble, then shook it so it rattled. "All right, Ifrit!" I shouted up to him. "It's time for me to confess. I found something else in the roc's nest, something you'd be very interested in. I've got it in here!"

The Ifrit turned his full attention from Kaz-alrhun to me, an evil glint in his enormous eyes. "This is a trick, little mage!" he announced—totally accurately, I could have told him. "You said you found nothing but those worthless jewels."

Maffi, I noticed out of the corner of my eye, had spotted the jewels and was picking them up, rubbing off the filth on his sleeve and eyeing them appreciatively.

"And this!" I said, shaking the bottle again. "If you don't believe me, have a look."

"You're just trying to trick me into there," said the Ifrit. Right again, I thought. "But the joke's on you, little mage! This bottle has no stopper—not that even a stopper would hinder me!"

I continued holding the bottle up toward him, trying not to tremble. With a shrug, the Ifrit suddenly started going misty around the edges. "I'll see what you have in there, and if this is all a trick, this time I really will slay you!" His face lit up in a fierce grin. "Painfully, too. Though perhaps you should thank me. This way you will not have to live the rest of your miserable human existence!"

His voice faded out as his enormous frame finished dissolving into smoke. The smoke, a dark green smudge in the clear air, shot into the bronze bottle. And I slapped the great seal of Solomon across the opening.

"What is this? This is just a pebble!" came the Ifrit's voice from inside, tiny now, not much more than an insect's whine. But he was rattling the seal, in spite of my best effort to hold it tight to the mouth of the bottle. "Do you think you can hold me inside? Well, prepare to die, for—"

Kaz-alrhun's voice drowned out whatever else the Ifrit was saying, speaking heavy syllables I did not recognize—close to the Hidden Language, but certainly not the Language I had learned at the wizards' school. King Solomon's seal burned hot for a second, and light flashed from the gold. I held on grimly in spite of the sharp pain in my hand. Kaz-alrhun stopped speaking, and the seal ceased to rattle across the bottle's mouth. The Ifrit too was silent.

Then the mage said, "You need not clutch the bottle quite

so tightly, Daimbert. The seal shall not separate itself while my spell holds."

"And the Ifrit—"

"Is bound there until someone shall loosen the seal to free him."

But I didn't loosen my grip, not yet. "What was that spell you just said?"

"The activating spell for Solomon's seal. I know you western wizards are a little backwards in your knowledge, but I had expected you, Daimbert, to know his seal when you saw it!"

Oh, I did all right. "I know what *else* I recognize when I see it." I glared at him, furious, forgetting my leg, forgetting my burned hand in my anger. "I recognize you maneuvering me. You had heard this seal was in a roc's nest and that the Ifrit was seaching for it. So you sent me after it, conveniently showing up just in time with a bottle. Now you're going to expect me to hand the Ifrit over to you, being properly grateful for your spell."

Maffi turned toward us, hands full of jewels. "And are you not properly grateful? Is this not what you came to the East to find, a captive Ifrit who would do your bidding?"

I held the bottle toward him so he could hear better. "He doesn't sound likely to do anybody's bidding."

"—first your feet, then your calves, and then your thighs!" the Ifrit was shouting in his tiny insect-whine voice.

But Kaz-alrhun looked thoughtful. "You may retain the bottle—and the binding seal—at your need, Daimbert. And I do not even ask for your thanks in restoring your companions."

He said a few quick words in the language that was not quite the Hidden Language, and the two black dogs immediately turned back into Hadwidis and Gwennie: exhausted, bleeding, and ragged, but thoroughly young women again. I shook my head in admiration for the mage's abilities. He had transformed them into dogs and transformed them back, and I still didn't have the slightest idea how his spells had worked.

Maffi was at once all solicitation. He had the women sit down, salved and bandaged the dog-bites with an emergency kit he produced from his pocket, and presented them with the jewels, saying that the stones for which I had nearly been pecked to death by nestling rocs were intended as compensation for their troubles. The two appeared dazed, though Gwennie took the jewels in her lap.

Hadwidis put both arms around her. "You saved my life," she murmured. "Those dogs would have killed me. Thank you." Both turned to glower in my direction, as though this were my fault.

Other than making sure they were not badly injured, I had no time yet for them. I was not through with Kaz-alrhun. "You're not answering me," I said, low and hard, "because you can't deny what I'm saying. You just wanted me to do your messy work for you. But your plans won't succeed, because I'm keeping this Ifrit, and Solomon's seal."

The mage chuckled then, not insulted in the slightest. "I fear I may be learning the true nature of your feelings for me, Daimbert, without even the necessity of planting rumors of my death! But do not let your rage build so; it is too hot here for that. If you think that my information was so good as to know exactly where Solomon's seal was to be found and how to trick you into finding it for me, you imagine more than even I have ever accomplished.

"Of course I knew," he continued, "that the chances might now be excellent for finding the golden seal you now clutch so tightly to you. I told you as much yesterday. It has been treasured, stolen, lost and found, bought and sold, all over the East for over two thousand years. At only a few points in its history has it fallen into the hands of a mage who knew even a fraction of Solomon's magic, enough to activate the great binding spells inherent within it. But the rumors have been building these last months, in Xantium and all around the Central Sea."

"Rumors that it was in a roc's nest," I muttered.

"Not that specific, Daimbert," with a flash of his gold tooth. "But I calculated that if we mages had heard of it, then an Ifrit would also have done so. He would be just as interested as we—although for different reasons. I only knew for certain how to contact one Ifrit, but I also knew for certain that if I contacted him I did so at peril of my life. When you said that you sought to meet with an Ifrit I realized how dangerous it would be. As you recall, I attempted to talk you out of it."

My own recollections were somewhat different, but I let it pass.

"My hope was that the Ifrit would know where the seal was located, even though I did not. Thinking of your own resourcefulness, I also hoped that you might be able to trick him into leading you to it. You succeeded even more quickly than I had anticipated. Perhaps I should have thought to check all the rocs' nests within five hundred miles of Xantium, though the prospect were daunting."

"Um, where are we exactly?" I said, not wanting to give up righteous indignation just yet. But between my relief at being alive and his matter-of-fact answers, I was finding it harder and harder to keep the fury going.

"Nearly two hundred miles east of Xantium, I would calculate. Not where I would have looked first for a roc. But you have succeeded, Daimbert! It was my confidence in you that made me decide, when your purple beast abruptly took off from my house, following you wherever you had gone, that I should bring a bottle as I came in pursuit."

"You can't have your bottle back," I said. "Not as long as there's an Ifrit in it."

"Of a certainty, Daimbert," he said with another chuckle. "What would I do with an imprisoned Ifrit? At the moment he would seem to be threatening to tear you apart rather than grant you wishes for freeing him again, but perhaps you may teach him better manners back in your little kingdom of Yurt. I have some lead at my house; it would be best to have the bottle properly sealed."

"I'm still keeping Solomon's signet," I said stubbornly.

III

Off in the distance, I saw a dark shape with an enormous wing-span, moving majestically toward us. "The roc's chicks must be hungry again," I said. "Let's get out of here before it arrives." With me astride Naurag and the rest of them riding Kaz-alrhun's flying carpet, we headed back toward Xantium. Gwennie and Hadwidis were ignoring me pointedly.

Our shadows rippled below us over miles of rocky scrub, with the occasional village or meandering stream to break up the sameness of the landscape. I had the Ifrit's bottle in my pocket, where he was just barely audible. From the occasional word I caught, he seemed to be making up new and imaginative tortures to apply to me before finishing me off.

I tried unsuccessfully to arrange my leg in a comfortable position and stroked Naurag's neck. I told him what a good flying beast he was, and how he could have all the melons he wanted as soon as we got back to Xantium. If he hadn't come after us, pursued by the mage, I might still be dodging between Ifrit and roc. For that matter, if Kaz-alrhun hadn't known the spell to activate Solomon's seal, I might be dead already.

To distract myself from the pain in my leg, I speculated in a rather desultory way about all the different forms of magic. The mage's spells were different from mine, and also different from Theodora's fire magic, or the terrifying magic of blood and bone practiced by the dark wizards of the Eastern Kingdoms, or the herbal magic which had been more prevalent in the West before the advent of the school, much less the magic of the Ifrit, who did not seem to use spells at all, but could transport us hundreds of miles in a few excruciating seconds. School magic, I was beginning to think, was only one of a myriad possible ways to move through magic's four dimensions, and must have been given the form we now took for granted by the old wizard Naurag.

Was there anything in these other forms of magic I might possibly use against Elerius—ignoring for the moment the detail that I didn't really know any of them very well? By the time we got home it would be over two weeks since my funeral. I wondered uneasily what had been happening while I was gone and what I would have to do about it. Aiming the Ifrit's bottle at Elerius, prying off the seal, and then standing back struck me as one appealing strategy.

Elerius would be hampered by no longer being able to operate out of the school, but he still had his kingdom— Hadwidis's kingdom. No telling how many of the various wizards from around the Western Kingdoms would follow him. I suspected that he had been working on gaining their support for years. The school had always been the focus for wizardry, even since its foundation some two centuries ago, but that had never meant that we wizards were inclined to line up all on the same side.

And meanwhile, what was happening in the City? Presumably Elerius was no longer in the running for mayor, but that only meant that the mayoral election would have become suddenly much messier. The City had always taken the presence of the wizards for granted, but how would a rift among the school wizards be affecting those who lived below the school's white spires? And since Elerius's candidate for bishop had been elected just before my funeral, then I guessed that a bitter divide was developing there as well, as the cathedral priests looked with new suspicion at the man they had chosen as their spiritual leader.

And what of the armies I had seen in Caelrhon? Who was planning to invade whom, and what part did Elerius intend his undead soldiers to play? I had a feeling I was not going to like the answers.

It was dark by the time we reached Xantium, but the lights flickered like fairy-land as we banked over the city. It was quieter now than during the day, and through the distant bursts of song, sudden arguments, and children's shouts, I could hear the waves splashing gently in the harbor. The flying carpet dove downward toward Kaz-alrhun's house, and I followed more sedately on Naurag.

"I shall accompany you back to the West," Maffi announced as we ate a late supper of cold eggplant and lentils. "I have never seen the fabled Western Kingdoms, with their unusual customs, exotic foods, and strange magic. But if I am to become a great mage, perhaps even as great someday as my most revered master here," with a quirk of his lips and a sideways glance at Kaz-alrhun, "then I need to expand my knowledge of all of God's creation. And besides," smiling toward Gwennie, "there are other attractions in the West as well!"

Gwennie and Hadwidis, exhausted from their ordeal, leaned against each other, taking occasional bites of lentils. They gave no sign of having heard this last, but then Gwennie had already ignored Maffi's earlier suggestion that she lean her head on his shoulder. Since the women were also ignoring me and seemed intimidated by Kaz-alrhun, they stayed pretty much out of the conversation.

I had hoped that by the next day they would feel sufficiently recovered that we could start back toward the West. But instead the next morning I woke with my leg burning like fire, and Gwennie, solicitous now, announced that I had a fever and could not travel. The one good thing about being wounded, I thought somewhat groggily, was that one got forgiven. I sent Maffi off to the market with as explicit instructions as I could, to find a certain kind of herb that should help against fever and inflammation. But in the meantime it looked as if we were staying in Xantium a while longer.

The first day wasn't too bad, other than the pain, which persisted even through broken sleep. Maffi returned with a variety of herbs, none of which looked right to my bleary eyes, and an offer to bring a doctor, which I refused. Gwennie, announcing that no self-respecting household could function properly if run by automatons, took over the responsibilities of the constable Kaz-alrhun apparently hadn't known he needed. The first thing she did was to order new drapes and new scrub brushes, telling the mage to expect the bill and that, once she had had a good look at the kitchens, she expected to be placing quite a few more orders.

Maffi, trying to persuade me that the obviously worthless herbs he had procured were really what I wanted, also told me that the automatons who normally did the cooking were huddled in the courtyard behind the fountain. Gwennie did not wait for whatever new pots she thought the kitchens lacked to get started there. It was not for nothing she was a cook's daughter, I thought, slurping down the best chicken soup I had had in months. Maybe soup could count as still an additional form of magic.

But by the second day the leg was much worse, impossible to put weight on, and I was too fevered to take any more soup. The spells against pain were hard to work, because I kept getting lost in the middle, and they only seemed to transfer the pain from my leg to my head. "The bone is cracked, not merely strained," Gwennie pronounced and had Maffi go for a surgeon whether I wanted one or not.

He was a wizened little man, gray-haired and dressed in black, with enormous strength in his hands. After probing delicately around my leg for a moment, he took hold of it briskly, ordered me to cling to the bedpost, and gave it a yank that felt as though he was ripping me in two.

But once the red pain had finished pouring through, I felt strangely light-headed and comfortable. The surgeon strapped the leg to a splint with a few quick motions. "God be praised, the bone is sound and had not started to knit in the cracked position," he told me, gathering up his things. "Rest in bed a few days, and keep from walking more than a few steps for two weeks."

For a second as he moved the light chain around his neck swung free of his shirt. I had expected to see a cross on the chain; instead it was a six-pointed star. He was one of the Children of Abraham.

Quickly, before the comfort of having the bone set could fade, I levered myself up on my elbows and scribbled on a piece of paper. "Here," I said, showing it to him. "What do these symbols mean?"

I knew I hadn't drawn them very well, but I had had to do it from memory, because the face of King Solomon's seal was still tight across the mouth of the Ifrit's bottle and I wasn't about to pry it off for a better look.

The surgeon squinted at my drawing in surprise. "They are not symbols but letters, the writing used by Moses to record the first account of humanity's creation and sins, and of our ancestors' covenant with God. Did you know you have written all the letters backwards? The words, however, are meaningless whether read backwards or forwards—are you sure you have written all the letters in their correct arrangement?"

I wasn't, but even more likely was that Solomon's words of power which he had inscribed on his great seal were not the sort of words someone would recognize without already being a magic-worker. Maybe Solomon had first regularized the magic that was still studied in the East, the same way that Naurag, many centuries later, had done the same in the

West—only using a different language. I thanked the surgeon and let him go; no chance there of learning the magic inherent in this seal for myself.

Enough for now that I had the Ifrit captive. I kept the bottle under my bed, not trusting either Kaz-alrhun or Maffi not to take it, the former to gain the Ifrit's power for himself, the latter to show off to Gwennie. As I slept fitfully I still thought I could hear the Ifrit ranting, though he was now starting to repeat himself in his threats.

The following day I sent Maffi off to the market with new instructions for herbs to find. He still couldn't locate precisely what I wanted, thus further reducing my respect for a thieves' market that couldn't even produce the simple plants that grew on western hillsides. But several of the herbs he did bring back had enough potential that by evening I was able to rally both my strength and my knowledge of herbal magic to activate a spell against inflammation. I was starting to feel nervously that the longer I stayed out of the Western Kingdoms the worse the situation there would be.

We ended up staying in Kaz-alrhun's house in Xantium for over a week. I saw our host very little; I didn't know whether, sick, I simply failed to provide diversion, whether he was trying to stay out of Gwennie's way, or whether he was off discovering new and interesting details about the affairs of the world, which he had no interest in sharing with us.

Maffi, however, took to coming and sitting by my chair, once I could sit up for long periods, trying to persuade me that he really enjoyed Gwennie's cooking, even though the word "bland" kept appearing in his praise for her dishes, and getting me to teach him school magic. Some of it, especially the elaborate illusions, produced effects which fascinated him. But in many other cases he would say offhandedly, "Oh, I already know a better spell for that."

That was fine with me. "So what spell did Kaz-alrhun teach you for this effect?" I would ask casually, and Maffi was more than happy to demonstrate. I had always known my knowledge of school magic was inadequate beside Elerius's. My only hope might lie in learning kinds of magic of which he had never dreamed.

Gwennie stayed busy, supervising the household the way she thought it ought to be supervised, and Hadwidis followed the older woman around. By the time I was able to hobble unaided into the kitchen, Hadwidis, demonstrating the useful skills taught her in the nunnery, had tied an apron around her waist and taken over much of the cooking, though she was much better on vegetable dishes than on anything with meat in it.

The two women also went out every day to see something of Xantium. Gwennie arranged, through Maffi, to sell just one of the jewels from the roc's nest, and she and Hadwidis found themselves with more than enough money to buy whatever they wanted in Xantium's markets.

Hadwidis came regularly to sit with me in the evenings and tell me about sailing over the city with Maffi on the flying carpet, or shopping in the bazaars, or watching a pageant put on in the plaza, or a professional sword fight there, or having a glass of wine under an arbor in an inn's courtyard while a flute player played in the background. Maffi paid most of his attention to Gwennie, but he was certainly not above complimenting Hadwidis on her appearance when she put on something new. One day she came in to see me wearing big hoop earrings and with her eyelids painted iridescent blue. It would be very hard after this to get her back into the nunnery.

On the other hand Gwennie, in spite of all the excitement of being in an exotic place, seemed to be thinking wistfully of Yurt. Or at least I was. So I was very glad when one morning I awoke to find my leg feeling much better and announced that we were heading home.

Kaz-alrhun reappeared as we were packing. The last thing we did in his house was to seal the Ifrit's bottle properly, with lead, stamped with Solomon's seal and strengthened with the mage's spells. Even Kaz-alrhun could not read the words of power on the seal, though he certainly knew how to activate them. It didn't seem to slow the Ifrit down, and indeed he seemed to be inventing even more horrible things to do to me, but I felt at least slightly more secure. And with the seal off the end of the bottle, now I could study the letters carved into it.

Until the very moment we left I kept expecting Kaz-alrhun to demand Solomon's great seal from me. As near as I could tell, he had maneuvered me into meeting the Ifrit at least in part to obtain the seal, and yet he seemed slow to claim it. I even checked it with probing spells as we finished loading the last of Hadwidis's purchases onto the flying carpet, fearing that the mage might have stolen the seal from me and substituted something different. But its strange, ancient magic was unchanged. The only explanation was that the mage had some subtle, long-range plan that involved me keeping it.

We left Xantium with me on the purple flying beast and Gwennie and Hadwidis on the flying carpet with Maffi. I didn't entirely trust his presence, feeling fairly sure he was prepared to send all sorts of interesting information about us back to Kaz-alrhun, but I could use all the help I could get.

As we soared from the courtyard of the mage's house, Kaz-alrhun waving jovially after us, I felt a fierce exhilaration. Broken leg or not, I had come to the East with the wild-eyed plan of mastering an Ifrit, and it appeared I had done so. Now all I had to do was figure out how to use it against Elerius without getting myself killed in the process.

IV

We flew faster on our way back toward the Western Kingdoms than we had on our way east. Naurag flapped along briskly with only me riding, and the magic carpet seemed easily capable of keeping up. I stretched out my leg—merely strapped now, rather than attached to a splint—along the flying beast's back.

We followed not the route along which we had come, which would have taken us west along the Inland Sea and then up the rivers that lead north into the heart of the Western Kingdoms. Rather we took a more direct route, across the Eastern Kingdoms that lay inland, between Xantium and the high mountain range which we in the Western Kingdoms considered the beginning of the East. Here the castles were more heavily fortified than anything seen in the West since the Black Wars; dust clouds along the roads marked marching troops of armed men; and the prevalent scrubby woodland suggested that most of the rural population not directly under the protection of a fortress had either been killed or else had given up and moved away.

I had been gone from Yurt for close to a month. Anything could have happened, and I needed information. It was only an idea, and even finding the place was not easy. The last time I had crossed the Eastern Kingdoms had been on horseback, not flying, and everything looked different from the air. My memories of the location were also more than twenty years old, and I was not even sure what I sought would be visible.

But after two frustrating days of criss-crossing the rocky upland where I was sure it must be, I spotted it: a black obsidian castle, rising jagged from a hilltop, its windows glowing dully like eyes and its great doors an open mouth. The sun shone overhead, but the black stone seemed to throw its own shadow in all directions, sheltering the land from the light.

With a quick word I paused Naurag, hovering, above it. I could have sworn I had searched this very hill the day before. But then the flying carpet had been with me, whereas this afternoon I had told Maffi to take a break from the tedious and unprofitable search—Gwennie had said she and Hadwidis might try to find a stream in which to bathe, which possibility Maffi had found intriguing.

And if the castle had indeed been here yesterday, but hidden, then that meant that someone was interested in meeting me—but not anyone else. The autumn air was already chilly here in the Eastern Kingdoms, but suddenly it seemed even colder. I rubbed my sore leg absently, working up my courage.

Twenty years ago the dark wizard Vlad had made this castle the center of his principality. He was gone now, but it looked as though another wizard had taken up residence here—doubtless another eastern wizard imbued with the magic of blood and bone. I had known less magic two decades ago than I knew now, I reminded myself, and I had not had a friendly flying beast to help me get away fast if necessary. But I had still escaped alive, which ought to mean I could always escape again.

Besides, I needed an artifact which might still be in the castle. I touched my heels to Naurag's sides, and he flew us down to land in front of the gates. The spikes from the raised portcullis could have been teeth, ready to snap me up as I entered the castle's maw.

Reluctantly I left Naurag outside. With his wings he would have been a very tight fit in the dark corridor which stretched beyond the nail-studded doors. He looked around dubiously, clearly regretting this entire trip and wishing that we had stayed in the valley by the little lake up in the land of wild magic, along with the melons and the butterflies. I could see his point.

A ditch so deep I couldn't make out the bottom gaped immediately before the castle, but the drawbridge was down. Slowly I crossed, my feet echoing, then passed beneath the portcullis. I took one step inside, then another, forcing myself not to limp. It was now as silent as though I were a mile underground, not on top of a hill. Even the sound of my steps was swallowed up at once.

But if this castle had been invisible yesterday, then there was an active mind at work here. I lit up the moon and stars on my belt buckle; they made a faint glow that gave me the courage for a few more steps. So far, then, spells of light were still working. A spell to reveal the presence of the supernatural indicated no demons nearby either. And if I glanced over my shoulder I could still see the open doors, a short distance behind me, but before me all was blackness.

I realized I was listening for the regular tap-tap of approaching feet. But the man I half expected to see was dead and dismembered, many years and a great many miles from here. If he was coming down that corridor anyway, the voice in the back of my head commented, I should be on Naurag's back, heading out at top speed.

Now I was a dozen yards down the corridor, trying to remember exactly where I had last seen the artifact I needed. One of the rooms down this corridor, I thought. If whoever had taken over this castle after Vlad's demise didn't want to show himself, then maybe I could snatch what I needed and be gone before he was any the wiser.

A sharp creak cut the air behind me. I whirled to see the great doors slam shut, cutting off both light and escape.

And then I did hear footsteps, coming briskly, still far off but approaching rapidly. My first thought was to smash the doors open with magic and flee wildly, but I hadn't spent two days looking for this castle to run at the first hint of danger. I put my back against the cold stone wall and waited.

I saw the candle flame first, a soft yellow glow that seemed lost amid shadows that were nearly solid with lack of light. Then the dimness above the flame resolved itself into a face, long and white, a face that was smiling. The lips were strangely red in the candlelight.

This was a much younger man than Vlad, I told my wildly beating heart. And it looked as if he had been born with all the body parts now attached to him. He *couldn't* be as bad as that half-dead prince.

And then the man before me smiled, showing dozens of needle-sharp teeth. "A western wizard, as I hoped," he commented, as though speaking to someone else. His voice was cold and flat in spite of the smile, and it echoed up and down the corridor around us. Another few steps, and he was staring into my eyes. His were purple and completely round. "Might I query, might I guess, that you are Daimbert of Yurt?"

There didn't seem to be any use in denying it. "Yes, I am," I said, just managing to keep the tremor out of my voice. "But I'm afraid I don't know your name."

I saw then who he had been addressing before speaking to me. On his shoulder perched a lizard, dead white and three feet long, including the tail. Just like having a purple flying beast for a companion, only smaller, I tried to reassure myself. It cocked an eye at me and flicked a long tongue.

"I am named Basil, but you may call me Count," the man said, slipping his lizard a slimy morsel of something. "And this is my pet, Bone."

A pet, I told myself. A man with a pet couldn't be too bad. I would offer to buy the artifact from him if he still had it; I had never been comfortable anyway with the idea of stealing it. In half an hour I would be safely on my way again.

"Bone prefers to eat human corpses," Count Basil continued conversationally. "But unfortunately we're all out at the moment."

So much for feeling reassured! The lizard was staring at me again, doubtless contemplating whether it would be difficult to turn me into a corpse. Dead white as if it and its kind had never seen the sun, with its master's eyes round and dark as though for seeing in the night, neither of these were creatures of day. Surreptitiously, behind my back, I flicked a quick flame into existence, just long enough to scorch my fingers and reassure myself that the magic of light had not yet deserted me.

But it had been Vlad who had been overcome by spells of light. This was a different wizard; I couldn't expect to escape from him the same way. And very oddly he was, it appeared, trying to be friendly.

"I would offer you refreshment, Daimbert," Basil said politely, "but I fear you would not like what I eat and drink." Even without knowing what it was, I had to agree with him. "I am so delighted to meet you after so many years! I would introduce you to my other pet as well, but little Blood does not come out during daylight. Besides, he usually terrifies my visitors. Come and sit with me a moment."

He led me to a room that was strangely familiar—Vlad's old sitting room. It was hung with folds of velvet, worked black on black, that seemed to absorb the light. Bodiless hands floated around the room's periphery, holding more candles, but nothing could penetrate the shadows.

And then on a black marble table I saw it, what I had hoped to find: the face section of a skull, the eye sockets set with crystals.

Putting itchy fingers into my pocket, I sat down on an uncomfortable chair by a cold fireplace, thrusting out my sore leg before me. "Glad to meet you too, Count," I mumbled, much too late.

Basil didn't seem to mind. "You see, Daimbert," he said, sitting across from me and leaning forward, "I owe you a debt of gratitude. I understand that you were responsible for the death of Prince Vlad."

I jumped at the name but tried to appear calm. "Well, not exactly," I said, half an octave too high. "I didn't actually kill him myself."

He waved my objections away with a slim white hand. The nails, like his lips, were a deep blood red. "The details are unimportant. He left here to pursue you, but instead of your death he found his own. Not merely the half-death with which he had long lived, but a final one," with what was probably supposed to be an ironic chuckle. "And with his castle empty, I was able to claim it for myself.

"In years past," he continued, "I had had to give myself in miserable service to older wizards, but now, though younger than most, I rule as equal to them all. Do you remember Vlad's apprentice Cyrus?" I nodded without speaking, remembering all too well. "When Cyrus left for the West, Vlad took me on as his assistant, which was an improvement from where I had been." I didn't like to imagine where he had been if Vlad was an improvement. "I even hoped that within fifty years or so I might be able to succeed to this castle. But then Vlad went west himself and died in Yurt! So my success begins with you, Daimbert, and I have spent much time in thinking how I might express my gratitude."

I made what was supposed to be a humble and dismissive noise, but not too dismissive—I wanted that crystal-eyed skull.

"Those of you from what you call the Western Kingdoms cross the mountains into our lands but rarely," he continued, "unless you are on some sort of quest or pilgrimage. Are you on your way to Xantium, Daimbert, or even to the Holy Land? Perhaps I could accompany you, to add my store of magic to yours, for I am sure there are spells known to me that are unknown to you. Certainly you are expert in your western magic of glass and steel, but there is much in this earth which responds best to a different magic."

I turned my face away so he wouldn't see the expression of horror. I was not going to face Elerius accompanied by a dark eastern wizard, who would be stopping to find corpses for his pet every time I looked for melons for Naurag. At my funeral Joachim had said I was good at making friends; if this was the result of my personal charm, I would have to try harder to make enemies.

He misinterpreted the turning of my head. "He's looking at the skull, Bone," he commented to the lizard on his shoulder. I was looking at the skull so I wouldn't have to look at him. "This," he continued to me, "is a good example of powers I believe you western wizards do not possess. Take it, hold it to your face, and look at the map."

This was what I wanted, but I still felt heavy reluctance as I rose and held the face of someone long dead up to mine and looked through the crystals in his eye-sockets. On the table was spread a map of the Eastern Kingdoms, and as I looked through the enchanted skull it came to life before me. In spite of the room's dimness, it now seemed brightly lit. No longer a mere detailed map, it became a surface on which I could see motion, merchants and troops moving on the highways, smoke rising from chimneys, forests bending in the wind.

It took a minute to get used to the skull, to learn to control where one looked, for a quick flick of the eyes could send one's vision shooting across scores of miles. The closer I looked the more detailed the map became. At last, peering, I could make out a tiny red rectangle, which must be the flying carpet, lying beside a stream where three people splashed. They seemed unconcerned that they might be watched by wizardry.

Then the hill just above that stream must be where I was now. I shifted my gaze cautiously. The hill was there, all right, and the miniscule form of a flying beast floated just above it, but the hilltop was empty: no black castle, but only barren rock.

"Marvelous, is it not," said Basil as I pulled the skull abruptly away from my face. "He seems quite impressed," he added to his pet.

"We're not on the map," I said accusingly. I still hadn't managed to make my voice come out right.

"Of course not, Daimbert," his purple eyes very round. "My castle is not drawn there, and most of the time I keep it invisible. It reduces the number of unwanted guests," with another chuckle.

And usually you want guests only if Bone is hungry, I thought but didn't say. Instead I commented, quite truthfully, "This is wonderful magic. We have nothing like it in the West."

"I shall certainly bring it with us," he said, then added, as though in sudden concern, "But it only works with the magic map of this region. Perhaps I shall be able to modify it so that it may assist you in your quest."

I too hoped it could be modified—it wouldn't be much use to me otherwise, because I really didn't want to know what was happening in the Eastern Kingdoms. But in the meantime I had to dissuade him from coming along. "I appreciate your offer of assistance," I said airily, "but you really need to stay here. After all, you don't want another wizard moving in while you're gone!"

He gazed at me as though not quite trusting my tone. "I can leave protective spells in place," he said. "Vlad's worked until his death. Now, tell me, Daimbert, where are you going?"

It was easiest to tell the truth. "I'm not on a quest. I've been in the East, but I'm heading home to face an enemy. He's a school-trained wizard like me, so I'm afraid your magic wouldn't be much help."

Basil bent toward me. I wished he wouldn't—his face, up close, appeared horribly artificial, as though he were not even really a man but perhaps a lizard in disguise—and a hungry lizard at that. "But that is exactly how I can help, Daimbert. As I understand—and you realize that the stories which came back from the West were *very* confused—you were able to overcome Vlad with magic different from anything he had expected. We can overcome your enemy with the same sort of surprise. After all, when all of you in the West have worn grooves into the flow of magic through all working the same spells the same way, what would be more devastating than discovering magical forces coming from an entirely new direction?"

I didn't like to admit it, but he was right. I had known all
along that I wasn't going to be able to succeed against Elerius
by matching him spell for spell. That was why I had first tried
to find the Dragons' Sceptre, and why I had then gone looking for an Ifrit—whose bottle was currently hidden among
some rocks a mile away. Access to magic different and more
powerful than anything Elerius knew was my only hope.

My imagination leaped ahead, seeing myself at the head of
a disparate army: the Ifrit, Count Basil, Kaz-alrhun armed
with all the magery of Xantium, maybe some witches with
fire magic, a few more flying beasts if I could tame them,
even one of the old, retired wizards whose training predated
the school, wielding his herbal spells—

Basil must have seen that he was persuading me. "You see,
Daimbert," he confided, "I perhaps know more about this
enemy of yours than you may suppose. One of my old friends
lives in the kingdom where your opponent was once Royal
Wizard."

I went stiff, my backbone feeling as though an icicle had
just been drawn down it. All this suddenly had the feeling of
an elaborate trap which Elerius had prepared for me. "Just
how much," I said through stiff lips, "do you know?"

V

Back before he had taken up his position in a powerful
kingdom with an aging king and an all-too-pliant queen,
Elerius had been Royal Wizard in a kingdom on the western
slopes of the mountains: an enormously wealthy kingdom
whose royal court was deeply sunk in evil. The chancellor of
that kingdom had kept in touch with Vlad, in fact had helped
steer our party toward this very castle when Vlad had decided he wanted something from us.

Though Vlad was gone, and the evil king was gone, and
even Elerius had resigned as wizard there over twenty years

ago to accept his present post, the chancellor must be maintaining his contacts in the Eastern Kingdoms. This explained how Basil knew what had happened to Vlad and knew that I had had a hand in it.

"I understand that one of you western wizards is trying to make himself the absolute ruler of all of your kingdoms," said Basil, showing dozens of pointed teeth—either a grimace or an unsuccessful smile. "He would not have minded my assistance, either."

In a sickening second I could see it all: Elerius enlisting the aid of someone like Vlad, to help him go up against Zahlfast and the school. In return he would promise full access to his own magic. Because he believed his goals were ultimately good, Elerius would not hesitate to forge an alliance even with someone so evil that Hell itself might hesitate to take his soul. And then, after a war that would make the Black Wars seem like a carnival tournament, just when he and this demonic eastern wizard were settling in to rule jointly, Elerius would have a curious accident ...

"But I do not trust him," said Basil.

I stopped looking at the pictures my imagination was producing and looked fully instead at Count Basil: a white-faced wizard sitting in a dark room with a man-eating white lizard on his shoulder, but not Vlad, not a demon incarnate, perhaps only someone who genuinely wanted to help.

"Of course, I don't trust him either," I said. Basil, I realized, must be about my age. If I had grown up in the Eastern Kingdoms instead of the City in the West, would I now have a pet named Blood who terrified the visitors? "But what is the basis of your distrust? Surely your gratitude toward me for my small role in securing you this castle could not outweigh what he must have offered you."

As I spoke I fought against the irrational fear that there was no point whatsoever to this conversation, that Basil was merely keeping me talking long enough for Elerius to capture my friends and the flying beast and discover where I had hidden the Ifrit's bottle.

"I heard that he was present when Vlad died but did not play the role you did in overcoming him."

I shook my head slightly. That was not nearly enough.

Basil smiled again—and this time I was fairly sure it was meant as a smile. "Someone who needs help on his road to power will always promise a partnership. But somehow, it is curious how often it happens, the man awarded with the partnership will have a strange accident …"

I thought this over. Apparently Elerius had been here before me, and Basil had rejected his offers. This wizard had spent his whole life surrounded by the intrigues of the Eastern Kingdoms and had served at the courts of cruel and bloody wizard-princes. This kind of distrust must be second nature to him.

"Then why are you willing to trust me not to kill you the way you believe I killed Vlad?"

"Because you are reluctant to take my help—even though I know you would not be here if you did not want it." He paused to slip a morsel to his pet lizard. "If you planned to kill me soon anyway, forgetting the oaths I gather all wizards trained in the West have to take against bloodshed, then the distaste you wizards of glass and steel always feel for our magic would have been in comparison very easy to overcome."

He understood me far too well. Even assuming I could ever capture Elerius, what could I threaten him with? Apparently everyone throughout the civilized world knew that good old Daimbert wouldn't really hurt a fly.

I took a deep breath and tried harder not to show what Basil discreetly called my "distaste" for him, his magic, his castle, and his pet. I would have called it horror and revulsion myself, but one had to be polite. "You are right, Count, that I need help, and you may be in a position to offer it. But before I accept your assistance, welcome as it might be, I need to know: what will you want in return?"

His blood-red lips twitched in a small smile: proud of me for being cautious. But then he leaned forward, white hands clasped together, lightless eyes extremely sober. "A promise from you, sworn on magic itself: when you are the head of organized wizardry in the West, you will not, as I realize that other wizard plans to do, use the conjoined forces of all of you school-trained wizards to conquer our kingdoms east of the mountains."

I didn't need to hear this again. Everyone from the old Master to Elerius to this strange pale-faced wizard seemed convinced I could become head of the school. Just because I wanted to stop Elerius didn't mean I wanted to make his ambitions my own—in fact, just the opposite, as I would have hoped would be self-evident.

Apparently not. I smiled as genuinely as I could. "I will be happy to swear such an oath, because I have no intention of heading organized wizardry. Even if I did, our school's purpose is to help mankind, not invade other parts of the world.

"But—" I added quickly, before Basil could jump up and start his packing to come with me, "—you may be able to help me best from right here." The white lizard cocked a disapproving eye at me, but Basil's face stayed dead still. "You were reluctant, I know," I hurried on, "to let your castle be seen by the people who were with me yesterday, and yet they're going to be with me for the rest of the trip. I would much rather have you here than someone like Vlad, and you don't want to take chances on another wizard moving in."

"You know, Bone," Basil commented to his pet, "I do not think he wants us to come with him."

Now I had hurt his feelings. I knew from his insistence that his castle stay invisible that he was deeply reluctant, when it came to it, to leave darkness and solitude for sunlight and other people. Yet it must be lonely sometimes even for him, with no company but a white lizard. "You could help me best," I said brightly, "by letting me have this magic skull."

He insisted for several minutes that he would not mind associating with other people—though I tried to suggest, without actually saying so, that many of these people would feel enormous "distaste" for his pet. He was also reluctant to part with the skull, especially since he remained convinced that all it would show me was the Eastern Kingdoms. But Vlad himself had made it, not Basil, and Basil might not know all its tricks—or so I fervently hoped.

But after a quarter hour of discussion, during which I tried to convince him that I personally would be delighted with his company, even though my companions might be a bother, Basil agreed to stay where he was but to let me have his magic artifact.

"After all," he said to his lizard, looking on the bright side, "making a new one will keep me happy and busy for a while. And finding a new skull for the face section shouldn't be too hard, should it, Bone?"

I swore the oaths he wanted, hating the solemnity of swearing to something which I knew would never be an issue anyway, and took the skull in both hands. As I looked at it I tried to reassure myself that since Vlad had not sold his soul to the devil, the one bit of evil he had never undertaken, I would not be endangering my own soul in using it.

"Now you have made me feel guilty, Daimbert," Basil said suddenly. "You helped me gain my castle by killing Vlad, and you have promised not to invade our kingdoms, and all I am offering you in return is an artifact which may not serve your purposes. Here. Let me give you this instead. I am hoping for an apprentice of my own some day, so I have started composing a primer of the magic of blood and bone. It will be easy enough for me to write out a new one. This one is for you."

Startled, I took it and pushed it in my jacket pocket with no more than a glance. Another handwritten book of old spells. Maybe I would have done better all along if I had just concentrated properly on studying modern technical magic.

"Thank you very much," I said as graciously as I could manage on short notice. "And one last thing. Everyone in the West thinks I'm dead. Please don't mention my visit to your old friend the chancellor." Or, I added silently, to Elerius. The pit of my stomach remained convinced that this was all an elaborate plot to capture me.

But Basil smiled. "Of course not, Daimbert. It would be returning evil for good to betray you when you have just sworn to leave me my castle and my peace. Do come by when you have finished defeating this other wizard and tell me of your adventures. Perhaps, for you, even Blood will agree to come out during the day."

His pet lizard Bone was taking another morsel of something, clearly thinking it was not so tasty as I would be, as I staggered down the corridor toward the doors. They swung open at my touch, and I was back blinking in the sun, as the obsidian castle faded into invisibility behind me.

We were at least a hundred miles from Basil's castle before I waved to Maffi on the flying carpet that we should set down for the night. Evening was coming earlier and earlier these days, and the western sky, above the mountains we could now see rising to the west, was streaked with red.

"I'm going to have to adjust the skull's spells," I told Maffi as we munched on the last of the cucumber salad Kaz-alrhun had sent with us. Just as well; the salad had become limp, and the flat bread into which it was packed was stale. "I'm sure it was designed to work only with the enchanted map of the Eastern Kingdoms, but I need to make it show me the West."

I had kept the account of my visit to the obsidian castle to a bare minimum, and now, with Basil far behind us and

Naurag's warm flank between us and the wind, I could speak almost casually.

"Try drawing a map of your own," suggested Gwennie. "Try drawing Yurt."

Homesickness, keen and unexpected, hit me as I sketched the shape of the kingdom, the location of the castle, the roads and rivers, the plateau cut by the valley of the Cranky Saint.

"Don't forget the nunnery," put in Hadwidis.

Elerius had never threatened Yurt directly, but as I drew I knew in my heart that I was opposing him for the sake of my kingdom and my family, as much as for any principle. *This* is where Elerius's influence must never come.

But when I looked at the map through the crystal eyes of the skull, it refused to come alive. All I could see was a series of pencil marks, hard to make out in the dim light and slightly distorted by the crystals. Yurt lived but not on paper.

"When we mages of Xantium need to communicate over long distances," said Maffi confidently, "we say certain words over deep pools, and can see the person with whom we wish to communicate." I was happy to let him try, but his 'certain words' had no effect here.

Hadwidis had been watching quietly. "Don't try to do it all at once," she suggested suddenly. "Start by making your own map of the Eastern Kingdoms. If you can make the skull work at all, you can then start working on other places."

"What a good idea," I said, rousing myself to give her a grin and tousle her hair. She had been out of the nunnery long enough that her hair was worth tousling.

It was now so dark that we had to work by firelight, me drawing and the other three arguing about where the rivers ran which we had crossed over today. I emphatically drew Basil's hill complete with the obsidian castle. The one part of the map on which we could all agree was the woodland clearing in which we now sat.

"Let me try this now," I said, again holding the skull to my face. The map remained stubbornly ill-lit and unfeatured, but for a second I thought I caught a hint of a spell, almost a trailing thread—

"That appears akin to something I know," said Maffi, serious now, not simply trying to persuade me of the superiority of his training with Kaz-alrhun over mine at the school.

I still thought of him as the boy he had been when I first knew him, but he was, I reminded myself, probably older now than I had been when I first came to Yurt as Royal Wizard. I nodded and shifted to give him room beside me. We each held the skull in one hand and, mind to mind, worked together at teasing out its magic. What I had spotted was more than a trailing thread; it was the beginning of a spell shaped in something very like the magery of Xantium, though with some odd twists—

"There," said Maffi suddenly, breaking the mental contact. I wiped my forehead with my sleeve. His mind had been even stranger than I expected. But between us we had found the tiniest gap in the magic of the seeing crystals, a gap apparently meant to be bridged by the ensorcelled map Basil had had on the table beside it, but which might be filled in with certain other spells instead… And I thought we had it.

"I shall attempt the map now," Maffi said, then grinned. "You know," he commented with a wink for Gwennie, "I would have to characterize you of the West as *strange*." I let him have the skull, and he bent over the map. There was a long silence.

It was night now, and the piece of paper on which I had drawn my map was no more than a firelit rectangle. The wind was rising, sighing in the trees and bringing back the suspicions I thought I had left behind at Basil's castle, that Elerius was cautiously and invisibly approaching. Hadwidis put her hand on my arm, and I squeezed it.

Maffi pulled the skull from his face, his eyes huge. Worldlessly he passed it to me, and I bent eagerly over the map. Instantly it came to life.

It was a disquieting life, lit by more than the fire. Parts of the map were extremely sharp, including the obsidian castle with its jagged towers, and most of the road we had followed both on our way there and leaving. In other places a smoothly-running river simply disappeared, though I knew I had drawn its entire length, only to reappear again after an unfeatured, misty gap. Those parts of the Eastern Kingdoms which I had not tried to sketch, that is most of them, also faded almost immediately into vague whiteness. The skull must be able to bring to life only those parts of the map which were drawn to correct scale—and the misty gaps were the parts over which we had argued.

And then, moving my eyes very carefully, I saw us. It was extremely disconcerting to see oneself from the outside. I stared, fascinated, at the miniscule fire, the four tiny human figures, and the large, dark and shadowed shape which I recognized after one startled heart-beat as the flying beast. The miniature trees of the living map bent and swayed with the trees above us. Though I stared until my eyes ached, I could make out no enemy creeping up on us.

I pulled it from my face. "Let's try Yurt."

It didn't work. Though this map was much better than my sketch of the Eastern Kingdoms, it refused to come to life. Maffi and I tried further adjustments on the spells, without effect. Gwennie and Hadwidis gave up and went to sleep while we were still passing the skull back and forth, saying, "I think I have an idea," and "Let me try just one more spell."

I pulled out the primer of the magic of "blood and bone" which Basil had given me, but in flipping through its pages by firelight I saw nothing about far-seeing skulls. Spells worked with bodies dead three days, seven days, seven years were all there, as were constructions built on dragons' teeth, spells to sicken from miles away, but nothing useful—now, or I thought, ever. I thrust the book back in my pocket and returned to school spells and improvisation.

Exhausted, Maffi and I stopped at last. I looked up at the sky, where a star peeking through the clouds could have been the watching eye of someone else with his own magic skull. As I watched the clouds shifted, and I could see that the star was not an eye but a shoulder of the Hunter, rising in the east over Xantium. Feeling hunted myself as I wrapped up in a blanket, I only hoped that our failure to see Yurt didn't mean that the kingdom no longer existed.

part seven ✤ armies

I

From the Eastern Kingdoms we headed straight west, over the high range of mountains that separated eastern and western lands. I kept Naurag fairly close to the ground, following the passes. The high peaks towered over us, shutting out half the sky. The stinging wind off the eternal ice fields that topped the peaks was frigid and tasted of snow.

We made camp for the evening in a relatively sheltered valley at the feet of the highest mountain. "Could people even *live* up there, Wizard?" Gwennie asked, craning her neck.

I considered. "You wouldn't be able to breathe," I said at last. "There's less and less air the higher you go, and you wouldn't have any breath for climbing." A wizard, I thought, could probably fly up there with magic, perhaps creating some sort of spell to trap and bring air with him. But wizards are too practical to want to freeze to death three miles above the surface of the earth.

"Perhaps this trip will give me a new appreciation for the summer sun of Xantium," commented Maffi as we tried to cook supper over a fire whose heat was sucked away by the bitter night sky. When we awoke in the morning, folded two to a side under Naurag's warm wings, it was to see the ground lightly dusted with white.

Maffi considered it enormously exotic, and Hadwidis, declaring that they never let her build snowmen in the nunnery, promptly built one, using up most of the snow around our camp in the process. But I couldn't enjoy it. I had still not gotten the skull to show me anything beyond the Eastern Kingdoms, and as I tried another spell this morning, even those lands seemed oddly faded. I rubbed my eyes, wondering if this was just due to glare off the new snow, but when I tried again my penciled sketch of the region east of the mountains still only resolved itself into a misty approximation of the living scenes I had been able to see before.

Basil had tricked me, I thought. He had given me a worthless artifact, made me swear not to attack him to forestall my trying to take its value out of his hide, and was probably thinking that when I came, peacefully, to complain, he could feed me to his lizard. But my certainty that it was hopeless did not keep me from trying new spells. I *had* to find out what was happening at home.

Naurag was inspired by the cold air under his wings to fly even faster, so in another day we were able to leave the highest peaks behind us and start down into the foothills. The first kingdom we would reach in the West, I recalled, was Elerius's former kingdom. He was long gone, and the evil king who had ruled there was dead, but I didn't want to take a chance on the royal chancellor. According to Basil he was still there, and even if he had not been warned of my coming he would probably still recognize me.

So in spite of all three riders on the flying carpet waving and pointing to indicate that we should stop and ask hospitality at the enormous castle that sprawled at the mountains' knees, I led us onward, to another cold camp but a safe one. Here at least the snow had not yet to begin to blow.

"I have another idea to coax this skull into compliance," Maffi announced. I let him have it, along with the map of Yurt, not expecting him to have any more success than I had had up in the mountains.

But the moment he had the crystals before his eyes, he gave a shout. "God be praised, it is working!"

I snatched it from him without even a word of thanks and pressed the skull to my own face. He was right. Before me Yurt came to life.

"We mages of Xantium have many abilities," said Maffi airily, trying to suggest without actually saying so that his magic had finally made it work.

"I think," said Hadwidis loyally, "that Daimbert had done all the spells correctly, and you just triggered it."

"No, no," I said absently, staring until my eyes hurt. "I think the skull just has a limited range, and can only show you the region where you are. It's a good thing, Maffi, that we didn't spoil its inherent spells trying to work on it." But even as I spoke my mind was far away.

There was the white castle of Yurt, banners flying from the towers. There was the brick road that led down the hill into the woods. There was one village, and another. There was the nunnery of Yurt. If I shifted my gaze cautiously, I could see the limestone plateau into which the river which bubbled up by the Cranky Saint's shrine had cut its deep bed. It all looked very peaceful.

I lowered the skull and looked toward Gwennie, sitting still and white-faced. "Nothing seems to be happening there," I said. "No marching armies, no volcanic craters, no fire-blackened woods."

"Can I see?" she asked in a small voice.

I had been about to raise the skull to my face again, but I nodded and handed it to her instead, hiding my surprise. Most people who are not trained as wizards prefer to watch from a safe distance, and Gwennie had never shown any inclination before to try a spell.

Even now she hesitated, holding the skull with the very tips of her fingers. "If it will work here in the Western Kingdoms," she said, "why didn't Vlad bring it to Yurt when he came, rather than leaving it behind in his castle?" She was trying to speak casually, but she gave an involuntary shiver, both I guessed from holding something Vlad had made and from her memories of his magic. Hers must be as vivid as mine.

"He didn't have a map of the West," I said. "Remember, he had trouble even finding Yurt." And I wished he'd had a whole lot more trouble. "And once he was there, it was easier just to look around than to try to create a map of what was right before his eyes."

She nodded and took a deep breath, then lifted the skull to look through the crystals. She looked for several minutes, not speaking, and finally lowered it.

"The king is not at home," she said at last, somewhat distantly.

"He might be inside the castle," Hadwidis suggested. A glance indicated she was itching to try the skull herself. "So you couldn't see him."

Gwennie shook her head, handing me back the skull and wiping her fingers on the grass. "His royal flag is not flying," she said. "Ever since I have been constable I have made sure always to fly his flag when he is in residence."

I met her eyes. Both of us were wondering where he was—and if he had decided to try to find adventure in my absence by galloping off after Elerius.

Hadwidis started to lift the skull from my lap, then stopped. "I really don't need to see what's going on in the nunnery of Yurt," she said. "I already have much too clear an idea. I'm going to draw *my* kingdom."

The wind kept catching the paper, and the flickering firelight gave her little enough to see by, but she drew determinedly, tongue between her teeth. "I may not have been there for a few years," she said, "but I was born there. The nuns didn't make me forget."

In fifteen minutes she had drawn a fairly detailed map, the area around the royal castle the most sharply-drawn, the villages and a seaport sketched more roughly, the rivers traced carefully, hills, valleys, and forests indicated with a tangle of pencil strokes. "Now, I'm going to see what my mother is doing. The nuns wouldn't let me go home even for my father's funeral, but they can't stop me now!"

She took the skull mask gingerly, peered through the crystals, then gave a startled cry and dropped it. But she snatched it up again before I could react and raised it again, this time more slowly.

We waited, holding our breaths, for her to speak. Her eyes, distorted by the crystals, flicked up and down, back and forth. Then abruptly she hurled the skull aside and threw herself into my arms.

"It's horrible, Wizard!" she cried, on the edge of tears. "Why did the Cranky Saint want me to leave the nunnery? Why couldn't I just stay there? Does he expect me to deal with *this*?"

Gently I eased her out of my lap and took up the skull myself. I had wanted to know what was happening in the Western Kingdoms, and now I was going to find out. An old saying flashed through my mind, about not asking a question if you don't want to learn the answer.

As I put the mask to my face, Hadwidis's penciled map came alive, lit from within. It was night in her kingdom as it was night here, but as I looked through the skull light seemed to follow my gaze. There was the great castle where Elerius was Royal Wizard, where Hadwidis and her half-brother, Elerius's son, had grown up. The courtyard was packed with tents; an army appeared bivouacked there. Up in the towers magic lanterns burned, and through the windows I could see tiny figures passing back and forth against the light.

Cautiously, reluctantly, I moved my eyes from an examination of the dark towers to the surrounding territory. Here again were encamped armies, watchfires burning.

Armies! Tents and fires seemed to stretch to the horizon. Thousands of soldiers were there, tens of thousands. They were settling down for the night now, but sentries walked between the tents, and horses stamped and shook their manes. Shields hung from the tent posts. I doubted so many armed men had been assembled in one spot since the Black Wars. Feeling ill, I identified among the flags the royal insignia of Yurt. While I had been gone, Elerius must have retreated to his kingdom, protected by warriors and powerful spells, and much of the rest of the Western Kingdoms were assembling on his doorstep.

That they had not yet overpowered Elerius with their superior numbers suggested that his protective spells were holding. Either that, or human armies were reluctant to march into battle against undead creatures of hair and bone. And how many wizards might have joined him, to add their magic to his?

"They're attacking my mother and my little brother," Hadwidis said brokenly, and Gwennie tried unsuccessfully to comfort her.

It would take months, I thought, to starve Elerius out, much too long to keep an attacking army the size of that one calm and quiet. The kings of the West, delighted to have an excuse for war after generations of peace, must be eagerly anticipating an open battle. All too soon, one of the kings would charge, then all would charge, and it would be impossible to restore peace out of the resulting carnage.

For several minutes, Maffi had been trying to get my attention. At last I handed him the skull and closed my eyes, trying unsuccessfully to get the image from my mind. I had been thinking I needed to find a way to keep Elerius from becoming head of the wizards' school. That would have been hard enough, but now I was also going to have to find a way to keep thousands of eager warriors from killing each other.

I had no answers, but the question was unmistakeable. Was this apocalypse necessary?

II

All of us now were eager for speed, but Naurag didn't like to fly at night, and even Maffi was reluctant to pilot the flying carpet through darkness across kingdoms he didn't know. We were still nowhere near either Yurt or Elerius's kingdom when I decided late the following evening that we had to stop for the night.

I had recognized a castle. It was a small castle, built on a bridge arching across a placid river, where a family of swans swam and sheep grazed by the riverbank. The castle had a very distinctive roof: bright blue tiles, and gold leaf reflecting the last rays of sun from the peak of each tower. We had stopped there twenty years ago on our way to Xantium; the castellan, I recalled, had had a mother who was fourth cousin or something to King Paul's father, the old king of Yurt, and he had been delighted then to put us up.

The same castellan was still there, grayer but still hospitable. He didn't remember me, but he did remember old King Haimeric. "So how did that quest of his ever turn out?" he asked, while his servants bustled around to prepare rooms for us. We had left Naurag and the flying carpet over the next hill, but we must still have appeared a rather ill-assorted and scruffy bunch, standing inside the front doors on his blue-veined marble floor.

"It was exciting and dangerous," I said truthfully, "but in the end I think we all found our hearts' desire."

"Well, I was very glad to welcome your group then," he said cordially, "and I'm happy to welcome all of you for Haimeric's sake. I'm afraid we've already had dinner—would you mind if we brought trays to your rooms? We do want to hear in the morning about your adventures, however. We see very few travelers, since we're well off the main routes. And you say you're coming from the Eastern Kingdoms? It must be quite a journey on foot!"

Hadwidis, at least with a scarf on, now looked more like someone who had had a disastrous haircut than a runaway nun, but I still would have had trouble explaining why a wizard and a man with the olive skin of the East were wandering westward, without any apparent means of transportation, accompanied by two young women. Fortunately he didn't ask. His servants showed us to small but gracious guest rooms where we could hear the river rippling below and told us that our baths would be ready in just a few minutes.

"Let me show you something, Wizard," said the castellan proudly as the other were getting settled. "I've recently had a telephone installed!"

I made polite sounds; magic telephones had been common in the Western Kingdoms for over fifty years, but a remote castle like this, which didn't have its own wizard, might be well behind the times.

"I had the Royal Wizard come out from my king's court this summer to install it," he continued, showing me a very ordinary glass telephone sitting on a red velvet cushion. "I believe he had just graduated from that wizards' school of yours. A very serious young man he is. His name, I believe, is Levi."

The name was familiar. I didn't know very many of the younger wizards—other than Whitey and Chin, and I wouldn't say we had ever been properly introduced. But the name Levi teased my memory— Then I remembered. Levi was one of the few of the Children of Abraham ever to study western wizardry.

Most of the teachers at the school had probably been brought up as nominal Christians, but since they made a point of being above issues of the Church, Levi's religious background would not have concerned them in the slightest. I wondered without much curiosity whether it still concerned him.

"I made sure," the castellan continued, "that he put the Daimbert-attachment on my telephone."

"Daimbert-attachment? Oh, yes, yes!" With difficulty I managed to turn the surprise of hearing my own name into a burst of approval. Most telephones these days had a far-seeing attachment, such as I had invented when first out of school, but I had not before realized it was named after me. The time when my major concern about the school was whether they were going to let me graduate—or retroactively take my diploma back—seemed impossibly distant.

"Do you happen to know," the castellan asked with a frown, "if it's named for the same wizard Daimbert as the one they're all talking about these days?"

All talking about these days? I made a noncommittal murmur, doubtless confirming his opinion that I was mostly inarticulate. Who was talking about me, and what were they saying? Clearly in the time I had been gone more had been happening than a skull and an ensorcelled map were likely to tell me.

I excused myself and started toward the guest rooms, hoping that a hot bath would restore some rationality. Behind me I could hear the glass telephone ringing.

The castellan caught up to me at the door to my room. "I'm afraid I didn't catch your name—is it Daimbert too? It's a more popular name among wizards than I realized!"

Elerius had found me, I thought. Well, too late to wonder how he knew where I was or to try to evade him again. Nothing to do but face him. I licked my dry lips and squared my shoulders. "Yes, I'm Daimbert."

"You have a telephone call."

But the base of the glass telephone showed not the black-bearded wizard but rather Joachim. The bishop of Caelrhon was smiling as I had seldom seen him smile as I gasped out, "Hello?"

"Welcome back to the living, Daimbert." It would have been gratifying to see how extemely pleased he was to be talking to me, if I hadn't been so startled.

"Um, well, I've never actually been gone," I mumbled.

"So I gather."

"But how did you know?" I burst out. "How did you find me? I hadn't know myself that we would be stopping here until an hour ago." If the bishop could find me, Elerius surely would be next.

"Your daughter told me."

"Antonia!" She had seen me alive and well before I left Yurt for the East, but I had never expected her to start telling everybody.

But the bishop said, almost apologetically, "She did not feel she could lie to me when I asked her. I do not believe she has told anyone else—not even Theodora. You see, Daimbert," he went on when I did not respond, "I was worried about my god-daughter. Death is always particularly difficult for children to accept, yet if they do not accept it the healing cannot begin. And Antonia continued to act as though she thought you were coming back. She did not mourn, she did not seem distracted from her normal activities, she did not come to ask me why God had taken you or if I was sure you were in heaven—which, in fact," he added dryly, "I was, in case you were about to ask."

I hadn't been about to ask him anything.

"So I requested that she come to my office in the cathedral for a discussion today," Joachim continued.

Today. That meant that Theodora and Antonia were still safely in Caelrhon, not with the armies besieging Elerius's castle.

"She and Theodora have been living in the cathedral this last month, you see, at my invitation. I hope you don't mind, Daimbert. But I thought that even Elerius would not attack them there. They have gone out only for errands and for Antonia's schooling. It was when I talked to her today that she informed me that you were hiding from Elerius but had a secret plan.

"I am sorry to tell you, Daimbert, that at first I did not believe her. This is not because I have ever suspected your daughter of being less than truthful, but rather because the force of my own sorrow seemed so strong against the faith of a child. As a bishop, I should have known better. This evening I prayed to Saint Eusebius, prayed between sorrow and hope that I might know the truth. And I must have slept, exhausted with uncertainty, for the saint appeared to me in a vision."

For a moment a shadow passed across his image in the glass telephone. I had never seen the Cranky Saint face to face, and I could only be glad that it had happened to the bishop, not to me. A feeling like tiny footsteps went down my spine. What plan could the saint have, and why did he persist in being so interested in me?

"He told me where I might find you," said Joachim, smiling again. "I remember that little castle well from our quest with old King Haimeric. A pleasant resting spot on a dangerous trip. Are there still swans in the river outside the guest room windows?"

I took a deep breath. "Yes, the swans are still here. But what's been happening in the West? I—I understand that armies are gathering in Elerius's kingdom," not wanting to get into long explanations about the magic skull. "How many wizards does he have on his side? Is it going to be open war? And what's this about everyone talking about me?"

Joachim abruptly looked more sober, though he still kept smiling as though he couldn't help himself, every time our eyes met. "Your information is correct. Half the kings of the West have declared war on Elerius, including King Paul of Yurt. Because you served him, he is in fact considered the leader. I understand that at least one of the principal teachers of your school is opposing him, but Elerius also has wizards who support him. It all began at your funeral—were you really there, Daimbert, as Antonia says you were? If I had known you were listening, I might have tried to say something laudatory about you."

Years ago I had decided Joachim had no sense of humor. More recently I had concluded he had one after all, but I could never predict what he might find amusing. "What's this about Paul being the leader?"

"Well, once it became clear at your funeral to that old teacher of yours—Zahlfast, is that right?—that the school's late Master had designated you as his successor, and we thought Saint Eusebius was telling us that Elerius had killed you, it was decided that all opposition to Elerius would be carried out in your name. I might," looking somewhere over my head, "have had something to do with the decision. So Paul, as the king most closely associated with the martyr Daimbert, has rallied the other kings. Oh, you'll also be pleased to hear that any differences between Paul and King Lucas of Caelrhon have been healed, now that Lucas realizes that the enemy is not wizardry in general but one wizard. And I'm sure you'll also be pleased to hear that the new bishop of the great City has realized his association with Elerius has stained him, and he has already resigned."

Since I really didn't care who was bishop of the City and had never had much use for King Lucas, I wasn't as pleased as he seemed to think I should be. Especially I didn't like the idea that the grim army I had seen gathered around Elerius's castle was preparing to make war in my name. "It can't be allowed to come to fighting, Joachim," I said quietly. "First the warriors will kill each other, then the wizards will start, and no one anywhere in the West will be safe. The war must be stopped before it begins."

He nodded, his enormous dark eyes holding mine. "That is part of the reason I am so happy to see you, Daimbert, even aside from my joy in knowing that our years of friendship have not ended after all. Because I know that you will be able to stop Elerius without bloodshed."

III

That last, I thought as I numbly replaced the telephone's receiver, was not something the saint had suggested to him. A saint would have had too much wisdom to suggest that a single, mildly competent wizard was going to stop a war that might be breaking out at this very moment. That was Joachim being wildly convinced, on the basis of whatever Antonia had told him, that I had a plan.

I didn't have a plan. All I had was a flying beast, a couple of books of spells, the rightful heir to Elerius's kingdom, and an Ifrit who was planning to dismember me the moment I opened his bottle.

When I emerged from my bath, the door to the women's room was closed, and Maffi was snoring peacefully on the far side of the chamber the castellan had given us. I set the candle on the table and took a few bites of the cold meat on the tray. Maffi had eaten most of the roast beef but left me all the ham.

Then I pulled out the ancient book of magic that I had carried to the dragon's den, to the Ifrit's lair, and back to the Western Kingdoms. Someone who had mastered dragons must have an idea how to overcome a supremely capable wizard.

Or, I thought, also setting out the volume Basil had given me, maybe eastern magic, repellent as it seemed, might give me some ideas. I finished the ham and started reading.

I awoke with my face pressed against parchment pages, my neck stiff, and the candle guttering by my hand. I pinched out the flame and rolled into bed for a few hours' sleep. Basil's spells were written in letters that had taken some deciphering, and as far as I had gotten they appeared better designed for someone like Elerius, who was not too squeamish about processes, than for me. And the old wizard Naurag seemed to be entirely silent on the topic of overcoming superior wizards, because he himself had been superior. In his day, I feared, even though he had apparently reminded the old Master of me, he would have been one of the wizards assisting Elerius by setting up powerful protective spells against King Paul and me.

But when I awoke again, before dawn, it was with an idea. I scribbled a note, tiptoed past Maffi's bed, eased the window all the way open, and flew out over the river. A mist obscured the riverbank, and a soft splash could have been a muskrat or the swans.

I flew straight up, over the mist, climbing into the morning sunlight until the air in my lungs started to thin. Using a far-seeing spell, I scanned the countryside in all directions. It was as vivid as Vlad's map of the Eastern Kingdoms when seen through the skull, but this was no product of magic, only itself, a landscape just awakening from sleep. From this height I could see for scores of miles and pick out several castles and manor houses, but only one big enough to be this kingdom's royal seat.

It was just barely late enough that one could decently ask for admittance when I reached the castle gates. I tried to straighten up a bit so as not to look too disreputable and finally had to add a layer of illusion to hide my worn and travel-stained clothing. Illusion also made my beard look tidy and brushed, since my comb was back with the luggage. The drawbridge of the royal castle was just being lowered for the day. Plenty of knights here, I noticed; we must still be far enough away that this king saw no reason to lead his troops into battle, either against or in support of Elerius. I crossed into the castle courtyard and asked to see Levi, the Royal Wizard.

He was eating breakfast in his study, tea and cinnamon crullers, when the castle constable announced me. A wave of homesickness hit me. I had done the same in Yurt for thirty years.

He looked up, smiling, and for a second I hoped he was going to offer me a cruller. But instead he froze in the middle of lowering his cup, slopping tea onto his flagstone floor. "You're Daimbert! You've risen from the dead!" Slowly, he started inching his chair backwards across the floor.

"I never actually was dead," I said crossly, not having time for this. "And I'm not a ghost," I added when his eyes stayed wide and round. "I need your help." I brought out King Solomon's seal, where the words of power were written in symbols I could not read. "I gather these are the letters originally used by Moses?"

Levi recovered a little after a moment, when I did not burst into spectral manifestations, and put his teacup carefully down. "What do you have there?"

I hooked a chair with my foot and sat down at the opposite side of the table. It took a little explanation, and I was starting to feel a desperate urgency. We needed to get to Elerius's kingdom immediately, and I also started wondering uneasily what Maffi might be doing back at the little castle. I had left the Ifrit in his bottle there among my luggage, worried that if I could learn from Levi to read the words of power on Solomon's seal, I might accidentally release the Ifrit while practicing. I didn't entirely trust Maffi not to start experimenting with the bottle on his own.

"So you see," I concluded, "to an ordinary learned person, even one who recognized the symbols, these words are unreadable, just as someone who had never learned the Hidden Language couldn't pick up a book of our western magic and start reading out spells. So I need someone who both understands the ancient writing of the Children of Abraham and is trained in magic. That is, I need *you*."

Levi still wouldn't touch the seal. The idea that it had belonged to King Solomon impressed him more than any spells that might be inherent in it. But he let me put it on the table and looked at it thoughtfully. Rather belatedly, he offered me tea and a cruller. Not enough cinnamon, I thought, biting hungrily into it. I noticed he was watching me out of the corner of his eye, to assure himself my spectral body really was eating.

At last he took a piece of paper, leaned closer to the gold seal, and started drawing. I was interested to note that he worked from right to left in reproducing the seal's symbols. His drawing was very careful and meticulous—just what you'd expect, I thought, of a wizard fresh from his training in the school's technical division. "The forms have changed over the centuries," he muttered, more to himself than to me, "but I am unlikely to mistake this one, or this one. And if this is indeed a vowel mark, and not just a scratch—"

"The signet is unscratched," I said. "Look at it. As smooth and clean as the day it was made. The spell's a binding spell, designed to hold fast whatever is sealed with the signet, if that's any help. I assume it's related to the binding spell they teach us at school, but this one will hold even against wild creatures of primordial magic."

But he was still drawing. I waited for several minutes, watching him try several different transcriptions. At last he looked up with an expression of triumph. "I think now I understand the words inscribed here, but I hesitate to speak them. After all, Solomon was the only man who ever filled all three functions, of king, of priest, of magic—" He broke off in the middle of a sentence, staring. "Daimbert, you *are* dead!"

My chair crashed to the floor as I jumped up and swung around, prepared to see Elerius. But the room was empty except for Levi and myself. "I'm as alive as I ever was," I said in irritation, turning back.

"The illusion of life is falling away," he mumbled with an expression of horror.

I looked down at myself and snorted. "Not the illusion of life, but the illusion of clean clothes. Take my hand. Feel me. Why are you so convinced that I'm a ghost?"

"You were eaten by a dragon at the instigation of Elerius," he said faintly.

"Then where are the teeth marks?" I demanded. The voice in the back of my mind wondered if the Cranky Saint, who *had* been eaten by a dragon, had identified with me because of the way I faked my death.

Levi took several minutes more of persuasion, but finally he returned to the seal. Young wizards, I thought in disgust. We teach them enormous earthly power, but any whiff of the supernatural still gives them the willies.

"I hesitate to speak the words," he finally continued, "both out of respect for Solomon son of David, and for fear of what might be bound by them."

"Good point," I said. "It would be nice, for example, to be able to get the door open again during our lifetimes. The crullers wouldn't last us nearly that long."

He gave me a dubious look, then seemed to decide if I was capable of joking I really wasn't a ghost after all. "But I believe the words, transcribed into the characters of the Hidden Language, would read like this."

I studied his piece of paper, stopping myself just in time from murmuring the words to myself. It wasn't any spell I recognized, though it suggested a much more powerful version of the magic lock we used in the west, and it had certain affinities to the spell I had twice heard Kaz-alrhun use. With this, if I ever got Elerius cornered, I might be able to bind him.

A test would have been useful, but I didn't dare try it any more than Levi did. "Thank you," I said, standing up. "You have helped me enormously." I thought of asking him not to tell anyone I was still alive, but it didn't seem worth it. I doubted a junior wizard at an out-of-the-way kingdom was spying for Elerius, and if he was, well, Elerius would know the truth very soon anyway.

Levi frowned. "Tell me again how you knew that I could help you read this spell."

"I'm acquainted with one of the castellans in this kingdom—the one for whom you installed a telephone this summer."

"So you were just passing through, and you just happened to stop there, and he just happened to mention that one of the few Children of Abraham trained as a wizard lived right down the road."

"That's right," I said, starting to feel uneasy. "Just a coincidence."

"Doesn't that seem to be ascribing a lot to coincidence?"

It did, now that I thought about it. "There's only one explanation," I said at last, not liking this at all. "The Cranky Saint. He's maneuvering me."

Levi rose to see me out. "You realize, of course, that we do not believe in the powers of saints."

It wasn't until I was half way back to the castle where I had left the others that it occurred to me to wonder whether by "we" he meant the wizards or the Children of Abraham.

Back at the castle, the swans swam peacefully. This corner of the Western Kingdoms, I thought, might still escape destruction if war broke out, because the rest of us would have killed each other off long before the fighting spread this far. Now all I had to do was to make sure Yurt escaped as well.

The castellan and his family were plying my party with questions about our adventures. With Hadwidis worried about her mother and Gwennie thinking about King Paul, it was mostly left to Maffi to relate some of the marvels of Xantium.

I shot through the breakfast-room, tossing off an excuse, and gathered up our luggage for departure. The Ifrit's bottle was exactly where I had left it, sealed with lead inscribed with the words I now could read. Maffi hadn't touched it after all, and I felt guilty for having doubted him.

"It appears that I chose the best possible time to visit the West," he told me as we left at last, refusing the castellan's offer to lend us horses. We walked over the hill to where we had left the magic carpet and the flying beast. "Kaz-alrhun will regret having missed the excitement."

I could have missed the whole thing without regret myself. But I didn't seem to have much choice. We flew on west as fast as Naurag could fly.

We kept on as the sun sank, burning in front of us, casting the shadows of the hedgerow trees below far across the stubble of the fields. We kept flying as the sunset flared, then slowly faded, and the stars began to come out above us. And at last we saw the bulk of Elerius's castle, shimmering with spells, rising against the dark sky, with enemy watchfires burning all around.

An encampment of that many men will never be silent, but at this time of the evening it was fairly still, the clearest sounds being the occasional whinneys of the horses and the calls of the watchmen to each other. I flew Naurag directly next to the carpet and shaped an invisibility spell to cover all of us.

I had never tried to make so many different things invisible at the same time before, and the fringe of the carpet and the flying beast's wings kept emerging from the spell. But Maffi realized what I was doing and added his own magic to fill the gaps in mine. We didn't want to be shot full of arrows as we came in over the encampment.

The spell worked fine against the watchmen among the army's tents. We flew, unseen, over their heads, aiming toward the center where King Paul's standard flew. But if the armies didn't spot us, the wizards did.

IV

The carpet abruptly buckled, losing height rapidly. The women screamed—Maffi may have too. I abandoned the invisibility spell in preference for a lifting spell, in a wild effort to keep the carpet from crashing. My invisibility spell was being ripped from us anyway; only Maffi's spell on the carpet's fringe and on Naurag's wings remained.

Responding at last to my desperate magical commands, the carpet recovered itself ten feet from the ground and landed fairly gracefully, though Hadwidis's packages of new clothing tumbled off. Naurag folded his wings and came in smoothly, looking around with interest at the fire-lit camp, doubtless wondering if anyone had some melons.

I whirled, furious, to find the wizards who had come so close to getting Gwennie and Hadwidis killed. And there stood Whitey and Chin, the old Master's pet pupils, looking inordinately pleased with themselves.

"You didn't think you'd fool us twice with the same trick, did you, Daimbert?" asked Chin proudly. "Ever since you slipped away from us that time by making yourself invisible, we've been working on detecting invisibility spells in action and disabling them. Is that a real flying carpet?"

"You knew I was coming?" I demanded. Perhaps I had been wasting my time pretending to be dead.

"We found out just this morning," Whitey chimed in. "And nobody knows but us. Do you remember Levi, who graduated last summer? We've patched a phone connection through from the school to here, and he phoned us from his kingdom. Somehow, though he sounded rather incoherent when we talked to him, he'd found out you were alive—and all the time we'd thought you were dead!"

"If you were just trying to spot me," I said, unmollified, "why did you almost make the flying carpet crash?"

"That wasn't us," said Whitey without concern. "Elerius and the wizards with him are blocking all spells from working, next to his castle walls, and I'd guess he is doing the same for anything in the air. He hasn't touched our magic, though."

"And," said Chin with badly-concealed pride, "we've been working on very special magic, something the old Master first gave us as a project last year—to make illusions that will last a very long time."

"Great," I muttered. "So we'll send illusory armies against Elerius's quite real warriors." Maffi was looking around, intrigued; Gwennie strained to spot anyone from Yurt; and Hadwidis became suddenly shy, discovering herself in the middle of a crowd of interested soldiers, including many emerging from their tents clad only in their long shirts, to find out what was happening.

"Um, while you were dead, Daimbert," added Chin, abruptly much more serious, "did you happen to hear that Elerius has defied the masters of the school and declared himself the true head of all wizardry? And indeed of the Western Kingdoms?"

"But you'll be able to stop him!" said Whitey enthusiastically, without giving me a chance to respond. "After all, the Master made you his heir. That's why we didn't go along with the rest of the younger wizards and join Elerius. When Zahlfast took ill we knew it was up to us. So we've been working on our spells, and we're going to be able to assist you. We'll stop him together." He really was, I thought with an inward groan, a very young wizard.

Before I could find a way to break it to him gently that just because the Master had wanted me to succeed him didn't mean I had the slightest idea of what to do, I was distracted by a murmur moving through the crowd. "Daimbert! Daimbert lives. Daimbert has come back from the dead. Daimbert lives!"

Shivers went through me at the sound of the voices, first a few, then many, first spoken in terms of surprised acknowledgment, but then within a few seconds turning into a triumphant chant. "Well, wait!" I tried to say. "You see, I wasn't really—"

It was no use. The chant almost immediately had nothing to do with me. Sleepy soldiers crawled from their tents and took it up. Several began banging their swords on their shields in rhythm. Even without magically amplified hearing, I thought wildly, those with Elerius in the castle must surely hear and understand.

And then I saw King Paul, striding through the encampment with his helmet cradled under one arm and his breastplate flashing in the firelight. He seemed somehow taller and more mature than when I had last seen him—maybe it was the armor. He saw me, stopped short while a smile of disbelief and joy lit up his face, then tossed his helmet aside to crush me in his mailed arms.

"You're solid flesh and bone! You've come back from the dead to save us!" he cried, letting me go but continuing to grin. I cautiously checked my ribs for cracks. "I always knew that Yurt had the best Royal Wizard in the West, but now all the other kings will know it too!"

It was going to be difficult to get anyone to believe I hadn't really been dead. In fact I had returned from death once, years ago, something that very few people outside of Yurt had ever known; I seemed now to be getting the credit for it a generation too late. My ruse with the air cart appeared to have worked all too well.

King Paul looked past me to my companions. Naurag he seemed to take as an air cart in the flickering fire light. "This is Hadwidis," I said, pushing her forward, "a princess who is the rightful heir to this kingdom." I left out entirely her career as a nun, and the issue of her rightful inheritance seemed to pass Paul by. I could see him preparing to introduce himself and to welcome her to this encampment, on the assumption that if she were with me then she must be an excellent person.

Then he saw Gwennie.

The grin stayed on his face, but for a second it looked completely unnatural. She hesitated herself, half-hidden behind Hadwidis, an arm around Naurag's neck.

Then Paul's smile became altogether genuine again as he sprang toward her. "Spending some time with an old friend!" he said with a great laugh. "You might at least have told me it was the wizard we were all mourning!" He grabbed her in a bear-hug as he had grabbed me and whirled her around. Gwennie gave an undignified squawk as all the air was squeezed out of her, but she was smiling as widely as the king. The soldiers watched with approving interest.

Paul set Gwennie down and abruptly became uncomfortable again. "I am delighted to see you in good health," he told her formally. I realized I still, after all this time, had his diamond ring in the bottom of my pocket, but the middle of a military camp was not the place to produce it. "Won't you introduce me to your friend?" Paul continued. He looked properly at Maffi for the first time, a handsome and rather exotic-looking man the same age as Gwennie, and his eyes narrowed.

I had no time to worry about anyone's love life but my own. If everyone—including, very soon, Elerius—knew I was back, then I could not let Theodora go another night without knowing too. "Where's that telephone you set up?" I asked Chin. "I have to call my wife."

King Paul of Yurt, King Lucas of Caelrhon, and a dozen other western kings sat in a circle around a watchfire, talking. On one side was the encampment, starting to settle down again after the excitement of my arrival; on the other was an empty mile that separated their armies from Elerius's castle. Firelight reflected from the kings' armor, and the shadows dancing across their faces made their expressions impossible to read. They were ready for a battle which I knew would leave the fields of Elerius's kingdom scattered with their bloody corpses.

Coming back from talking to Theodora, I squeezed in next to Paul. Hadwidis, Gwennie, and Maffi sat behind him. For a moment I wondered if this kingdom had ever before had so much royalty gathered outside its castle, but then I remembered—of course it had, at the time of the old king's funeral. But then the kings had assembled to mourn the passing of the man who had ruled here, and now they were gathered to oppose the man who had set himself to replace him.

Zahlfast, I gathered, had been overcome by the excitement, which meant that the only wizards here were Whitey and Chin, who hadn't even graduated yet. Leadership of the army was thus in the hands of the kings. They were arguing, several, including Lucas, convinced that an immediate midnight attack was the best course, while others urged caution.

"He's got those *things* fighting for him, Lucas," one king said darkly. "You weren't here yet when we first attacked," and for a second I could hear all sorts of other unresolved quarrels behind his words, "but I for one don't want to face them again—and many of my best men will never have the chance to fight *anyone* again. Let's give the wizards a little more time to disable them with their spells."

"I don't trust those wizards," Lucas retorted. "How do we know they won't turn against us given a chance—or join Elerius the way they tell us so many other wizards have? We wouldn't be hearing so many thing about how Elerius is 'stronger' than they are if they just had their minds on their magic for a change."

I looked around surreptitiously for Evrard, King Lucas's Royal Wizard, to see how he was taking this, but didn't see him. I hoped this didn't mean he had joined Elerius. But he might well have, the voice in the back of my mind pointed out. He had always admired him. In which case I wasn't just fighting against Elerius, who I knew as my enemy; I was also against Evrard and doubtless many other wizards whom I had always considered my friends.

"If you are so rash, Lucas," said one of the other kings roughly, "as to want to try unaided steel against black magic, I shall not be ashamed to wait here for you."

Lucas growled and reached for his sword. He had always been touchy, but this went further; it seemed to me that the fierceness and pride he was at such pains to demonstrate were not really his but the product of what he thought a warlike king should be like. It was much too late now to go back and tell his childhood nurse not to let him hear such stories.

Paul put a hand on his arm. "Let's hear what Daimbert has to say."

That stopped Lucas, as indeed it stopped them all. They turned faces suddenly still with awe toward me. In the ten minutes I had been on the phone my legend seemed to have matured. From snippets of conversation I had heard while walking back, the Cranky Saint had redeemed me from death so that I might free the West from the scourge of Elerius and his minions. At least so far, I wouldn't have to cleanse the populace of their sins while I was at it.

How could I possibly lead all these powerful kings? I hadn't even had much luck leading Maffi. But I did know that neither charging headlong against Elerius's castle, nor waiting for Whitey and Chin to come up with better spells than those of the wizards inside, was likely to work.

"The Cranky Saint has sent you a wizard to lead you," I said, thinking that soon I might have to believe it myself. "The wizards in that castle have been misled by Elerius, the same way that his knights have been misled. But when we win," just barely not saying, "if we win," "then we'll have to make our peace with all his followers, wizards and warriors alike."

"So what are you planning to do, besides defend the good name of wizardry?" demanded Lucas, just barely keeping his tone from being insulting. I probably should have been gratified that not everyone was awestruck by my miraculous appearance here, but I wasn't.

"I'm going to go talk to Elerius," I said, firmly and clearly, wondering even as I spoke what I could possibly say to him. "He's always claimed that he wants to rule in order to benefit humanity, and it must have occurred to him that there cannot be any benefit in a repeat of the Black Wars."

"How are you going to get in?" one of the kings asked.

For a moment we were all silent, looking off toward the castle, just visible against the evening sky. "I'll find a way," I said with more confidence than I felt. "And he'll *have* to listen to me."

"If you think you can reason with him, Wizard—" the king started to say.

"Not reasoning," I snapped back. "Threats. I shall threaten him with my powers. And I hope you don't imagine that I came back from the dead to betray you all!"

The one time I actually had come back from the dead, it had not been with any startling new powers, but none of these kings would know that. I stood up. "I'll go tonight— now. He may have thought he could defeat your armies with his spells and his undead warriors, but he reckoned without *me*."

With the Ifrit's bottle in my pocket, I rose from the ground and flew toward the distant glowing lights of the castle, wondering what I could possibly do to match my bold words.

The spells against flight which Elerius had erected around his castle caught me a quarter mile away. Fortunately I was ready for this and was only a few feet above the ground when all my flying ability evaporated.

It wasn't a true magical shield, I thought, picking myself up and trudging across the dark ground toward the castle gates. It would have no effect, for example, on an army. But— It might slow down dragons. Elerius must fear that I had obtained the Dragons' Sceptre after all.

I allowed myself a small grin. Let him imagine I had a hundred dragons lurking a few hills away. I wondered briefly why the spell hadn't affected Naurag's ability to fly, but then Naurag wasn't a dragon. If Elerius was so concerned about dragons, I might be able to work them into the conversation even while trying to reason with him. In spite of what I had told the kings, I did intend to try reason first, but I was certainly not above threats if I thought they would succeed.

And if that didn't work, I was putting an alternate plan together in my mind. I didn't like it at all, but at least it was a plan.

The ground under my feet might once have been a wheat field. Now it was trampled and ruined. A battle had already been fought here, I reminded myself, and for all I knew I was walking across the graves of some of the west's bravest and most foolhardy warriors.

The castle bristled with magic, and I paused, wondering how I could possibly get past protective spells far more powerful than anything of mine. But I need not have worried. The drawbridge swung down and the portcullis, creaking, rose before me. Clearly I was expected.

I hesitated a moment, trying unsuccessfully to see what was in the black passage beyond the portcullis. This was worse than Basil's castle in the Eastern Kingdoms—there all that awaited me was a wizard with a man-eating lizard on his shoulder. In here was a wizard who imagined he could save the world by destroying it.

Maybe, I thought, still hesitating, I should have had Hadwidis draw a detailed map of the major rooms of her castle, so that I could, by using the ensorcelled skull, have had an idea of what Elerius was up to before I arrived. But then I shrugged and forced my feet forward. My leg twinged, but I ignored that too.

The castle was dark, but as I entered, all around I could sense powerful spells, spells that must be keeping a potential dragon attack away and observing the royal armies. I saw no one, not the queen mother or the young prince about whom Hadwidis was so worried, and none of the dozens of wizards Elerius might have with him. But doors opened before me, magic lights flicked on, and as I strode forward the lights behind me went out and the doors slammed. I kept my head up and one hand in my pocket, trying to walk the way a man would who might at any moment brandish the Dragons' Sceptre.

The halls and the doors were leading me straight up to Elerius's study. I considered improving my appearance with illusion as I had when visiting Levi but rejected the idea; I had looked ridiculous as the illusion faded, and I needed my attention for far more important things than lace cuffs. How many wizards would Elerius have standing by him, I wondered, ready to neutralize any spell of attack I might try, even before the words were fully shaped? Or how many knights might he have positioned, whose swords could pierce me before I could paralyze them all?

The study door opened before me without anyone touching it. Lamplight spilled out into the dark hallway. My feet, acting on their own, stopped moving. "Come in, Daimbert," said Elerius's voice. "I've been expecting you for weeks."

I took a deep breath, closed my eyes for a quick prayer to the Cranky Saint in case he really was trying to help me, and forced my feet forward into the doorway.

No hordes of wizards or knights with drawn swords awaited me—just Elerius. He sat in a large chair in the middle of the room, arms crossed, looking expectantly toward the door.

The only person with him was a boy, a boy Antonia's age. His shock of dark hair was the exact same shade as the wizard's beard. He slid off his own chair as I came through the door, landing somewhat awkwardly—I realized with a start that one of his legs was ever so slightly twisted. But I had no time to think about that now. He looked up at me haughtily but then spoiled the effect by smiling. "Hello, Wizard. Are you the famous Daimbert?"

Elerius answered for me. "So he is, Prince. And he has come to join us."

V

Join them! Elerius thought I might still be talked into becoming his co-ruler, and he called the boy Prince. So I had two pieces of useful information already, I thought, turning around a chair and straddling it backwards, leaning my arms on the back and doing my best to give him a wizardly glare. He wasn't planning to kill me immediately, and he had not yet told young Walther that he was his father.

"I'm afraid your wizard has misled you, Prince Walther," I said to the boy, who seemed surprised that I knew his name. Now I just had to hope that the pounding of my heart wasn't as loud in the room as it was in my own ears. "It is true that I am Daimbert, but I have not come to join your wizard but to oppose him. And he has not been expecting me for weeks but only for an hour or two."

"You told me Daimbert was our friend, Wizard," said Walther uneasily, stepping back closer to Elerius. He was a tenderly-raised young prince, I thought, with none of his father's supreme self-assurance. I couldn't hurt him myself any more than I could have hurt Antonia, but I might be able to maneuver Elerius by hinting that at any moment I might do so.

Already I could tell that this conversation was not going the way Elerius had planned. I would have smiled if it had not been so deadly serious. He had arranged to meet me alone except for his son, as a demonstration of his goodwill and his trust in me. Instead of being swayed by the loving family picture of the two of them together, I must suddenly seem like someone dangerously likely to say things he didn't want the boy to hear.

"I am ready to be a friend to both of you, Prince Walther," I continued, deliberately not looking toward Elerius because I knew it would annoy him. So far, my voice was staying fairly steady. "But friendship will be on my own terms, or else I am your enemy." I had the initiative and I didn't dare lose it—Elerius's ability to plan and prepare must be slipping, what with trying to run a war, but at any moment he might regain control. "First—and this is fundamental—he must give up his mad plan to dominate the West. You can see all those armies out the window for yourself, Prince. They would happily be friends with you, but not until your wizard yields himself to me."

Elerius interrupted before I could start laying out the terms of surrender. "Come, Daimbert, you're going to give the prince the wrong impression if you keep on talking like that! We cannot be enemies. I mourned as much as anyone when I believed you dead. You certainly did a good job of making the air cart look as though you and it had been chewed by a dragon—I would be interested to learn, some day, if you really were bitten by one. I know you never found the Dragons' Sceptre, or you'd have brought a horde of dragons with you—" Was that real knowledge or just bluff? "—but your trip to the northern lands could easily have killed you. When you came to your own funeral, without dragons and therefore unsuccessful, I realized your death had just been a ruse, and I was delighted to know you had survived your adventures—but then you disappeared again!"

"What do you know about my presence at my funeral?" I snapped, then realized that by going on the defensive I had already given him the chance to regain the initiative in this conversation.

"Your invisibility spell or whatever you were using worked perfectly," he said airily, smiling with his lips while his tawny eyes stayed sober and calculating. "But you're carrying something in your pocket, something with a tracing spell attached to it—you had it in your pocket when you visited me in the City and, I thought, agreed to work with me. I recognized the spell just as I was leaving Yurt, but I left so rapidly that I couldn't investigate."

"Actually I refused to work with you," I mumbled. Paul's ring. I had put that tracing spell on it myself, to help me find it if the women to whom he offered it kept throwing it away. "I may have let you believe I would help you run the world after the old Master died, but that was only be to be able to get away."

But if Elerius had known since my funeral that I was alive, he still hadn't had any idea where I had been. I tried glaring again.

"In spite of your protests, Daimbert," he continued in tones of calm rationality, "it is clear that you wouldn't have walked straight into this castle, all by yourself, if you weren't intending to join us. Do these protests about being my enemy satisfy your conscience over some oath you gave to the kings before you came here?"

I pulled back my lips in the semblance of a smile, which only succeeded in worrying Walther. "That's because you think I'm like you," I said. "I'm not. You should know better." For a second Elerius's confident smile cracked, as he did realize better. "You would have happily lied in my place if you thought that betraying the western kings would have been best for them in the long run. And you would never willingly walk into danger, because who would put your doubtless excellent plans into operation if you weren't around to do so yourself? But I'm surprised you haven't noticed that my own vision of a better future for the world doesn't always require a world with me in it."

"You have always had something of a penchant for self-sacrifice," Elerius said uneasily.

But that was my final plan, which I hoped I didn't have to use. Time to try reason, while I again had him off-balance. "So accept that I'm here alone, but here as your enemy," I said firmly. "But not irredemiably your enemy. There's still time, Elerius, to give up this war. You wanted to become the new Master of the school, and you would have if you had not been so precipitate in claiming the position as your right. Did you ever really think the teachers would elect someone else? But you did make a serious error when you quarreled with Zahlfast. Penitence and submission would have been a much better option—you could still have become Master eventually, even if you had to wait another twenty years."

"It's much too late, Daimbert, for me to be penitent," he said with a wizardly glare of his own. "The school will elect you as soon as they hear you're back from your presumed death."

Jealousy, I thought. Completely misplaced, of course. But half a heartbeat later I realized that something was wrong here—or else I had missed something crucial. I didn't want to ask him anything because it would lose me what little momentum I had, but I had to know. Maybe his jealousy would obscure his judgment. "Why would the school elect me? I thought you had all the teachers here, working with you, with the single exception of Zahlfast."

"Most of them are still in the City," he said in a low voice, looking away. I could tell this stung. "They haven't joined the kings, but, unlike a lot of the younger wizards, they have also refused to support me."

"Then think of me as speaking with the voices of those teachers," I said, trying to sound matter-of-fact and sympathetic. If I had drawn a map of the City instead of Yurt I might have known this already. I couldn't dig at the wound to Elerius's pride that the defection of the West's most important wizards must represent—if I did, he would never listen to me. "I'm sure they're as sick at all this as I am. None of us—starting, I know, with you—want to see a disagreement between wizards lead to more bloodshed than we've already had, especially not the deaths of the worldly leaders whom institutionalized wizardry should rather help and guide."

The last was gratuitous, intended to appeal to Elerius's own vision of his mission. But he did not react as I hoped. Instead he shot me a vicious glance. "So what are you offering instead, Daimbert? That if I agree to leave this castle you'll *graciously* engage to talk to the teachers at the school, to see if they'll agree that, after you become the new Master, they'll allow me to become your helpful little assistant?"

I had never thought of it at all like that. Once again, he was assuming that I was like him. But he was far more bitter than I had expected. Haughty defiance I had been prepared to face—not anger and jealousy because his best plans were rejected.

Walther spoke up then—for a moment I had nearly forgotten him, standing silent next to his father on his thin, slightly crooked legs. "But Wizard," he said to Elerius, "aren't *I* supposed to be your helpful little assistant? Isn't that why you've been teaching me magic?"

For a second Elerius's expression changed, and he gave the boy a smile and rested a hand briefly on his shoulder. "That's right, Prince," he said while I wondered if he was about to have Walther turn me into a frog. I'd better not lose track of the boy again.

"You forget," I said quickly, "that I have no interest in heading the school, with or without assistants. At this point,

I'm sure the teachers would all agree that we'd be better off if the school didn't have a single head at all—or at most a person with enough administrative authority to make sure the tradesmen's bills got paid, but nothing like absolute power. If you think about it, that's really how the old Master functioned." I took a deep breath and spread out my hands in a placating gesture. "There's still time to be penitent, Elerius, to rejoin the school and eventually play a role in shaping its policy, along with all the rest of us."

Maybe I shouldn't have said "us." But this was as reasonable as I could get. I wiped my sweaty palms on my trousers and waited for his answer.

I didn't have to wait long. Anger darkened his face, and he started to rise from his chair. Only Walther's presence, I thought, kept him from summoning lightning to fry me to a crisp. It was not good to have the best wizard in the West angry with me.

"No!" he shouted, then paused, taking a deep breath. Walther took a step away as he slowly sat back down again. "No," he said more quietly, "I have no interest in your 'penitence.' You've been spending too much time talking with men in the church—weaklings, all of them, without enough courage to take a firm stand on anything except for so-called sin." I recalled that his hand-picked candidate as bishop of the City had already resigned. "If the teachers of the school, sitting in their classrooms fretting about tradesmen's bills, don't want to join me, then I shall defeat them all! This collection of royal armies at my gates will not take very long; then I shall turn my magical powers on the wizards. They shouldn't take much assurance from the school's protective spells—after all, I helped design them."

"You're going to kill everybody, knights and wizards both, who stands in your way?" I said in horror. "Elerius, are you insane? This is *not* helping humanity!"

He had glanced toward the window as though planning the great stroke that would reduce the armies outside to ashes. But now he shot me a sharp glance from under peaked eyebrows. "I would not have stood this insult from any other wizard, Daimbert. But you are the only man who has ever been able to disrupt my plans so consistently and so thoroughy. When I learned the old Master wanted you as his heir, I understood why at last."

If so, it was more than I'd ever understood. Elerius was speaking more calmly now, but there was a note of bitter coldness in everything he said.

"Your sometimes bumbling exterior," he continued, "must hide abilities equal to mine—maybe even greater, because I have long suspected that the Master had learned secret lore from earlier generations of wizards which he never taught at the school, and which even my years of research have not uncovered."

"Bumbling exterior" I let pass without comment—could he possibly be saying that he thought I was as good as he was?

"I allowed you to come here unmolested, Daimbert, because I have continued to hope that you would agree to work with me. Even now I do not entirely despair of you. Be reasonable, so that I need not turn to threats."

His voice was softer now, insinuating. "Haven't you often wished that academic magic was not so limited? We struggle to learn the most difficult spells, are exhausted in working them, and even then we can accomplish but a fraction of what we envision in imagination. But if the two of us worked together! Then there would be no further need to consult the wishes of others or engage their participation, when we could do everything ourselves. You with the secret knowledge the old Master gave you, me with my mastery of all known branches of western magic—we shall dominate the world!"

I had a very clear idea of what Joachim would say—

Lucifer and the fallen angels must have talked like this just before their fall.

But then the implications hit me. I sprang backwards, knocking the chair over, no longer caring who had the initiative in this conversation. "Elerius! This is black magic you're advocating. You've sold your soul to the devil!"

VI

Young Walther was almost as terrified as I. He retreated rapidly in the opposite direction. I stood with my back against the locked door, the boy with his back against a window, and Elerius sat deserted in the middle of his study.

He actually managed a chuckle. "That would certainly justify all the evil things you've thought of me over the years, wouldn't it! But no, Daimbert. My soul is still my own. As is my pride—which would suffer irrevocably if everyone knew my best effects were not due to my own magic but to the workings of a demon. Go ahead and check for the presence of the supernatural. You'll not find it here."

I checked at once, the same spell I had used in Basil's castle. Here, as there, I found no demonic influence, not even the faint taste of evil lingering at the edge of perception from a demon trying to hide itself.

"Come back, Prince," Elerius continued, fairly under control now and smiling. "I'm sorry if the wizard frightened you. But he won't hurt you." Walther returned slowly, not crying but right on the edge of doing so.

I righted my chair with hands that just barely did not tremble. "Black magic or not, Elerius, you're still searching for powers beyond anything human."

He shook his head, still smiling. He was back in charge of the situation, jealousy and bitterness thoroughly concealed. "You're sounding like your priest friends again, Daimbert. You know I've warned you about that. And very soon I shall stop giving you any more second chances to change your mind and join me! Know that, with you or not, I *will* become ruler of the West. If you persist in being finicky about bloodshed, then I shall let you leave here alive, charged with telling all those kings and wizards to cease their opposition to me at once. That way I shall not have to kill anyone else, which of course would be my own preference too."

Reason had failed—time to try threats.

"I shall neither," I said clearly and conversationally, "join you in world domination nor try—unsuccessfully, I'm sure—to persuade anyone else that the world would be best if you ran it. I've given you a chance to end this without destroying yourself or anyone else, but now I shall have to destroy you."

He looked startled at this wild claim—but it was not entirely a bluff.

"You're so good at discovering things in people's pockets," I continued, fierce and grim now. "Tell me what I have in mine!"

He would have been wondering this ever since I came in the room. A magical object is normally hard to detect if it is not functioning, but in my pocket I had a bottled Ifrit, even now struggling and shouting tiny threats that I had long since ignored. A wizard as good as Elerius would have spotted it at once without necessarily knowing what it was.

"Where have you been," he demanded, "to be carrying something like that?"

"Still don't know what it is?" I asked teasingly, keeping an eye on Walther—Antonia would have been putting a spell together to work the object out of my pocket.

"If this is something the Master gave you instead of me—" he started to say, with another flash of jealousy. But he stopped himself and started over, though his good-humor now was entirely unconvincing. "Don't tell me you're planning to issue hollow threats against me in my own stronghold, Daimbert."

I jerked the Ifrit's bottle from my pocket. "The threats will not be hollow."

The bronze bottle lay heavy in my hand, shaped like a cucumber, green with age, sealed with lead imprinted by Solomon's dread seal. For a moment the room was dead quiet, still enough for the Ifrit's high, thin voice to carry. "I shall pluck the living nerves from your face, cast your body half way to the sun, set lizards into your guts—"

Both Elerius and Walther stared. The boy would never have seen such a bottle before, but I knew Elerius had. "Surely," I said, allowing myself to sound patronizing for a change, "you recognize an Ifrit's bottle when you see it."

Elerius actually blanched. For one second I enjoyed the rush of triumph, the knowledge that at least for this moment he feared me. But I brushed the sensation aside almost immediately. This was not about proving my own abilities, but about Elerius recognizing the inherent limitations in his.

"These are the choices," I said, speaking slowly to give my words added weight. "Either you immediately surrender—give up your resistance and throw yourself on the mercy of the school—or else I release this Ifrit from his bottle. Listen: you can tell he is eager for release! With the first of his wishes he will grant me, I shall blast you and your castle into pebbles. I shall ask the Ifrit if he will spare the boy's life, but I will make no effort to save yours!"

This was pure bluff. The Ifrit was no more ready to grant me wishes now than he had been when I first tricked him into the bottle. But Elerius did not know this. "Come, Elerius," I continued when he seemed to hesitate. "For all your talk of augmenting wizardly powers so that we can rule in absolute authority, you know that the Ifrit is more powerful than you or any wizard ever has been or ever can be."

Still he seemed to hesitate, watching me intently. Did he doubt my willingness to act? Did he know that all my talk of wishes was false? Did he sense my extreme reluctance to kill anyone, including him?

The silence between us stretched out. Earlier I had felt half-frozen with fear; now sweat ran down inside my shirt. He kept his tawny eyes fixed on me.

I broke first. "Dear God, Elerius, don't make me do this!" Because this wasn't a bluff any longer.

Slowly, giving him every last second to change his mind, I reached for the edge of the lead seal and started to pry it open. In one second the Ifrit, furious with all the frustrated rage of an enormously ancient and enormously powerful being, who had been created to help shape the world but who had been tricked into complete helplessness, would burst from the bottle. In two seconds he would have destroyed this castle with all its inhabitants, Prince Walther, Elerius, and me.

"Stop!"

I stopped.

Elerius's words came out low and rough. "Give me the bottle, Daimbert."

I clung to it with both hands. "*You* are surrendering here," I said, my voice trembling. "Not me."

He rose then, for the first time since I had come in the room, and shifted his chair. The chair had concealed it, but I could see it now: a pentagram drawn in chalk.

In horror and despair, I nearly dropped the Ifrit's bottle. When he spoke again it was so quietly I could hardly hear him. "Don't you make *me* do this."

"You can't mean it," I managed to gasp. "You're not going to summon a demon!"

"I will if you do not surrender the Ifrit."

Should I give him the bottle and make a run for it, letting him discover for himself that the Ifrit was bent on destruction rather than granting wishes? But I immediately rejected the idea. It would be bad enough to sacrifice myself in making sure that Elerius too was dead. But I could not give him the means to end his life—and Walther's—while saving my own.

Besides, I did not trust the Ifrit not to become all accommodating and friendly if Elerius was able to get his attention in the bottle, to explain to him that he who was opening the seal was not the same person who had closed it. Elerius with an Ifrit beside him would be almost worse than Elerius with a demon.

He bent to touch up a few spots where the chair had scuffed a slight imperfection in his pentagram. Walther was again backed up against the window.

"You just told me," I said desperately, "that you didn't want to let anyone think your magic was not all your own."

"It would indeed be a blow to my pride," he said quietly, with a glance back at me over his shoulder. "But better to sacrifice my pride than not to take the rule that is rightfully mine."

"I don't believe you! You're bluffing!"

"A bluff? I am completely in earnest." He rose and dusted off the chalk on his trousers. His voice, louder now, filled the room, and at his voice the magic lanterns began one by one to go out. "By Satan, by Beelzebub," he cried, "by Lucifer and Mephistopheles!" And as he spoke the lines of the pentagram began to glow.

part eight ✣ the cranky saint

I

STOP!"

Elerius stopped.

For a wild second I thought that I myself had spoken. But it wasn't me. It was Prince Walther.

He was shaking hard, but he moved determinedly toward the pentagram. The light from the few lamps still burning cast wild shadows across the room. The prince's walk had only the slightest limp, and his chin was raised in a desperate attempt at hauteur. "You warned me," he said through the tremor in his voice, "you warned me against black magic yourself, Wizard. Don't do this! Daimbert is our friend."

"A friend," I added from between dry lips, "who will be able to get the seal off the Ifrit's bottle far faster than you will be able to negotiate with a demon for the sale of your soul."

"I think," said Walther in a low voice, cocking an eye at me and still trembling, "Daimbert doesn't really care if the Ifrit kills him too, as long as it kills you."

Where had the boy gotten such a good insight?

"You will notice," said Elerius slowly, "that I have stopped the incantation to summon a demon."

I let out a shuddering breath. "Good," I said as clearly as I could. "Now erase the pentagram. You will notice that I still have my hand on the lead seal."

Elerius pulled his black eyebrows down heavily. "I am not yet ready to yield, Daimbert. I shall simply stand to one side."

It wasn't good enough, but there wasn't a lot I could do. "Order all the wizards with you to return to the school! Agree that you will stop this resistance to the kings and the masters of wizardry!"

But he was not defeated—only calculating his next move. "You and I can continue to make demands of each other, Daimbert, that the other will refuse to honor, until Prince Walther falls asleep from boredom. Why do we not instead agree now, rather than hours from now, that we have each other stalemated?"

"And what would a stalemate mean?" I asked cautiously.

"That we would separate, you with your Ifrit, me with my pentagram. You can return to those obstinate western kings who still believe they can order the world's affairs better than a wizard could, and I shall continue to plan their destruction, but without the use of black magic. I really would prefer not to invoke a demon, you realize."

I realized nothing of the sort. "The prince comes with me," I said levelly. "Or there's no agreement."

But this wasn't just a discussion between Elerius and me. "No!" cried Prince Walther, pulling back his shoulders and glaring. For a second I caught a glimpse of Hadwidis's stubbornness in her half-brother. Their mother, I thought irrelevantly, must be a queen one obeyed at all costs. "I am the royal heir to this kingdom and this castle!" Walther declared. "I shall defend them against anyone, warrior or wizard!"

And die with your father if I figure out how to get the Ifrit to obey me, I thought. But I nodded to the boy because there was nothing else I could do. "How can we trust each other not to attack the second the other's back is turned?" I asked Elerius.

"We shall both swear oaths," he said calmly, in charge once again. "Swear to me, Daimbert, on magic itself, that you will not use the Ifrit's powers to attack me."

"Not something so sweeping," I said, careful because I

knew he had to be plotting something. "The Ifrit is my ulti-mate weapon in this war, and I can't give him up."

"Then give me forty-eight hours' truce," said Elerius briskly. "Neither of us shall attack the other for a space of two days. That should give me the time I need to prepare the cas-tle's defenses so that even an Ifrit could not penetrate them."

He again exuded confidence, even rationality—yet the pentagram still glowed beside him. "What," I said carefully, "will you swear upon, Elerius? I don't trust you to swear on magic. You've already broken the powerful oaths all of us had to swear in the school not to harm mankind."

That startled him, at least momentarily. "Well, I—"

I interrupted. "Swear on Prince Walther's life."

There was a long silence, during which the boy's eyes went very wide. But then Elerius shrugged. "Of course. I shall be happy to swear on his very being not to summon a demon, either now or later. I shall swear such an oath as soon as you have sworn yours."

I should have known better. It was late at night; I had just come back from an arduous trip to the East; I was being hailed as miraculously resurrected; and my leg was still not entirely healed from my run-in with the roc. But still I should still have spotted the fallacy in Elerius's proposition.

In the heavy syllables of the Hidden Language I swore the enormously solemn oath he wanted, not to use the Ifrit to harm him, his castle, or his armies for at least forty-eight hours. He kept his eyes on me the whole time, as though waiting for the slightest deviant word. "Now you," I said roughly, thrusting the bronze bottle into my pocket.

And then he laughed, his head thrown back, and fire blazed from his fingertips. "You have sworn, Daimbert, but I have not! And now I have changed my mind!"

My hand shot to the lead seal on the bottle, but I froze without loosening it. I had just sworn, in the most powerful terms a wizard could swear, not to release the Ifrit.

What was a broken oath, I thought desperately, compared to the danger of the world's most powerful wizard working with a demon?

But I could not do it. My fingers had no intention of obeying me. I had believed in wizardry and magic down to my bones since a very young man, and I could no more break an oath sworn on them than I could have duplicated any of Elerius's other feats.

Madly I tried a paralysis spell, to stop him from speaking, but he was ready for me and brushed my magic aside with the ease of brushing away a fly. Spinning around, I tried to wrench the study door open, to escape in the few seconds I might yet have. It was no use. The door was shut fast with magic. "By Satan, by Beelzebub," the words rose behind me, "by Lucifer and Mephistopheles!"

On the far side of the room I spotted Prince Walther, terrified, trying unsuccessfully to open a window a hundred feet above the ground. I doubted he yet had learned how to fly, and anyway the window was magically locked. I crossed the room in long strides, making a wide detour around the pentagram, and wrapped an arm around the boy. He was too young to have to meet a demon, or to see the wizard he had believed good turn to evil. He pressed himself, shaking, against me, and we both waited with averted eyes for the inevitable.

Behind me in the room there was a great crack and a flash of light. The demon is here, I thought with a kind of dead resignation. I had met a demon twice before and felt no need to look. In a second my nostrils would be assailed by the smell of brimstone.

The scent of roses, months out of season, drifted across the room.

My head jerked up, and I reflexively clutched Walther tighter until he cried out. The light in the center of the room was rapidly growing brighter, until its brilliance was almost unbearable. The light washed out the glow of the magic lamps and of the pentagram, filling Elerius's study like water filling a pond.

In the center of that light stood a figure. But it was not a demon. It was a saint.

An old bearded man, burning with light, leaned on a staff in the center of where Elerius's pentagram had been a few seconds before. But the pentagram was gone, the chalk dust blown to the far corners of the room. I noted wildly that the man needed the staff because one of his feet was missing its big toe.

Visions in dreams I had often heard of, and had been very glad that I had never been visited with such a vision myself. But I knew now the true, annihilating terror of actually meeting a saint. The air of the study was soft, perfumed with flowers, more gentle than the air of the enchanted valley in the Land of Magic, and all I could feel was primordial fear. Dazzled until I was almost blind, so overcome that my bones felt like water, I gazed with living eyes on Saint Eusebius, the Cranky Saint.

He rapped his staff hard, and the tower swayed around us. "What do you think you're doing, young man?" he rasped out, glaring at Elerius with a fierce frown. I would have whispered a prayer of gratitude that the saint was angry with Elerius, not with me, but somehow I couldn't pray to someone who was so palpably right in the room with us. "Thinking of yourself again," the saint declared, "and of no one else! This kingdom belongs to my spiritual daughter, who bears my name in religion, and I do not want a demon in it!"

Elerius staggered backward, clutching a chair for support. The times I had met a demon I had thought there could be nothing more terrifying. I had been mistaken. The supernatural power of good was just as overwhelming as the supernatural power of darkness, and one could not even console oneself that that power was ultimately wrong. If there was any evil in the room, it was in us.

Elerius's face was completely white, but still he managed to gasp, "How did you get in here? This castle is protected by powerful spells, against dragons, against—"

The Cranky Saint interrupted him with another sharp rap of his staff. "I am not affected by your natural magic. You have certainly been taught, young man, that magic is only effective in this world—and let me tell you, it is well past time for you to start thinking about your soul's welfare in the next!"

I fell to my knees, pulling Prince Walther down with me. "This kingdom doesn't belong to anyone's daughter," the boy mumbled, stubborn even in terror. "It belongs to me."

The saint swung toward us, and I pressed my face against the floor. Walther, half under me, must have been nearly stifled. The saint said, somewhat more mildly, "I think, Walther my son, your destiny lies elsewhere. My spiritual daughter may not always be as obedient as I would wish, but she does try to follow the path of goodness, unlike some people, and I intend her to rule here."

My eyes squeezed shut, in fear, in reverence, in reaction to the blinding force of the light pouring from the saint. "Dearest Lord," I murmured, wishing I had, even once, asked Joachim for the correct way to address a saint, "I thank you for your mercy, your benevolence, your answer to my poor prayer—"

"Call no one Lord but God," the saint snapped, but then his voice softened for a moment. "Your prayers are not unheard, my son, but it is above all two others who have reached me with their constant imprecations: Bishop Joachim, and the woman who has taken the name of Sister Eusebius."

Elerius, half hiding behind a chair on the far side of the room, peeked out and said, "You can't keep me from summoning a demon. That would violate human free will."

"It would do nothing of the sort," said the saint with a snort. I lifted my head—I could just bear to look at him as long as his eyes were not fixed on me. "Don't you wizards learn anything about metaphysics? Certainly we allow you to make your own decisions, even damn your own souls if that is your determined choice. But if humans call for our aid, of their own will, it is certainly within our powers to respond. Or," and he glowered until I, in Elerius's position, would have used a spell to sink bodily into the floor, "did you think that demons could be summoned, but that humanity was somehow immune from the influence of saints?"

"Well, no, Your Sanctity," muttered Elerius, eyes averted, with no more idea of how to address a saint than I had. "But I thought—"

"I do not care what you erroneously thought," announced the saint with another snort. "I found you here in the process of breaking the most solemn oath you could imagine—and the detail that you had not yet spoken the words does not make it any less solemn! Perhaps that is all that I should have expected from you—although I hope you do know it is within the power of your will to seek the good! I must say, I was very disappointed with your conduct at Daimbert's funeral. Instead of reverently commending his soul to God, all you could think of was asserting some claim of worldly authority, completely disrupting a sacred ceremony!"

"But Daimbert wasn't dead!" Elerius protested, sweat running down his face.

"You didn't know that," the saint shot back, "and, indeed, you hoped he was. Do not try to deny it! Do you think I didn't know your inmost thoughts, your wicked hope that if he did not intend to help you he would be killed? No, you are clearly not one to be trusted. Therefore I intend to keep this castle safe from demons until my spiritual daughter can reclaim it. You may stay here as long as you like, but I shall be watching! Any further attempt of yours to summon a demon here, in defiance of the oath you should have sworn, will utterly fail.

"Beyond that—" and he spun toward me again with another rap of his staff "—you are left to your own devices. I may have helped you and guided you a few times in the last few weeks, Daimbert, my son, but you are now approaching a difficult test. Demons I can save you from, at least demons summoned by Elerius, but I cannot save you from yourself."

I made an affirmative mumble, wondering wildly what he could mean—did he think that *I* was about to summon a demon?

"As for all this nonsense about running your wizards' school," the saint continued, "I have not the slightest interest in any of it. Work that out if you must, but set yourself above all, all three of you, to work out your souls' salvation! And be assured that you shall do so with absolutely no demons here."

Strong winds swirled around the Cranky Saint, even here in Elerius's tightly-sealed study, lifting his gray beard and whirling his cloak as he began to glow even more brightly. Elerius on the far side of the room had buried his face in his arms. Another enormous crack rent the air, and even through my eyelids I could see the great burst of light that accompanied the saint's transit from this world into the world of the supernatural.

And for a second, in spite of all my terror in his presence, I felt a tearing sense of loss. I had, for a few moments, been in the presence of supernatural good, and the ordinary world reasserting itself around me, material, neither good nor evil but fundamentally confused, was achingly empty without that goodness.

But I had no time to consider the sensation, for as soon as the saint disappeared Elerius's magically-locked window flew open, and I found myself plucked from the floor and Prince Walther wrenched from my grasp. My own spells were completely ineffective. I was catapulted through the air, sailing away from the castle far faster than I could have flown myself—even faster than Naurag could have flown.

The Ifrit's bronze bottle was still heavy in my pocket—not that his power could ever be even slightly comparable to that of a saint. My dazzled eyes blinked hard, trying to readjust to the darkness through which I flew. I was able to identify the army's encampment ahead, toward which I was speeding. The fire around which the kings had taken counsel was still burning, though low now, and only a few soldiers waited there, leaning on their spears.

The saint's power let me go then, leaving me feeling even more naked and alone than when he disappeared. I dropped the final thirty feet under the power of my own magic, to land next to the startled guardsmen.

It was only then that I realized that my leg was completely healed.

II

As the exalted savior of the western kingdoms, I had been given my own tent. There I lay awake for hours, missing Naurag's comforting warmth, even missing Maffi, next to whom I had slept on the whole trip back from Xantium, and feeling less like an exalted savior than I ever had in my life.

A miracle had been worked on my behalf, a miracle I didn't dare tell anyone about, but which made me feel that everything I did from here on had better be worthy of such a great concession. Joachim I could have talked to about the saint, but the bishop wasn't here. I rolled over for the dozenth time, trying unsuccessfully to find an angle where I

could close my eyes without seeing the overwhelming burning goodness—and irritated frown—of the Cranky Saint.

The dawn reveille woke me from an uneasy doze. I rolled
out of my tent and nodded in response to the respectful
greetings of the guardsmen, wondering how even more
respectful they would be if I told them I had been talking to
a saint. The early morning sky was dark and lowering, heavy
with stormclouds.

I shivered, looking around the encampment. The rows of
tents and banners stretched far in all directions. Knights were
scrambling from their tents, rubbing their eyes and shivering.
I had sent a message to King Paul when I got back last night
that Elerius would not listen to reason, but I was afraid the
kings would take that as an excuse to start the war at once. If
I couldn't find some way to stop it, the brute strength of
thousands of men would be thrown against the spells of a
handful of wizards. Even if Elerius wasn't demon-assisted, I
felt a queasy certainty who would prevail.

Unless— Unless I could find some way to fight Elerius's
undead warriors without involving human soldiers. I leaned
against a flag pole, tapping my foot and thinking hard. I had
never tried making any such warriors of my own, had never
before even contemplated doing anything of the kind, but I
might—might—be able to do so. My predecessor as Royal
Wizard of Yurt had once made a creature from dead bones
which would move of its own volition, and I still had his
notebooks.

This thought cheered me enormously, until I remembered that Elerius, in happier times, had once visited me in
Yurt and systematically read through those very notebooks.
He would thus be able to find any flaw in the magic propelling the creatures I made, and then dismantle them—after
all, even *I* had been able to improvise a way to stop my predecessor's monster, after it had killed him.

And it was no use trying the same approach I had used then on Elerius's warriors, because his would be substantially improved, imbued with some of the dark spells Elerius had picked up from eastern wizards during his years in the kingdom next to the mountains—even picked up from Vlad. Vlad's own monstrous creations had eventually been stopped, when they had showed up in Yurt years ago, but Elerius would have had ample opportunity to develop spells to overcome any weakness there as well.

No use, then, matching him spell for spell, where I was bound to lose. My only chance lay not in dismantling his warriors, but rather in using entirely different magic to make even better warriors of my own.

And I had just had an idea.

King Paul was drinking tea from a tin mug when I found him. "Do we have any alternatives, Wizard?" he asked me soberly. "If Elerius won't agree to stop this war, do we have any choice but to start it?"

He was not quite so eager, in the early morning's chill light, to start killing people as he once might have been. Nothing like facing real bloodshed, I thought, to make a restless young king rethink the fun and glory of going to battle—not to mention the responsibility of being treated as the chief king among them all. Now I just had to make sure that the bloodshed he was facing in his mind stayed hypothetical.

"I have a plan," I said with more confidence than I felt. "I'm going back to Yurt today, to look at my books, but I think I can make some soldiers that will match those inhuman creatures of Elerius's. If the unliving destroy each other first, it should make things substantially easier for the living."

Paul gave a sudden grin, though his emerald eyes remained serious. "I knew you would find a way to stop renegade magic!" He offered me a rather stale piece of bread, all he was having himself, which I wolfed down. "You didn't really return from the dead, did you?" he added thoughtfully. "This was all a ruse, though I must say a very good one!"

"Have you been talking to Gwennie, sire?" I asked though a mouthful of dry crumbs.

The king poured me a mug of scalding tea. "She told me one or two things about your trip, after you left for the castle last night," he said stiffly, not looking at me. The lovers' reunion, I thought, must have hit a snag—doubtless the same snag that had hung up Paul's original proposal, to say nothing of Gwennie's justifiably wounded feelings at knowing that the king had followed up his proposal to her with one to the Princess Margareta.

"But how long will you need to be in Yurt?" he asked then, putting the fate of the western kingdoms firmly ahead of his own love-life. "I can stall the other kings for a day or so, but some of them—especially Lucas—are pretty hot-headed. And if the kings who already tried to face the undead monsters get into a quarrel over their manly courage with those who arrived later, I don't trust them all not to start fighting each other. That would certainly help Elerius!"

"I'll be back tonight," I said, swallowing the last of the tea and feeling more confident by the moment. It must have been twenty-four hours since I had last had something to eat—facing a saint was always bad enough, but I had had to do so on an empty stomach.

And tomorrow evening the truce I had sworn to Elerius would be up, and I could try attacking him with the Ifrit— assuming, of course, I figured out how to do so in the meantime.

"Then I'll see you tonight," said Paul and grinned again. "It's good to have you back, Wizard."

But I didn't leave at once after all. I had just lifted into the air to start flying inland, intending to stay well away from the castle where Elerius's magical defenses kept flying spells from working, when I spotted something purple, flying fast toward me out of the cloudy eastern sky.

Where could Naurag have possibly gone? The last I had seen the flying beast, he had been with Maffi and Hadwidis, being closely observed by several curious knights. He had flown so far and so fast on our trip west from Xantium that I had thought to leave him here today, but it looked as if he had gone somewhere on his own.

Quickly I shaped a far-seeing spell, and then realized it wasn't Naurag after all. It was an air cart. And riding in it were my wife and daughter.

I laughed out loud with surprise and joy. I should have known that the two of them would want to join me, for all my firmly telling Theodora last night to stay safely in Caelrhon. Antonia had become quite proficient in the spells that commanded the cart, during her trips back and forth between Yurt and the cathedral city. My search for creatures out of the old magic could wait a little longer.

But as I flew to meet them, I realized something was wrong. Theodora was gesturing emphatically, but not toward me. The air cart had altered direction, and its wing beats were no longer taking it toward the kings' encampment.

Instead it was heading straight for the castle. And it was picking up speed.

My insides went cold as I madly doubled my own speed. I tried shouting encouragement, but my words were carried away by the wind. Agonizingly slowly, I drew closer, but not close enough. The air cart flew on steadily, its head with its unseeing eyes and wired jaws held high. With my far-seeing spell I could tell that both Theodora and Antonia were trying new commands to regain control of the cart, but it was no longer listening to their spells. Theodora looked down, over the cart's side, but they were several hundred yards up, much too far to jump, and neither of them had an entirely reliable grasp of flying spells when they were under pressure.

That cart was governed by school spells, and the world's greatest practitioner of school magic was drawing them toward him. I had faked my death in the first place to avoid something just like this, but it appeared I had made everyone sad needlessly, only to have Elerius use my family as a pawn in the end.

What would he *do* to them? My imagination provided half a dozen horrible answers, from painful dismemberment to killing them outright and using their dead bodies to make new warriors. And he wouldn't even have to carry through with any of it—all he had to do was threaten. At this point a demon was unnecessary for his victory. In five minutes I would be back at the castle, promising any assistance he wanted and giving him the Ifrit, just to assure my family's safety.

But then I heard a trumpeting call. Someone else had joined the chase. Not Whitey and Chin, doubtless still snuggled down in their blankets. Not any of the warriors, itching to fight but with weapons useless against wizardry. It was Naurag.

The purple flying beast chased after the air cart, faster than I could fly, his wings beating mightily. And as he flew he called.

And the air cart hesitated. It responded to school spells, but the cart was the skin of a flying beast, and the call of its own kind was even stronger than the spells that the original wizard Naurag had shaped to control flying beasts and air carts. The purple flying beast trumpeted again, whether in warning, in greeting, or even in yearning I did not know. Did he even realize the cart was not alive?

But it didn't matter. Caught between summons to fly in opposite directions, the air cart came to a dead stop, hovering. Thirty more seconds, and I dropped into it, between my wife and daughter.

"I'll block Elerius's spell," I gasped even as I hugged them both. "Try to get us out of here."

Naurag flew around and around the air cart, bringing his head in close as though sniffing it in surprise. But I had no time to wonder if my flying beast was startled to find the object of his amorous pursuit so unresponsive. Working fast, I started countering the spells coming from the castle. At this distance, even Elerius was not too powerful for me to oppose. Antonia again gave the magical commands, and the air cart turned obediently and started slowly toward the encampment.

For a moment Naurag hesitated, hearing that magical summons himself. But I couldn't rescue him too—it was all I could do to keep Elerius's spells from reaching the air cart.

Twenty yards we flew, forty, a quarter mile. Naurag turned toward us, flew a few strokes, stopped to look back over his shoulder, flew another short distance after us, and stopped again. As a living creature, he had a choice the dead air cart did not have, but the old wizard who had first created those spells had known flying beasts extremely well. Was Elerius going to fight us every inch of the way? I wondered as I muttered spells through clenched teeth.

But then the spells of summons stopped abruptly. Were we out of range, or had Elerius decided to conserve his energy for something even worse?

No matter. The air cart surged forward, then flew down in a stately spiral to land triumphantly in front of King Paul. Naurag came in next to us and started nuzzling the cart again. I jumped out and threw my arms around his neck, telling him what a fine and brave, what an excellent flying beast he was, and how many melons he deserved. Antonia was immediately interested, and sprang from the cart to look at Naurag from all sides and reach up to pat him.

But Theodora, climbing out more slowly, just took my hand a little shakily, with only a faint curtsey toward the king. She did not burst into tears, which I might have done in her place—in fact I felt like sobbing now myself in relief.

I turned to King Paul. "Excuse me, sire," I said, my voice unsteady. "I had hoped to be well on my way by now, but I'm afraid I've run into a bit of a delay. It may be tomorrow before I'm back from my trip—because I'm going to wait a little while to leave."

Paul nodded, a bit wistfully, but then after a few seconds straightened his shoulders and said, "Of course, Wizard," in hearty tones. "I should be able to keep the rest of the kings from getting too restless for at least another day."

And with my arms around Theodora and Antonia I went off to try to find a quiet spot in the bustling camp to talk to them, but mostly just to hold onto them.

III

I flew on Naurag toward Yurt, my heart lifting at knowing I was going to see the kingdom again after all. The flying beast, carrying me rapidly eastward, seemed to be trying to convey the suggestion that he had never been the slightest bit interested in a dead air cart. Autumn colors had come on while I was in the East, and the hills over which I passed were tinged with red and golden, almost luminous on this cloudy day. The queen would be surprised at my return from the dead; I just hoped she hadn't had my rooms cleaned out and given to someone else.

But even before consulting my books I had to check for something else: dragons' teeth.

It had been my first year in Yurt when a dragon attacked the castle on Christmas Day. I had managed to kill it, through the assistance of my predecessor as Royal Wizard and also a fair amount of sheer dumb luck. I had tried not to dwell on that hair-raising adventure, and time and other dramatic events—including my own recent experiences in the dragons' valley in the north—had pushed it toward the back of my mind, but the memories were still uncomfortably clear whenever I stumbled across them. One never forgets one's first dragon.

The stable boys had sawed up that dragon's carcass and buried it down in the woods below the castle, and in a few years the ivy and saplings had grown thick over it. But in the very oldest spells, dragons' teeth were the first ingredient for unliving warriors.

Or so I had heard, though nothing in my predecessor's notes had ever hinted at such an ingredient. He had never used them himself, nor, I believed, had Elerius. After all, dragons had not been found in the west for a very long time. Previous to the one I remembered so vividly, probably the last to visit Yurt had been the one who had eaten almost all of Saint Eusebius, leaving only the Cranky Saint's big toe.

But the primer of dark magic Count Basil had given me spoke quite confidently of dragons' teeth and the uses to which they could be put. The count was right that the only way I was possibly going to be able to oppose Elerius was to try a form of magic that he knew nothing about—now I just hoped I could get that magic to work.

A cold rainstorm met me as I flew, but I managed a spell to keep the rain off, and the darkest clouds had slid away from the sky by the time I saw the white towers of Yurt's royal castle on a hilltop before me. One would never know from the peaceful scene that, down in the cellars, was a hole that led to Hell—a hole dating from the same period as the dragon. An arching rainbow stood for a moment over the highest spire, which I took as an excellent omen.

The woods below Yurt's royal castle had begun to shed their leaves. I could catch glimpses of the castle's whitewashed outer walls through their branches as I hunted for dragons' teeth. The air bore the sharp, autumnal scents of rain, earth, and dead vegetation, but along the woods' edges, where fields ran up to the trees, late asters still bloomed.

It took me half an hour to find the right spot, probing magically for bones that might still bear some of the imprint of the great creature to whom they had once belonged. The first time I thought I had found the dragon's remains the aura seemed somehow wrong, and when I dug with a stick in an earthy mound, which my magic told me was full of bones, I brought only beef bones to light.

Beef bones? Some long-forgotten garbage pit, I decided, dropping the T-bone I had picked up and wiping my hand on my trousers. The dragon must be somewhere else.

I found it at last, the spot well away from the castle. Again I started digging with a stick, decided that was too slow and too undignified for a wizard, and recklessly used powerful spells to throw cubic yards of dirt aside at a time.

It had been thirty years, and there was not much left of the dragon other than the bones—even its scaly skin survived only in patches. But anyone coming across this skeleton, tumbled about as it was, dug up and chewed by foxes and badgers over the years, would have known that this was no garbage dump—unless the dump of monstrous giants. The massive ribs still survived at least in part, the long leg-bones, the thin, lightweight bones that would once have supported the wings, the long claws—and the teeth.

I tugged at the teeth, longer than my hand, working them loose while being careful to avoid the still-sharp points. I didn't like the way the skull's empty eye sockets looked at me, or how the dead jaws gaped, disarticulated. Even Elerius, I told myself, could not suddenly reclothe these bones with flesh and skin and put a living, ferocious brain back into this empty skull. But I still felt better once I had assembled a pile of teeth and could throw dirt back across the dragon's remains.

Now that I had the teeth, all I had to do was figure out what to do with them. Lifting them with magic so I wouldn't have to handle them any more, I headed up the hill and home.

Between my funeral, where everyone had spoken so well of me, and this homecoming to Yurt, where everyone in the castle, from the queen to the stable boys, was first stunned and then overjoyed, I could be in serious danger, the voice in the back of my head commented, of thinking myself something special. Even the flying beast received a great deal of attention and some of the melons he so richly deserved.

But I had no time to enjoy hearing how much everyone had missed me. It was already late afternoon, and I still had to figure out how to make warriors out of a pile of sharp and dirty teeth, how to control them, and how to get them to a castle two hundred miles away—all before either Elerius attacked the royal encampment outside his castle, or the kings got so restless they decided to attack themselves.

My study was disconcertingly neat, and for a moment I really did fear that the queen had been cleaning out my effects, until I remembered that Theodora had gone through my papers. She didn't seem to have removed anything, other than the old Master's letter naming me his heir, but she had demonstrated a flair for organization generally lacking amid her cloth scraps and pattern pieces in Caelrhon. All my books were shelved in rational order, my own notes placed tidily in folders in the drawers, and my pens and pencils lined up, ready for use.

I immediately destroyed the pristine order by piling my desk with books: old Naurag's register, Count Basil's primer of the gruesome magic of blood and bone, my predecessor's notebooks, even the books belonging to a long-dead ducal wizard who had died well before I even came to Yurt. I slapped the two volumes of *Ancient and Modern Necromancy* on top of the pile in the hope that a little school magic could give at least a semblance of calm and order to the old undisciplined magic—and to Basil's dark spells. The Cranky Saint could not foresee the future, I reminded myself, could not say for certain what I might or might not do, but he was clearly worried that I would find the enormous power of evil too tempting in my fight against Elerius, and I didn't want to take any chances.

Ancient and Modern Necromancy did indeed talk about dragons' teeth—I knew I had heard about them even before coming to Yurt as a young wizard. However, the reference was buried in a chapter on outmoded, messy practices interesting chiefly for their historic value, to show how far organized wizardry had come. No wizard today would ever dream of making undead warriors, the book announced dismissively, not like some of those misguided wizards back before the Black Wars. Besides, it asked rhetorically, wouldn't a wizard who had successfully killed a dragon for its teeth have enough power already that a restless army that would not listen to reason would be more of a hindrance than a help to him?

I didn't like the part about a restless army that would not listen to reason. My dragons' teeth were supposed to create a force to go up against Elerius, not wander dangerously through the Western Kingdoms. *Ancient and Modern Necromancy* pointed out in a final note that such warriors could not bear the light of the sun, which would decrease their dangerousness but also their utility. Oh, right. I knew that.

The queen herself knocked on my study door to ask me to accompany her into dinner, finding me with my fingers in my hair, staring at the much more upbeat discussion of dragons' teeth in Count Basil's volume. Here at least was a spell to transform and activate the teeth, which *Ancient and Modern Necromancy* had failed to provide, but he too was quite discouraging about the effects of daylight.

Dinner thoroughly distracted me, at least briefly, from thinking about dragons' teeth. A roaring fire kept the autumn chill away, the brass choir played, the steaming platters held the most delicious food I could remember eating for months, and the chaplain led everyone in a prayer of thanks for my miraculous safe return. "Next time, Wizard," said the queen with a smile and a twinkle in the emerald eyes she had passed on to Paul, "if you're planning to die, warn us that you're also planning to come back to life, so that we can skip the mourning period and go straight to the celebration!"

But as soon as I had finished dessert—raspberry pudding, my favorite—I rose to return to my books. So far I had managed to avoid having to give a speech, but I didn't want to press my luck.

I turned now to my predecessors' notebooks, thick with references to herbs I didn't know, and dotted with cryptic references to some other spells he had worked out, which I didn't understand either. But he had determined, over long months living by himself after I had replaced him as Royal Wizard in the castle, that it was possible to make a creature from old bones that could endure the sun. The more I read the more it seemed that I ought to be able to do this—improvise a combination of old herbal magic and eastern magic to make my own warriors who would fight Elerius's.

But I liked the idea less and less the more I read—even the most optimistic reading of Basil's spells suggested they would be almost uncontrollable, once given motive force, and I didn't want to have to kill Elerius's knights. Especially since they were really Hadwidis's knights.

No way to tell unless I tried. The castle was dark and silent as I made my way out into the courtyard, carrying a magic lamp. The light made a yellow stripe across the cobblestones that reached Naurag: asleep, floating a few feet in the air, his head under one wing.

But his head popped out as I approached. I rubbed his forehead and swung onto his back, carrying the dragons' teeth in a bag. "So far," I told him, "you've seen dragons, an Ifrit, and great armies. How would you like to watch me make dead creatures move without life?"

IV

Far from the royal castle I flew, up toward the high limestone plateau at one end of the kingdom. Cut into the plateau was the narrow bed of a river, flowing out of a cave sheltered by a grove of trees. That grove was both the home of a wood nymph and the site of the shrine of the Cranky Saint.

Neither was in evidence, late on a dark November night. The hermit who served the shrine always used to have a group of apprentice hermits, I remembered, but it was too dim to make out their huts. This valley still held some of the intense magical forces left over from the world's creation, which was why the wood nymph lived here—and which was why I hoped my spells might work if I tried them here. Leaving Naurag and the magic lamp at the edge of the grove, I lit up the moon and stars on my belt buckle and made my way cautiously between black rivulets of water.

I came around a beech tree's ghostly white trunk and saw it: the shrine of Saint Eusebius. On a rough stone altar sat his reliquary, shaped from gold into a giant toe. Even on a moonless night it glowed.

Down on my knees in front of the Holy Toe, I murmured a quiet prayer—quiet because I didn't want to wake up the hermit whose hut backed up to the shrine. I asked the saint, as fervently as I could, to keep his eye on the undead warriors I was about to make, and to destroy them and keep them from hurting anyone else if they ended up killing me at the moment of their creation.

Back under the night sky, a few hundred yards from the shrine, I shook the teeth out of the bag and considered them by lamplight. I doubted that God, looking at the muck from which He formed Adam, had felt anything like my reluctance. But this was no divine creation—and I was fairly sure that, if I asked Joachim, he would tell me that humans should not try to make themselves like God by doing what I was about to do.

Was this what the saint had warned me against? I didn't have much choice. I lined up the teeth and started on my spells.

Count Basil's spells worked spectacularly here in the Cranky Saint's valley. As I spoke the slow, heavy syllables of the Hidden Language, the teeth stood up, transforming themselves with startling speed, from something I had wrenched out of a dragon's dead jaws into something which—at least when viewed through shadows—looked almost human. I added the spells my predecessor had worked out, to keep such creatures from dissolving in the morning sun. As the magic infused them they all shook, but then went still again.

They stood silently as though watching me, unliving, unbreathing, unmoving but ready to move. I shivered and stopped my spells, leaning against a beech and watching them in return. Basil had run together in his primer the spell to shape the creatures and the spell to activate them, but his version of the Hidden Language was close enough to what they taught at the school that I had spotted the transition point and emphatically stopped when I reached it.

Almost indestructible, Basil's primer called them. But if mine were indestructible, then Elerius's warriors must be as well. Arming them would thus only make them dangerous to the castle knights, not to other creatures like them. And the whole point of risking my life and soul to make these creatures was to stop Elerius's.

Well, if they couldn't stop the undead warriors now guarding Hadwidis's castle, then maybe they could immobilize them. Primordial muck was going to be necessary after all.

I raised gobs of mud from along the edge of the river and slathered it all over my man-like dragon's teeth. But the mud would dry out. Stick-fast weed, that's what I needed. Down along the stream I went, looking with the lantern until I found a patch of weeds, still growing tangled and robust this late in the season. I plucked a double handful and hurried back, half-afraid the creatures would be gone, but they still stood silent and waiting. Again using magic, I ripped up the weeds and flung the pieces against the mud. A few words made the combination of leaves and mud not just sticky but very sticky—almost anything that touched it would be trapped.

Again I paused, catching my breath after working so much magic so fast. The next obvious step was to march them down to the coast, but I felt a deep reluctance to put them into motion. Maybe the Cranky Saint had good reason to worry about me—I couldn't help but think how much easier all this would be if I could just use a demon's power to blast Elerius and his castle to smithereens, rather than having all the mess of trying to make a viable army out of dragon's teeth.

A touch fell on my shoulder.

I leaped five feet and spun around, wildly shaping protective spells against— Against a ragged man with a long beard, leaning on a staff.

Not the saint, I realized after a terrified second, but a man younger by some fifteen hundred years: the hermit who lived here. He hadn't had the beard the last time I saw him, but that had been a long time ago. "Are you dead, my son?" he asked me pleasantly.

I leaned back against the tree and tried to slow down my heartbeat. "No. Or at any rate, not yet."

"You are the Royal Wizard of Yurt, are you not?" he continued. His voice was rough, as if little used, but he certainly was taking advantage of an opportunity for conversation. "Perhaps the account I heard of your death was mistaken. The duchess's daughter came to the shrine of the Holy Toe to pray for your soul, but my conversation with her was very brief, so I must have misunderstood."

If I survived, I made a mental note never to fake my own death again. It made too many explanations necessary. For the moment I skipped the explanations. "I'm here to work some magic. I was hoping not to disturb you."

"I see many curious things here," the hermit said gently, "from the wood nymph to visions of the saint to creatures that I am never sure later I really saw. So you must forgive me for wondering if I might now be seeing a dead man. Though I must say," frowning toward my warriors, "those are some of the strangest things I have seen lately."

"Me too," I agreed. I took a deep breath, preparatory to setting them into motion, then changed my mind. There was no way I could get them to obey me long enough to march obediently to Elerius's kingdom without getting into trouble along the way. I was going to need help. But in the meantime I had to lock them up safely. "Would it disturb you if I put them into the cave?"

Carefully, one at a time, I lifted the dragon's-teeth warriors and transported them inside the mouth of the cave from which the river flowed. I lined them up so that they did not quite touch each other, not wanting them stuck together when I came for them. I also didn't want them suddenly activated when I wasn't here—for all I knew Elerius might have tracked my movements and be planning to set them loose the moment my back was turned. I erected a mat of branches across the cave mouth, held it in place with a magic lock, then slowly pulled out King Solomon's golden signet.

The Ifrit in his bottle I had left behind in the royal encampment, not daring to expose him to the intense magical forces of this valley, but the seal I had brought with me. I didn't have any molten lead—mud would have to do this time. The hermit watched with interest as I pressed the seal into a dollop of mud and spoke the activating words I had learned from Kaz-alrhun. The mat of branches shivered and went stiff. As I stepped back, I could catch a glittering shimmer of magic from the mud. No undead warriors were going to get out of the cave through this entrance.

"As I recall," said the hermit with his gentle smile, "many years ago when I was still an apprentice hermit, the other apprentices and I offered you hospitality at our huts in the grove. Would you accept my hospitality again?"

Back when he had been an apprentice I had been a much less experienced wizard, having neither a flying beast nor an air cart, and the long flight back from the valley to the royal castle had seemed much too hard to attempt late at night. Or maybe I was just getting too soft in my old age to find appealing sleeping on a hut's dirt floor, with the cold, dank wind coming in the open doorway and only a crust to look forward to for breakfast.

"Thank you," I said, "but I could not dream of disturbing your devotions." It might be for the last time in my life, but I was going to sleep in my own bed in Yurt again.

But by midmorning I was back in front of Elerius's castle, talking again to the kings. "I've created my own army of undead creatures," I told them, leaving out the detail that I wasn't sure I could control them, "and as soon as I transport them here we can attack."

"What did you make them out of, old wine bottles?" asked King Lucas sarcastically. Reverence for the wizard who had miraculously returned from the dead seemed to be fading rapidly. I didn't dare ask Lucas whether his own royal wizard was back at the school or holed up with Elerius, but in either event he seemed to have lost any respect for wizardry he might once have had.

"I made them out of dragons' teeth," I said evenly, which at least silenced Lucas. I could hear several of the other kings asking each other in awestruck undertones how I could have possibly overcome a dragon—something I still sometimes marveled at myself. "And I'll be bringing them here this evening." At this I was pleased to note that several looked distinctly uneasy.

"Have you tested them in battle?" asked one grizzled old king, who wore a battered steel and leather helmet that might actually have seen service during the Black Wars.

Of course I hadn't. "Their enemies will not escape them easily," I said vaguely, trying to decide how I was going to get all the warriors down here without having them stick to every bush in half a dozen kingdoms. "With reinforcements on the way, I must ask you to wait until at least tomorrow morning to join the battle. Elerius would not listen to either reason or threats while he felt himself secure, but if my army can neutralize his we may still be able to avoid killing very many more of our men."

In the meantime, what was Elerius doing? His castle was silent and ominous. The sun had emerged today, but its rays were sharply slanted even in the middle of the day and did little to warm the chilly air. Leaving the kings arguing strategy, I went and found Hadwidis, sitting with Antonia, Theodora, and Gwennie beside her, staring toward the castle as though she could evict Elerius by gaze alone.

I sat down next to the runaway nun. "I saw your brother," I told her quietly. "He believes he is the heir to the kingdom, but he is learning magic with Elerius."

"Has he been turned to evil like that wizard?" she asked with a sideways glance toward me, then returned her eyes to the castle. A former nun, I thought, would still think in terms of good and evil. I wondered if she was regretting leaving the nunnery, in spite of her frustration with the restrictive atmosphere there, and in spite of the shove out the door the Cranky Saint seemed to have given her.

"He just seems like a serious boy," I answered, "who wants to learn magic but has a pretty clear sense of magic's limitations." I was most certainly not going to tell her about

Elerius's efforts to summon a demon—or his false agreement to swear, on Walther's life, not to summon one. The saint had definitely shown up just in time.

"This is going to be terrible for him," she said, not looking at me. "But I know now that the saint's purpose for me all along has been to make me reveal what I know, to keep my mother from going to her grave impenitent, with her sin unconfessed. She must already be realizing the magnitude of her error, seeing her former lover turn to evil."

I must say that I had never before considered that the queen's adultery might be the problem behind all this.

"Why did you never tell me about Maffi?" Antonia interrupted by asking from my other side.

I smiled at my daughter and gave her a squeeze. I really should be starting back toward the valley of the Cranky Saint with Chin and Whitey, in the hope that advanced wizardry students would do where I really needed another competent wizard. "I hadn't known you would ever meet Maffi," I said to Antonia, "and I'm afraid at some level I assumed he would always be the boy I had known before—don't tell him that!"

"He is not a boy," replied Antonia, in her best I-am-not-a-little-girl voice. "And he knows lots of magic. We were talking about different kinds of spells while you were gone."

He was going to be jealous that I didn't use him, but it couldn't be helped. I needed someone with whom I could easily work mind-to-mind because he had been trained in the same school I was. "You know," I said to Theodora over the girl's head, "I'm not sure this is the best place for any of you. An army encampment is a dangerous place for women at any time, and now that—"

Hadwidis broke in, still not removing her eyes from the castle. "I'm not leaving, Wizard, with an enemy in the castle where I should be queen. Gwennie shall stay with me."

I turned to look at her properly, the blond hair starting to grow in thickly now, the determined set of her jaw, and realized that she had picked up more on our trip to Xantium than some new clothes and blue eye-shadow. When she left the nunnery she was ready to become a bar-maid rather than let herself be made queen; now she was determined to take over the rule that was rightfully hers.

She might almost have heard my thoughts, for she added, "You helped me, Wizard, when I had no one to trust, and I shall not forget that." I noticed she was delicately passing over her attempt to seduce me—something I too preferred to leave in the past. "But I need no more help in reclaiming my rightful castle—no more than the help that I know Gwennie shall provide at my side. The easy solution, I knew, would be to marry one of these royal warriors assembled here and spend the rest of my life at his castle, but I want my own back. Get that wizard out, and I shall do the rest."

Gwennie gave me a worried glance. Worried about the girl's well-being, I thought, since Hadwidis didn't seem to be competing for King Paul, unlike most of the other well-born young ladies of the West. I shook my head and turned back to Theodora.

But she put a hand over my mouth before I could speak. "If a runaway nun can stay in an army encampment, a witch can too. I hope you weren't planning to tell us to take the air cart, and nearly get captured with magic again!"

"Well, no—" Time to stop stalling. I pushed myself reluctantly to my feet. "I'm going to need the cart anyway, to help get my undead soldiers here."

V

The air cart was scarred and battered, covered with the imitation dragon bites I had carved into it, up on the borders of the land of wild magic. I had to admit the fang marks were pretty authentic—looked like they'd cleaned up the blood, however. Still, the cart was ready to fly wherever I commanded it. Naurag, whose will was his own, was showing signs of incipient grumpiness, especially since he no longer wanted to have anything to do with the air cart, but a few gourds restored his good temper. With Whitey and Chin I flew off toward the kingdom of Yurt again, this time to get my warriors.

Elerius made no attempt to stop us. He must be watching my every move, I thought, but he was too far away to over-hear conversations, even with the best magic—besides, I told no one, even the young wizards, what we were doing. Let Elerius worry himself, I thought with jaw set, as to what I could possibly be planning.

With Naurag flying fast, in the hope of more gourds, and the air cart magically speeded up, we were able to reach the kingdom in only a few hours. The two young wizards had been properly obedient—at least most of the time—ever since learning that I was the old Master's choice as successor.

The saint's valley was as quiet as when I had left it the night before, and my seal across the cave entrance was intact. Elerius hadn't followed me here, then, I thought with relief, pushing aside any lingering doubts whether Whitey and Chin might secretly be thinking that Elerius would have made a better choice as the Master's heir. I had to trust them because I had no alternative.

When I used my palm print to release the magic lock and broke the dried mud seal, the warriors stood as I had left them, unmoving, unbreathing. That was a relief. I hadn't told my young helpers, but I had been turning over in my mind all the way up here the possibility that they might decide to come to life by themselves.

"Let's get these out one at a time," I said, "without letting them stick together. And no mock battles with them!" when I thought I saw an overly-enthusiastic expression on Chin's face. "These aren't toy soldiers."

Just what I needed, I thought. Supposed helpers who were

ready to play. But the two became very sober as they helped me transport the warriors out onto the grass at the base of the cliff. The creatures were short but solid, their arms heavy and powerful, their faces unfeatured except for lifeless eyes.

They stood in silent rows, absolutely motionless but giving the impression that at any moment they would burst into action, as ferocious and implacable as the dragon from whose teeth they were made. "By the way," I said to the two young wizards, as casually as I could when my own heart kept pounding hard, "after you graduate, don't give up when you discover how little you actually know. There will still be plenty of time to turn you two into half-decent wizards."

Now came the hard part. For this we needed Naurag and the air cart for more than comfort in flying. We weren't going to have enough attention to spare from the soldiers to be able to fly properly ourselves. Instead we needed all our magic to lift the soldiers.

We had to link our spells, working mind-to-mind. It was horribly difficult because we had to keep the warriors separated from each other. One tipped over while we were trying our first lift, and it rose covered with leaves and pebbles. Two swung too close at the second attempt and bonded firmly and irrevocably together. But at last, concentrating and sweating in the cold air, we had them all raised up about thirty feet, in a reasonably stable configuration, and started the long flight back toward Elerius's kingdom.

As I gritted my teeth, willing the dangling warriors to remain together, the wind to remain gentle, and the student wizards to stay attentive, I thought I saw one of the warriors blink.

No. Impossible. My imagination. I bit back an exclamation that would have broken the others' concentration and ended up with all the warriors tangled in the brush below. The creatures' stares were all blank and unseeing. I steadied my breathing, never letting up on the spells, and hung on tight to Naurag's neck.

We flew slowly, avoiding villages and castles, staying far enough up that the creatures did not become tangled in the trees, low enough not to tax our thinly-stretched lifting spells any further than we had to. Twice I could have sworn I saw from the corner of my eye one of the warriors blink, as if the magical currents within the hermit's valley had somehow brought it to life. But each time that I spun around to stare, aghast, I saw nothing but a stiff, unliving creature, and Whitey and Chin gave no sign of seeing anything unusual.

It seemed as though I had been flying back and forth over this route dozens of times in the last few days. This time was the hardest. The clouds overhead became lower and darker all afternoon, leaving only a thin clear area off to the west, where the sky toward evening turned as green as the sea. It had still been morning when we left for the valley; and now, four hundred miles later, we arrived in darkness.

We set the warriors down carefully at the inland edge of the army encampment, away from the castle. I didn't dare go any closer, for fear that Elerius might again try to seize control of the air cart. Soldiers with flaming torches came out to stare and exclaim over what we had brought.

Whitey and Chin collapsed where they stood. It was almost a physical relief to break contact with their minds, which had struck me all day as sloppy and greasy. But as I leaned against Naurag's flank I realized I was not through yet. I still hadn't worked out how I was going to control the warriors, but they had better be out in front, ready to march in the vanguard, because I very much doubted I could get them to detour in an orderly way around the camp, and I didn't even want to think about them, alive, marching through its center. With no energy to try more than one at a time, I slowly started moving the warriors through the air, over the royal encampment, to set them down in a line facing the enemy.

I had to work fast, before the last of my own strength

went. If there were any chance they were going to come to life during the night, then even more reason for them all be on the same side of the camp, the side toward Elerius.

From the corner of my eye I caught motion, a small, slim person running toward me. "Let me practice my lifting spells," said Antonia. I nodded, concentrating too hard to speak, and she immediately began, using the same skills she had used on a volleyball in the castle courtyard, in a distant time that could have been years earlier. Teeth set in her lip, she lifted one of the warriors, carried it through the air in a great arc a quarter mile long, over the soldiers and horses and tents and watchfires, and set it down on the camp's opposite side, on the edge of the trampled no-man's territory. She gave me a quick grin and started the spells for another. After a moment I realized she was moving hers faster than I was moving mine.

"They're impressive, Wizard," said King Paul behind me, which made me jump. But it was good, I thought as I nodded to him, for the commander of this camp always to know what was going on in it. "Dragons' teeth, you said? They're almost like—you remember that time." I did indeed. "But why are they so still?"

"Not activated yet," I said shortly.

Antonia was now experimenting with two warriors at a time, carefully keeping them spaced so they didn't stick together. I gave up trying to help her and just took deep breaths.

"Well," said Paul, looking out toward Elerius's castle, "I've told King Lucas and the rest that they can expect to attack at dawn. Do whatever you need to do to get these creatures activated, and I'll match your magical monsters against any-one's!"

He turned his back on the castle and the warriors then, his head cocked to listen to a distant challenge; it sounded as if someone had just ridden into the camp. The king hurried off to investigate. But I had no time to wonder who it was or what message he might bring. In the flare of the torches I was quite sure I had just seen one of my creatures move.

A quiet voice spoke beside me, Theodora. "That one's trying to wake up."

I was so tired that for a moment my mind went blank. Would a paralysis spell work? Would I have to disassemble it altogether? If it woke up would it bring all the rest of the warriors to life?

It stopped twitching abruptly. Startled, I checked with magic. It had a very tidy if rather unorthodox binding spell wrapped around it.

"There!" said Theodora. "Now aren't you glad you didn't send the two of us away?" Sometimes it was very useful being married to a witch.

I hugged her, weak with relief as well as exhaustion. "Then as long as you're here, could you help Antonia and me shift the rest of these?" which really meant, help Antonia. "And for God's sake, stay back out of their way!"

In a few minutes we had finished moving the last one. Antonia told me she had checked, and none of the others were showing any signs of life. I was too tired to do anything but take her word for it. "First thing in the morning," I said, "we will give them life, and we'd all better hope they charge in the right direction."

There was a murmur behind us, and I turned to see, picking their way through the tents by torchlight, King Paul, accompanied by the bishop.

The bishop! For a moment I was too delighted to do anything but gape. Joachim had been my best friend for years, even before I met Theodora, and when I decided to oppose Elerius it had been with the bitter knowledge that I might never see him again. And though he might never know it, according to Saint Eusebius it had been in part the bishop's prayers that had brought the saint to the castle just in time to save Elerius's soul and my life. "Good to see you, Joachim," I said, too overcome to be able to produce anything beyond a platitude.

But he, much less disconcerted than I, stepped forward and seized me in a hard embrace. "Thank God we are together again!" he said. "Don't ever pretend to die again, Daimbert, without first warning me!"

"I've tried to tell him the same thing," said Theodora.

"And you," he said to her with a smile, "don't leave the cathedral again without warning me either. One minute you and Antonia were safely under the Church's protection, and the next I knew one of my priests told me you had gone running out and were seen flying away in the skin of a purple winged creature!"

"We had to come help him," said Antonia. "Do you see all those warriors over there? I put them there myself!"

The bishop contemplated them thoughtfully. Arms upraised, mud and weed stuck all over their thick bodies, they waited for the command to attack and kill. Joachim was going to chide me for making creatures of war, for presuming on the creative powers of God. I just knew it.

But when he turned toward me again, deep eyes shadowed from the firelight, it was to say, "So was it to learn the secret of making these that you disappeared?" I looked for a frown and it wasn't there. Instead he was smiling again. Some time, I thought, I might have to explain to the bishop that just because he liked and respected me, he didn't have to assume that everything I did was for an excellent reason.

But not now. "Well, in some ways they were an afterthought—" I started to say. First I had been going to use the Dragons' Sceptre against Elerius, then the Ifrit, and dragons' teeth had been my fallback position when nothing else worked. But it was too complicated, and I was too tired. "Yes, they represent my secret plan."

"And Elerius will be very surprised in the morning!"

added Antonia.

"Could you shrive us all at dawn, Father, before we go into battle?" Paul asked quietly.

We started walking slowly back into the center of camp. One of the knights from Yurt hurried up to say that a tent had been made ready for the bishop. Had he ridden here alone, I wondered, without any of the priests and soldiers who were supposed to accompany a bishop everywhere? I would ask him in the morning.

But all the plans for what we would do in the morning were wrong.

Suddenly there was a shout behind us, and exhausted as I was I spun around, fearing to see my soldiers springing to life and running wildly across the trampled earth.

It was worse. Elerius hadn't waited until morning. His own unliving warriors were upon us now.

part nine ✥ the princess

I

THE TRUMPETS SOUNDED behind me in the camp, and men poured out of the tents, falling over each other as they scrambled into their armor. Shouting, clanging, trying to find their fellows by torch light when sleep still lay in their eyes, the armies of the west prepared for battle. The war cries of a dozen kingdoms rose above the tumult.

Elerius's unliving warriors, which I had last seen on a deserted island offshore from the great City, marched toward the camp. They were made of hair and dead bones, and their only features were their glowing eyes. Ungovernable and violent as when Elerius first made them, they were only a hundred yards away and moving inexorably toward us.

What was that spell of Basil's? And *where* was his book? In my pocket? In the air cart? Able to see nothing but those advancing warriors, I wildly slapped my pockets, found the book, realized it was going to be impossible to read Basil's handwriting by torch light if I couldn't stop shaking, yelled for Whitey and Chin—

And heard a voice speaking next to me, words almost but not quite the Hidden Language that I knew. At those words, all the dragons' teeth warriors began to twitch.

Maffi stood beside me, concentrating hard on creatures made with no magic he had ever learned and giving them movement. All but the one that Theodora had bound spread their arms and stamped, but they made no move to attack. Maffi added another spell, which made the creatures whirl their arms wildly but still stay where Antonia had put them.

I blinked and was suddenly calm again. The sound of Maffi's words had nudged my panic-stricken brain. If Elerius had carefully created his warriors without the use of school magic, so that they could advance across the deserted fields where he had stopped all school spells, then Basil's spells should work here as well. I rattled off his activating spell, and the dragons' teeth surged into motion.

A war cry came almost in my ear, and I whirled. King Paul, riding his stallion, had gathered the cavalry around him. Horses reared, and drawn swords flashed in the firelight. In a remarkably short time, the knights of the western kingdoms had armed and were ready to face whatever Elerius sent toward us.

"No! Wait!" I cried. "Sire, listen to me! Don't charge—not yet!"

I couldn't see the king's face behind his helmet, but he pulled up his stallion at once. "Daimbert prepares the way for us!" he yelled over his shoulder. "Wait for Daimbert's signal!"

That wasn't exactly what I meant, but at least they stopped, the sweating horses jostling each other, as Paul's command was shouted back rank by rank through the army.

My warriors—with one exception—were off with Basil's spell, heading without anger or fear, only emotionless violence, toward the monsters Elerius had made. Theodora said something, and the last of my warriors, freed of her binding spell, sprang after the rest. Thuds, dull clangs, and scrapes marked the meeting of forces, but creatures without mouths cannot shout.

"My spells for automatons work but poorly on these creatures," commented Maffi in disappointment.

Better than anything of mine worked when my brain wasn't functioning at all. "Thank you for what you did," I said, attempting, without much success, to speak normally. The field before us was dark away from the torch light. "Can you see if they're destroying each other?"

He shook his head. "I perceive them not." I tried a magical flash of light, but Elerius must still have his defenses against school magic very well in place, for the spell dissolved ten yards from where we stood, doing little more than deepen the shadows around the undead warriors.

I glanced over my shoulder. Most of the knights had lifted the visors on their helmets and were watching me intently, expectantly. Clearly to stay quietly here, waiting to see if any of the creatures Elerius and I had made would come this way, was not an option for Daimbert, glorious savior of the west.

Antonia and Hadwidis would be back in the crowd somewhere. I didn't need to see their faces to know they would be watching just as expectantly. "Come on," I said to Maffi, convinced I was heading toward my own death but almost too tired to care. "Let's go find out."

I stumbled with exhaustion and had to lean on his arm as we started across the rough field. Unable to fly in the area governed by Elerius's spells I realized how easy magic had always made life for me. Normally I didn't worry about walking into danger—I could always fly out. But now if Elerius's warriors broke through mine, or he took control of mine with his spells, Maffi and I would have no recourse but running, and I didn't think I would be able to run very far.

Close at hand I heard a rapid clicking noise—Maffi's teeth were chattering. I looked toward him, but he merely shrugged with one shoulder. "It is colder than I had anticipated in your western realms," he said, his flashing smile unconvincing.

The creaks and clanking ahead of us grew quieter rather than louder the closer we got—maybe there was something wrong with my ears. There seemed to be something wrong with my eyes too, for even as we approached, slowly, cautiously, ready to flee at any moment, I couldn't resolve individual warriors, but saw only vast untidy masses of darkness. The night air blew damp and piercing toward us.

Maffi stopped, and I stopped with him. "They are no longer fighting," he said quietly.

Had they formed their own monstrous alliance, the voice in the back of my mind asked, to destroy their makers, both Elerius and me? It took a moment of terror and despair to realize what had happened. But then I felt a second's wild exhilaration. My plan had worked.

Writhing on the ground, pressed as tight together as welded pieces of steel, were Elerius's warriors and my own. His, stuck fast to mine, were still trying to march toward King Paul's army. Mine, powered with Basil's spell, were trying just as determinedly to march toward Elerius's castle. The net result was mounds of creatures kicking ineffectively but not—at least for the moment—about to kill anybody. Use of the stick-fast weed, an old bit of simple magic out of herbal lore, something I had picked up years ago when a very new graduate of the school, had stymied both Elerius's carefully-wrought spells and my own much more ad hoc dragons' teeth.

"We'll have to dismantle them," I said, suddenly feeling confident again. "What do you use when you no longer need an automaton?"

"Daylight," said Maffi firmly. "These spells require daylight."

I actually doubted that they did, but I could see his point. "Maybe we could erect some sort of magical shield around them for tonight," I suggested uncertainly, "if such a thing would work here." I didn't want Elerius coming out after I was asleep and finding a way to separate them and reactivate his.

But putting any further activity off until morning was suddenly not even to be imagined. From Elerius's castle came war cries and the harsh clang of swords being beaten against shields. Elerius might no longer be opposing us with undead warriors of hair and bone, but he had plenty of living warriors of flesh and blood.

I spun around and shouted for King Paul. I tried magically amplifying my voice, but Elerius's spells against magic kept my spells from working. It didn't matter. Paul heard me.

In a few seconds Maffi and I were surrounded by the warhorses of our army. Men gripped flaring torches in mailed fists as they galloped toward the enemy. The horses screamed and reared to avoid us and the mounds of unliving warriors, and for a moment iron-shod hooves flashed by our unprotected heads. Then the horses jostled, found their footing, and shot away toward the enemy.

I put my hand over my eyes. I didn't need to see this. Distant sounds of battle indicated that the armies had met. The Black Wars, the wars that had so sickened the West that there had been nothing been minor skirmishes between kingdoms ever since, were going to fade in comparison to the massive blood-letting about to take place.

After a moment I said to Maffi, "We're going to have to move or drag these warriors further from the castle, somewhere we can get a little light. Did Kaz-alrhun teach you any lifting spells that Elerius might not be expecting?"

Maffi took a deep breath. "Perchance I can work without light. If I am to try spells, let them be the spells to deactivate an automaton."

The two masses of unliving warriors still struggled in each others' grip, so we stood well back as Maffi started mumbling spells. From the distant battle came what sounded like shouts of triumph among the screams and the clashes of metal on metal. Somebody must be winning, I thought dully, looking at the ground at my feet because it didn't seem worth looking anywhere else.

And that winning somebody, the thought struck me, should be the armies under Paul's command. Hope made me lift my head, though I still couldn't see anything. There were thousands of men in the army that had dedicated itself to my memory, whereas Elerius couldn't have fit nearly that many into his castle. He would not have been concerned about the size of his human army because it was supplemented by his undead warriors, not to mention his own spells and those of whatever wizards he had with him. But his magical warriors were out of action, and the forces he had erected against my spells worked equally well against his.

"Ha!" said Maffi suddenly, and one of Elerius's warriors collapsed into bits of stinking bone.

But, freed of the obstacle in its path, the dragon's teeth warrior against which it had been bound started forward again—marching this time not toward a foe, but toward the rear of Paul's army.

I stumbled after it, snatching at spells. As long as I could avoid school magic, *something* must still be working. Maffi had managed to disassemble something made by another wizard, made with spells that had only a tangential relationship to the magic he knew himself, and yet he had succeeded. Exhausted as I was, I ought to be able to deal with a warrior I myself had made.

The third almost-random series of commands in the Hidden Language worked, and the ferociously advancing creature stopped, quivered, and became nothing more than several long, razor-sharp teeth, lying in the dirt churned up by the cavalry.

"Let us coordinate our efforts, Daimbert," said Maffi, taking me firmly by the arm as though I were a recalcitrant student. I stood beside him meekly, working to remove the semblance of life from my warriors at the same time as he worked on Elerius's warriors. The two sets of creatures were not perfectly balanced—sometimes one of mine would start slowly pushing its way successfully forward, toward the clashing armies, and sometimes one of Elerius's would make a break toward the camp of the assembled kings. Scurrying around the writhing, dark mass of undead bodies, we were just able to stop those who threatened to escape and to break the spells that gave them motion.

It was excruciatingly slow, because our timing had to be perfect to destroy both warriors at once, and Maffi told me in disgust that no two of Elerius's creatures was put together precisely the same way—doubtless to foil somethng like what we were now doing. But somewhere in the back of my brain was the thought, which would have been joyful if I had had the energy to pay attention to it, that even Elerius's best spells could not stand against the combination of herbal and eastern wizardry.

We kept on working, slowly, carefully, knowing that if exhaustion made us sloppy we would not live long enough to get away. I tried to calculate when we might finish rendering all the warriors inactive, mine and Elerius's both, and reached the conclusion that it would be sometime tomorrow afternoon. "That can't be right," I thought, shaking my head, but felt too muzzy to try the calculations again. Besides, they might still give me the same answer.

Someone came racing toward us from the camp, surprising us so much in the middle of a spell that two warriors nearly got moving again before Maffi was able to bind them.

It was Hadwidis. "They've escaped!" she cried. "I saw them coming!"

"Who? What?" I managed to say from between parched lips.

"My mother and brother! I used that magic skull thing again to see what was happening in my castle, and I saw them slipping out through the postern gate! Come with me, Wizard! I have to go to them!"

I looked helplessly from her to Maffi, but the latter gave

me a shove. "I would rest a moment from these spells," he said. "Go, and we shall resume on your return." Hadwidis took my arm and almost pulled me across the broken land, toward the clash of armies.

But not quite toward them. She angled around the base of the castle, running tirelessly while I staggered along behind. The ground was rough, dotted with rocks and little streams that would have made for difficult going even in daylight, even it had not been heavily trampled by mounted men, but she led the way through the darkness in perfect assurance: this was, after all, her kingdom.

We were close to the castle now, whose dark walls rose sheer above us. Elerius was up in there—but he might not be able to see us magically with all school spells still blocked. A delicate stairway, only wide enough for one person, curved down the castle's side. Between us and that stairway, through the shadows, I could see two figures approaching.

Hadwidis skidded to a stop, abruptly shy. Almost she hid herself behind me for a second, though I couldn't imagine what protection or wisdom I could offer at this point. "Hello, Mother," she said stiffly.

The figures stopped abruptly, then the smaller one took a few steps forward—I would have guessed it was young Prince Walther, except that he walked erect, with no hint of a limp. "Who is there?" he said in a voice that would have been haughty had it not come out so high.

Her answer was low and expressionless. "Your sister."

"Hadwidis!" It was Walther after all. I could make out his features as he sprang toward us. "The saint has answered all my prayers! You're back to help me as I prepare to become king, and look! My leg is healed!"

The Cranky Saint had become *way* too active for my tastes, especially since he seemed more interested in making Hadwidis queen than in stopping Elerius's ambitions. I stood quietly aside while the brother and sister embraced, and she turned, awkward again, toward her mother. No one paid the slightest attention to me.

"You have left the nunnery?" the queen asked, her voice sharper than I would have expected from a woman being reunited with her daughter after years of separation. She was, as well as I could tell through the shadows, still a very attractive woman, much too well dressed to be scrambling around a muddy field at night. "Was leaving deliberate on your part," she added, "or did the abbess find your conduct unacceptable?"

II

A strained silence hung between mother and daughter for a minute, broken by the distant sounds of battle. But then Hadwidis laughed. "I'll tell you the whole story when I've got you safe," she said briskly, taking charge. "Come on! We've got to get you further away from Elerius while he's still distracted."

She took each by the arm and dragged them away from the castle, while I tried to keep up. "What do you mean," the queen demanded, breathing hard at the pace Hadwidis had set, "by saying you need to 'get us away' from Elerius?"

"He *sent* us away," provided Walther, "for our protection. Although I do think …" His voice trailed off without finishing the sentence. He still wanted to believe in Elerius, I thought, in spite of what he had seen, and that wizard must have given him some sort of innocuous explanation for why he had tried to summon a demon, but there were definitely doubts in the boy's mind.

"What—?" Hadwidis almost stopped for a moment, then shook her head and forced her mother and brother to redouble their speed. I started falling behind. Trumpets sounded from the field of battle. Rallying the cavalry, I thought—or sounding retreat.

But what could Walther mean by saying that Elerius had sent them away? The queen had once been—and presumably still was—his lover, and Walther was his son. Was he planning to destroy Paul's army, now at his very gates, by blowing up the entire castle?

In which case, I thought grimly, he would blow up a lot of young, misguided wizards along with it. And there was nothing I could do about it.

"You look quite disreputable, Hadwidis," commented the queen, panting in an undignified manner. "I do hope you are not about to tell me that you have become a camp follower for the invading armies."

"What's a camp follower?" asked Walther, but no one told him.

Instead Hadwidis laughed again. "Of course not," she said, leaving out of the story her brief plan to become a tavern wench in Caelrhon. "King Paul has treated me with every courtesy since I arrived here."

"King Paul? Is he the one commanding this invasion? If so, I need to speak with him at once."

"Excuse me, my lady, but I don't think you'll want to wade into that battle in search of him," I said, managing to catch up again. "Paul will be in the front ranks."

We all paused and looked a minute toward the torch-lit battle that still surged around the base of the castle. "Highly improper," the queen pronounced. "The life of a commander is more important to any war effort than some boyish dream of glory." I wasn't going to say so but I had to agree with her.

Hadwidis squinted at her mother through the darkness. The distant flare of torches beneath the heavy sky gave everything a lurid quality. "I hope," she said quietly, "that you are acting as Elerius's ambassador, come to offer terms of surrender. I don't know what he's told you, but he can't possibly resist much longer. After all, we have Daimbert on our side."

My name did not seem to register. Elerius had told his son about me, I thought, but perhaps he had not told the queen. Or else she did not deign to pay attention to a wizard she considered so much inferior to her own. She lifted her head with the same stubborness as her daughter and said, "I am indeed an ambassador, if any ruler survives to whom I might speak. But I come to offer terms for the *invaders'* surrender."

A slightly different story, I thought, than Walther's version that they were sent away for their own protection. I had a sudden doubt whether the queen was acting entirely on Elerius's behalf or might have some deep plan of her own.

Hadwidis, continuing to tug her mother forward, focused on a different issue. "Do not call these invaders," she said fiercely. "This is *my* army, for I am the rightful queen here!"

The queen started to say something and changed her mind. Walther looked wildly from one to another. But before any of them could continue the topic, they were interrupted by a great roar from the sky. Something streaked above us, flaming like a comet, then altered course and plunged straight down before us.

Right where Maffi and all the undead warriors had been. I stumbled forward, wildly calling his name, temporarily forgetting Hadwidis and her family. Had Elerius summoned a demon to destroy the one wizardly ally on whom I could rely?

But it was not a demon. It was the Ifrit.

Freed from his bottle, even more enormous than I remembered, he dropped from the sky surrounded by a sheet of flame, straight into the middle of where my warriors and Elerius's struggled against each other.

How had he gotten free? A great boom shook the land, and even through my fear I could feel the magical currents swirling madly, as powerful spells were broken up. I staggered backwards as scraps of hair and bone and broken shards of dragons' teeth exploded in all directions.

Then with another great roar, the Ifrit rose and shot away, toward the castle. He was loose but, for the moment, he had let me live.

I didn't have time to wonder about it. None of the bits that had flown by me had looked like pieces of Maffi. I groped forward cautiously. Off in the distance, the shouts from the battlefield had changed their tone. Behind me, their differences forgotten, the queen, prince, and princess of this kingdom clung desperately together.

Maffi lay flat in the mud, unmoving. But when I touched his shoulder he jerked and lifted his head, his teeth a white flash in a filthy smear. "Kaz-alrhun warned me that I might find your Western Kingdoms rather dull," he commented. "I must remember to chide him for this, for he was quite mistaken."

"That was the Ifrit," I said in amazement. "He destroyed all the warriors but left you untouched. All those spells we were working on—he dissolved them in five seconds!"

"And he is not done," said Maffi, gingerly pushing himself to a sitting position. "By the Prophet, I am glad I need not spend the next eighteen hours taking apart another's automatons!"

So his calculations on how long it would take had come out the same as mine. "What do you mean, he is not done?" I demanded.

Maffi lifted a muddy arm. "Look."

Again streaking the sky, the Ifrit had reached the castle. I wished desperately for a far-seeing spell and suddenly found that I had one. School magic was working here again.

Hadwidis, I thought, was not going to like it at all if the Ifrit destroyed her castle—and neither might the Cranky Saint. I held my breath, waiting to see the towers torn from the castle like a toy ripped apart by a peevish child. Even with a reliable spell working for me again, it was hard to see through the dimness, but the brightly-lit windows of the castle stayed solidly in place.

Instead, I saw the Ifrit's fiery shape abruptly shrink and pour in through one of the windows. The castle vibrated with a note like an enormous bell, swaying as though floating on a wave rather than built on solid rock. And then all the windows and doors were flung open.

The battle that had been raging at the castle's feet ceased. Had I been that close to the castle I would have been in total panic, but the blowing horns sounded as though they were giving rational orders.

Rational orders to get as far away from there as possible. In a second all the armies turned, Paul's and for all I knew Elerius's men as well, and galloped back toward the royal encampment at a furious pace.

The thundering hooves would be on us in just a few moments. With reserves of terror-driven strength I thought I had exhausted hours before, I half-lifted, half-dragged the royal family as fast as I could toward the safety of the tents and the still-burning campfires. Maffi on their other side helped pull them along.

"Did you know something like this was going to happen?" I shouted at him. "Were you experimenting with the Ifrit's bottle while I was gone?" But he seemed not to hear.

I turned back toward the castle once I was sure Hadwidis had recovered enough to be in charge again. With my far-seeing spell I could see people pouring both in and out of the castle's gaping doors—mounted knights jostled wildly to enter, but emerging were two dozen wizards.

I shouted to them, my voice magically amplified to boom over the broken and muddy field like the sound of the doomsday trumpet. "Get away from there! Escape while you still have your lives! Come to the camp, and you will be pardoned! It is I, Daimbert, who calls you!"

As long as I was supposed to have returned from the dead,

I thought with a small smile, I might as well get some use out of my supernatural status.

The next moment I had to lift myself into the air with the last of my strength, to avoid the army rushing toward me. I tried unsuccessfully to find Paul in the great confusion of armored men and horses racing below me. For all I knew they too thought they were obeying the call I had sent toward the young wizards.

Hovering, I looked again toward the castle and thought I could see the wizards, strung out in an untidy line, moving nervously across the broken, empty fields. Good enough. If they had once turned their backs on Elerius, they would not suddenly run again to him.

But where *was* Elerius, and how was he reacting to the Ifrit's destruction of all his defenses? For that matter, why hadn't the Ifrit just started killing everyone in his path the moment he broke free of the bottle?

It was all far too confusing for me to work out in my present state. But as if in answer to my question, just as I was ready to turn away and drop the far-seeing spell, light flared at the top window of a tower—Elerius's study. And out through the window shot the Ifrit, his body swelling to its normal enormous size the moment he was through the opening. In one great green hand he held Elerius.

And he threw him: threw him like a boy throwing a ball but far faster, far higher, so that he shot up and away and disappeared into the night sky.

The Ifrit turned, slapped his hands together as though satisfied, and flew directly toward me.

This was it, then. At least I had gotten Elerius out of the castle before I died, so maybe the teachers in the school would have some luck now tracking him down and capturing him.

I closed my eyes for a quick prayer and opened them again. But the Ifrit was now aimed in a direction that would, by a small measure, miss me. My own despairing readiness for death gave way to new horror, as I realized that he was not in fact after me. He was instead heading for the camp.

He and I reached it at the same moment. The camp was in complete chaos, as the men and horses who had fled from the Ifrit suddenly found him among them. His giant bare feet set down on top of tents as men dove for safety, and he strode among them, avoiding the fires but nothing else.

"I have fulfilled your commands, Mistress!" his voice boomed above me. "And I have come back for my bottle."

Mistress! Who could he be talking to? But in a second I spotted the person standing in front of him, not substantially taller than one of his green toes. I should have known. It was Antonia.

"Have you really fulfilled all my commands?" my daughter demanded, looking up with her braids tossed back over her shoulders. Tucked under one arm was the bronze cucumber-shaped bottle in which the Ifrit had been imprisoned. "You said I would get two wishes, and so far I don't think I've gotten more than one."

The Ifrit bent to scoop her up in one gigantic hand. She balanced easily, holding onto his thumb. "You may have freed me, little Mistress," he grumbled, "but you cannot change our agreement so easily! First, I destroyed all those undead warriors. That was one wish. Then I nullified the spells of the chief mage in the castle and expelled him from it. That was two wishes. And finally, I accomplished all this without killing anyone, not even the trickster mage who imprisoned me, whom I had sworn before God to rip into tiny shreds, so slowly that he would live far beyond the normal short span of you mortals, but so painfully that he would pray each day for death. That is three wishes."

"That wasn't a third wish," said Antonia briskly, her voice high and tiny compared to the Ifrit's. "It was a condition of the first two wishes. Now that you mention it, I guess you really *did* grant me two wishes, but I still see no reason to give you the bottle."

The furrows in the Ifrit's massive forehead deepened. "And I see no reason to refrain from killing the trickster mage, who I see is conveniently handy."

I would have yelled up to Antonia except that my voice didn't seem to be working. Besides, I didn't know what I should yell. I found Solomon's golden seal in my pocket and considered brandishing it, but it wasn't going to do a lot of good unless the Ifrit were already inside a bottle, which he most indubitably was not.

Antonia considered coolly. "All right. How about if we make the agreement this way. You grant me three wishes— the three you've already given me—the first two in return for freeing you from the bottle, the third in return for letting you keep it. But remember! Before I'll hand the bottle over, I'll have to have some assurance that you won't kill the wizard or anyone else here!"

"I have lived," the Ifrit growled, his voice as deep as the grumble of an earthquake, "since the earth was first formed, and yet you, a mortal whose life I could crush out in a second, dare ask me for assurances?"

"Yes," said Antonia. Her voice had gone up an octave, but she did not hesitate.

The Ifrit stamped one gigantic foot, scattering the soldiers who had started creeping closer, and brought his cupped hand up toward his face. A gigantic yellow eyeball glared at Antonia from only a few feet away. "I hope you are not next to tell me that you are from Yurt."

"Caelrhon and Yurt both," she said, pressing herself back against his fingers, as far from that eye as possible. "Aren't you supposed to protect and not harm people from Yurt?"

The Ifrit growled again, and his fingers twitched as though he really was about to crush her. But instead, after a second that seemed to last for hours, he nodded his massive head. "You are my mistress no longer. But I swear to you on the dread name of Solomon, son of David, that I shall not slay the trickster mage with the slow death he so fully deserves."

"Good," said Antonia. "After all, he's from Yurt too."

Slowly he lowered her back to the ground. From the corner of my eye I saw the young wizards who had been working with Elerius straggling into camp. Antonia hopped from the Ifrit's hand, then slapped the bronze bottle into it. "Good to meet you!" she called up, on her best manners.

The Ifrit did not return the courtesy. Instead, with a final great stamp of his foot, he launched himself into the sky, and shot away in a fiery blaze, streaking eastward like a comet across the dark sky until we could see him no more.

Theodora and I reached Antonia at the same time and dropped to our knees beside her. With four arms wrapped tight around her, she looked from one of us to the other. "Now aren't you glad I'm here?" she asked proudly.

III

All I wanted to do was sleep. Even asking Antonia how she had possibly been able to master the Ifrit could wait, though my bones felt like water as I thought about how close we had come to having an infuriated Ifrit destroy this entire corner of the Western Kingdoms. But the young wizards were all looking at me, their eyes round in the firelight. I noted that Evrard, Royal Wizard of Caelrhon, was among them.

I pushed myself to my feet with Theodora's help. Joachim appeared beside me and supported me with a strong arm under mine. The knights of the royal armies made a great circle around us. To my enormous relief I spotted King Paul among them, apparently unhurt. I had lost track of Hadwidis and her mother and brother, but they must be back in the crowd somewhere. With the bishop on one side of me and Theodora on the other, and Antonia standing proudly in front, I beckoned the young wizards forward.

They hesitated, some shame-faced, some trembling in fear. Evrard spoke at last, in a shaky voice unlike his normal good-natured tone. He had been my friend for years, and he seemed the only one of the wizards worried about me as well as about themselves. "Are you—are you dead, Daimbert?"

At this point I probably looked a lot like a walking corpse. But I shook my head. "I am alive as you"—surely something of an overstatement—"and indeed was never killed by the dragon." Elerius must not have told the wizards who had joined him that he knew my death was faked—an indication, I thought, of how little he trusted them, or still feared my potential influence. "But I would not be here were it not for Saint Eusebius." Better give credit where it was due.

Evrard looked back uneasily at the rest of the wizards, but he was the most senior one there, and the rest of them shoved and nudged him. "Well," he said with false heartiness after a moment, "we knew the Master intended you to head up the school after him, but Elerius told us that the old man must have been losing his judgment in his final months. Elerius was clearly mistaken if you've got an Ifrit and a saint working for you!"

"Also two witches," provided Antonia, politely including her mother in her boast.

"I'm sorry, Daimbert!" Evrard continued, his tone more genuine. "I must say I never thought of you in years past as a particularly good wizard. That's why I thought I'd better fol-low Elerius. I know now I was wrong!" he added as two of the other wizards poked him in the back. "Especially since you've overcome him! Is it too late to join you?"

They were all looking at me expectantly now. My next duty, I realized, was to find a diplomatic way to reintegrate these wizards into organized magic, in a manner that would make them realize the extent of their folly in allowing Elerius to create a rift in the school, which had almost led to a new outbreak of the Black Wars: only worse, because instead of stopping the fighting the wizards would have been abetting it. I also had to find a way to make the teachers of the school receive these properly penitent young wizards back, to start healing the rift Elerius had created.

I couldn't do it. I just couldn't do it. If I were the kind of wizard the old Master thought I was, I would have been able to start the diplomacy at once, in spite of my exhaustion. Instead I just shook my head. "You can't 'join' me," I said, having to force myself to speak above a whisper. "There are no more sides. There is only organized wizardry. You'll have to be penitent, and you'll have to ask the forgiveness of the masters of the school. Talk to the bishop. He'll explain it to you."

Theodora kept me vertical as I staggered off toward my tent—fortunately one of the ones the Ifrit's giant feet had missed. Whitey popped out of the crowd to say, "We're telephoning the school now, Master. Do you want to talk to the teachers first, or should we tell them the news ourselves?" But I waved him away, too tired even to correct him for calling me Master.

"I've won," I mumbled as I collapsed into the blankets. "I've done what the Master wanted me to do after all. I've defeated Elerius."

But as my eyes fell shut the voice in the back of my mind pointed out that I had not in fact defeated him at all. I had separated him from the wizards who were assisting him; I had separated him from his son; and I had driven him from his castle. But the Ifrit had told Antonia that he had not killed anyone, and that must include Elerius.

Hurled violently through the air, landing miles away, once he recovered his wits enough to use a flying spell, he might not have his defenses and his allies but he still had his abilities—and he was always the best wizard of any of us.

At this point, any hesitation about using a demon would be long gone. And the first thing he and his demon would do would be to hunt me down and inflict on me tortures that would make in comparison the Ifrit's abandoned plans for me seem like a stroll through the flowers of a summer meadow.

"So Maffi helped me," Antonia explained. She sat on the tent floor beside me while I lay, propped on my elbows, in my camp bed. Early morning light came through the canvas. I wasn't sure how long I had slept, but it had not been nearly long enough. But if my daughter had not wakened me now evil dreams soon would have.

"Freeing the Ifrit was Maffi's plan, then?" I prompted, stifling a yawn. Left behind while I went first to create and then to transport my dragons' teeth warriors, Maffi was much too active a young man to have let enforced idleness drain his initiative.

"Of course not," said Antonia firmly. "It was mine. He explained to me about the bronze bottle when we found it here, though I must say he didn't make it clear enough just how scary the Ifrit would be."

"So you were scared?" I asked with a smile. "To me you looked perfectly confident, standing there in the Ifrit's hand ordering him around."

She gave me a grin. "Well, I had to make him think I wasn't afraid. It's the same as with dogs. But I was terrified! My insides hurt so much I could hardly breathe, there at the end!"

"You and me both," I agreed. Chiding her for irresponsible behavior didn't seem to be working as well as I had intended. Maybe Theodora would be firmer.

It had been just about forty-eight hours, I realized, between when I swore to Elerius to give him a two-day truce and when Antonia had released the Ifrit. Elerius might imagine I had done so myself—if it gave him reason to worry, wherever he was, so much the better.

"We could hear the Ifrit even inside his bottle," Antonia continued, "cursing both you and the mage Kaz-alrhun. That's why, when I decided we might be able to use him against Elerius, I knew I had to be the one to open the bottle. The Ifrit would know right away that Maffi was Kaz-alrhun's pupil, because their magic is the same, but he would never know I was your daughter, because I'm a witch instead of a wizard."

And Maffi, who was indeed a true pupil of Kaz-alrhun, would have calculated that even if everything went completely wrong, his chances of escape would be at least marginally improved if someone else had pried the seal off the bottle. My insides went all cold again.

"Anyway," Antonia went on, "Maffi gave me suggestions on what to say to get the Ifrit's attention even before I let him out, and exactly what to tell him about breaking Elerius's defenses—including being very sure that the Ifrit knew I didn't want anybody dead. But he wasn't with me when I went ahead and opened the bottle, so I had to improvise the part about destroying those warriors. That's why the Ifrit was able to get me confused for a minute over how many wishes he had granted me."

"If he's got his bottle now," I said slowly, "then it's going to be very hard for any other mage or wizard to imprison him again."

Antonia nodded vigorously. "That's what he told me. He didn't like it in the bottle. He told me that even before I let him out. It must be awful for someone so big to be squeezed into such a little space. It's a good thing I realized I could use the poor thing against Elerius, or I might have had to let him out anyway."

I closed and opened my eyes, taking a deep breath. There didn't seem to be much helpful to say to this. Maybe Elerius had been right about one thing, and it was time to start Antonia's real wizardry training. She had the tricks of magic down just fine. Now all she needed was the sense of consequences and responsibility.

And the school had managed to teach even me some of that, though I still sometimes had doubts about Whitey and Chin. Maybe now that I had weakened Elerius the masters of the school would be able to do the rest. Once they had captured him—especially if it took the demonology experts to do so—I would have a quiet conversation with them about admitting their first girl student ever.

The tent flap was pushed back, and the bishop put his head in. "I thought I heard voices," he said with a smile. "If you are awake, Daimbert, there are several people here who would like to speak with you."

It didn't look like sneaking in an extra hour's sleep was an option. I sat up, started trying to straighten the torn and filthy clothes I had slept in, and decided it was hopeless. "Talk to you later!" said Antonia with a new grin and darted away.

Pale sunlight and cold air came into the tent along with Joachim. I noticed he was wearing his formal scarlet vestments and looked composed and well-brushed, even though he must have had even less sleep than I had. Jostling behind him were the two dozen young wizards who had been with Elerius.

Evrard again was nudged forward as spokesman. He stroked his red beard for a minute, trying unsuccessfully to look wise and wizardly. Someone nudged him again.

"We come to you to confess the full error of our ways," he said then, speaking too fast, as if rattling off something memorized. "We beg you in full penitence to accept us as your followers, as you take your rightful place as the head of the wizards' school. We will never again try to reach beyond the boundaries so wisely established for wizardry, to help mankind but never to set ourselves over them. We will always be mindful to be sure that you, as our leader, also do not pass these boundaries, but we foreswear rebellion and desertion until all efforts of reason and persuasion have failed. Recognizing our failure and our limitations, we beg you to reinstate us within organized magic at the lowest possible position, so that in hard work and obedience we might make ourselves worthy."

If he had smiled as he finished I might have had to slap him for such a sanctimonious confession. Coming to me as the new head of the wizards' school, indeed! But his blue eyes were genuinely troubled. I frowned, an expression doubtless made worse by the headache building behind my eyes, and the corner of his mouth gave a convulsive twitch.

"I really am sorry, Daimbert!" he burst out, sounding like himself now. "And we all are! Just like I said!"

Over his head I caught the bishop's eye. Although I was probably the only person there who could have spotted it in the angle of his cheekbones or the glint of his deep-set eyes, he was pleased.

Well, I thought gloomily, at least Joachim hadn't made the wizards put anything in their confession about throwing themselves as miserable sinners on the mercy of God, though I didn't like his assumption that now that I was back I would accept the position as the old Master's heir. It looked as if the bishop had done all my work for me, in reintegrating the rebellious young wizards back into wizardry's organization. Now all I had to do was to make sure they stayed properly penitent once they realized that the great and marvelous Daimbert, miraculously returned from death, had no intention of becoming their Master.

"All right," I said, standing up and pushing my hair back. "I'm glad you've all seen reason. You still have to persuade the teachers, of course, but—"

"You mean you'll take us back?" cried one of the younger

wizards in the back row, in an eager voice. "You won't cast us out of organized wizardry after all?"

"Um, well, no. That is, *I* won't. It's really up to them. I'm so glad you're penitent." I could hear myself starting to babble and decided to stop while I was still ahead. "Later today we'll all go to the City, and we can talk to the teachers to see if they agree."

And the school's defenses might be able to protect me from Elerius, when he came looking for me. I started feeling prickly unease, wondering how much time I had left before he attacked, and if the Cranky Saint really would keep him from summoning a demon.

I tried frowning again, which stilled what I considered an inappropriately frisky murmur starting to run through the assembled wizards. I had no desire to punish them harshly, but I didn't want them getting complacent either.

"You can all begin your first act of penitence at once," I said gravely. "It will be to tell Whitey and Chin—no, I know those aren't their real names, but you know who I mean, and yes, I know they haven't even graduated yet, but deferring to them is part of your punishment—to tell them everything you know about Elerius's defenses and plans. Talk too to Maffi—he's the eastern wizard here in camp. And see if you can get word to any of the kings who might have opposed King Paul's army that Elerius's might is broken, and that even his wizardly assistants have deserted him. Now, if you all will excuse me, I would like a private word with the bishop."

Abashed, they trotted away. If I was going to send Antonia to the wizards' school to learn responsibility, I was going to have to hope she didn't learn much from that group.

IV

When the tent flap dropped back into place, Joachim turned his enormous dark eyes on me. "How can I help you, Daimbert?"

"Thank you," I said, rubbing the last of the sleep from my own eyes. "You've already helped me. I'm not sure what you told them, but it seems to have worked."

"Counseling contrition is what I was trained to do," he said with a gleam of what had to be amusement. "Are you forgetting that I am a priest?"

I shook my head. Someday I really might understand his sense of humor. "I haven't forgotten. But tell me. What happened in the battle?"

"It was not as deadly as we had feared," he said, serious now. "The royal armies won, of course—the armies that march in your name. King Paul had ten times as many men under his command as did the war-captain from the castle. I believe Elerius's strategy had been to have those unliving magical monsters decimate Paul's troops before battle was ever properly engaged. When you instead destroyed them—"

"Actually just stopped them," I put in. "With Maffi's help."

"—and the royal armies rode up in full strength, most of the castle troops retreated, and some who were not quick enough were captured. I do not believe more than two dozen men were killed on both sides—which is two dozen too many, but substantially fewer casualties than for the battle I understand was fought here a week ago. King Lucas was wounded, and I heard him this morning boasting about the scar he would have to show his grandchildren, won during Daimbert's War. King Paul was untouched, though he rode in the forefront of battle and, I believe, slew several men himself."

There were several points here to which I might have responded. Out of all of them, I chose the term of Daimbert's War. "Joachim, I don't want a war named after me!"

"Not even a short, successful war?" For all I knew he was being humorous again.

"Well, if it might turn out successfully, it certainly hasn't yet. Elerius is gone for now, but he'll be back. If he survived the Ifrit, he'll soon be assembling new forces. And I assume the forces from the castle are holed up in it again."

"For the moment," agreed the bishop "But not for long. There will be a confrontation—or perhaps a ceremony—this morning at which I have been asked to be present. After the battle last night I had a long conversation with Gwennie, who I was very pleased to see again, as I have known her since she was a little girl in Yurt. She gave me an idea which I shared with the assembled kings; they have been meeting since before dawn. Then this morning I have been speaking to a delightful young lady who greatly admires you: Hadwidis, or, as she told me in confidence, Sister Eusebius."

I asked in amazement, "Do you realize she is a runaway nun?"

"Yes, of course, but this sin puts no stain on her admiration for you. And while certainly I cannot condone in the normal way of things an avowed nun leaving the cloister, in her case I believe she had no choice—remember, I have had a vision of Saint Eusebius myself. After we are through here, I shall have to go at once to the nunnery of Yurt and speak to the abbess about her. Hadwidis has asked me to help her in something which for another might be a defiant rejection of the cloister, but for her will be painful penitence."

He reached for the tent flap, preparing to go out, but I put a hand on his arm. "Joachim, please wait. There's something I need to tell you. You're the only one I can talk to about this. Saint Eusebius appeared to me."

He turned back sharply then, his eyes burning. "Not in a vision or dream?" he asked quietly. "But face to face?"

I nodded. "Face to face."

I told him about it briefly: Elerius's aborted attempt to summon a demon, the saint's abrupt appearance, his words to me, and the healing of both my cracked leg and young Prince Walther's lifelong limp. "I've faced a demon twice, Joachim," I concluded, looking at the floor, "but I think this was even more terrifying."

"Evil we can recognize in ourselves," he said, even more quietly. "But fallen as we are, absolute good always seems to rebuke us—even when God and the saints, through their chastisements, also offer us divine mercy."

"It may be strange, Joachim, but the only thing that has made me capable of functioning the last few days, rather than giving way to terror and awe after that appearance, is knowing that I am not the true object of the saint's attention. He's really more concerned with Hadwidis than he is with me, because of her being named for him in the nunnery. I can't tell her that, of course, and I hope you don't feel you have to either: she wouldn't be chattering with you about some ceremony if she were contemplating the active presence of a saint. He's helped me enormously—I wouldn't even be here if it weren't for the saint being cranky with Elerius—but mostly he's left me alone."

"God does expect us to do our best to work out our own salvation," the bishop commented, "even if we could never do so unaided."

I didn't want to think about salvation; I still had to concentrate on what to do with Elerius, and all my best plans seemed to involve danger to my soul. "Well, I've actually been aided a lot lately," I said, looking up again. "Everybody has been treating me as a great hero—including you, who ought to know better—but I've done almost nothing. The undead warriors are gone, the western armies have stopped fighting, and Elerius has lost his grip on the younger wizards and on his kingdom, but it's had nothing to do with me. It was all done by the saint, the Ifrit, you, and my daughter."

"And what we all have in common," he said, holding me with his eyes, "is our friendship with you." He smiled then.

"But come. Hadwidis will be growing impatient. You will say that she is accomplishing this on her own, but she too is your friend."

I emerged into a camp which Hadwidis's mother seemed to have made her own. The queen sat grandly in a chair in the center as though sitting in a throne, her son by her side. She surveyed the assembled kings with an imperious gaze. Hadwidis stood back a little, chewing her fingernails.

"Am I to understand, then," the queen was demanding of Paul, "that you consider me a prisoner of war? And that you will require that my knights surrender the castle on penalty of my life? Because if so, this is not at all the way I understand royal prisoners of war are to be treated!"

"Not at all, my lady," said Paul. The king looked as sober as I had seen him in years, his eyes rimmed dark with fatigue. He was not wearing his armor for the first time since I had returned from the East. Almost he looked like the losing rather than the winning commander in what I refused to consider Daimbert's War. "You are free to go whenever you like."

"What about Prince Walther?" she demanded, a protective hand on his shoulder. "I cannot believe your supposed magnanimity would extend to the rightful heir to this kingdom! Or are you expecting him to issue the surrender you appear unwilling to accept from me?"

"Well, no," said Paul uneasily. Then he spotted the bishop and me, and for a moment his face lightened. But only for a moment. "This will all become very clear in just a few minutes," he said quickly and stepped aside.

There was something going on here, something the kings had worked out. I suspected that the bishop had been instrumental, but if I didn't watch it I would again be given all the credit.

Joachim came forward then, and even the queen seemed somewhat abashed under the dark intensity of his gaze. "I speak here not as someone on one side or the other of battle," he said in a clear voice, "for those in God's service can never be part of battle. My only side is that of right and justice. Members of this army have asked me for my spiritual counsel, but if you would prefer, my lady, we can defer proceedings until the bishop of this kingdom could be summoned."

She looked uncertain for a moment, suddenly having to deal with a bishop when she thought she was only going to have to face down kings of kingdoms smaller than hers, men she considered her inferiors. But then she waved the issue away. "I have never had much use for our bishop," she announced. "If you are here to offer these kings' terms, I will be happy to hear you."

Prince Walther had been looking uncomfortably from side to side, but he gave me a quick smile before turning back to the bishop.

"I am here for quite a different purpose," said Joachim. "I am here as spiritual supporter of the oaths of the Princess Hadwidis."

Hadwidis hesitated a second, then squared her shoulders and came forward. She had put on a silk dress from Xantium, in which she shivered, and had apparently made some attempt to regulate her short, unruly hair. She stood before the assembled kings and war-leaders, chin up, a girl not all that much older that Antonia, wearing a thin dress that gave her a boldness they would never have allowed in the nunnery. She opened and closed her mouth, scanning her audience with an expression almost of disdain. I knew her well enough to realize that she was in fact almost too terrified to go on. But she did go on, and I thought her performance one of the bravest things I had ever seen.

"I come before you," she said at last, "before the western kings and before my own mother and brother, not due to my own ambitions, but to the urgings of a saint. Saint Eusebius, the Cranky Saint of Yurt, never liked me very much, but he did love me. And he wanted me here, to do what I am about to do."

She paused then, looking around again while the armies waited in silence. Some of the men watching her wore a livery unlike anything else in camp—the livery of this kingdom, I realized. These must be the prisoners, but they were not bound in any fetters, even though they were well-scattered, and each one was closely attended by a knight of the victorious armies. Banners snapped in the cold air above us.

"I'm sorry, Walther," Hadwidis said at last. "I know you thought all your dreams were coming true. But instead your troubles are only beginning."

The queen seemed finally to realize what was happening. She started to rise from the chair in which she still sat, but Joachim gave her a rather cold nod and she slowly settled back again.

Hadwidis leaned toward her brother now, ignoring everyone else. "I know this is very painful, but I have to tell you. You are not the heir to our kingdom."

I had expected some sort of shouted protest, but the boy and his proud mother only went white and waited for the rest.

"You see, Walther, you are not the king's son—not the son of the man you always thought was your father. You are the son of the wizard Elerius."

At this the queen could contain herself no longer. "Outrageous girl! What is the origin of these lies? I cannot believe the nunnery taught you—"

The bishop cut her off. "Princess Hadwidis had feared you would dispute her word. Therefore I am prepared to witness the oaths of both of you." Tall, formal in his scarlet vestments, carrying with him the full authority of the Church, he stared her back into her chair with burning eyes.

"Both of you will swear on the Bible," he continued, "telling the truth as best you know it. I also have with me a vial of the water from the shrine of Saint Eusebius, a relic I have carried with me since my days in Yurt. Swear to the truth, and God and His saints will judge where real Truth lies."

There was a brief pause in which no one moved, then Hadwidis stepped up to the bishop, her back straight and her hands shaking. The queen rose slowly then, bright spots of color on either cheek, and stood beside her.

For the moment, everyone had forgotten Prince Walther: that is, everyone except Antonia. From the corner of my eye I saw her dart forward and take his arm. "It's all right," I heard her whisper. "The bishop and my wizard will make sure everything is all right."

I admired my daughter's concern for others, but her assurances would not help. From Walther's point of view, everything was about to be all wrong. I turned back toward Joachim.

He held his heavy Bible in both hands, the vial of holy water tucked into one palm. The queen shot her daughter a venomous look as Hadwidis put one hand on the Bible. But the latter had eyes only for the bishop.

"I swear," she said in a low voice, "I swear that what I speak is true. I am my father's only true-born child, though I would have been much more content in the nunnery than as queen of this kingdom. My mother lay with our Royal Wizard, and from their coupling came my brother Walther."

I sniffed surreptitiously for the scent of roses. If the Cranky Saint was going to put in another appearance, I wanted to be ready.

But nothing happened, other than a sigh running through the crowd, and the queen standing even straighter and growing even redder.

"Will you confirm this, Mother?" Hadwidis asked at last.

But she was stubborn. Not more than a day or so ago, I

thought, Elerius would have been telling her she would soon be empress of the West. Their son might have become nominal king in a few years, but she and her lover would both have known where the true power would lie. And abruptly an Ifrit had ended all her plans.

"I will not confirm this," she said, a little too loudly, "because it is false!"

"Will you so swear?" asked the bishop, holding out the Bible politely.

The queen didn't quite dare scowl at him, but I could tell she would have liked to. Elerius would have taught her lack of respect for the Church—if justifying her adultery in her own mind had not already made her persuade herself that religion contained little useful. On the other hand, there were a great many people watching her intently, and it was hard not to respect Joachim. She lifted her chin, in a gesture very like one I had often seen in her daughter, and slapped a hand on the Bible. "I swear before God—" she began.

Now was the time for the saint to appear. I squeezed my eyes shut.

But there was no flash of light, no scent of roses. Instead, I realized, opening my eyes again, there was sudden silence from the queen.

She stood before the armies of the West unable to go on, opening and closing her mouth in a not very good imitation of a fish. The Cranky Saint had no need to waste his time exploding into sight before us. His influence, or the queen's guilty conscience—or both—had kept her from swearing falsely.

V

"If you would like to withdraw a false oath, my daugher," the bishop said kindly, "and swear instead to the truth, I am certain the saint will return the power of speech to you."

The queen was not yet ready to yield. A few more attempts at speech, with her hand both on and off the Bible, yielded nothing more. Hadwidis suddenly stepped up beside her mother, embraced her, and led her back to her chair.

King Paul, realizing that the next was up to him, took Hadwidis's hand and led her away from her mother, back to the center of the circle of shocked and attentive kings and knights. "You are here before many of the highest lords of the West, my lady," he said, "those who must accept you if you take your place on this kingdom's throne." My exhausted brain had finally worked out what this series of oaths was supposed to demonstrate: Paul couldn't leave Elerius's armies in the castle, even if without the kingdom's regent, and the only way to get them out was to persuade them to follow a ruler opposed to Elerius. "Our acceptance of you as our co-ruler, however, will be valid only if your position is established both by heredity and by the support of the powerful nobles who would serve you here. One question first: how old are you?"

"Eighteen," she said, sounding defiant because she was almost incapable of speaking at all. "I came of age this year."

"Then if you are your father's sole heir, and you are ready to inherit, then the regency is over," said Paul, with a side-long glance at the queen. "We will need to assemble your kingdom's greatest lords for your coronation."

Walther had been standing with my daughter's arm protectively around his shoulder, as silent as his mother. But now he said, his voice thin and high, "All our dukes and counts are there in the castle."

"Then we shall assemble them here," said Paul. "Perhaps we should send a delegation."

"Walther and I shall go," announced Hadwidis. "They'll remember me from when I was a girl, and they certainly all know Walther. They will listen to us. Mother?"

But the queen was not moving. I recovered enough from my stupor to realize that there was no need for them to walk all the way back across the broken fields and offered them a ride on Naurag. In a short time, the prince and princess had been admitted in through the front gates of their castle, while I waited outside with the flying beast, alert for anyone shooting at us from an arrow-slit.

But the great nobles and knights of this kingdom were no longer in a warlike mood. They must, I thought, have been promised glorious victory, in a great battle they would have dreamed of in the same way that Paul or King Lucas had dreamed of glory. Instead, Paul's armies and the Ifrit had reduced what should have been their greatest moment into a humiliating and terrifying retreat, barely in time to save their skins. They emerged from the castle gates within less than half an hour, waving a white flag to show they were not about to reopen hostilities, and rode slowly toward the great encampment of those they had made their enemies.

A central tragedy of this war had always been that they all knew each other. Most of the kings present had attended the funeral of Hadwidis's father. Many had relatives among the nobility of this kingdom; Paul himself had cousins among the region's castellans. The men from the castle waved their white flag defiantly, sitting their horses at the edge of camp, not wanting to appear to capitulate too easily, but there was no concealing that it was a relief to everybody.

By the time we arrived at the camp, Paul had arranged everything for Hadwidis's coronation—with, I noticed, Gwennie's help. She and the king were not looking at each other, but between them they had organized all the great lords by position, put a red cloak over a camp chair to stand in for a throne, and set up a table with a crown on it—doubtless one of the kings', for it looked far too large for Hadwidis. Her mother was still sitting silently, almost forgotten now. I didn't know what the normal coronation ceremony was for this kingdom, but we clearly were going to have the ceremony of Yurt.

Paul had not brought his own crown with him to war, but he had cleaned and put on his silver breastplate, which gave him a somewhat formal air. He was not, however, wearing his sword. "There is no more fighting here," he told those from the castle, speaking quietly, almost as if their battle of the night before had never happened. "We do not expect a surrender, because we do not seek to conquer—only to restore the friendship lost through the renegade wizardry of one who temporarily led many others astray. Come and join us as we prepare to recognize the daughter of your late king as your new queen—a recognition we cannot give without you."

Blaming it all on renegade wizardry, I noticed. It might be a way to allow those who had fought for Elerius to make peace with the armies at their gates without too much humiliation, but I didn't like the possibility that we might soon be back to kings distrusting organized magic.

Hadwidis spoke earnestly with the bishop for several minutes while final preparations were made, then everyone became quiet except for the trumpeters, who blew a festive fanfare. She walked slowly out in front of everyone and stood supporting herself on the arm of the improvised throne.

"Your royal highnesses, lords and ladies," said Paul into the silence at the end of the trumpet fanfare. "We are assembled today for the coronation of a new queen. Hadwidis is the daughter of your late king, born to rule. For several years this kingdom has been governed by a regency, but now that she has come of age the time for that regency is over! She has not recently lived among you, but now that she has returned I trust that you will all learn both to respect her and to love her."

The ceremony abruptly put me in mind of my own funeral. It would be just like Elerius to come back, invisible, to observe what was being done to his kingdom. And after I had taken Hadwidis all the way to the East with me to keep her out of his way, I didn't want her blasted with lightning in the middle of her own coronation.

Surreptitiously I started probing with magic. Nothing there. I found Theodora's mind and cocked an eyebrow at her across the crowd. She shook her head—she hadn't been able to find him either.

Which either meant that Elerius was off somewhere else, plotting his revenge safely distant from an Ifrit he might think was still with us, or else that he had become good enough to conceal himself not only from another school wizard but also from a witch who was actively looking for him.

"Princess Hadwidis's mother," said King Paul in a pointed fashion, "will now swear to her legitimacy and fitness to inherit this kingdom's rule."

The queen had been staring off into space as though completely unaware of the proceedings around her, but Paul had given her no choice. She rose and came forward, opened and closed her mouth experimentally a few times, and suddenly found that she could speak again.

"I swear to you that Hadwidis is the true-born daughter of our late king, my husband," she said, with a glare for Prince Walther, as though being Elerius's son was somehow all the boy's fault. "As his only child, she will take up a rule that is hers by heredity and right."

At King Paul's coronation, his mother had continued at this point, asking for the assent of the assembled nobles of the kingdom, but the queen showed no sign of wanting to participate further. Having sworn truly, she retreated, leaving Paul, a foreign king, to preside over her daughter's coronation.

He gave Hadwidis a reassuring smile, but she did not seem to notice, standing stiffly without meeting anyone's eyes. "Do you all agree that she should be your queen," he asked his audience, "to lead you in war, to lead you in peace, to lead you in wisdom and judgment?"

There must have been counts and dukes and powerful castellans among the men from the castle, but they all looked more like battle-weary warriors than rulers of authority, and they also all seemed somewhat in a daze at the pace that events in their kingdom were moving. But when the kings of the neighboring kingdoms began to murmur, "We agree," "We agree," they all enthusiastically joined in, if somewhat belatedly. Some were eyeing Prince Walther and whispering, still not clear why the boy they had always thought of as the heir was suddenly excluded. I wondered exactly what Hadwidis had told them to bring them here.

"Come forward, then, Hadwidis," Paul said in a loud voice, "and receive your crown!"

She came forward slowly, almost hesitantly, but her back was still straight and her chin firm as she went down on one knee before him. "These are the duties of kingship—or, in your case, queenship," Paul continued, concentrating as though trying to recall the exact duties he had pledged himself to a dozen years earlier, "to rule with justice and dispose with mercy, to guide the powerful and aid the weak, to eschew evil counsel while hearkening to wisdom, to lead your country to honor and your people to God. Do you promise, Hadwidis, to do all these things?"

I had the feeling that the formal list of royal duties to which Paul had sworn had been much longer, and that he was either forgetful or condensing, but on the other hand he seemed to have covered all the key issues.

"I promise to fulfill all these duties faithfully," said Hadwidis, almost too quietly to hear.

Paul lifted the crown, then, and set it carefully on her head. It slipped rather rakishly down over one eye, but she quickly pushed it back up and settled it firmly on the tops of her ears. "Rise, then," he cried, "Queen Hadwidis!"

She got slowly to her feet, Paul's hand under one arm. Slowly she seated herself in her throne, and slowly lifted the sceptre of authority which Paul handed her. I had a feeling there was supposed to be a sword involved as well, but I didn't think the morning after a battle, when knights from both sides of the fighting were standing shoulder to shoulder, would have been the best time for anyone to start brandishing a naked blade.

With only slight prompting from Paul, Hadwidis said, "With the aid of God and the counsel of all my people, I swear that I shall guard you, lead you, and rule you justly. Come forward, then, my faithful followers, to renew your allegiance to the crown." They came forward, still rather stunned, to kneel at her feet and, holding up clasped hands, recite the long oath of allegiance. As each finished, she put her hands around his, drew him up, and kissed him formally on both cheeks.

I spotted Gwennie across the crowd. She was watching the king of Yurt suspiciously, and I could have sworn she was tapping her foot as he continued to hover at the new queen's elbow.

The swearing of oaths took a long time, and the sun mounted high in the sky above us before all the nobles over whom Hadwidis would rule had sworn their fidelity to her. Prince Walther came forward last of all to pledge himself to his sister.

She hugged him hard and patted his hair. Antonia was standing only a few paces back. As Walther stepped away from the throne, his eyes rimmed red, my daughter whispered, "Don't worry. Even if you're not a king you can be a wizard. Being a wizard is much better. I'm going to be one myself."

"Let us join in the singing of a hymn," said Joachim, "and pray to God for the new queen's safety and good governance." The trumpeters found a note, there was only minimal confusion over which hymn we would sing, and enough people there knew most of the first two verses that the singing added further dignity and beauty to the service.

When the singing and prayers were over, Hadwidis broke into a smile for the first time today, as though realizing that her coronation had gone smoothly and that she really was queen now. "My people! My friends from throughout the West!" she cried, arms upraised. "I thank you all for your support! I believe that at the end of a ceremony like this it is normal to celebrate with a great feast, but we mostly seem to have camp food available here, and I'm not sure what condition the castle kitchens are in." There was an appreciative chuckle.

"However," more soberly, "I would like at this point to make two announcements, important enough that you all need to hear them. The first is very painful for me to tell you. As many of you may know, I was for years a nun. In making my oaths today to serve you as your queen, I have broken my oaths that I took in the cloister." There was a disconcerted murmur through the crowd; the departure of a princess for the nunnery had happened long enough ago that most people here had forgotten about it, even if they had been wondering all day about the sudden appearance of a new heiress.

"Therefore," said Hadwidis, "I shall take an additional oath now. I shall rule my kingdom because that is the will of the saints, but I shall take no husband. I shall live and die as virginal as I would have as a nun."

The murmur was louder now. Several of the great lords, who had been eyeing the pretty young queen with interest, looked deeply disappointed. But I could see Gwennie's face, and she was beaming.

"My other announcement," said Hadwidis, pushing on without giving the whispering a chance to die down, "concerns someone who has assisted me enormously in the past weeks, from the time I left the nunnery until I arrived at this camp."

Embarrassed, I thought that I did not need any further recognition for what had not been particularly unusual actions.

"This person has both encouraged me with her words and guided me by her example, as I sought to find my true path."

Her words and example? So Hadwidis didn't mean me after all. I felt unaccountably disappointed.

"Gwendolyn of Yurt, please come forward."

Gwennie, surprised as I was, stepped hesitantly out of the crowd, still wearing her travel-stained clothes.

Hadwidis took her firmly by the arm. No longer shy, her voice rang out. "Gwennie befriended a confused and frightened girl who had left the nunnery but did not know yet where her duty lay. Her friendship made me realize the responsibilities from which I could not run, the joy that comes from doing what one must."

Gwennie shot her a quizzical look, as though thinking, "I did? Really?"

"I wish therefore to reward her, as best I can. I thought first to make her wealthy, but she is already wealthy, having brought home great treasures from the fabled East."

This was news to almost everybody. The jewels I had taken from the roc's nest, I thought. I wasn't quite sure at what point they had become Gwennie's, but I certainly wasn't going to object. Several of the younger lords who had been disappointed by Hadwidis's announcement that she would never marry started looking at Gwennie with new interest.

"Therefore I shall, as my first act as your new queen, perform an act that only a king or queen can perform. I grant to you, Gwennie, the status of nobility! Come forward, then, Countess Gwendolyn, and pledge your allegiance to the crown!"

Gwennie, looking dismayed, did not at first move. But King Paul's head came up sharply, and his green eyes took on an intensity I had not seen in them even as he prepared for battle.

I looked around for Hadwidis's mother, to see how she was taking this. But she was not there. The chair in which she had sat was empty.

Now that I thought about it, it had been some time since I remembered seeing her, since before this kingdom's greatest lords began their oaths of allegiance. Feeling uneasy, I looked around, both with my eyes and with magic, without finding her.

Gwennie had been persuaded to come forward now, but was trying to explain to Hadwidis that, as much as she appreciated the offer, she could not become a countess of another kingdom while she was still royal constable of Yurt.

Where could the queen have gone? Did she, for example, know where Elerius was? As I started further magical probing, I was interrupted by Whitey and Chin hurrying up.

I had not seen these two student wizards all morning. Maybe they could help me search for the queen, I thought, but they didn't give me a chance to ask.

"Daimbert, Daimbert!" Chin panted. "We've just gotten a telephone call from the school!"

"Yes? You did call last night, didn't you, to tell them we'd gotten Elerius out of his castle?"

"Yes, yes, but we didn't know then where he'd gone!"

I suddenly felt cold all the way down to my toes. "Where has he gone?"

"That call, Zahlfast said he thought it was the last call they'd be able to get out. Elerius has seized the wizards' school!"

part ten ✢ dragons

I

"Now stay calm!" I ordered, completely panic-stricken. "Tell me exactly what happened!"

"Elerius has seized the school," Chin repeated dully. "The old Master wouldn't like this at all."

"But how?" I demanded wildly when the two student wizards just stared at me in mute despair. "Didn't anyone try to stop him? When did this happen? Why didn't you tell me before?"

I got it out of them at last. They had spoken last night with some of the teachers, who had been encouraged to hear that the rift in wizardry might soon be mended. Then this morning the jerry-rigged telephone here in the camp had rung with a message from Zahlfast.

"You knew he'd been sick," said Whitey. "Well, he was in the infirmary, separate from the rest of the wizards, and when they spoke to him mind-to-mind, to warn him what was happening, he just had enough time to get a call out on the infirmary phone."

"Elerius himself redid most of the school's protective spells over the last few years," provided Chin. "He said he would strengthen them against all enemies. He let us work on just one little part, as a class exercise, and those spells were impressive! Well, apparently he left some sort of magical back-door for himself, that he never told us about, because there was no warning he had arrived at the school until the teachers and students found the protective spells turning the other way around. From what Zahlfast said, all their own magic was disintegrating, and all their doors were locked. So they're all in the school with him, but they're trapped!"

Leaving me outside the school, with my only possible helpers a group of young wizards who had never learned the modern technical spells any better than I had. Elerius would grow to be as old as the Master had been before we worked out a way to break his defenses down.

"At least while he's in there he can't do anything," said Whitey more cheerfully. "He's as much a captive of his own spells as the teachers are."

Oh, he could do plenty, I thought. Starting with summoning a demon.

I went over in my mind the appearance of the Cranky Saint to Elerius and me, as much as my thoughts shied away from the memories. The saint had been angry because Elerius had been ready to break the promise he had made, for a forty-eight hour truce before he threatened to use a demon again, and because Saint Eusebius did not want a demon in the castle he intended Hadwidis to inherit. Well, the forty-eight hours had been up last night, and Hadwidis and the men who had pledged themselves to her were preparing to ride over to her castle and take charge, starting by assessing the damage from the Ifrit and from war. The saint might still be amenable to desperate prayers, but I couldn't count on it.

And in the meantime all the teachers and the school itself were hostage. Shortly Elerius might be telephoning me himself, to order me to cooperate and the young wizards to surrender, or he would start killing the teachers one by one, beginning with Zahlfast.

Saint Eusebius had been right. One need not sell one's soul to the devil to damn it eternally.

The only thing to do was to get out of here before he started telephoning with his demands. "Get the other wizards," I said grimly. "We're going to the City, now."

"Yes, Master," they squeaked, impressed, and scurried off. I found Theodora to say good-bye, just a quick kiss because this time it really might be good-bye forever, and I couldn't stand it any more. Within ten minutes I was mounted on Naurag and soaring toward the City, the young wizards flying along in a ragged squadron behind. Several seemed intrigued at the idea of a living air cart, even in the middle of our desperate situation, and would have chatted with me about how I had tamed him if I had let them.

The only bright spot, I thought during the short flight, was that Elerius might think I still had the Ifrit under my control. While he wasted time trying to create spells against an enormously powerful being who had already returned to the eastern deserts, I might be able to think of something.

But my mind stayed discouragingly blank as the City's towers rose before us. I didn't see any way I could improvise a means to break down carefully forged technical spells; even in my student days, I had never properly understood them.

On the surface, everything looked normal. Scudding clouds came off the sea to sail high over the harbor and sailors' and merchants' quarters to catch themselves on the highest white spires of the school. Ships bent before the wind, and faint came the sounds of people and commerce.

But the school itself was silent, and no magic lights burned in its windows. No voices, no scraps of illusion floated up toward us. A quick probe revealed no escaping spells, and I could not reach the minds of any of the teachers inside. From the silence this could have been a nunnery instead of a school for wizardry. I tried a little more vigorous magical probing and still found nothing—for all my spells could tell, the school no longer existed.

We stayed well back. None of us knew what kind of defenses Elerius might have mounted. It might be a much more complicated version of the already horrendously-complicated spells against magic, which could result in all of us toppling out of the sky if we got too close. Or it might be sheets of fire that would burn our flesh down to charred bone in seconds.

"He's got the whole library in there," said Evrard, as though I might not have thought of that myself. "With enough time, he'll work out whatever spells from the whole world he doesn't already know."

"Let me try something," said another of the young wizards. He took something from his pocket—a bread crust, I thought—and sailed it toward the school's highest spire. With a small puff, it turned into white vapor, not fifteen feet from us.

We all backed rapidly to a safer distance, then hung in the air again, swaying slightly in the breeze. Whitey and Chin, growing tired, took firm grips on Naurag's neck. I realized they were all waiting for me to think of something.

If I wasn't careful, if I angered Elerius, this really could be the apocalypse I had mistakenly thought the Ifrit and the Cranky Saint had helped me avoid. My first concern was for all the teachers trapped inside, but if Elerius destroyed the school with them in it, he could start a fire-storm that would destroy the City as well. Any slight hope of his of becoming reconciled with the school and all its teachers again was now gone. He either had lost his mind in a mad desire for power—or he somehow imagined he could rule the world while keeping the world's best wizards locked up for the rest of their lives.

"You were with him," I said to Evrard. "You know he always has a plan, and a fallback strategy. What was his fallback plan?"

But neither Evrard nor any of the other wizards had been privy to his plans. "He just said he had a final strategy that he preferred not to use but that would ensure victory if all else failed," Evrard provided. That, I thought, would have been the demon.

No whiff of the supernatural here, but then there was no whiff of anything. "Elerius!" I shouted, and even magically amplified my voice was carried away by the wind. "There's still time to surrender!" There was no answer, but then I had expected none.

We set down in a little plaza halfway down the hill from the school to the harbor. Curtains twitched in windows facing onto it, and several people hurrying down the steep streets toward the plaza turned around abruptly and headed away again. The City was used to wizards, but not to purple flying beasts.

"This is the time to show just how penitent you are," I told the young wizards sternly. Most of them had only graduated from the school a few years earlier and had been serving in the courts of castellans and lesser lords around the Western Kingdoms, until Elerius offered them a chance for what they considered much more spectacular power. Whitey and Chin, who had never aided Elerius, stood to one side being smug.

"You all helped Elerius create and maintain the spells that kept school magic from working near his castle," I told my penitent assistants. "Whatever spells he's thrown up around the school must be based on similar principles. So I want you to start analyzing them and seeing if you can find a way to reverse them. And you," turning to Whitey and Chin with a frown that wiped away their smugness, "you worked more closely with the Master toward the end of his life than any other students. He had doubts about Elerius and may have had some sort of project of his own to counter him. You told me you were working on projects for him—now get to work!"

"We left our notes in the library," Whitey started to protest, but I cut him off. I actually doubted this group could come up with anything, but one of them might stumble across the right spell by accident. After all, I had done so more than once myself in my early years as Royal Wizard.

After a little confusion, the challenge of overcoming the spells of a wizard of whom they all stood in awe actually seemed to inspire the young wizards, who were soon busily consulting with each other, both verbally and mind-to-mind, and every now and then trying a phrase in the Hidden Language. Twice the flagstones that paved the plaza surged upwards with a grating wrench, then settled back into place, as two separate experimental spells were badly aimed. The young wizards grinned and shrugged.

I thought of, tried, and rejected half a dozen approaches of my own while the sun, a lighter patch in the cloud-covered sky, slowly sank toward the sea. We were left alone in the plaza below the school until I heard hoof-beats moving determinedly toward us.

This was a person who didn't care if a group of wizards and a flying beast had taken over the plaza. It was the queen, Hadwidis's mother.

The dress that had been elegant the night before was now torn and stained with hard riding. She was heading straight up the narrow street that led to the front gates of the school. The plaza was no more for her than a widening in that street, and the presence of a group of wizards there irrelevant. Curtains twitched again at the queen's passage. Ignoring us, she projected fury in every angle. The horse she rode was lathered and stumbling, but she kicked it past us and steadily upward.

"Keep on working," I said hastily to my supposed assistants and hurried after her. Elerius might choose to pretend I did not exist, but the queen was hard to overlook. If I had no success against him with magic, I might be able to reach him through her. His lover, the mother of his son, she was a proud woman who had now been unceremoniously stripped both of her grandiose hopes and even of her ruling status. And in her eyes it would all be Elerius's fault.

We arrived at the main school door, with me flying so close to the queen's shoulder I might as well have been riding the same horse. The door was on the far side of a pleasant plaza, set about with fountains and fruit trees. Still the queen ignored me—either she didn't know or didn't care that the war her soldiers had just lost had been named for me. She reached for the great bell-pull; normally one of the younger wizards would be in attendance during the day, one of the older ones at night, to greet whoever climbed up the wizards' hill. I held my breath, wondering if Elerius would blast the queen into vapor with his magic.

But she remained solid while, far-off, the bell sounded mournfully. When there was no immediate answer, she rapped impatiently at the door with her riding crop, then tugged at the bell-pull again.

This time there was finally a response. The door began to glow a vivid red, as waves of heat suddenly beat out from it. I backed up hastily, but the queen's horse was too tired to move. A booming, disembodied voice said, "Get away from the door."

I wasn't completely sure if that were Elerius or just some spell, voicing a warning to anyone who dared touch his magically-protected door. But the queen had no doubts that he was just inside. "I shall not leave!" she replied sharply. "Elerius, I order you to come out at once!"

There was a brief pause. The door grew no cooler. "Daimbert, get away from the door," said the voice.

Even the best talking magical door was unlikely to recognize all wizards by name. I was back beside the queen in a second. "Elerius!" I shouted. "Listen to me! I'm giving you a final chance. Release the teachers and come out, and I'll personally guarantee that—"

But I didn't know what I could guarantee. That the teachers would forgive him? Not likely. That we wouldn't kill him? No wizard had killed another wizard since the Black Wars, and even for this I doubted we would do so again—and Elerius knew his history of wizardry much better than I did. That I would try to distract the queen from her entirely justified indignation?

"—I'll guarantee that I won't turn the Ifrit on you!" I finished, much too tardily.

The queen didn't give Elerius a chance to respond. Still paying me, her obvious inferior, no attention at all, she said from between clenched teeth, "You said you loved me. You said that nothing would give you more joy than for us and our son to rule the West. You told me that I was your ambassador, the only one you could trust to deal with the enemy. And yet at the first hint of real danger, you were gone! I will have you know that everyone in the West is now snickering about you and me, and my daughter has just been crowned queen in my place. I shall have explanations from you, and I shall have them now!"

In Elerius's place, I would have doubled the protective spells on the door. But maybe, somewhere in his heart, he loved his queen as I loved Theodora. Because he answered her, and even through the boom of his voice's magnification he sounded wheedling.

"Now, dearest lady, do not be so upset. I'm very sorry for how it turned out, but it's not as bad as you think. In fact—"

"I do not," she said, icy now, "intend to discuss this while standing in the street like some spurned drab. Open this door now!"

"Well," he said, in a tone that sought to suggest that he was always reasonable, "I can't very well let you in when there's a wizard with an Ifrit in his pocket standing beside you."

She turned her haughty blue gaze on me. "Step aside, Wizard," she said dismissively.

"Elerius, listen!" I cried. "I don't have an Ifrit any more! He's granted his wishes and he's gone!"

Just for a second I felt a magical touch—Elerius probing for the bronze bottle. I threw up mental shields against him, but the touch was gone in a second. It wouldn't have taken him long to discover what he wanted to know.

And if he had spotted Solomon's signet, he would not have known what to make of it—but it was most certainly not an Ifrit.

"I am waiting, Elerius," announced the queen.

Evening was setting in rapidly now. Normally someone would be coming up the street to light the magic lamps the school had installed all along the street that led to its main door, but nobody ventured out now.

The door before us had continued to glow hot, but now, almost imperceptibly at first, then rapidly, the waves of heat ceased to pour from it, and its color returned to its normal shade. I held my breath, feeling more than seeing the magical barricades come down. Faint below us I heard a triumphant whoop—the young wizards must have sensed it too, and thought it was somehow their doing.

Slowly, slowly, the door swung open. Inside it was dark, the hall empty. The dark entryway and Elerius's unseen presence were ominous, but if I was ever going to get inside the school, this was my one chance.

The queen swung down from her horse and stamped inside. I was so close to her that she must have been able to feel my breath on her neck. I barely had both feet through the doorway when the heavy door slammed shut behind us, and all the locks clicked into place.

II

It was pitch black, and all my magic was gone. A brief attempt to reach Evrard's mind was as unproductive as if I had never studied any wizardry at all. The magic lights were, naturally, not working. As soon as the door closed everything had gone completely dark, so that without sight or magic I would not have known if Elerius were two paces from us.

What was Elerius using to power his spells? He had needed a cohort of young wizards in his castle to keep my magic from working, and here he was by himself, opposed by the best wizards in the West, and he was still neutralizing their spells. No wonder I hadn't been able to find any trace of the school teachers' magic from outside: Elerius had stopped all their spells before they began.

And was continuing to do so, even with the very same young wizards who had once been his assistants now outside probing for flaws in his magic. The one bright spot was that in these conditions most of the magic Elerius knew would be as inaccessible to him as it was to me.

The queen was not about to let a little darkness deter her. I kept on her heels as she stormed down the passage that led from the front door. "There are two steps up here, my lady," I said, "and the passage then curves left."

She must have heard me because she avoided tripping on the steps or hitting the wall, but all her intent was focused on finding Elerius.

If the magic lights weren't working, I thought, and Elerius didn't want to show himself at a window, he might well be operating out of the big lecture room, lit by skylights, up toward the top of the school. It was a long climb up there, especially in the dark—student wizards worked on their flying spells in part to make the ascent more easily. But I had never become particularly proficient at flying until after I left the school, and I still knew every step, though my student days were now decades in the past.

Where were the student wizards? I wondered as we scrambled up the steep stairs. There had been a number of students at the school when the old Master died, but no one had mentioned them recently. The problem with being thought dead was that one lost all track of current events.

The teachers must have sent them home, which at least meant they were out of the direct line of fire.

We came up the last flight of cracked stone steps, seeing faint light in front of us. Other than turning where I told her to turn, the queen had given no sign of even realizing I was with her. But as we entered the large, unnaturally quiet room, with its rows of seats carved with the initials of generations of wizardry students, and the chalk dust hanging in the air, she turned toward me. She was breathing hard from the ascent but still had enough breath to say sharply, "Thank you for showing me the way, Wizard, but I would prefer to speak with Elerius in private."

"So would I," I said. "First we have to find him."

In the twilight shadows lurked in every corner. Normally, as well as the noises made by students creaking in their chairs, whispering, coughing, flicking pages in their textbooks, and scribbling notes, there was a constant faint sound from the skylights: the whistle of the wind, the rattle of a dead leaf on glass. But except for the sound of our own breathing, everything now was dead silent. The room was full of memories of lectures, by Zahlfast, by the old Master, by other teachers—even a few by me. Surely, it seemed, all that magic must be accessible here, but my spells still didn't work.

Into the silence came the faint sound of a footfall. Both the queen and I whirled, to see Elerius up on the dais, stroking his black beard and looking at us from under peaked eyebrows.

"Just a moment, my dear," he said to the queen, one palm held out. His voice sounded almost normal, but not quite—his confidence had been broken by the double blow of the saint and the Ifrit, and he didn't have it back yet. "There has been a brief detour on our path to triumph, but I can explain my new plans to you as soon as I am through with Daimbert. Could you leave us?"

"I," she said, very cold, "shall not leave without first receiving satisfactory answers."

"Very well. But this may possibly prove unpleasant."

He took two steps down from the podium, now looking only at me. I was right. His confidence had been broken. His thoughtful tawny eyes held something I had never seen in them before—pure hatred.

He was still trying to sound normal, especially with the queen there, but was rapidly becoming less successful. "If you have come with one more of your pathetic attempts to make me yield to your authority, Daimbert, I am afraid it is much too late." He had gone far beyond jealousy that the Master preferred me. Telling him it had been my daughter, not me, who had used the Ifrit to drive him from the castle would only make things worse.

"This is my school," he continued from between clenched teeth. "Neither the saints with whom you claim friendship, nor any magical creatures from the East, shall take it from me. You have disrupted my plans for the last time! Even if I do not succeed in persuading the West that everyone would be better off in yielding to my leadership—something of which they will see the wisdom much more clearly once you are gone—I shall have the satisfaction of knowing that you will never lead them either."

So much for my first plan, of making one final effort to talk him out of here. Stalling for time while I tried to come up with a second plan, I said, "Magic's stopped working here. We both know you could defeat me if it came to a contest of spells, but until you break your spell against spells, we may be reduced to the undignified alternative of wrestling on the floor. I'm not sure the queen would enjoy the spectacle."

He glanced quickly toward her and made no effort to tackle me, though I flexed my newly-healed leg to be ready, just in case. He answered quietly, but the threat of violence gave a harsh undertone to his words. "A contest of spells will not be necessary. You are now utterly alone, and this time none of the friends of whom you're so proud will be able to help you. In a few minutes you shall accompany me to the school cellars, and what we find there shall destroy you utterly."

My heart, still beating hard from the climb, hammered wildly. He's summoned a demon, I thought. And the saint, having answered my prayers once, was leaving the rest of this up to me.

"Dear God, Elerius!" I burst out. "If you kill me—" Was he really planning to kill me in cold blood? It was hard to doubt his ability to do so. "—how will you ever persuade any of the teachers to follow you?"

"When you are gone," he said, even more harshly, "they shall have a final chance to agree to my authority, or they and the entire school shall be destroyed as well."

Back when the Master said he wanted me to succeed him, I had tried to object by pointing out that I had no idea what the school kept in all those locked rooms down in the cellars. My objections had been even more pertinent than I realized. It looked as though I was finally going to find out.

I pulled back my lips in a desperate effort at a smile. "Goodness, Elerius, you almost had me believing you there for a minute!" I knew very well he wasn't joking, but maybe if I suggested he was, it might still give him a chance to back down. "But I am sure you aren't planning to sacrifice yourself."

He bent toward me, glaring through the dimness. "It would be worth it, if I took you with me."

The queen interrupted—for a second I had almost forgotten her, and her voice behind us made me jump. "Perhaps you are not the man I thought you were, Elerius," she said, speaking clearly and loudly from one of the student seats. "Threatening to kill a wizard who you imagine has been responsible for your own failures, preparing to destroy the wizards' school you had told me you would be so proud to head—all this sounds to me like an admission of failure!"

That stopped him as nothing I could have said would have. "No, no, of course not, I said I would explain," he said hurriedly, again with a faint pleading note. "This is triumph! Don't you understand?"

"I understand nothing," she said in a voice toneless with anger, "but that you have betrayed my affection."

Maybe I could get out of here while she distracted him. Half a dozen steps, I thought, and I would be at the top of the stairs. I was sure I could run down them faster in the dark than he could. And when I reached the door, the door he had somehow magically sealed—

"Don't try to run, Daimbert," he said as my foot quietly began to move. "You will never get the doors open." He wasn't looking at me, but he didn't have to—he would have been running himself under the circumstances.

So what was I supposed to do? I thought, looking at the back of his head. Something he wouldn't think of doing himself, like throwing myself headfirst down the stairs so that I would be dead of a broken neck before he had the satisfaction of killing me?

He might accuse me of a penchant for self-sacrifice, but I had a powerful penchant for survival. I would somehow have to reach the teachers, wherever he had sealed them. Zahlfast was in the infirmary, according to Whitey and Chin—that at least I thought I could find in the dark. With several of us working together, we might be able to find a way—

So, the voice in the back of my mind asked sourly, did I think that if the teachers couldn't break through Elerius's spells by themselves, my own patchy knowledge of herbal and eastern magic would be enough to do the trick?

"You were right, I realize now," I heard him babbling to the queen, "to point out that it was silly of me to worry so much about the school these last few months. Once I have destroyed it I shall no longer be distracted, and you and I shall set ourselves up in a much better kingdom than the one your daughter has so rudely seized. In fact—"

He never had a chance to finish. The floor under our feet gave a sudden jerk, as though for a second Elerius's spells had faltered. I reached for my magic, but it still wasn't there.

But something was different. Had Evrard and the rest of them found a chink, no matter how small, in Elerius's protective spells? I looked up at the skylights, where the last of the day's light still lingered.

And saw a flash of flame, a yellow set of talons, and an enormous eye. The school was under attack by a dragon.

III

The floor jerked again, and just for a second sounds reached us from outside: a dragon's roar, the scrape of mighty claws on the roof, and, faint in the distance, what could have been shouts of triumph.

Elerius gave a strangled cry of dismay and sprang for the stairs. If dragons were about to come down through the skylights, I could see his point. I grabbed the flabbergasted queen by the elbow and pulled her after him.

"Coward!" she shouted after his retreating back as we stumbled down the dark staircase. "Will you save your skin and abandon me?"

"He's not abandoning you, my lady," I said, though I couldn't have said why I still felt compelled to defend Elerius. "He's hurrying down to the school cellars to work on the magical defenses."

She ignored me. We could hear his footsteps, moving far faster than hers, growing far and faint before us. If he had sold his soul to the devil in return for protection, it must not have commanded a very high price, or else a dragon would never have gotten within miles of the school.

Could Evrard have possibly summoned a dragon? He had

never had what I considered particularly good sense, but this went far beyond what even a marginally competent wizard with an over-active imagination should come up with. And how had he gotten a dragon down from the land of wild magic so rapidly?

We were most of the way down to the level of the front door when all of the magical lights suddenly went back on, and whatever powerful spell had blocked my knowledge of the Hidden Language dissolved away. "Hah!" I shouted, from the sheer pleasure of having my magic back. With the lights on I could see again, but the feeling of opening my eyes from blindness went far beyond vision.

The queen stopped, blinking in the sudden glare, but I pulled her on with new speed. Elerius must have shut down his spells to keep magic from working here in order to use the force to power his spells against dragons. But that meant it might be possible to find and rescue the teachers.

The front doors were locked, but I had learned the spells to unlock them back when I was still a student, sneaking in after a long evening down in the taverns. A few quick words in the Hidden Language, and they swung open. The horse the queen had ridden in on was still there, but the street, that had been empty when we came in, was now packed with citizens staring upward, open-mouthed. Below us I could hear the city's alarm bells ringing wildly.

"Straight down the hill, my lady," I said, giving her an unceremonious shove. Above us I heard new roars and scrabbling sounds. My view was blocked by the bulk of the school itself, but I saw a red tail, a green wing, and flames shooting from several different points. How many dragons could Evrard have possibly summoned? "Get as far away from here as you can!"

"I shall not—" the queen started to announce, but I had already slammed the door, leaving her outside. Now to find the teachers before the dragons dismantled the school.

It had been a while since I had lived here, and I had never spent much time in the infirmary, but my feet knew the way. Some of the other teachers had become my friends over the years, but Zahlfast had been my true friend since I graduated—and, although I had not realized it at the time, even before. I shot down the halls, down turnings and steps, past offices and seminar rooms, past the entrance to the cafeteria, and skidded to a halt at the white door that marked the suite of rooms where sick students and members of the faculty rested and were treated.

I wrenched it open and burst into rooms smelling strongly of alcohol and medicinal herbs. A row of narrow beds were lined up, empty mattresses bare—except for one. Far overhead came crashes and thundering roars. The floor shook and shook again. If Elerius was trying to set up spells against dragons, they weren't working.

For a second I did not recognize Zahlfast, whom I had always thought of as a figure of strength and authority. He was out of bed but leaning on the headboard. The tall red hat that was always on his head was nowhere in sight. He wore a nightshirt and looked in it much thinner and more frail than I remembered. His fingers on the headboard went white with tension as he struggled to keep his feet while the whole school swayed around us. We are wizards! I shouted mentally. We're not supposed to get old!

Zahlfast's eyes had been downcast, as if in resignation, but then he looked up and saw me.

"I'm alive. I was never actually dead," I said hastily, seeing the shock building. Faking one's death really was more effort than it was worth. I didn't want an old man, especially one already made ill by the unsuccessful struggle to keep organized wizardry together, pushed into apoplexy by seeing a ghost apparently welcoming him into the afterlife. "Elerius has lost control of the school's defenses, and we're under attack by dragons. I've got to get you out of here before the whole structure comes down around us."

I lifted him with magic and transported him toward the doorway, trailing a sheet. That last crash sounded closer. Zahlfast shook his head hard and seemed to recover momentarily. "I can walk," he said shortly, then unexpectedly smiled. "I should have known, Daimbert, all the way back during that disastrous transformations practical of yours. Saving the school by attacking it with dragons was exactly what you would think of first."

I had never, even for a minute, planned to attack the school with dragons, but there was no time to go into that now. "I'll get you to safety, then try to find the rest. Do you have any idea where in the school they are?"

He was on his own feet now and wrapping the sheet around his shoulders like a cloak. "In the library. They had all gathered to try to decide what to do next, after the telephone message came through that Elerius was out of his castle. So when he showed up here instead, it was easy for him to capture them all."

"I'll get them as soon as you're safe," I started to say again, but he cut me off short.

"Aren't you surprised, Daimbert, that they haven't already come rushing down the halls, now that Elerius is distracted from most of his spells? I'll have to go with you. The library has its own set of protective spells—I put them in place myself, years ago, with the help of an especially bright student named Elerius. He's turned the spells inward to prevent the faculty's escape, and even now I'm sure they are struggling to derive a countervailing spell, starting from first principles. I never let the knowledge of my protective spells spread, thinking the library would need to be defended from any wizard who went renegade—never realizing the worst renegade would be my own star pupil."

We hurried as best we could back up the stairs and toward the library, though several times we were thrown against a wall by the force of the building's swaying. It couldn't hold together much longer, I thought. Once all the magic lights went out for ten seconds, then came back on. Scrapes and creakings came from below us now as well as above, and a deafening roar suggested an entire tower had toppled. It should have been full dark outside, but whenever we passed near to where a window had been—and glass now lay in shards—sheets of dragon-fire lit up the sky. Twice parts of the ceiling fell into a corridor through which we had just passed.

"I've given my whole life to this place," Zahlfast was mumbling.

"To the teaching of wizardry. Not to the building," I said firmly, though my own heart felt wretched at seeing it being pulled to pieces around us.

The library, however, seemed untouched, the corridor leading to it free of rubble, even the sounds of disaster and collapse sounding more distant. Zahlfast sank to the floor by the door and for a moment leaned his head against the wall, his face gray.

"Master," I said quietly, bending over him, "if you can just tell me the spells I'll try them, you shouldn't—"

He looked up at me with a glint of anger from under shaggy eyebrows. "I'm not as far gone as you seem to think, and I'm not the Master. You won't saddle me with that! If we survive you'll be the Master here, Daimbert—or should I say, *Frogs?*"

Stung, I stepped back, and after a brief pause he started on spells. In a moment I stopped being indignant enough that I began to try to help him, working mind-to-mind.

But what did he mean by using that old teasing nickname I had hoped had been forgotten for decades? And where had he learned magic like this? I didn't know about the rest of the faculty, but it would have taken me many months to try to work out the spells he had set up around the library—the spells Elerius had used to capture the teachers.

Zahlfast had built an unusual twist into his spells, one I had never seen before, though I immediately realized how Elerius could have turned it around, to keep people from getting out of the library as well as to keep others from getting in. Zahlfast worked steadily; he might be old but he had not lost track of how he had put this particular piece of magic together. Quickly he untwisted his spells, disentangled them from other bits of spells, and set the whole magical edifice into reverse.

He was doing all the real work. All I had to do was murmur a few words of the Hidden Language at appropriate moments to keep the spell structure from collapsing around him as he forced his way furiously through magic's four dimensions.

Even amid the grating of stones against each other, the breaking of the spells around the library came with an almost audible 'pop.' The door swung open, and the best wizards of the west tumbled out, undignified and clutching armfuls of books to their chests.

But I had eyes for none of them. Zahlfast had slumped against the wall again, his eyes shut and his breathing shallow.

"Why didn't you tell him I was still alive?" I demanded, not finding the most polite way myself to greet my old teachers. I lifted him carefully in my arms; he seemed to weigh almost nothing. "He was sick, he was horrified to see me coming into the infirmary like an apparition, and he's used the last of his strength freeing you because you weren't alert enough to spot Elerius coming!"

They let my rudeness pass. "He's down in the cellars," said one teacher, an expert at mental communication. "Still not working with a demon," said another, one of the demonology experts. "Let's grab the books and go!" cried a third.

His view prevailed. But even with all their lifting spells

working together, they could not carry more than a fraction of the library's contents, down the narrow corridors toward the main doors. Not all the teachers were even carrying books; two were carrying between them a heavy box that I hoped held the school's accounts and bank deposit receipts. Books dropped, fluttering, whenever we had to negotiate a sharp corner or a particularly steep staircase, but no one stopped to pick them up. "We'll have to come back," said the librarian, worried.

There were plenty of upper doors, but we hurried on toward the lower levels: no one wanted to go out into a night lit by dragon-fire.

"They're not my dragons," I panted, though no one except Zahlfast had accused me of summoning them. "I think Evrard must have somehow gotten them here."

"Evrard skipped the whole section of the curriculum on dragons," a teacher said crisply. "Got a waiver from the Master himself—a big mistake, I thought at the time." I said nothing, having skipped the same section myself. "He won't have known the spells to summon dragons."

But someone had. We were taking a short cut through a series of sitting-rooms some of the teachers used in the evenings, and the windows, still intact, suddenly shattered as an entire dragon's snout was thrust through, all hot breath and great yellow fangs.

"Daimbert!" a voice shouted, a voice I didn't recognize. I didn't stop to find out who it was.

Clutching Zahlfast to me, I redoubled my speed. He hadn't moved since we left the library. Scattering books behind them, the teachers flew down the corridors, and in a moment we shot out into the street at the school's main level.

A dragon hovered, slowly flapping enormous leathery wings, in the air directly above us.

We dove back toward the doorway, but I was stopped by a voice that seemed to come from the dragon. "Daimbert!" it shouted again.

Dragons can't talk. Still trying to keep Zahlfast right side up, I peered upward. Someone was actually *riding* the dragon, perched on its back at the base of the wings, a tall person with a mane of silver hair. In his hand he held something long, something that glittered with magic—

It was Gir, the elf from the land of dragons, and he wielded the Dragons' Scepter.

I thrust Zahlfast's motionless form at the other wizards. "Get away!" I shouted at Gir. "Get the dragons away from the school!" And I shot upwards, dodging the barbed tail of the great dragon, and settled onto its scaly back behind him.

Gir glanced at me quizzically but shouted something himself and gestured with the Scepter. The old wizard Naurag had dreamed of starting a school, I thought, and his own magic had just destroyed it. The alarm bells were still sounding wildly, but the fire brigade wasn't going to have much luck against dragons. With a final blast of flame that melted the mortar between the bricks of the front of the building, Gir's mount gave an almost lazy flap of its wings and rose up into the black sky.

"It is good to see you, Daimbert," said Gir, as though this were a friendly social visit. All around us dragons snorted small flames, and on all their backs I could make out white-robed shapes. "It has been a great many years since we have been in the lands of men, and it has changed much."

Years ago it probably wasn't overrun with dragons, I thought. I spotted the window that had, not very long ago, been the window to my room at the school. The glass was gone, and the roof above was peeled away.

"We owe mastering the dragons, such as we have, to your example," Gir continued. "A great challenge, and I fear it took us longer than we had hoped."

"Me?" I gasped in horror.

"Your obvious friendship with the purple flying beast, the one you named for the old wizard Naurag, made us realize that we had been short-sighted. We had seen the dragons only as a danger, though a danger that also protected us. Why not, we began to think after you left, why should we not tame the dragons and ride them as you had your flying beast?"

"These aren't tame," I said between dry lips. The dragons kept wheeling, making to descend again toward the City, and being jerked up again by the magic of the Scepter. Frustrated, they snapped at each other and at each others' riders with razor-sharp fangs.

Gir shook his head regretfully. "It may never be possible to make them our friends as you have befriended the one you call Naurag. But as we attempted at least to learn to ride them, the thought came to me: you had sought the Dragons' Scepter originally to use against a too-powerful wizard named Elerius."

"I remember telling you that," I mumbled. Even without dragon claws and dragon fire, the school below us was continuing slowly to disintegrate, a tile sliding suddenly free from the roof, a chimney toppling, a wall beginning to buckle. With a far-seeing spell, I could see that the teachers had retreated a safe distance down the street—it looked as though several were having to restrain the librarian from going back in.

"We recalled," Gir added calmly, "a time, perhaps a dozen years ago, when a wizard summoned a great number of dragons out of our northern land and down to the lands of men. His spells were very powerful—he drew the dragons from their valley even before we were aware of it, though we have always attempted to keep them safely there. And we began to think that that wizard might have been the same as the Elerius of whom you spoke."

I nodded, realized he couldn't see me, and said, "Yes, that was he."

"I regretted then letting you return here without the Dragons' Scepter you so obviously needed, or even any offer of assistance. Perhaps we have been too comfortable, too complacent—too selfish. Thus, as soon as we had mastered the dragons enough that we thought we could control them on a long flight, we determined to start south. A great burst of magic, which stirred up the dragons even thousands of miles away, told us your need was great."

The Ifrit, I thought. Nothing like his power had been seen in the West since the early days of the earth.

"And when," Gir continued, "we found the City where the old wizard who had given us the Scepter once lived, we also found here a group of young wizards. They told us the wicked Elerius was inside, so, since the dragons were restless anyway, we thought we should attack his fortress."

The rumbles and scraping sounds below us had steadily been increasing in volume. A rising damp wind pushed against weakened walls. Now, very slowly, those walls began to tilt. Stones that had stood solidly in place for centuries shifted and broke free of their mortar. The remaining turrets waved wildly for a moment, and then, almost majestically, the wizards' school, the center of organized magic, collapsed with a deafening roar.

IV

There had been a number of embarrassing failures in my career as a wizard, starting with the disaster that had gotten me the nickname of Frogs. But this was the worst yet. I could blame it on Evrard and the rest of the young wizards, on the dragons, on Elerius himself. But assigning blame only distracted from the central fact, that the real one to blame was me.

I stared dully down, listening to the shouts from the citizens of the City, the people who had managed for years to carry on ordinary lives in the shadow of the school, and now faced dragons and disaster. I could think of only two factors that kept this from being a total failure: Elerius must be dead, crushed in the rubble, and none of the teachers, after this, would possibly want me to be Master of whatever fragments of organized wizardry remained.

Joachim might think it an advantage that people whom I met became interested in my cause. It just showed how wrong even a bishop could be.

"Our work here seems done," said Gir, looking down at the plumes of dust and smoke rising from the rubble. "We mean no harm to the people of this city, now that the evil wizard's fortress is destroyed. Perhaps we should return to our own land."

And he probably expected me to be properly grateful. "Well, the cafeteria's no longer serving," I managed to say, "but if you're hungry maybe I could get you something down at the wharfs—"

But Gir just smiled and tossed back his silver hair. "We brought our own fruit with us. Thank you, Daimbert, but I am not sure what these dragons would do here if I were not constantly alert. Contact us again if we can help you further!"

"Any time," I mumbled, slid from the dragon's back, just dodged a snap of its great jaws as Gir rapped it reprovingly with the Scepter, and descended slowly toward the remains of the school. With a final wave, Gir and the other elves shot away into the night, their dragons lighting up the sky with a last sheet of flame.

The destruction seemed confined primarily to the school itself and to the area that had once been the elegant plaza at its base. The fires the dragons had set seemed to have been put out by the school's building stones falling on top of them. The teachers stood, white-faced, in a little group, hardly seeming to hear the surrounding shouting and commotion. The librarian was turning over the books they had managed to rescue, barely keeping from sobbing. "First the Master. Now this," another teacher said, his voice breaking.

And there was even more than the loss of the school and its Master to leave them in despair and shock, I thought. All these teachers had assumed for years that, whenever the sad time came that they needed to elect a new head, they would be voting for Elerius. Even though Zahlfast had talked them out of their support for him, unlike the younger wizards who were ready for excitement whatever the cost, the older teachers had yet to come to terms with the deep betrayal they had experienced—betrayed by their own best judgment.

Evrard came sauntering up, followed by a much more abashed-looking group of young wizards. "Even Elerius's magic couldn't stand up to dragon-fire!" he said, very pleased with himself and stroking his red beard. "I must say I was terrified when all those dragons appeared, until I spotted the dragon-riders and realized they were asking for you! The school's got a lot of old memories buried in the mess, but now that you're Master you'll build it back better than ever. The plumbing, for example, was never—"

I cut him off short. It had been my own fault that the young wizards were sitting outside the school, trying to find ways to break through its defenses, but I wasn't going to let Evrard boast about it. "This is the greatest disaster that has ever befallen wizardry," I said coldly. "We haven't just lost the school building; we've lost untold numbers of books of magic—"

"There must still be lots of copies of the new, printed ones," Evrard said airily, "and who wants the old ones anyway?"

"—as well as whatever magical artifacts were kept in the cellars. It will take years for institutionalized wizardry to recover."

"Well, at least we've gotten rid of Elerius," said Evrard, uncowed.

"And," I said, seeing an additional glimmer of hope, "his library in his old kingdom had thousands of books, enough to fill at least some of the gaps caused by the destruction here. Since he won't be needing his magical volumes now—"

But one of the teachers lifted his head slowly, as though unbearably weary, and froze me with the same look with which he had, years ago, frozen me in class. "Elerius is still alive."

I sat down amid the rubble, my head in my hands. I had compounded the destruction of the school by letting Gir leave too quickly. This is where we needed dragon-fire, to burn through the school's foundations, down to the root of the hill to wherever he was hiding. My conversation with Elerius and the queen had made one thing very clear, the one thing I had kept hoping I could avoid: we could not rest while he was free.

Zahlfast had recovered a little in the cold air and roused himself to look toward me. "Even dragon-fire couldn't get him out of the cellars," he said as though reading my thoughts—for all I knew, he really was. "There are artifacts down there out of the old magic, created with spells stronger than anything we can work today, that would hold off even dragons."

Something left from the old wizard Naurag, I thought. Something he'd doubtless created up in the land of magic toward the end of his life, to protect his own home in the City now that he had given away the Dragons' Scepter, and which, along with so much else, he'd failed to mention in his ledger.

"We could just leave him down there," Evrard suggested uncertainly.

But no one else liked this plan. "You have no idea what other magical artifacts are down there," one of the teachers told Evrard sternly. "If he has gone completely renegade, he could decide to destroy half of the Western Kingdoms."

I turned to Zahlfast and knelt beside him in the street. "You knew a way into the library, Master," I said quietly, talking fast before he could reprove me again for calling him Master. "You've been at the school longer than any of us. Do you know anything—any secret passage, any spell, any magical force—that could cut through into the cellars?"

He shivered and closed his eyes. For a moment I feared he had fainted again. But when he spoke his voice, though thin, was clear. "Now that the Master is dead," he said, eyes still shut, "I know this school better than anyone. There used to be a way. I believe I can still remember the magic to find it again. It was a passage concealed with magic, shut with spells. The old Master—and the only Master, Daimbert!—and I built it years ago, a shortcut, we thought, down to the cellars and the powerful objects concealed there. I do not know that Elerius ever learned of it."

"But where is it?" I asked eagerly. The rest of the teachers, I noticed, did not look eager at all for this information. Once again it looked like avoiding apocalypse was up to me.

He gestured almost aimlessly. "Here. Under the street where we are now. The entrance lies under the paving stones."

"Then let's find it," I said determinedly. "If we're ever going to get Elerius out, it will have to be now, before he has a chance to build new and stronger defenses of his own."

The other teachers still looked reluctant. "I think that Zahlfast—" one said uncertainly.

The old wizard interrupted him, his voice creaky but resolute. "I think that Zahlfast wants to see if his passage is still there. I have been doing powerful spells since before you learned your first illusions, and I am not so sick that I have lost my command of wizardry! The magic to open the passage will not kill me. If Daimbert is willing to go in, then I am willing to help him find the way."

I wouldn't have characterized myself as "willing" to go in, but Zahlfast had given me no choice. Some of the other teachers lifted him out of the middle of the street, and several of us used magic to wrench paving stones up and out of the way. That was the easy part.

At first I couldn't detect any secret passage, and really didn't want to start digging around in the damp gravel, but Zahlfast seemed to know what he was doing. He leaned on his elbows, concentrating hard. And then slowly, his voice creakier than ever, he began speaking in the heavy syllables of the Hidden Language.

This was no spell I knew, though it had certain affinities to spells in the old wizard Naurag's ledger. It was enormously complex—I would have known even without hearing the strain in my old teacher's voice what effort it took to shift magic's four dimensions like this. I had planned to help, but realized immediately that while Zahlfast was moving earth and space I was best off out of the way.

As he spoke, an opening grew in the center of what had once been a street: a round opening down which the gravel rattled. It swirled momentarily, almost like an illusion, then became solid. I tried to peer down it, both with my eyes and with magic, and could find no bottom. I looked uncertainly toward Zahlfast. The light was dim, but I could see sweat standing out on his forehead in the freezing air.

"The passage is stable," he gasped. "The opening is still where I remember it, and it still leads all the way down. If you're going to go, Daimbert, go!"

"But should I—"

He shook his head without waiting for my question. He was panting now. "I don't think I can hold it open much longer. Go!"

None of the other teachers seemed ready to challenge me for the right to go down through a tunnel kept open with faltering magic, to meet a renegade wizard who intended to kill me. Already, I could see, Zahlfast was having trouble keeping his opening in place. I grabbed and squeezed his hand in case I never saw him again.

And was startled to hear his voice in my mind, as sharp and as raspy as when he spoke aloud: "Take me with you."

No time for discussion. I grabbed my old teacher around the shoulders and dove, head-first, into darkness.

V

A floor, faintly lit with a magical glow, came up to meet us, and I caught myself with a flying spell to land with only a small thump, setting Zahlfast down beside me.

The instant we were out of the passageway it disappeared, closing over our heads with a rumble and a last fall of gravel. The shortcut's gone, I thought, knowing Zahlfast would not have the strength to work that spell again. That meant that the only way back out was the regular way, the stairs down which Elerius must have come—and which, if they were not completely blocked by rubble, he would now be guarding.

I spun around, ready for an attack, but at first the cellars appeared rather innocuous. The corridor in which we had landed was whitewashed and fairly featureless, uniformly lit, and as dead silent as though a whole City were not built a few dozen yards above us. I strained for sounds of Elerius—or of some horror out of the Black Wars—and could hear nothing. The rows of heavy oak doors, all closed tight and faintly glittering with magical locks, gave no hint either of menace or of the school above that had so recently been destroyed. There were none of the signs of active life and wizardry that had permeated the school: no desks with salacious spells carved into them, or books set aside with a salamander marking someone's place, or the slowly dissolving remains of an illusion, or a forgotten cup of cold tea.

Only once had I been down here, while still a student, when one of the teachers had sent me here on an errand to find another one of the faculty. At that time a blue baby dragon had been kept in one of the cellar rooms, but I had only had a glimpse of it then, and I had heard that it had died a few years later.

Zahlfast sat catching his breath and rearranging the sheet he had wrapped around himself. It gave me a momentary shiver in its likeness to the winding sheet around a corpse, but he seemed, at least for now, somewhat stronger. "If I'd told all those other faculty members I was coming with you," he said, pleased with himself, "they would have tried to give me an argument."

"But why didn't you bring one of the more knowledgeable teachers instead of me?" I asked. "I've been off in Yurt for years, and have no way of knowing what's in these cellars. Wouldn't it have been better to have someone here who actually understood the dangers?"

He looked at me sideways from under bushy eyebrows. "No. All of the rest of the teachers understand the dangers far too well. We have at most an hour or two until Elerius starts breaking through some of the magic locks down here. I didn't want to spend that hour or two arguing that averting the potential danger to the City and all the kingdoms around was worth the very real mortal danger to ourselves."

Very real mortal danger! I thought but said nothing. After all, I had claimed all along that the only way to oppose Elerius was by being dead.

I helped Zahlfast to his feet, and we started walking slowly. He leaned on my arm, his sheet dragging behind him. "Doesn't look like Elerius has gotten over here, yet," he commented.

"What is down here, Master?" I asked, ignoring his snort when again I called him Master. "What things did the teachers find necessary to lock away from the students?"

"And sometimes each other?" he added with another snort. "The old Master started the collection, artifacts of great power that had been made by his teacher or his teacher's teacher." Naurag, I thought. "I believe there are a number of powerful objects here as well which were first created by those wizards' contemporaries. He and I always regretted that those old wizards weren't very conscientious in writing down their spells, but they were probably better than any wizard since—until Elerius."

This was a glum thought. I didn't answer.

"Then, when he started the school after the Black Wars," Zahlfast continued in his school-teacher voice, "he had all the wizards of the West bring him the weapons of terrible destruction which they had forged for use in those wars. Many he merely destroyed. For others, he carefully disentangled the spells in his search for new and different ways to order magic's four dimensions. By the time I joined him, and the school was already taking its first young wizardry pupils, all that were left were those most interesting for demonstration purposes—or those most terrible, where even the best wizard might find it difficult to control the forces such an artifact would unleash. As a one-time pupil here, I'm sure you can appreciate why we didn't want to allow the students easy access."

"Um, yes," I muttered, thinking of Evrard—and myself.

"Over the years, an occasional creature from the land of wild magic might appear in the lands of men, and some of those we captured and locked in the cellars as well. A few decades ago there was even a collecting trip up north, but it was not considered a success and not repeated."

As we slowly passed the series of identical and unmarked doors, I found myself wondering uneasily which one might hold a miniature gorgos, which an artifact second in power only to the Dragon's Sceptre, and which dark instruments of death, and hoping that the magical locks were able to hold them. If any of us emerged alive from this, proper identification tags on the doors should be a first order of business.

But then something Zahlfast had said a moment ago struck me. "You said you expected Elerius to break through the magic locks! I thought it was impossible to break one."

He gave me another sideways look. "I wondered when you would think of that. The Master decided a few years ago, when he recovered from his last serious illness, that it was a mistake to have all these doors keyed only to his palm print. Without him, none of us would ever be able to open them again. So he rekeyed them all, using two palm prints, his own and that of the faculty member he then thought most likely to succeed him—Elerius."

"But wouldn't you still need both people's hands to open the lock?"

"One should. But the magic of the lock is weaker by being divided between two hands. The old Master counted on Elerius being able to find a way to break down the spells once he himself was gone."

"Do you know how he could do that?" I asked, intrigued.

Zahlfast shook his head slowly, and when his answer came it was so quiet I almost didn't hear him. "I'm not that good a wizard."

That made two of us. We walked on in silence for a minute. I was thinking that there was at least one artifact down here to which Elerius already had access, the one with which he had threatened to destroy me. Could he be lurking behind this door, I thought, looking both up and down the corridor, or that one? I tried a prayer to the Cranky Saint in an effort to calm my panicked heart beat. At the moment even he, bursting in with a blaze of celestial light from the realm of the supernatural, would have seemed like a friendly face.

These cellars must be solidly built; only a few cracks in wall and ceiling suggested that tons of masonry had collapsed on top of them, and the magical lights still functioned smoothly. The corridor intersected other passages, with no indication of which might lead to the stairs. We turned right at the first intersection, left at the next and the next, and in a few minutes I had lost any sense of where we had come in.

When the sound began, it was at first so faint I didn't notice it. But then I realized that neither my old teacher nor I were making a hissing sound. I looked at him questioningly, but he had already stopped, his head cocked.

"I feared as much," he said quietly. "I wondered why we had not seen him yet, if by some chance he didn't realize we were here. No, Elerius has declined to meet us."

"And that sound—" The hissing was closer now, and the temperature of the air in the corridor was dropping rapidly.

"When he decided to break a magic lock, he did not choose a door at random. He chose one door on purpose. I thought it might take him two hours, but I overestimated. He has it unlocked now."

Zahlfast leaned more heavily on me, and we waited as that sound slowly approached. "Whatever you do, Daimbert," he said between his teeth, "do not look it in the eye."

The corridor walls on either side were now white with frost. Even the cold could not conceal the smell that began sliding toward us, a smell like an open grave. Added to the hissing came a constant click-click, of talons against the floor.

Ahead of us another corridor crossed the one in which we stood. The magic lamps that lit the cellars cast a shadow, a shadow of the creature which proceeded it past the corner: not very big for something of such horror, it walked on chicken legs, feathered wings emerging stiffly from its sides, but its head and tail were those of a serpent.

A basilisk. A creature of wild magic that should never have come to the land of men in the first place, and if it could not be destroyed should have been permanently locked away. And now Elerius had loosed it on us, and, after it had frozen us or turned us to stone, it would find its way out to do the same to the rest of the people in the City.

"Do not meet its eye," said Zahlfast again, just as the serpent head came around the corner.

Shivering uncontrollably, I stood as stiff and motionless as though the basilisk's gaze had already turned me to stone. My own eyes averted, I heard its taloned feet coming steadily toward us.

They freeze the air around them, I remembered from a long-ago lecture held in a classroom that no longer existed. They turn to stone those who meet their jeweled eyes. And they bite with the bite of death those they neither freeze nor transform to stone.

Zahlfast might have been old and sick, but at least his terror had not paralyzed him. He began speaking in the heavy syllables of the Hidden Language, a binding spell, more complicated and far more difficult than anything I had ever been taught at the school. For a second the click of chicken feet on stone ceased, then, more slowly, they started moving toward us again.

Solomon's spell. The binding spell that would hold even an Ifrit in a bottle. I opened my mouth and found it almost too dry for speech. The dragging talons were coming closer. I tried again.

And shouted the spell that Levi had written out for me, the spell that Solomon had engraved on his golden signet. For a second the corridors echoed to my words, which seemed to come back at me from a dozen directions, and in that second the voice in the back of my mind asked how it felt to have paralyzed all of us.

But I hadn't. I moved both arms at once, almost toppling Zahlfast, then took a step forward, my eyes still averted.

"*Where* did you get that spell?" he demanded, his voice creakier than ever. "Whatever you did," he continued, "it worked—the creature cannot move now. And its serpent teeth cannot bite. But its eye could still turn us to stone."

We sidled toward it, trying to judge its location by its shadow and sideways glances that stopped just short of its head. Zahlfast was shaking far harder than I was. But he ripped a strip off the end of his sheet and, awkwardly because he couldn't watch what he was doing, wrapped it around and around the basilisk's serpent head.

"I'll look first," he said at last, and I watched his face as he turned his head, gazed for a rapid second, gazed longer, and finally looked toward me. "The bandage holds."

The frost was melting back off the walls, and the smell was receding, as I looked too: at a creature messily wrapped in a rag, a rag that completely concealed its eyes.

Zahlfast let out all his breath then and sat down on the cold floor. "By all the powers of magic, Daimbert," he said after a minute, "what spell was that?"

"Um, something out of the really old magic. King Solomon's own binding spell." It was too complicated to explain.

"I never did hear where you were when we all thought you dead," my old teacher said, with the faintest hint of a smile. "If we are not truly dead at the end of this night, it would be worth hearing. I thought all those years ago at the transformations practical exam, when you approached those frogs in such a spectacularly lame-brained way, and then got out of your mess so brilliantly, that you would either end up as one of the most innovative and successful wizards of your generation, or else would destroy the school. I never imagined until today that you would do both. Help me up. Elerius will not long delay once he learns what we have done to his basilisk."

I gave him a hand up off the floor, then was appalled when he picked up the basilisk by its stiff little chicken wings. He held it distastefully, well out in front of him. "And how long did you think," he said with a sideways glance, "before Elerius came to recover it, if we did not take it with us? Besides," and for a second he almost chuckled, "if we suddenly come upon him, we can threaten to whip the rag from its eyes."

We kept on walking. We seemed to have been walking a very long time, yet the corridor looked always the same. Zahlfast was constantly trembling now, but he shrugged off the arm I tried to offer him. "Best only one of us be in living contact with this beast," he said. "If we can find the room from which Elerius freed it, we can throw it back in and lock it with our own palm prints."

"But don't you know where the basilisk was kept?" I asked.

"No," he snapped between shivering teeth, "because I don't know where we are. I thought I knew, and we have taken all the right turns, yet ..." His voice trailed away, then he suddenly snorted. "Illusion. We have been done in by the simplest trick. Elerius has changed the appearance of these corridors just enough that we could walk in circles in here for weeks and never find our way out."

Illusion I could deal with. It had been a subtle spell, one designed to leave no impression of its presence, but obvious once I looked for it. I broke the spell with a few words. The corridor looked to me exactly the same.

But it looked different to Zahlfast, for he lifted his head with new confidence. "Now I know where we are. A few more turns, and we will be at the stairs that used to lead up to the school."

The stairs to which Elerius would know we would have to come sooner or later, and which he would therefore have carefully fortified against us.

But he might be there himself. The whole purpose of being in the cellars, I reminded myself, was to find him.

Suddenly the floor around our feet came alive: scorpions, snakes, spiders, six-inch cockroaches. I stopped dead in horror, but Zahlfast kept on walking. "More illusions," he announced.

I swallowed the bitterness of revulsion and broke this illusion as well. The creatures disappeared as quickly as they had come.

"Of course, there *are* real cockroaches down here, but nothing that size—" Zahlfast was just saying, when I heard a new sound.

This one was almost metallic, a creaking and scrabbling of something very large coming toward us from down a side corridor. I put a hand on Zahlfast's arm. Illusions do not make noise.

After the basilisk I had thought I was prepared for anything. But I was wrong. I was not prepared for a cockroach ten feet high, filling the corridor from side to side, waving its tentacles and coming on fast.

part eleven ✤ hell

I

a PARALYSIS SPELL! I thought wildly. King Solomon's binding spell! Could I work that powerful a spell a second time down here without seriously weakening the walls that kept the ceiling above us? Would the basilisk's stare freeze the cockroach in its tracks as it would have frozen us?

While I was flailing around desperately trying to find the right magic, Zahlfast was already at work. He rattled off a spell, and the enormous insect stopped advancing. But it waved its tentacles and stared at us with its multiple eyes. It looked hungry. I wondered if we could feed it the basilisk.

Zahlfast spoke again, and abruptly it was gone. A small, brown, normal-sized insect scuttled across the floor. I took one step forward and crushed it beneath my sole.

"Good work, Master!" I said, attempting to sound nonchalant and scraping the residue off my shoe. "How did you manage to shrink it?"

Zahlfast had closed his eyes, swaying for a moment, then took a deep breath. I put an arm under his elbow without comment. I knew he wouldn't say how he really felt, and he didn't want me to seem to be fussing over him, but this constant series of spells must be a serious drain on a man already old and sick.

"It was in fact quite simple, Daimbert," he said after a moment. I noticed he hadn't had the energy to chide me for continuing to call him Master. "Elerius had transformed an ordinary cockroach into one swollen to extraordinary size.

All I had to do was to reverse his spell. I hope you haven't forgotten that I am the head of the transformations faculty!"

"If he's resorting to transformed insects," I said, "he must not have managed to break any more magic locks. Either that—or he himself is frightened of what might be in the rooms."

"With good reason," said Zahlfast.

We kept on walking because there didn't seem to be much else we could do. It was bitter cold down here, even with the basilisk immobilized, a coldness that seeped into my bones. I was so tired that I thought that if I dared sit down I might fall asleep and never wake up—and it must be even worse for Zahlfast. I wondered with a kind of flat despair if Elerius might be long gone from the cellars, and if we would die from cold and exhaustion before we were able to find the way back out again.

I almost missed it. We were trudging down another corridor, when I realized that one of the doors we had just passed was not locked.

Silently I motioned to Zahlfast, then put my back to the wall next to the door and probed again. Definitely no magic lock here. Still no direct indication of Elerius, but he had to be somewhere. He would have had to unlock a door to go inside; I put a hand flat on it, trying to tell if he was in there— or if this room was just empty.

I couldn't be sure. Zahlfast stayed well back, holding the basilisk, also unsure. Very delicately I started turning the knob, preparatory to swinging the door open with a bang.

Still no sign of life. I gave the door an abrupt push and ducked back out of the way of whatever he might be using to defend himself.

But still there was nothing. Cautiously I put my head around the corner, and saw—

"What is it?" I asked in wonder after a moment. "Is this something left from the Black Wars?" In the center of the room was a great swirling mass of color, pouring from what appeared to be copper rods and steel wheels.

Zahlfast came up beside me to look. "That's nothing out of the old magic," he said with a snort. "That's something developed here by the technical division, only a few years ago. One powers it up with magic, and then it can keep a spell going almost indefinitely."

Someday I really had to stop feeling my whole mind go blank whenever someone mentioned technical magic. I took a step into the room. "What's it doing?"

Zahlfast frowned, probing. "I think he was using it to augment his own powers, first to keep any spells from working within the school, then, unsuccessfully, to strengthen the school's defenses against dragons. Now—" He frowned again. "I don't know what it's doing now."

"Nothing any good," I said firmly. "How do I turn it off?"

The one advantage of technical magic is that, even if you don't understand it, you can usually operate it fairly easily. With a few suggestions from Zahlfast, and only one pinch when I got my fingers too close to the copper rods, I managed to turn off the apparatus. It sighed, and the swirling colors subsided. Now it was only a collection of metal cogs, rods, and tubes, dead and without motion.

Far down the corridor, I heard a shout of fury.

"Maybe he had a second basilisk, and it's bitten him," I said hopefully.

Zahlfast shook his head. "There was only ever the one."

But Elerius must still be down here. With his apparatus turned off, maybe the two of us might even stand a chance against him. I took Zahlfast firmly under the elbow, and this time he did not try to shake me off. We walked quickly, down one corridor and then another—and saw a door standing open.

We stopped, looked at each other, and looked toward that door, slightly ajar, a faint light emerging from inside. I didn't dare even whisper—but then it would not have been difficult for Elerius to spot us, even silent as illusions. I pointed toward the doorway and lifted an eyebrow, inquiring if my old teacher knew what had been stored in there.

But he seemed to interpret my question differently. He slid his elbow out of my grasp and handed me the basilisk.

In my surprise I almost dropped it. Its wings were stiffer and sharper than I expected, and it seemed to weigh as much as something ten times its size. No hissing—Solomon's binding spell held it tightly. By the time I had recovered, and made sure the face was aimed away from me, in case of any slippage of the rag over its eyes, Zahlfast had started forward.

He had thought I was asking who of us should go first, and he was volunteering.

He walked straight to the door and swung it all the way open. "You know better than that, Elerius," he said in his school-teacher voice. "Put that down and come out."

Put what down? Curiosity overcame reluctance. Still holding the basilisk in front of me, I took two steps forward. Zahlfast stood in the room's doorway, leaning against the frame. "Without the augmenter working, you'll never be able to make that function," he said crisply. "It's designed for two wizards."

I had no idea what he had there, even after I stepped up next to Zahlfast. It looked like nothing more than an old clay cup, sitting by itself in the middle of the floor. But there was something about that cup that seemed almost unbearably sinister. And behind it, clutching a crumbling leather-bound ledger, stood Elerius.

He had changed, was my first thought. He no longer looked like the most fearsome wizard in the West. Deprived of his kingdom, deprived of his lover, deprived of the respect of the wizards' school, his black hair stood wildly on end, and his hazel eyes were not calculating but wild. But if he no longer thought he was acting for the best, the voice in the back of my mind pointed out, there was no telling what he might do.

"You will notice," said Zahlfast, his voice calm on the surface though I could hear the enormous strain underneath, "that Daimbert has the basilisk. You do not want him to have to remove the rag from its eyes. I'm sure I don't need to tell you that when it turns you to stone, even I, with all my abilities, will be unable to transform you back. Now, come out and give up this mad plan. Neither one of us will act as the second wizard."

"If I don't try to channel it," Elerius said, low and harsh, "then I don't need a second wizard." He opened the ledger, keeping a wary eye on us.

I had no idea what they were talking about. My first thought was that he had somehow gotten hold of old Naurag's ledger, but I realized then that this was a different book. Not a library book, clearly—it must be something stored down here along with whatever that cup represented. When I probed, I could see the magical influence it cast without understanding it at all. It seemed more sinister than ever.

Zahlfast stiffened. "This is the way of despair, Elerius," he said quietly. "I know you don't want to end your life as well as those of all the people in the City—and all the wizards in the West."

"I don't care," said Elerius, and he looked past our old teacher's shoulder straight at me. "As long as Daimbert dies, I really don't care what happens to me or anyone else."

Zahlfast addressed me without taking his eyes off Elerius. Almost casually he said, "It is time to use the basilisk."

It was impossible to hold it upright using only one hand. I had to balance it against me, its sharp wing feathers digging through my jacket, to free up a hand to start unwinding the torn sheet.

But when I commanded my hand to move, it stayed inert, clutching a corner of rag.

Had the dark powers of the basilisk leached onto me somehow, freezing me in place? But the rest of me could still move. Or was Elerius somehow paralyzing me? But all his attention was aimed toward Zahlfast—and toward that ominous clay cup.

It wasn't Elerius who was stopping me. I was doing it myself. I couldn't cold-bloodedly turn him into stone anymore than I had been able to set the Ifrit on him. I cursed myself for a sentimental fool with no strength of character. It didn't help.

But he had far fewer scruples. With a last scowl for me—and perhaps a sneer for my weakness—Elerius started on spells. He had to go slowly, marking his place in the ledger with a finger as the syllables rolled from his lips. As I listened to him I knew, from experience, that in several places he was improvising his way across gaps where unusual herbs were designed to go.

But the spell was working. Still clutching the basilisk to me though its cold had numbed all one side, I realized what he was doing. The magic that had been embedded, untold centuries ago, in that clay cup would slowly open a hole in the earth a thousand feet across and a thousand miles deep— a hole that would swallow not just the ruins of the wizards' school, but the City around us.

No spell is unique, and all magic has recognizable elements, even though some of the old herbal magic is very far from the technical magic of glass and steel. I spotted similarities, only slight but similarities still, between the spell Elerius was working and the spell Zahlfast had used to get us down into the cellars.

The difference was that my old teacher's spell had not required the layers of old magic laid down in the clay cup— magic that Basil would have described as the magic of blood and bone—and had opened a passage only three feet across and a few dozen feet deep. That, and the fact that Elerius was trying, by himself, to work a two-wizard spell, that even in the most capable hands required one wizard to help shape and position the chasm as the other's magic created it.

I struggled desperately to unwrap the basilisk, to freeze Elerius before he could complete the spell. This time the strip of sheet became all tangled, blinding the monster worse than before.

Zahlfast gave up waiting for me. He had seen the similarities in the spells as well. And slowly, his voice quavering, he sought to find the words of the Hidden Language to oppose Elerius.

This was no magic that I had ever learned. I set the basilisk down, facing into the room, and tried again with both hands to remove the rag. Now my fingers were almost completely numb, and I fumbled helplessly as I tried to take hold of the strip of cloth. Zahlfast beside me was speaking louder and louder but slower and slower. The tension between the two spells became sharper, until it was almost visible.

Elerius, his nose buried deep in the ledger, was almost shouting his own words of the Hidden Language. The clay cup slowly began to rise, spinning as it left the floor, and its center was a spinning vortex.

I abandoned the basilisk and tried a few spells of my own, but I was so exhausted that nothing I tried seemed to work. Zahlfast never stopped, however, forcing out each syllable. His voice was now no more than a croak, but he kept on going. I gave up on being a wizard and wrapped my arms around him, just trying to keep him from falling.

The clay cup was spinning so fast now that it hummed, and the vortex at the center, when I dared look at it, seemed ready to suck us into oblivion. Zahlfast's one advantage was that he knew his spell, whereas Elerius was constantly having to consult his book and improvise ways to get over the book's gaps.

Zahlfast's voice was growing fainter. I reached out to him, mind to mind, and for one second could hear his thoughts. "There, Daimbert, and there—"

And I could in that instant see it, the structure of the spell built into the cup which was now creating the vortex, and the way Zahlfast had constructed his counter-spell to oppose it. With a desperate effort, I forced myself into magic's four dimensions, pulling bits of spells together that I had learned from half a dozen wizards and mages in both East and West. My voice echoed in my ears, and before my eyes, blurry now, I could see the cup's smooth rotation changed into jerky motion.

Zahlfast spoke again, a whole string of words in the Hidden Language. With both our spells working together, the cup abruptly broke free of Elerius's spells, rose toward the ceiling, and exploded into dusty fragments. Elerius was left crouched on the ground, his face and beard spattered with dried clay, and even the ledger he held disintegrating into powder in his hands.

But I had no time to enjoy the triumph, for Zahlfast had gone limp in my arms.

"Zahlfast? Master? Are you—" I couldn't ask if he was all right because he very clearly wasn't. He drooped with no sign of hearing my voice.

I tried mental communication, and found a flicker of consciousness. He was trying to say something but could not speak, and even to speak mind-to-mind was an enormous effort. Close to his thoughts, I could feel darkness coming up around him, and reflexively jerked back my own consciousness, but not before I thought I had understood his final words.

He had told me, "Good-bye, Master."

Slowly I sank to the cold floor, trying to position Zahlfast in a comfortable position across my lap. His thoughts had slipped away beyond forgetting. For a few moments more, his chest still rose and fell. But then he stopped breathing.

II

I sat without moving for several minutes, my head drooping. Zahlfast's body gradually grew cold in my arms, and both the floor and the basilisk beside me could have been solid ice. Zahlfast had known, I thought. He had known that going to match spells with Elerius would kill him. But he hadn't cared, because the safety of the City was more important to him than his own life. I hadn't been able to save my old teacher— at most I had been able to help him where unaided he would have failed. And now I had to try to finish what he had given his life to do—stopping Elerius.

I pushed myself to my feet and furiously wiped a sleeve across my eyes, aching in every joint. I began to lift Zahlfast's body; I couldn't just abandon him here in the cellars. But where was Elerius? I hadn't heard him leave—for the excellent reason, I saw when I turned, that he was still here in the room, working on something, his back to me.

And then he spoke: "By Satan, by Beelzebub—"

I had thought nothing could make me move rapidly again, but I was wrong. I slung Zahlfast against the wall and threw myself bodily on top of Elerius's glowing pentagram. Wildly I rubbed at the chalk lines, while giving Elerius the best glare I could. "I thought the saint told you he would not tolerate demons," I said, and I was so tired that my voice came out an octave too low and without inflection—a voice from the tomb.

Elerius sagged backwards. He was, I saw, as exhausted as I was. I gave a quick glance over my shoulder in case the Cranky Saint with his staff and blazing eyes was right behind me. He wasn't, but I'd better press my advantage while I still had it.

"How do you do it, Daimbert?" Elerius was babbling. "How did you turn my son against me and destroy the queen's love for me? How did you summon the dragons without my detecting the spell? How did you defeat the basilisk and the most powerful objects out of both modern and ancient magic?"

Some of that had been Zahlfast, not me, but I didn't say so. I sat up in the middle of the half-effaced pentagram, letting my voice stay deep. "You told me yourself," I said, hoping this wasn't so big a fib that the Cranky Saint would turn against me. "You yourself said, Elerius, that I have powers you do not comprehend." Powers of integrity and friendship, I told my conscience.

He was panting now. "Well, you and all your saintly friends may keep me from working with a demon, but I don't need a demon! Come with me, Daimbert. I have something to show you."

I rose slowly and leaned over him, glowering. "Something with which you intend to kill me? As you already killed Zahlfast? Do not look so surprised, Elerius. I can read your plans in your face." I could barely see straight, much less read a plan in his expression, but it hadn't taken a very astute guess.

There was a limit to how far bluff would take me. Very faint, far above us, I heard scrapes and creaks. Clearly the school's ruins had not yet finished settling. "You come with *me*!" I said urgently. When this was all over, I thought, whoever tried to take over running organized wizardry had better figure out what actually was down here under the rubble and see about deactivating it. "We must leave before the final destruction of the school above us blocks these tunnels. We don't want to starve here while cursing each other."

He was still panting, but he seemed to have recovered at least a little of his composure. "Don't mind what I said to Zahlfast. I was just overwrought; I never really wanted you dead, Daimbert. Maybe I should simply surrender to the teachers—assuming any are still alive." This was exactly what

I wanted to hear him say, but as he spoke his eyes were calculating.

I took his arm and pulled him to his feet with a jerk. "First, find the stairs to get us out of here. You go first." I lifted Zahlfast's body over my shoulder, and for one moment Elerius did look genuinely repentant. He really had not meant his old teacher to die: unlike what he planned for me.

As soon as we were into the corridor, out of the room where Elerius had found the clay cup, I pushed the basilisk inside, slammed the door, and locked it with a magic lock, keyed to my own palm print. Let Elerius try to break *that* lock.

He looked surprised but said nothing. Instead he started down the corridor meekly and obediently. Suspecting a trick, I followed close behind. He might be heading straight toward other dreadful creatures or artifacts of dark destruction. I was barely able to stagger under Zahlfast's weight, and I doubted I could have matched spells with Elerius any better than could a kitten. But he didn't seem about to attack me either. We proceeded through the cellars like the friends we once had been.

Elerius led me first to an open door—the room where he had had the machine of technical magic with which he could augment his spells. "If these cellars are likely to collapse," he told me innocently, "the rest of the teachers will want to preserve at least this."

"I think I had better carry it," I said sternly.

"Do you want me to carry Zahlfast, then?" he asked, still all innocence.

I clutched my teacher's body closer. "No." I didn't trust Elerius not to try some horrible black magic with his inert form. "But don't turn the machine on."

He nodded meekly, not giving me an argument—either too frightened of a possible appearance by the Cranky Saint, or already thinking of a better plan—and led the way again, carefully carrying the awkward collection of tubes, rods, and wheels out in front of him. Turned off, it gave no hint of its magical powers.

"I have to keep walking," I told myself, because I would have fallen asleep if I had sat still. Intermittently, when I remembered, I murmured the words to break an illusion, in case Elerius was again trying to confuse me by altering the appearance of the cellar corridors. But the long stretches of white corridor and identical doors were disorienting, illusion or not. I wondered vaguely if it was yet morning outside.

At last Elerius stopped by a door that at first glance looked like all the others. "This is the way to the stairs," he said with a completely unsuccessful attempt at a smile. "If you rebuild the school, once you're Master, you might want to have the exit better marked. See? The door is unlocked." He pushed it open, and beyond I could indeed see a corridor with, far ahead in the shadows, a staircase.

"I wonder how badly the stairs are blocked," I said, keeping one eye on him as I tried to peer down that dim corridor.

"I know these cellars better than you do," Elerius said. "And you're burdened with Zahlfast. I think I had better go first, just in case there's any problem."

There was always reason to be wary with Elerius, I thought. "Oh, no, you don't," I said firmly. "*I* am going to take the lead here."

It was not until I was half way down the dim corridor toward the stairs, and heard the whirring of the magic augmenter behind me, that I realized I had not been wary enough.

I spun around, just in time to see Elerius shooting upward, working a variation of the spell Zahlfast had used to get us in here in the first place. The magic apparatus hummed and poured waves of colors across the dim white corridor.

"You, Daimbert," he shouted in fury, "can go to Hell!" And then he was gone, burrowing effortlessly through tumbled building stone and bedrock. Behind him the opening to his tunnel closed as tightly as if it had never been there.

I looked toward the stairs, partially blocked, but my only way out. I didn't have any apparatus to make it easier for me, I thought with a groan, trying to find the strength to work a few simple lifting spells. Even if the roof didn't collapse, it would take me hours to get out of here, by which time Elerius would be long gone.

The sun's rim was just rising into a sullen sky when I finally emerged from the rubble that had once been the school. I sat slowly down on a bit of stone that had probably once been a parapet. I was so tired I could hardly see, and my entire body felt scraped from repeatedly using magic to tunnel through tons of unstable stone and plaster.

Initially while I burrowed out I had feared everything would collapse on top of me, and then for a while I had rather hoped it would, thus saving me the trouble of ever having to do anything else. At least Elerius was not waiting to greet me; if he had been, I think I might have surrendered on the spot.

After ten minutes to catch my breath, I hefted Zahlfast's body over my shoulder a final time and wandered down the street in search of the teachers. They were no longer sitting in the streets; they must, I thought, have been taken in by the townspeople. The dragons and the Dragons' Scepter were gone, as was the Ifrit. And Elerius was gone too, but, I knew, already planning his return. I didn't know what else we could try to stop him.

Even staggering down the street with my eyes mostly shut, I couldn't help but notice someone wearing the blue and white livery of Yurt. I stopped, peering in the dawn light. The guardsman peered back at me. Bedraggled and covered with dust as I was, I must have been hard to recognize. On the other hand, I knew him—he was one of the knights of the royal castle of Yurt.

And then he did recognize me, started to grin widely, dipped his head respectfully instead, and mumbled, "It is an honor to see you, sir." He darted inside before I could answer.

The townhouse in front of which he had been standing was one of the more elegant on this street, faced with white marble and with a row of balconies, each displaying a potted orange tree, on its upper floor. The orange trees seemed to have suffered from dragon fire, and some of the marble was scorched, but the house was essentially intact. Inside the door the knight had left ajar I could hear high-raised voices, then, down the street, the ringing of a telephone. I leaned my forehead against the housefront and wondered if there was time for a small nap before anyone came back.

But I had done no more than close my eyes when I heard running feet, and King Paul burst out the door, half-dressed, trailing his sword in one hand, his face lit up by an enormous smile. "Wizard! You did it! I always knew you could!"

Something was wrong. It took me a minute to work it out. But then I remembered. "Excuse me, sire," I said thickly, "but you're not here. You're back in Hadwidis's kingdom."

I was, of course, mistaken. He smiled for a moment, shaking his head, then became serious. The seriousness looked more like a normal expression on him than it ever had before. "The war's over, Wizard, thanks to you. All of Queen Hadwidis's knights have accepted her, but she will be busy for weeks going around her kingdom reestablishing order and loyalty. There was no reason for us to stay there—to try to make glorious the remnants of a hideous war in which men had to die, some by my hand."

Other people poured out of doorways up and down the street, some fully clothed, some still in their dressing gowns, and all of them delighted to see me: the teachers from the school, the young wizards, most of the royal party from Yurt, Maffi, and my family.

Someone, I thought one of the teachers, came to take Zahlfast's body from me. At first I wouldn't let go—I had been carrying him so long, it didn't seem right to let someone else have him. The realization that he had died in the pursuit of Elerius took the smiles, pretty tentative anyway, off the teachers' lips, but everyone else was too happy to see me to be very deeply bothered by the death of an old man they barely knew.

Antonia danced around me. "Dragons!" she cried. "That must have been so exciting! I wish I'd seen them, but we got here too late. Can Walther come live with us? He has to be with his sister now, and I know he hates it. And do you know what we've been doing, Wizard? Maffi and I, we've decided we'll trick the Ifrit back into his bottle, and have him give us even more wishes. Now all we have to do is to find him in the East and get the bottle back from him."

I didn't have the energy to discourage her. I put my arms around Theodora and my face in her hair.

"You know," she commented, "several times recently you've raced off, every time without me, and every time you've reappeared battered and worn, lucky to be alive at all. To put it delicately, you look like you've been through Hell. Now, you're fairly smart, so I'll ask you to ponder this: aren't you starting to notice a *pattern*?"

The teachers were huddled together in the street, even the older ones looking to me as if they expected some sort of guidance. "Zahlfast died defeating something out of the old magic which Elerius was trying to use against us," I told them over Theodora's head. "Something that involved a clay cup." Several of them blanched. "We destroyed the cup together, but I'm afraid it was all for nothing. Elerius is still alive. He burrowed his way out of the cellars, and if none of you spotted him when he emerged, the saints alone know where he's hiding now."

"How are you going to find him?" a teacher asked.

I had no idea. The responsibility, I noticed, seemed to be firmly mine.

"While you and Zahlfast were gone, Daimbert—" the teacher added, then paused as if what he was about to say was distasteful, but pushed on anyway. "While you were gone, we decided it was well past time to elect the Master's successor. So we decided— We voted that if you came back you would lead us." He paused again. "I do need to be frank and tell you that, while you got far more than a majority of the votes, it was not unanimous."

My heart, if possible, sank even lower. Several of the teachers, including doubtless this one, agreed with me that I would be a terrible leader. By electing me, however, they had assured that I, and not any of them, would go chasing off after Elerius.

The only thing to do was to pretend I had not heard him and try to distract the teachers onto a different topic. "Elerius will be hiding very thoroughly," I said, "especially since he's got some sort of spell augmenter to keep us from finding him—and to help him spot us if we try to sneak up on him. If there was some way we could trick him into revealing his position …"

If there was, I couldn't think of it. Gwennie came running up the street from a house a little further down. She had pulled back on the bedraggled clothes she had worn on our trip to the East but had at least made an effort to comb her hair.

"Did you think we wouldn't all follow you, Wizard?" she asked with a smile. "It's not as fast as flying, but horses can travel rapidly if they have to! Hadwidis can manage without her new countess for a while."

Her new countess, I thought dully, thinking this ought to make sense. Then I noticed that Gwennie had gone immediately to stand next to King Paul—close enough that, without appearing to intend to do so, he could take her hand. The seriousness that, I had just started to think, looked good on a king was gone in an instant. She turned her head slightly toward him, and there was a sparkle in her eyes.

Oh. Yes. Hadwidis had ennobled her. It all made sense after all. "Did someone telephone the bishop?" Paul asked.

He and Gwennie turned together, hips touching, hands locked, to look down the street. "I think that's him coming," she said.

I fumbled in my pocket. After thousands of miles of travel, I still had Paul's diamond ring. I pulled it out from under King Solomon's golden signet. Maybe some of its binding power would rub off on the ring, to make a union of hearts that would last for a lifetime. "Here you go, sire," I said, handing it to him. "You probably were wondering whatever happened to this."

Paul took it with a pleased grin. Gwennie, however, turned up her nose in an unconvincing attempt at saucy disdain. "Haven't gotten over your fixation on rings yet, Paul," she asked, "after all that's happened?"

I had always thought Paul and Gwennie would make a good couple, if only there were not such a social gulf between them. It had taken a trip to the East with a runaway nun who turned out to be a queen, but Gwennie had come home with the roc's treasure and a patent of nobility, as well as stories of fabled Xantium. Theodora gave me a squeeze. She too knew—we didn't need to worry anymore about a queen for the king of Yurt.

But the only comment on the situation came from Maffi. He sighed deeply. "I traveled all the way from Xantium with two of the West's most lovely young ladies," he said in a low voice, "protected them and enriched them, and at the end one of them announces she's going to live like a nun, even though she's a queen, and the other one chooses some benighted local kinglet over me." At least he didn't suggest waiting for Antonia to grow up.

Joachim by now had reached us. Somehow the bishop's presence always made me feel calm, in spite of the spiritual intensity which surrounded him as palpably as magic had once surrounded the wizards' school.

"The old Master of your school," he commented, looking in the cold light of morning at the rubble, "would be surprised to hear that your rule as his successor had begun with the school's destruction. But you might take heart, Daimbert, to learn that not everyone in the City is blaming the wizards for all this excitement. I spoke last night with the priests of the cathedral, and they are convinced that they themselves are to blame, that God is punishing them for first being divided so long in electing a new bishop, and then for electing an unsuitable candidate."

"I need your help, Joachim," I said, still holding Theodora tight to me. I had had an idea. "Elerius is still alive, still plotting all our destructions. Now that he's out the cellars we don't need to wonder what artifacts of destruction he might get his hands on, but he's still the best living wizard in the West. He has all the advantages of natural magic on his side, so, short of the supernatural—"

The head of the demonology faculty interrupted. He had been standing with the rest of the teachers, watching my reunion with my family and friends from Yurt, but now he put his hand on my arm. "Daimbert, I know what you're thinking. Don't do it. It's not worth it."

Startled, it took me a second to realize what he meant. "No, I'm not going to summon a demon," I said hastily. "I'd have to give myself to the devil, body and soul, for him to agree to find Elerius for me, and at that point I wouldn't trust myself not to become so drunk on power that I would become even worse than he is." I'd had this discussion with myself too often in the past. The Cranky Saint was right. I wasn't going to get out of this without being tempted, and the idea that one could somehow serve a wholesome, useful function through the exercise of evil was the greatest temptation of all.

My plan was quite different. It was probably the most foolhardy idea I had ever had in a long career of them, but at least it was something that Elerius would never, ever anticipate. Other than being the product of a deranged mind, it was in fact an excellent plan, because it would make Elerius himself, all unsuspecting, bring me to where he was. "I'm going back to Yurt," I said.

"Giving up, Daimbert?" another of the teachers asked coldly. Another one, I thought, who had kept the vote for me from being unanimous. "Abandoning the problem of Elerius to us? I must say I'm not sure what the Master was thinking when he suggested you as his heir."

I smiled and looked past him to meet the bishop's eyes. "Neither do I. But at least he never imagined that I would give up." Going to the land of dragons hadn't worked, and neither had capturing an Ifrit, or even befriending a saint. But sheer stubbornness kept me going. "Elerius himself first gave me the idea on how to find him. I'm going to catch him if I have to go through Hell to do it."

III

I hadn't planned to take anyone else with me. But it soon appeared that I had no choice. "I don't trust the staff not to have made a mess of the accounts without a constable to keep track of them," said Gwennie, but the way she looked at the king suggested something quite different: her mind was less on paperwork than on planning their wedding.

I left the teachers to try to make sense in the morning light out of the school's destruction, and to see about Zahlfast's funeral, and headed back to Yurt. I rode on Naurag, Theodora sitting behind me with an arm around my waist, while Joachim, King Paul, Gwennie, Antonia, and Maffi rode the magic carpet.

My purple flying beast was irritable. He had been badly frightened by the dragons and seemed to have decided it was my fault. Several hoots he gave suggested unflattering comments about my ancestry, my morals, and my personal hygiene. Since I had to agree with him that it was indeed all my fault, I could do nothing but try to soothe him with soft words.

Whitey and Chin had insisted on coming along, saying that now that I was Master they needed to assist me as they had assisted the old Master. I had still, even after working with them on the undead warriors, not entirely forgiven them for their midnight capture of me on their one previous trip to the royal castle of Yurt, and made them fly along behind.

I was in something of a mental haze as we sailed over the kingdoms between the City and Yurt, half-dozing against Naurag's neck. What I was contemplating would have been appalling if I had not been so tired. With vague curiosity I wondered what would happen to my soul once I was dead.

I wanted to start at once, as soon as we arrived, but first everyone wanted to hear how Daimbert's War had turned out, in more detail than Paul had given the assistant constable on the telephone; then they had to marvel at the flying carpet and an exotic eastern mage, who immediately demonstrated how exotic he was through a series of spectacular illusions; then Gwennie had to start finding out just how badly castle organization had disintegrated in her absence; then there was covert but intense speculation among the staff about her and the king. Somewhere in the middle of it, while the cook was preparing a great feast and I was still ineffectually trying to have a private conversation with Joachim, Theodora wrestled me into my own chambers and into bed.

When I awoke again, a damp and colorless dawn was just breaking outside my windows. I sat up abruptly, knowing that if I was going to do this I had better do so before my nerve failed completely—or before it was too late. Theodora had been asleep with an arm across me, and I woke her too in sitting up.

"You still haven't told me what this plan of your involves," she said, leaning on an elbow and watching me dig through drawers for the luxury of clean clothes. "But I hope you realize I'm coming with you."

"You can't," I said, speaking briskly but without meeting her eyes. "The bishop won't let you."

"We'll ask him," she retorted. "He's in your study, asleep on the couch. You forget I had the opportunity for a number of conversations with him while you were off pretending to be dead. He's my friend too."

Joachim was already awake when we went into the study a few minutes later. Still exhausted, I didn't bother to light the magic lamps, and the bishop's enormous dark eyes merged with the shadows, making it impossible to tell what he was thinking as I told him what I intended to do.

"It's been thirty years," I said, "and Zahlfast and the old Master covered over the hole in the castle cellars and surrounded it with a triple pentagram. But it should still lead straight down to Hell."

The castle was silent around us. Everyone else must be sleeping off the triumphant feast that I had missed. But as a curtain shifted in a breath of air, the darkness at the room's edges appeared ominous. "I heard you tell those teachers," said Theodora warily, "that you weren't going to summon a demon."

"And I won't. But Elerius will. He didn't dare for a long time after the Cranky Saint appeared to him, but he tried again yesterday." Yesterday? The day before? I was losing track. "I rubbed out the pentagram before he could, some-how managing to intimidate him in the process—at least temporarily. But I observed that the saint did not appear to stop him this time, and he will have noticed that too. The only reason I'm sure he hasn't tried summoning a demon again in the last two days is that I'm still alive. But sooner or later Elerius is going to decide again that he needs the forces of darkness to get his vengeance on the teachers—and on me."

I paused and looked at Joachim. "I still don't understand why he hates me so much."

"Jealousy," said the bishop simply. "You are loved, and he is not. God binds us to each other with the same love that ties us to Him, and Elerius has enormous power but no love. You must remember the words of the Apostle, 'Though I have the gift of prophecy, and understand all mysteries, and all knowl-edge, and have not love, I am nothing.'"

"Yes, of course," I mumbled.

"When we arrived at the City," Theodora provided, "his queen was there. It was fairly clear that she didn't love him anymore." She started to smile and frowned instead. "You still haven't said what you're planning."

"Whenever Elerius does call a demon," I said, speaking slowly because in the morning light this was even more hor-rifying than I had originally thought, "anyone in Hell would know exactly where he was, and would be able to follow the demon straight to him." This part of the plan was still remarkably vague, but I thought I could probably improvise an appropriate spell when the time came. "We've got a hole in the cellars of Yurt that leads to Hell. It's been sealed for years, but there's no reason to think it's not still there. Where I need your help, Joachim," turning back to the bishop but almost unconsciously putting my arm around Theodora, just for the human contact, "is to know how I can venture, living, into Hell, and living out again."

I had been afraid Joachim would find this humorous, as he did so many incomprehensible things; or that he would just announce that Hell was the land of the dead, not the living; or say that these mysteries were not for those as spiritually backwards as wizards.

But instead he took me seriously, pondering with his chin in his hand. "There are stories, of course," he said at last, "usually told of those who later became saints, of visions of Hell: of a man or woman taken bodily into the infernal regions, for a sight of the torments of the damned with which to warn the living. I do not recall that these saints normally *chose* to make such a voyage."

"Suppose someone wasn't a saint," I said. "Suppose he did choose to make the trip himself. Could he come out again alive—with his soul intact?"

"Christ brought many souls out of Hell with him when He rose on the third day," commented Joachim, "but of course both they and He had been dead when they entered."

It wasn't a lot to go on. "In these visions," I asked thoughtfully, "is Hell very large? That is, would I be sure to notice when a demon was setting off to answer a summons from Elerius?"

"Hell," said the bishop definitively, "is *big*. Think how many wicked sinners there have been since the creation of the earth. Think how many more there will be before the final apocalypse. Hell must be large enough to hold them all."

"I wouldn't want to get lost," I mused. "If I couldn't spot the demon, at least I'd hope to find again the place where I'd gone in."

Theodora had been sitting silently, but now she stirred in the circle of my arm. "You're not serious, Daimbert. You have a strange sense of humor sometimes, but this has got to be the strangest manifestation yet." She was not laughing.

"I'm serious," I said, afraid that I really was. "Elerius is gone, maybe a few miles away, maybe a thousand. We won't find him until he and his demon appear to destroy us. That's why I have to do this. Even if I can't find my way back out of Hell, I'd rather go in there trying to do what is best, than to end up there anyway after Elerius has his demon kill me slowly and painfully. Especially—" I paused, then decided there was nothing for it, and pushed ahead. "Especially since this way it's only me, but when he shows up bent on evil he won't just hurt me: he'll go for you and Antonia."

"In that case," she said, speaking rapidly to cover a crack in her voice, "I'm coming with you."

I looked helplessly toward Joachim. He lifted his head, so that for a moment the faint light of morning illuminated his face. "As am I," he announced.

My first thought was intense gratitude that I had lived to experience such excellent friends. My second thought was that I couldn't possibly endanger anyone beyond myself in such folly. "You're the bishop," I protested. "You have to stay here and take care of the twin kingdoms of Yurt and Caelrhon."

"Also the City," he said off-handedly. "The cathedral priests offered me the episcopate when I arrived there, following you. I have not yet accepted. To leave Caelrhon for the City, with its responsibilities and burdens, could be hellish in itself. But you need me with you, Daimbert," and the angle of his high cheek-bones suggested he had found something humorous in this after all. "I'm the only one of us who's read all the saints' visions of Hell!"

And the saints would be sure to get him out again, I thought selfishly. I could cling to his robes or something when they came to save him.

Theodora was a different matter. "You have to stay here," I told her, "to take care of Antonia."

"She's sleeping in Gwennie's room right now," said Theodora. "Apparently it's a nostalgic visit, reminiscent of her first visit to Yurt when she was just a little girl—just seven or eight years ago to us, more than half a lifetime to her. She's almost grown up, Daimbert, and you can't have missed the fact that she has a mind of her own. I don't think she's going to need 'taking care' of much longer."

"Anybody who releases an Ifrit from its bottle," I said darkly, "seriously needs to be looked after."

"Regardless of Antonia," said Theodora, brushing her lips against my cheek, "when I married you, standing in front of the bishop, I promised to stay with you through better and through worse. You've slipped away from me before, but I'm not going to let you do so again. Going to Hell certainly strikes me as one of the 'worse' patches for which the oath prepares us."

"If we're going to do this," said Joachim, "it had better be immediately, before the rest of the castle wakes up and finds out what we're doing, before Elerius summons a demon without giving us a chance to follow it."

He rose and stretched, then gave me a somewhat quirked smile. "Knowing you, Daimbert, has certainly been the one of the most interesting aspects of my life."

I had been able to contemplate doing this only by keeping from thinking very much about the probable outcome. But at the bishop's words I went cold down to my toes. This sounded like something someone said when he assumed his life was effectively over.

We slipped out of my chambers and went silent as wraiths across the empty courtyard, to where a rusted iron door marked the entrance to the cellars. They had been dug, centuries ago, too close to the well, and were always damp. When I first came to Yurt the cellars had been locked for years. Now the door had stood open for still more years, and the first level of abandoned storerooms was used to grow mushrooms.

I had taken a magic light from my room, and it lit our way as we descended the stairs, past the mushrooms, to the dark, slick tunnels beneath. There were faint scurrying sounds in the distance, but other than that the silence of the tunnels was so heavy it roared in our ears, and the sounds of our feet against stone seemed like great slaps. "Tell me, Joachim," I asked quietly, "what's really on the other side?"

He looked back over his shoulder at me, his eyes catching a reflection of light. "On the other side, of course, is us sitting having a glass of wine together, talking with some amazement of how we were able to overcome Elerius."

That wasn't what I meant, but then he doubtless knew that. I lifted the light higher, and we kept on walking. Damp cold bit into us. Theodora's hand in mind seemed like the only warm thing left in the world.

At the very bottom of the cellars, past rooms and tunnels and slimy stone walls dripping with moisture, were sheets of wood and boards all nailed together, covering a spot on the floor. Three pentagrams encircled the spot; the chalk of one had been partially washed away by the damp, but the other two still held. Below, as I knew all too well, was a hole leading to Hell.

I closed my eyes and must have stood, incapable of movement, for several minutes, before Theodora asked, "What should we use to pry up the boards?"

I opened my eyes. "Magic, of course." Wizardry still made a number of things easier, including my own destruction. I set the light to one side and started ripping up boards with magic, then using a lifting spell to stack them against the wall.

The hole was exactly as I remembered it, utterly black and bottomless. Curling up from it, greenish in the lamplight, came a tendril of brimstone.

"This is your last chance," I said to the other two. "You really should not come with me."

Theodora did not answer but only held tighter to my hand. Joachim took my other hand. "Shall I count to three," he suggested, "and we can all jump together?"

IV

We seemed to fall for a very long time. When we jumped, feet-first, into the gaping hole, my eyes squeezed shut and I gripped the others' hands so tightly I could have broken their bones, expecting any second to smack into the floor of Hell. But there was at first no sensation at all. When I opened my eyes, all was dark, and I couldn't tell if we were suspended or still falling. Faintly in the distance I could hear blood-chilling wails, which sounded like the cries of lost souls—and probably were. Something brushed against us, something like a huge wing. Close by I heard a gnashing of teeth—either the despair of the damned, or else the pleasurable anticipation by some unspeakable winged monster of sinking its teeth into a new soul. Joachim and Theodora were totally silent beside me.

After what could have been a few minutes or a few hours, the sensation of hanging suspended changed, and we were very clearly falling again. Wind rushed by us, and a faint light glowed beneath our feet. We shot from darkness into light, and the next moment the three of us were standing on a dark and dusty plain, beneath a lowering sky. Off on the horizon dull orange flames were reflected against the clouds above. The land around us was unfeatured, except for the prospect straight before us.

There ran a black river, steaming and fetid, running so rapidly that swimming would have been hopeless. As the waves crested and broke against the rocks, I thought I saw, faint within them, traces of human shapes.

On our side of the river was a boat. And standing in the boat, leaning on a pole, was a hooded figure with no face.

"I think we have to cross that river," said Theodora in a small voice.

I didn't like the looks of either the boatman or the boat—too creaky, I thought, as likely to drop us into that polluted river as carry us across. "Maybe I can fly us over instead," I suggested.

But Joachim shook his head. "Magic won't work here."

Not believing him, I tried a simple spell of illusion—and found that my magic was gone. This was definitely going to make it harder to find and follow whatever demon Elerius might summon. Well, I had myself commented that only the supernatural was going to be any use against him.

"What happens," Theodora asked quietly, "if we try to cross in that boat and it capsizes in the middle of the river?"

"Then we drown, of course," said Joachim. "We can die just as easily in the netherworld as in the land of the living—probably easier. But there is nowhere else to go except across the river."

We slowly walked closer. A voice came out of the blackness of the ferryman's hood, a spectral voice that vibrated across the dead landscape. "That will be three silver pennies for the three of you."

Theodora groped in her pocket. "I've got it." I wondered what happened to the dead who hadn't thought to bring exact change with them. Theodora reached out to drop the coins into the ferryman's skeletal hand, her skin brushing against his.

He jerked his hand back so fast he almost dropped the coins. "You're alive!" he snapped, and raised his pole threateningly. "What are you doing in Hell?"

It was going to be hard to explain. I stepped as casually as I could between him and Theodora. "We're looking for someone."

He brandished the pole in my face. "I've only let a few of the living in here during all of eternity, and every time it was a mistake. All they wanted was to take the dead back out with them."

"We do not come for the dead," said Joachim, very stern, and for a moment even the ferryman seemed intimidated. "Our mission lies elsewhere."

"All right, then," the ferryman retorted after a brief pause, "you can go on with your 'mission,' but let me tell you right now. With or without the souls of the dead, once you cross this river you won't be crossing it back in my boat!"

"Then we are agreed," said Joachim, still stern. I glanced around, wondering how else we were supposed to get out of here, and looked upward in the hope of a last glimpse of the cellars of Yurt, whose deserted dank corridors now seemed positively appealing.

But there was no hole in the sky, no indication of anything but arid sand, lurid flames in the distance, and this black river.

Theodora scrambled into the boat and moved up toward the prow, and Joachim and I followed. The boat, as I feared, seemed scarcely capable of ferrying even one of us across, much less three. It shifted alarmingly under our weight, and small jets of foul water shot between the boards.

The ferryman pushed off with his pole, and we were immediately seized by the current, spinning around and almost crashing against a rock, from which he fended us off just in time. We sat very still, trying to keep out of his way, as he poled desperately. I couldn't help but notice that we seemed to be making no headway.

"The weight of flesh," the ferryman gasped, as a wave broke over the railing, "is more than this boat was made to handle!"

"We paid you in silver," said Joachim firmly, "and you agreed to take us. You cannot turn back now."

The boat spun again, and again as waves splashed high around us I thought I saw the shapes of human body parts, faintly outlined in the spray. The remains, I wondered, of those who had not made the crossing successfully?

But the ferryman kept on poling. He worked us out of one eddy, and in momentarily smoother water he was able to make a dozen yards of forward progress. Then the current hit us again, and we were swept downstream, far away now from where we had first begun to cross. Off in the distance I could hear a heavy roaring, as of this river pouring over a precipice.

Theodora's face was white, and her lips tight together. I squeezed her arm, wondering what would happen after we shot over the waterfall. Would we just continue our journey across Hell, being dead now, or would we have to start all over again?

The river banks were closer together here and steeper. Caught in another eddy, the boat spun right next to the shore—and then came joltingly to a halt, as the prow caught on a hidden rock. Theodora was thrown into my lap by the force of the impact.

"Out," said the ferryman. "All of you, out!" Water was now gushing into the boat—we were going to be in the river in a few seconds anyway.

A scrubby tree, that looked as if it had never borne a leaf, leaned over the bank, just beyond my reach. But Joachim, with his longer arms, stretched up and seized it. "Hold onto me," he told us, swung a foot over the boat's railing to plant it against the nearly vertical riverbank, and started to climb.

Theodora and I clung to his shoulders like children, and for a second the bishop seemed to have grown, twenty feet tall and enormously muscular. Then he had pulled his way far enough up the bank that we were able to snatch at branches ourselves, and drag ourselves to safety. Behind us, the boat, freed of our weight, leaped higher in the water. The ferryman did something in the prow, then started poling steadily and easily back upstream, without a backward glance.

We sat on the rocky ground for a moment, catching our breaths. "This was an even more idiotic idea than I thought," I said, wondering how Joachim had managed to grow like that, and shy to ask him. He looked perfectly normal now, wringing fetid water out of his vestments.

"As long as we cannot go back," he said, "we should go on."

The landscape still was dry and unfeatured, the occasional bush twisted and dessicated. "I somehow thought Hell would be more, well, violent," said Theodora, "not just have flames off on the horizon."

"We are not yet actually in Hell," said Joachim. "These are only the outskirts."

We started walking along the riverbank. Here we were on a high ridge and were able to look for what seemed many miles across the depressing outskirts of Hell. The sounds of the waterfall before us grew closer. Beyond the churning black river below us, I spotted another river, also aiming toward the waterfall, and on our other side, off across the stony plain, were the beds of two more. "These are the four rivers of Hades," said Joachim, sounding almost pleased, "just as I have seen them described."

"When people die," Theodora asked, "do they all have to make this entire journey, starting with the ferryman?"

"When I was dead," I provided, "I don't remember seeing anything like this."

The bishop looked thoughtful. "Hell is very old," he said, "the first creation of Lucifer when he rebelled against God and tried to make himself God's equal. All humans came here between the Fall and the time of Christ. Some of the earliest recorded visions of Hell took place before the beginning of the Christian era, and all mention the ferryman and the four rivers. With the coming of Christ, however, and the coming of salvation, I think that those who die with pure hearts skip this—and even the damned may not now start at the beginning." That would avoid the problem of not carrying silver pennies, I thought. "We, however, entered living."

We had now come so close to the waterfall that we had to stop talking because of its noise. All four rivers came together here, and the ridge along which we had been walking ended in a promontory, thrusting out into a chasm, down into which the stinking black water of the rivers poured. Arching over that chasm was a bridge.

It was narrow, spiked, and wet with spray from the roaring water. Its rusted iron span was no more than twelve or fifteen inches wide, and in the distance it seemed to shrink to the width of the hair. On the far side of the chasm, a quarter mile away, rose a castle's dark walls. Theodora and I looked at each other. Neither one of us liked the appearance of that bridge, but it seemed the only way on.

Joachim did not hesitate. He started across the bridge at once, placing his feet carefully between the spikes, his arms out to the side to keep his balance. The moment he stepped on the bridge there was a sharp sizzling sound, and for a second he stopped with a cry. He half turned toward us, and I saw that the silver crucifix he always wore around his neck was gone. But then he turned resolutely back toward Hell, and again started placing his feet between the spikes of the bridge that would take him there.

He was our guide, and our only hope of ever finding our way out of here. I gave Theodora what was supposed to be a reassuring smile and started after him.

As soon as I stepped on the bridge, I was hit by a powerful wind. Reeking with the scent of the fetid waters below, the wind made me sway so that for a second I almost lost my balance. I snatched at one of the spikes to steady myself, then jerked my hand back with a red slice across the palm.

For a second I went totally motionless, my knees refusing to move as I contemplated the drop into the roaring waterfall below. I took a quick peek, to see if I could see the bottom of the chasm into which the water raced, and could not.

Theodora spoke behind me, her voice low under the thunder of the water. "Hell doesn't want us."

I started to take a deep breath, almost choked on the foul smell wafting up toward us, and took a few quick shallow breaths instead. I couldn't spend the rest of eternity here, especially since Theodora, with her much better climbing ability, was waiting behind me to go on. If Hell didn't want us, that must mean we were on the side of right. By sheer will, I urged my feet forward.

Another step, and another. And then, strangely yet undeniably, the bridge was getting wider. The spikes shrank and seemed less sharp, and I was able to step without each step being an exercise in swaying and determination. Ahead, I saw that Joachim had already reached the far side. I didn't dare go too fast, for fear that I would fall when three-quarters of the way across and have made most of the difficult crossing for nothing. But in a few minutes of grim balancing I too was on the far bank, and Theodora was right behind me.

"Here," said Joachim, "is where we truly enter Hell."

Hell was guarded by a castle's soaring stone walls, as though it actually wanted to keep out the souls of the damned. But its gate was open. An inscription over it read, "Through me lies the way to eternal pain. Through me runs the path of the lost. Abandon all hope, ye who enter." Standing in the gateway was a enormous black hound with three heads.

Its six eyes were a bright red, and its fangs long and sharp. But it wagged its tail at us, its three tongues lolling from its mouths. "How are we supposed to get by *that*?" Theodora asked, staying back behind me.

But Joachim advanced confidently. "It shouldn't stop us. These walls aren't for us. They are to prevent the escape of the damned." And indeed as he advanced the dog stepped to one side. Its monstrous heads were on a level with the bishop's, and it gave him a quick lick with each tongue as he went by. I pulled Theodora rapidly past while it was distracted.

Two steps, three steps beyond the gate, and we were into Hell. Spreading at our feet was a lake of molten fire. I stopped and looked back at the hound.

Immediately it bared its fangs and began to growl, crouched ready to spring on me if I took even one step back. I turned quickly around and moved closer to the burning lake. Going on remained our only choice.

The heat from the lake beat against our faces, and the air was heavy with the smell of sulphur. "I hope we aren't going to have to resort to an inadequate ferry boat again," said Theodora.

But the bishop shook his head. "There should be a path around the lake."

I put a hand on his arm. "Who are those?"

Standing in the lake, up to their chests in burning pitch, were human shapes. They were clearer than the forms I had thought I had seen in the first river of Hades, but when I looked at them directly they faded. Only when I looked at them sideways did they gain any solidity. Fire licked at their naked skin, covered with raw burns and with bites from giant snakes that writhed in the flames. The human shapes twisted in pain, and their mouths moved as if screaming, but I could hear nothing.

"Those," said Joachim shortly, "are the damned."

"But I can't see them," I said, trying with sidelong glances to tell if any were people I had known. I really didn't want to meet Zahlfast down here.

"We are still alive," he said soberly. "I do not think the living can look on the faces of the dead."

"But if the living knew the punishments the evil will have to suffer—" said Theodora in horror.

"That's what we priests keep on trying to tell them," said Joachim. "Until the devil himself is redeemed at the end of infinite time, the wicked must suffer for their deeds in unquenchable fire. Come. Let us find the path."

We walked a short distance along the edge of the burning lake, Theodora and I clinging together and trying not to look at the dead. Then we came suddenly on two paths, both leading away from the lake: they ran next to each other for a short distance, then diverged.

The left one was smooth and wide, paved with flat white stones. The right-hand one was narrow and stony, leading between thorny bushes, marked by no more than a continuous row of pebbles. "I choose left," I said.

But Joachim shook his head. "From some of the accounts of visions of Hell, it is clear that if one keeps going, one will eventually reach the gates of Heaven. But this is only if one has followed the right paths through Hell. It may be that our only way back to the lands of the living lies through Heaven, and if so we want to get there."

I certainly had to agree. My stomach knotted at the realization of how even more dangerous Hell was than I had imagined. "But how do you know which road to choose?"

"The Bible tells us that strait and narrow is the road that leads to salvation. Let us take this one."

The path was so narrow that we had to go single-file, and so rough that sometimes we had to go on all fours over the rocks that littered it. Above us, clouds gathered gray and angry, with rumblings of thunder and flashes of lightning that threatened to ignite the sulphur in the air. But away to our left, I saw the wide paved path end abruptly at a monstrous set of jaws: jaws without more than a vestigial head or any body at all, but sharply toothed, gaping ready for anyone who had chosen the wide and easy path.

Our narrow path turned a corner and reached—a flower garden. Colors were bright, and the air, rather than reeking with sulphur, was soft and perfumed. I stopped and looked around suspiciously. "Either this is a sign that we've taken the right path, or it's another temptation to lead us astray."

"I think it means we chose aright," said Joachim, not sounding nearly as confident as I would have liked. "Perhaps we can rest here for a short time."

But barely had we sat down amidst flowering bushes when an ear-numbing shout assaulted us: "Living flesh! What do you think you're doing here?"

The tone was light, though loud: but even surrounded as we were by unquenchable fire, it made me cold with raw terror. A yellow demon bounced into sight beyond the garden, so short and round he would have been comical if any of us had felt like laughing. His feet were cloven and his tail barbed. His enormous mouth had heavy yellow teeth that looked ready for crushing bone. The dead had been hazy and hard to see—this demon was remarkably vivid.

"We are pilgrims," said Joachim, "wanderers in a strange land."

"Yes, most people find Hell pretty strange!" yelled the demon with a grin that threatened to split his head in half. "Couldn't wait for your deaths to have a look, eh? They do say people are just *dying* to get into Hell! Hah! Good joke, eh? How about a few pokes with my pitchfork, just to give you a preview of eternal torment?"

But Joachim held up his hand. "You cannot touch us, for we are not yet condemned."

I wondered desperately if this were true. The demon, however, frowned in frustration, then laughed once more. "Well, I'm friendly enough," he said, waving his pitchfork, "but not everyone you meet will be! All I would have done was to have a little fun with you. Now get moving, before I forget how to treat pilgrims. And take this as a gesture of my esteem!" He bent over, giving us a good look at a naked and hairy rump, as, arms linked, we hurried away again.

There wasn't much of a path anymore, only a rough track between thorn bushes, where burning pits appeared at every twist of the track. We saw demons standing hip-deep in some of the pits, whipping at hazy shapes that must be more of the damned. In other places huge cauldrons were set up, boiling, and demons stirred with their pitchforks, occasionally holding up a hazy skewered arm or leg as if to see if it were done. In still other places demons had wrenched the mouths of the damned open and were feeding them what looked, from a second's horrified glance, like their own rotted flesh. "I'm sorry," I said quietly. "I should never have let you come with me."

"We didn't give you a lot of choice," said Theodora, squeezing my hand. I winced; it was the hand I had cut on the bridge.

"But I realize now how foolish I was to think this could ever work," I said, my eyes downcast. "We'll wander through here for weeks, never come close to finding anything to help us against Elerius, get taunted by demons the whole way, finally starve to death, and then join the damned in the burning lake. That inscription at the entrance was right, in telling us to abandon all hope."

Joachim pulled me around almost roughly. "Daimbert. Look at me. This is despair."

"It's just good sense," I mumbled, flinching back from the intensity of his gaze.

"No. Hell is the source of despair. Even here we cannot be lost to God's mercy—unless we throw away hope."

"All right, all right," I said, half under my breath. "In that case, I *hope* we get out out of here before we starve to death."

"He's still about to give way to despair," said Joachim to Theodora. "We can't let him."

She put her arms around me. "I love you," she said firmly, though her lips trembled. "Where there is love there cannot be an end to hope."

I hugged her back and managed a smile. "I agree. I said I hoped we'd get out of here. Let's keep going."

It was hard to say how long we kept walking. Scenes of pain and torture kept repeating themselves. Some places demons ripped sinners apart with red-hot pincers; in other places wolves gnawed at their intestines. In one spot a demon hammered mightily at a glowing forge, and I could see the indistinct souls of the damned caught between hammer and anvil. In other spot demons tossed souls high with their pitchforks to be snatched by a monstrous many-headed beast, which caught them in its teeth, chewed them, and spat them out to be tossed again. The tormenting demons all seemed to be enjoying themselves hugely. Repeatedly I turned away, feeling sorry and sick, only to be able to see the damned and their tormentors even more clearly when they were just a movement at the edge of my vision.

I wasn't hungry, but I became progressively thirstier, as every stream here in Hell either burned with pitch or else was clotted thick with blood. I ached in every bone and sinew, but the general weariness became no worse no matter how far we walked. The stormy sky, made lurid by the flames between which we made our way, did not change; we were far from the sun and its circuit.

Every now and then a faint human shape appeared falling from the sky. Some were men and some women, some dressed in rags and some in silks—even some in priests' vestments. Bat-winged demons flocked up to seize them and strip them of their clothes, before tumbling them straight into one of the burning pits to begin their tortures at once.

The only real change in the landscape was that we appeared to be slowly heading downward, which I thought did not bode well if there was any chance we were going to emerge at the gates of Heaven. We could have walked a hundred miles, but here time and space had no meaning.

Most of the demons ignored us, having better things to do in torturing sinners than in taunting us. But then we were abruptly brought up short by a booming voice.

"Daimbert! How good it is to see you again!"

Leaning over us was an enormous horned demon, dozens of sharp teeth showing in a leer. Joachim had tried to tell me Hell was big. The first day here, I thought, giving way to despair after all, and I meet the one demon who knows me.

V

The demon bent down over his great belly, ignoring Theodora and the bishop. "You're a long way from Yurt, Daimbert," he said with an evil grin. "Too bad you didn't bring your daughter with you—now *she's* a tender little morsel. Twice I've almost had you for us, and now, behold! You've come here all by yourself!"

"Not to stay," I said obstinately when I found my voice again.

"Of course not," said the demon with a completely unconvincing attempt at good fellowship. "You just wanted to find out more about Hell, to see if all those torments the priests keep telling you about can possibly be as bad as they've led you to believe. Well, I've been watching you since you entered our gates, but I decided to wait to talk to you until I knew our little conversation could be the most effective. I know you, Daimbert. You're cautious, and probably even now you're rethinking the plan that brought you here—the plan to sell your soul in order to capture Elerius!"

I had been listening skeptically, knowing I was not going to get truth out of a demon, and trying to tell my wildly beating heart that, because I was already in Hell, his appearance here should not further terrify me. But at the mention of

Elerius I blurted out, "Where is he? What do you know of him?"

"I know where he is, certainly," said the demon airily, though his tone was belied by the miniature flames shooting from his eye-sockets. "Twice he's started to summon a demon, but both times something has intervened."

The saint and me, I thought but did not say.

"But Elerius is not so important now as you, Daimbert, and your desire to capture him. Well, I can reassure you about something I know is bothering you. All these sinners you see being punished—" with a wave of his clawed hand at the burning lakes "—are just your ordinary murderers and adulterers. We have a *special* place for those who sell their souls to their devil. It's not like the rest of Hell, no, not a bit! Do you recall passing a pleasant flower-garden? Well, it's like that, only even nicer. Those who sell their souls are the devil's special friends, and get to sit beside him on miniature versions of his iron throne. So, now that you know this, what do you say? Will you swap a soul that's pretty tattered already for defeating Elerius—and then eternity in triumph among us?"

"You're lying," I said between my teeth, trying desperately to keep them from chattering. Theodora was behind me, arms tight around my waist, her face pressed against my shoulder blades. "Now that I've seen Hell's torments, I'm even less likely to sell my soul than I was before."

The demon shook his massive head. "I've never seen such stubbornness." He was right that I was stubborn, but I wasn't going to grant him anything else. "Let me at least tell you what we're offering for your soul, before you throw your chance away! After all, that school of yours is full of demonology experts, but you'll be the only one among them who's actually been to Hell! And when you're Master—"

"I'm not going to be Master," I said, still between my teeth.

The demon shrugged. "Deny it all you like, but I know the secret ambitions of your soul. I've been watching you ever since you entered the gates of Hell, and I can tell you've become awfully discouraged. That means there are two separate things you most desire. First, you want assurance you'll leave here alive, and I can certainly grant you that in return for your soul—I'll even let your friends out too, for free! Secondly, you want to be the greatest wizard of all time, and with my help you will be. And after five hundred years as Master—or even a thousand, if you like—you can return here, to take up a special spot by Satan's throne!"

"Don't bother," I said brusquely. "I don't believe any of your lies. Any 'special' spot for those who sell their souls will be even worse than the rest of Hell."

"Well," said the demon, "if you don't believe me, why don't you ask your friend the bishop? I'm sure he'll reassure you that I'm telling the exact truth!"

I turned toward Joachim, and was horrified to see that he had turned his back on me, standing stiff and straight with crossed arms. I reached a hand toward him, but before I could speak a voice rolled through Hell's skies.

"By Satan, by Beelzebub," the voice said, "by Lucifer and Mephistopheles!" I recognized that voice. It was Elerius.

"Well, Daimbert," said the demon regretfully, "it looks like we'll have to postpone the rest of our little chat. Elerius is in Yurt, and I'm the one who answers summonses from there."

"Elerius is in Yurt," I repeated, and that thought was even more horrifying than the red and bloated demon himself.

"You may even have to think of something else you want in return for your soul," he continued, shaking his horned head, "because I'm certain Elerius will ask for the school in trade for *his* soul, and I can't very well sell it to both of you!

I must say, I'm not sure why heading an institution that's now a smoldering ruin should be so important to the two most powerful wizards now living, but we demons are only here to serve! Once Elerius has made the deal for his soul, I'll hurry right back, and I can show you the special place reserved for him—and for you too, once we reach our agreement."

I had been standing as if rooted to the spot, trying too hard to resist the demon's blandishments to think beyond them. But as he gathered himself for a great leap, Joachim suddenly swung around. With one arm, that had now grown fantastically to twice its normal length, he seized Theodora and me, while the other arm, even longer, he wrapped around the demon's bulging waist.

The demon leaped upward, sailing high over flames and chasms that stretched to the horizon in all directions. Dangling below the demon's red and bulging belly, swinging back and forth in the foul air, I felt I had gone beyond terror. In the center of Hell, in the direction we had been heading, there were no more flames, only a surface that glinted like ice.

Surrounded by ice fields sat a great dark something—or someone—at least a hundred feet high. I turned my head sharply away. If we were leaving Hell, I saw no reason at all to look upon the devil himself. The heavy clouds above rushed toward us.

The demon's head thrust into the clouds—and broke through a stone floor into the center of a pentagram.

We materialized with him, back on earth. Joachim let go the second we were through, and the three of us tumbled out of the pentagram. I looked around wildly and recognized the place. I had only been here once before, and my memories, though highly unpleasant, were vivid. We were in a long-deserted castle on the borders of Yurt and Caelrhon, in one of the few rooms that still had a roof.

Of course. Elerius knew this ruined castle well, knew that we were unlikely to start our search for him here, and yet also knew that he would be conveniently placed for whatever attacks he planned against my family.

Except at the moment he fell back, eyes round. His incantation turned into a shriek. His horror, I saw, was not for the demon he had summoned, but for us. His face dead white, he collapsed against the room's back wall, holding his arms up defensively in front of him. He made faint gibbering noises as I crawled toward him. He had, I thought, broken at last.

For a second I almost felt sorry for him. Three times he had tried to summon a demon, and three times something had gone wrong.

The corner of my eye caught a flash of white, and I turned to see a towering figure, burning with pure light, addressing the demon. "In the name of the Father, the Son, and the Holy Spirit, I order you back to Hell, never to enter this land again!" For a second I thought it was the Cranky Saint, making another opportune appearance. But it wasn't the saint. It was Joachim.

The demon shrank before our eyes, whimpering and whining. "But I never even—"

"Tell him," said Joachim to Elerius, great and terrible. "Tell him that you will not treat with him."

"Back! Go back!" Elerius cried, almost sobbing. "I don't want you!" And with a final burst of fire and brimstone and an almost overpowering stench, the demon reluctantly disappeared. I scrambled forward to rub out the pentagram.

Theodora snatched up the magical apparatus Elerius had brought with him from the City, while he was still stunned, and started rapid murmuring under her breath. I realized she was working one of her witch-spells, at least temporarily binding Elerius with magic that he would not immediately be able to counter. Magic, I thought. I could work magic again.

Still sitting on the floor, I shouted out King Solomon's binding spell, the enormously powerful ancient spell that could keep even an Ifrit imprisoned in a bottle, the spell that had stopped the dread advance of a basilisk. Tightly wrapped in magic, Elerius went rigid, his eyes still round.

But at the same moment, the ceiling above us began to sway. A spell that powerful was too much for a ruined structure standing up primarily out of habit. Slates tumbled down, and the pillars tilted. Grabbing Theodora and Joachim with magic, I shot backwards just as a whole wall smashed down, where a second before we had been.

The dust settled after a few minutes, and no more parts of the old castle seemed likely to collapse immediately. We were in an overgrown courtyard, and a frosty, sunny day of late autumn was just breaking. It wasn't Heaven, but it was close enough. "Is he dead?" asked Theodora.

I sought his mind—an easy task now that he could not put up shields against me. "Still alive," I said, "and I don't believe even badly hurt, though I think he's unconscious at the moment as well as unable to move. The stones fell in such a way that he's in his own little shelter. Between the stones and Solomon's binding spell, which may indeed have helped protect him, we don't need to worry about him for a long time. But, Joachim—" I turned toward the bishop and stopped, too awestruck to be able to ask him how he had learned to do such a convincing imitation of a saint.

He looked like himself again, pushing back his hair with one hand and starting to smile, a slow smile that worked its way up from his mouth to his eyes. "I think this is the 'other side' you asked about, Daimbert," he commented as calmly as if we had been sitting in his book-lined study. "We don't have the glasses of wine, however. And I am sorry to have lost that crucifix; the duchess's daughter gave it to me."

Theodora flopped back in the damp grass. "For the rest of my life," she announced, "I'm going to be the most perfect person you can imagine. I do not want to end up in Hell."

"We must all do the best we can," said the bishop, sober now, "but we cannot make our own salvation. We are all still miserable sinners, and must hope for the unmerited mercy of Christ. For example—" He paused, his eyes distant, but just when I thought he was not going to say anything else he went on.

"For example, I have spent my entire adult life as a priest fighting temptation, but I still had to turn my back on the demon for fear that he would make me an offer, and that I would find it too tempting. If he had promised me a successful rule as bishop of the great City in return for my soul, I would have had to reject not just his offer but the election of the cathedral chapter there, for my episcopacy would always have been tainted in my eyes. Yet as soon as I thought this, I knew that I *did* want the office, and that it was tempting me even without the active intervention of a demon. Therefore—"

I interrupted him with a laugh, suddenly feeling the weight of the fears of the last few months lifting from me. The hand I had cut on the bridge into Hell was completely healed. We've done it, I thought. We've done it! "Don't make it any more complicated than you have to," I told the bishop. "We did make it through Hell and through a demon's best blandishments."

The forces of darkness had tried to tempt me with the leadership of the school, and I had not been tempted. Which meant—which meant that I could choose freely, knowing that if I became the head of the school it was certainly not from a selfish desire for power. The teachers wanted me (or at least a majority did); both the Master and Zahlfast had died assuming I would be an excellent leader; and after Hell the burdens of administrative responsibility would have to be trivial.

"Tell you what, Joachim," I said. "If I become Master of the school after all, and they put me in charge of rebuilding because no one else wants the job, you can keep me company by becoming bishop of the City. Theodora, you'll have to come too, to help me keep track of our daughter. I think it's well past time her formal education in wizardry began."

"I shall always regret," said Joachim a little sadly, "not continuing on all the way through Hell, to see if the visions are recorded truly, and that when one reaches the devil's iron throne, frozen in eternal ice, there is a way to climb up to the gates of Heaven. It might have been my only opportunity to see those shining gates. And I now know, just from the momentary sensation of feeling absolute good working through me, how much I shall have lost."

Theodora rolled over on her stomach to look at him. "Father Joachim," she said sternly, but with a smile playing around her lips, "I realize this may come as a shock to you, but everyone who knows you knows that you'll be going to Heaven."

"But if you're terribly disappointed," I suggested, "you could always start the trip all over again, down in the cellars of Yurt. That reminds me—we'd better get the cover back on that hole before anyone gets in by mistake."

Joachim shook his head, slowly starting to smile again. "I am not impatient for a second glimpse of Hell. I think I can wait."

"In the meantime," said Theodora, sitting up, "what are we going to do with Elerius?"

"I guess we can't really leave him trapped in there to starve," I said regretfully. "I'll come back with Whitey and Chin this afternoon to get him. I've got an idea. But first, I want to see if the castle cook of Yurt has made any cinnamon crullers this morning."

With Maffi and my two young would-be wizardry assistants, it was remarkably easy lifting the stones off Elerius that afternoon. The last few were tricky, because I didn't want to risk crushing him as I shifted the slates that had protected him from the rest of the fallen wall, but at last he lay revealed, breathing shallowly.

"I don't like it that he's still unconscious," I said, worried. "The whole purpose is not to kill him. If I really am going to head the school, I have to be as different from him as I can be."

"Of course he hasn't recovered consciousness," said Maffi. "The spell binds him too tightly. Have you not wondered how an Ifrit could survive for centuries inside a bottle, without even eating?"

"Suppose I loosened the spell somewhat," I said thoughtfully, "so that a room, say, was all bound by it, and he was in the middle. Would he recover consciousness then? Would he need to eat?"

Maffi never liked to suggest he didn't know something. "That should allow him to recover," he said slowly, "without time truly passing for him. I can contact Kaz-alrhun, if you like, but he will tell you the same."

"He's in Xantium, and we're here," I said shortly. "Let's hope you're right."

We put Elerius's inert form on the magic carpet and flew him across Yurt, from the ruined castle to the valley of the Cranky Saint. Here, the heavy local concentration of inherent magical forces, left from the earth's creation, should make easier what I was going to try. The valley was exactly as it had been when we took my dragon's teeth warriors out of the cave. There had been entirely too many reminders of dragons lately, I thought. Around the sacred spring, bushes still put out green leaves, and the air was soft.

Ignoring the scandalized looks from the two young wizards, I knelt before the shrine of the Cranky Saint for a moment: thanking him for his help, asking him to help me just once more, and reminding him that, if Elerius escaped, he might take out his fury for being deprived of his kingdom on Hadwidis, the saint's spiritual daughter. The hermit appeared from behind a tree and smiled benevolently as we heaved Elerius into the cave.

"Now's your chance," I told Whitey and Chin. "Show me those illusions that last a very long time. Make them good."

They had already guessed what I wanted and were full of ideas. Maffi entered into the spirit of the activity, adding several automatons he fashioned on the spot, and then had to cover with illusion so that it was not immediately obvious they were made of nothing but stone and branch. Whitey and Chin were especially proud of an illusion that looked just like me, and they kept snickering every time I turned my back on them. When they had their illusions in place, I turned on the magical augmenter, concealed it with illusion so that it looked like a hat stand in the corner, and set it to keep both illusions and automata going indefinitely.

The sun had set, and a cold wind was whistling into the cave when we finished at last. I broke the spell that imprisoned Elerius, a more difficult process than I had expected, and which ended up requiring use of the golden signet for the final steps. He took a long, shuddering breath as though about to recover consciousness. The three of us darted out quickly. And both with the words of the spell Levi had taught me, and with the imprint of Solomon's signet itself, I sealed up the cave. Then each of us added magic locks, sealed with our palm prints, for good measure.

The first stars were appearing in the thin slice of sky we could see over the valley as we emerged from the cave mouth. The magic carpet was twitching, eager to be off again. But I looked back for a moment, sincerely hoping I would never have to see Elerius again in the land of the living. The next world, however, I decided I could deal with. If I ended up in

Heaven, I would be so happy that even he could not lessen my joy, and if I ended up in Hell, well, I knew from experience that there were even worse things there than he.

"In essence time itself will stop for him," I told Theodora that night, sitting in front of the fireplace in my chambers with her head on my shoulder. I had eaten a late supper off a tray after returning to the castle, and the fire provided a focus of warmth and light while outside the darkness grew cold. "But Elerius will never know it. If those young wizards' illusions work the way they're supposed to, he'll imagine a whole rich life for himself, probably including killing me, rebuilding the school, and dominating the world. I tried to impress on my assistants the necessity of keeping the spot secret, but I don't think even thirty good wizards acting together could break in there—at least not without Solomon's seal."

"You've been far more merciful to him than he would ever have been to you," she said.

"I'm just doing what you said you were going to do yourself," I said, giving her a squeeze. "I'm being the most perfect person imaginable. If you're going to end up in Heaven, I certainly want to be there with you, and returning good for evil strikes me as an appropriate way to start."

"Remember that," she said with a chuckle, "when you try to make your first act as Master of the school the admission of a girl, and all the other teachers start behaving obnoxiously toward you."

I kissed her. "You'll be there to help me, you'll recall," I said, "both to remind me to turn the other cheek, and also to remind the other teachers that if they want to dump all the responsibility on me, then Antonia's part of the package."

"Speaking of reminding," she said, "I meant to tell you. There was a telephone call from the City late this afternoon."

"They won't even let me finish taking care of Elerius before they think of something *else* they want me to do?"

"No. I think this was more in the way of warning. Kaz-alrhun showed up in the City. He's planning to fly on his own magic carpet up to Yurt first thing in the morning."

I shook my head. "I've always suspected Maffi of sending messages back to him, even though he's denied it. Well, the mage is just barely too late for all the excitement—or maybe he deliberately planned it that way."

"I don't think so, Daimbert. They put him on to speak to me himself—he congratulated me on our marriage, which he hadn't known about. But I don't believe he is coming out of idle curiosity. In fact," and she leaned back against my chest, "he said he felt it was imperative that the greatest mage the East has ever known—that's him, of course—should consult with the wise and mighty keeper of King Solomon's seal, the new leader of western magic. In case you didn't know, I'm afraid that's you."